The LAST ADVENTURE of the Scarlet Pimpernel

JACK CALDWELL

WHITE SOUP PRESS

White Soup Press, c/o Jack Caldwell, 3140 Sunset Beach Drive, Venice, FL, 34293.

http://www.cajuncheesehead.com
http://whitesouppress.com/
http://austenauthors.net/

ISBN: 978-0-9891080-6-5

Layout & design by Ellen Pickels
Front and back cover images: 123rf.com

Dedication

To Barbara,
my own Marguerite.

In Appreciation

To Debbie Styne, Catarina Cotic Belloube,
and Ellen Pickels for their endless hours
spent editing this work.

Author's Note

This work uses characters invented by the Baroness Emma "Emmuska" Orczy in her renowned Scarlet Pimpernel series and Miss Jane Austen in her series of Regency novels. This novel is intended to honor them and the immense pleasure they continue to bestow on the world.

This novel is not only a sequel to Jane Austen's *Northanger Abbey*; it is Book Two of my Jane Austen's Fighting Men series and a companion to my earlier book, *The Three Colonels*. It features characters from and references to events in that novel. While *The Last Adventure of the Scarlet Pimpernel* stands on its own, the reader's enjoyment may be enhanced by reading the earlier book.

—*Jack Caldwell*
Venice, Florida

Dramatis Personae

NORTHANGER ABBEY, GLOUCESTERSHIRE

Alexander Tilney: Major-General, British Army (retired), owner of
    Northanger Abbey.
Captain Frederick Tilney, Royal Horse Guards Blue, British Army:
    eldest son of General Tilney, formerly of the Twelfth
    Dragoons, now as part of the Blues assigned to the
    Household Cavalry Mounted Regiment, friend to Sir John
    Buford and George Blakeney.
The Rev. Henry Tilney: brother of Captain Tilney, rector of
    Woodston, a parish twenty miles from Northanger Abbey.
Catherine Morland Tilney: wife to Henry Tilney.

RICHMOND, SURREY

Sir Percival (Percy) Blakeney, Bart.: baronet and knight, very
    wealthy, and personal friend of HRH The Prince Regent,
    leader of the now-defunct League of the Scarlet Pimpernel.
Lady Marguerite (Margot) Blakeney: wife to Sir Percy.
George Blakeney: son and heir of Sir Percy, a student at Oxford,
    friend to Captain Tilney.
Violet Yvonne Blakeney: daughter of Sir Percy.

OXFORD, OXFORDSHIRE

Sir Robert Paisley: a student at Oxford, member of Clan Paisley.
The Honorable Brian Paisley: brother to Sir Robert.
John Thorpe: former acquaintance of Mrs. Tilney.

LONDON

Thomas Bertram: heir to Mansfield Park, Northamptonshire.

Colonel Christopher Brandon, British Army (inactive): owner of Delaford Manor, magistrate of Delaford, honorary position in the Life Guards, veteran of the wars of the French Revolution and the early Napoleonic conflicts.

Marianne Brandon: wife to Colonel Brandon.

Colonel Sir John Buford, CB, —nd Lt. Dragoons, British Army, earned the Bath for his service during the Peninsular War, friend to Captain Tilney and Colonel Brandon.

Lady Caroline Bingley Buford: wife to Colonel Buford.

Fitzwilliam Darcy: owner of Pemberley, head of the Darcy family.

Elizabeth Darcy: wife to Mr. Darcy.

Georgiana Darcy: only sister to Mr. Darcy.

Major Archibald Denny, British Army: attached to the Household Cavalry staff.

Sir Andrew Ffoulkes, Bart.: baronet and knight, close friend to Sir Percy and second-in-command of the League.

Lady Suzanne Ffoulkes: wife to Sir Andrew.

The Right Honorable Lord Hugh Fitzwilliam, 5th Earl of Matlock: head of the Fitzwilliam family.

Lady Alexandria Fitzwilliam, Countess Matlock: wife of Lord Matlock.

Mr. Manwaring: owner of Langford.

Annabella Adams Norris: wife to Randolph Norris of London, acquaintance of Captain Tilney.

Armand St. Just: barrister, London, brother to Lady Blakeney, former member of the League.

Marie St. Just: wife to Mr. St. Just.

Lady Victoria Uppercross: acquaintance of Captain Tilney.

Dorothy Wentworth: cousin to Captain Frederick Wentworth, RN.

The Honorable John Yates: brother-in-law to Mr. Bertram.

*HRH George Augustus Frederick, the Prince Regent of the United Kingdom: eldest son of the incapacitated King George III, estranged from his wife, Princess Caroline of Brunswick-Wolfenbüttel, friend and patron of Sir Percy.

*HRH Frederick Augustus, the Duke of York and Albany: second son of George III, Field-Marshal and Commander-in-Chief of the Forces.

*General Sir Henry William Paget, 2nd Earl of Uxbridge, British Army: member of the House of Lords.

*Lady Charlotte Paget, Countess Uxbridge: wife to Lord Uxbridge.

*Major-General Sir William Ponsonby, British Army: commander of the 1st (Royal) Dragoons.

*Major-General Lord Robert Edward Henry Somerset, British Army: commander of the Household Cavalry Brigade.

PARIS, FRANCE

Capitaine Honoré Bourgeois, French Army: former infantry officer, assigned to the Interior Ministry.

Citoyen Armand Chauvelin: the chief agent of the Committee of Public Safety during Robespierre's Revolutionary France.

Claudette: a maid.

Monsieur Lafarge: long-time clerk in the Interior Ministry, first for the French Republic, then for the Kingdom of France, once imprisoned with *Citoyen* Chauvelin.

Rateau: a resident of Saint-Malo.

Pierre St. Just: jeweler and cousin to Lady Blakeney and Armand St. Just.

Camille St. Just: wife to M. St. Just.

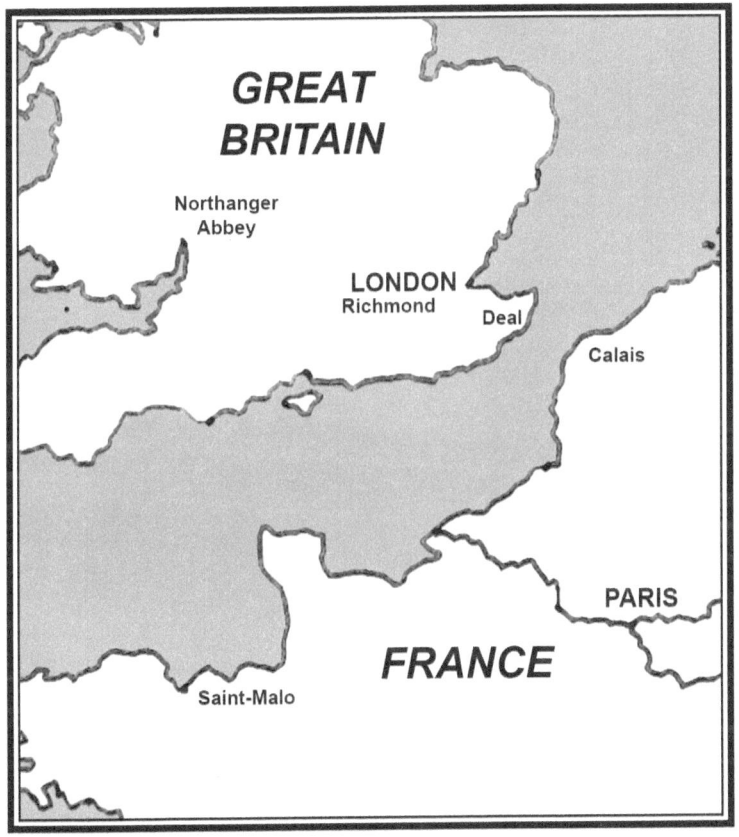

GREAT
BRITAIN

Northanger
Abbey

LONDON
Richmond
Deal

Calais

PARIS

FRANCE

Saint-Malo

Prologue

The prisoner sat upon his rough bunk as he had done every day of the five weeks of his imprisonment in the Temple. He stared up at the small window of his dank cell, a pitiful bit of light from outside barely penetrating the gloom. His musings were not interrupted by the sound of people moving down the hall, a noise he had heard far too often. He did not wish to contemplate their final walk to the tumbrels.

The scrape of the key in the lock caused him to turn. The door opened with a loud screech.

"Greetings, Lafarge! I have a guest for you!" cried the large, stinking turnkey. Into the small room he half-tossed a disheveled man who, tripping, fell hard against the wall.

"I present to you the mighty and feared *Citoyen* Armand Chauvelin! I know things are a bit cramped in here, but you will not have to suffer long, Lafarge. *Citoyen* Chauvelin, he has a rendezvous with Madame Guillotine in the morning!"

Lafarge helped the man to his feet as the jailor continued his taunting.

"First Robespierre, now you! Ah, but it is a wonderful day! I only regret I shall not see you shaved by the National Razor at the *Place de la Revolution*, Chauvelin, as I must be in Lyon tonight. So

I will say au revoir, *salaud!*[1] May you burn in hell!" Laughing, he slammed the door shut.

Lafarge resumed his seat on the lone bunk, eying the newcomer. Of middling height, the man ran his long fingers through greasy hair. His torn clothes seemed out of place adorning such a prestigious personage. Either the guards had been rough with him or his rags had been a disguise.

"So, you are *Citoyen* Chauvelin?" Lafarge knew nothing else to say.

Chauvelin glared at him and then looked about the room, straightening to his full height. "I am. Your name, *Citoyen*?" He spoke with an authority his present situation belied.

The man's abruptness did not bother Lafarge. He had heard such things many times before. "I am Lafarge. I work...I worked as a clerk in the city."

"Your crime?"

"None, now." As Chauvelin turned towards him, Lafarge continued. "I offended the wrong person down the street from my lodgings. I was denounced as an admirer of the *ci-devant*[2] aristocrats. I was awaiting trial, but now they tell me I am to be freed. My denouncer was himself condemned in the wake of *Citoyen* Robespierre's...fall. He went to the guillotine three days ago."

Chauvelin grunted and turned away towards the tiny, high window. "I knew how it would be. We are all turning on ourselves. First Hébert, then Danton, now Robespierre. Ah, well. Now Tallien is in control, and all of us who tried to defend *la Révolution* must pay the price."

Lafarge shrugged.

"Are you a patriot, Lafarge?" Chauvelin demanded to know.

"Yes. I wore the tricolor proudly. I have no love for the *aristos.*" He paused. "Do...do you think they will come back?"

Chauvelin laughed without mirth. "They will try, but no one

1 Bastard
2 French for "from before"; people or things dispossessed of their estate or quality; old-fashioned. In Revolutionary France it was a derogatory term for those who rejected Revolutionary ideals in favor of royalist sympathies

wants them. We are done with kings and courtiers. Tallien was as opposed to the *aristos* as any of us, no matter what he says now." Chauvelin looked over his shoulder at Lafarge. "They are no threat to the Republic, *Citoyen*. No, the danger comes from the north!"

Lafarge thought about that. "You speak of the English?"

"Yes!" Eyes alight, Chauvelin crossed the small cell and sat next to Lafarge on the cot. "The English have always been our enemy. Jealous of our prestige and power—of our culture, of our genius —they are always plotting against us. They stole our colonies in the New World. They stand against us at every turn. We must not rest until they have been put in their proper place!"

"There is not much we can do. *La Manche*[3] protects them."

"Yes, their accursed ships ply the waters of *La Manche* as though it belongs to them. But that will change. Even now, we are building the newest, fastest, most powerful ships in the world. Their time will come. But I speak of other threats."

Lafarge was curious. "What are those?"

Chauvelin lowered his voice. "Have you heard of *Le Mouron Rouge?*"

Lafarge's eyes grew wide. "The savior of the *aristos*? He is real?"

"Yes, I have fought him. I have seen him. He is as real as you and I."

"But...but if *La Terreur* is over, why should we fear him?"

Chauvelin raised his chin. "Have you no love for justice, Lafarge? This foreign criminal has dared to flout the laws of the Republic, delivering the *aristos* from their just deserts, and we should do nothing? Do not think France will be safe. No, those hated *aristos* will breed traitors, and the English will send them back to attack us. And *he* will be with them!"

Lafarge considered Chauvelin's words. Indeed, Lafarge considered himself a loyal supporter of the Revolution. Besides, those damned Englishmen had been France's enemy for centuries. Now, was his country to be endangered by them yet again? The thought roiled in Lafarge's empty belly.

---

3 The English Channel.

"What can we do about it?" he asked his companion.

Chauvelin stared at the floor. "I can do nothing. My labors end tomorrow morning." He shook his head. "I have no fear of death, Lafarge. It is easy—just eternal sleep. I only wish it were not…" He sighed. "The machine was designed for criminals, not patriots. If a firing squad awaited me in the morning, I would have no complaints. But to meet my end like a damned *aristo*? I am cursed." He turned to Lafarge. "But, if I cannot continue the fight, you can! You will take up my banner! You will see to it that France is kept safe!"

"How can I do that?"

"You will become my instrument. Once you are freed, you must take a position in government, one that will allow you to keep an eye open for the enemies of France. We have tonight. I will tell you everything I know. But first, you must pledge to me you will do this. Swear!"

The flame of fanaticism was ignited in Lafarge's heart. "I will do it. I swear on the grave of my mother."

Chauvelin sighed in relief. "Good! First I must tell you of the most dangerous man in England. Of him, you must be ever vigilant! Remember this name: Sir Percy Blakeney. He is an English baronet—one of their damned *aristos*. Do not underestimate him! He is clever, very clever." He laughed. "But he will not be looking for you. You will succeed where I have failed."

"Sir Percy Blakeney. Who is he?"

"You know him as *Le Mouron Rouge*—the Scarlet Pimpernel."

Chapter 1

Along the banks of a sleepy river, the budding branches of great trees hung in the early morning mist. The spires of the university were blanketed, giving the field where three friends were gathered the proper atmosphere for the events to follow. Spring had come early, and one of the figures stood in his shirtsleeves, swinging a sword back and forth against a patch of tall grass. His fellows watched nervously. The elder of the two, tall with black hair and blue eyes, crossed his arms over his broad chest.

"Tell me again how it is you always find yourself in this predicament, Frederick?" demanded an annoyed Colonel Sir John Buford.

The coatless man turned. "Buford, I am innocent of that lightskirt's accusations. I swear it." Captain Frederick Tilney's long blond hair was slicked back and tied in an old style queue.

Buford grunted. "That would be novel."

The third man, nineteen and much younger than his companions, moved his eyes between his two friends. "Frederick is right, Buford. We were there, do you not recall? The lady just walked up and began to denounce Frederick in the most disparaging manner."

"I was not talking about that, George," answered the colonel. He turned back to the other man. "I was witness to it. That is why I am here. But I am certain there is more to the story, is there not, Frederick?"

Frederick did not reply.

"Well?"

"All right." Frederick huffed. "Yes, I am acquainted with the lady—"

"Hold!" cried George Blakeney. "A carriage approaches."

"Well," sighed Buford, "remember what I asked you, Frederick."

"Of course," Frederick protested. "I do not want this fight any more than you."

The carriage pulled next to another one parked at the entrance to the meadow. The door opened, and four men stepped out. At once, they strode over to the waiting party.

A fat, middle-aged man in black with a powdered wig under his hat approached first. Carrying a small bag, he was obviously a doctor, and he separated himself from the others who had just arrived. "Captain Tilney?"

"I am he," Frederick answered. "Mr. Blakeney is my second. Sir John will act as Master of the Field."

"Why should it be him?" demanded one of the newcomers in a strong Scots accent. He could not have been eighteen.

"You challenge *me*, sir?" Buford spat the words in his most intimidating manner.

"There will be no more of that, Brian," said one of the others, also in a Highlander's lilt. "We agreed. Let us get this over with. Sir John, would you do the honors?"

The doctor stepped back as Buford took his position between the two seconds.

"Does Sir Robert stand by his challenge, Mr. Paisley?" he growled.

"He does, and he will have satisfaction!" cried the fourth man: English, portly, and red-faced.

Buford gritted his teeth. "You are not part of this, John Thorpe —unless you want to pick up a sword?" Mr. Thorpe blanched, and Buford returned his glare to the Hon. Brian Paisley, second son of Lord Paisley. "Well, sir?"

Mr. Paisley turned to his brother, who nodded. "Aye, he does, Sir John."

Buford turned to George Blakeney. "Does Captain Tilney have anything to say?"

George nodded. "I am charged to beg you hear my principal's words." With that, he motioned to Frederick, who took a step forward.

"Sir Robert, I stand by my assurances to you that I am innocent of the charge laid against me by your betrothed," he said in a voice far from humble. "I shall say that, during my acquaintance with the lady, I may have engaged in behavior that, while gentlemanly on the whole, might have inadvertently given rise to expectations that were not intended. If that be the case, I apologize to her and her family. It was unintentionally done, and I hope any pain suffered was but fleeting. However," he continued in a voice of steel, "I reject utterly any accusation that I behaved in an infamous manner with her."

"Lies!" cried Sir Robert Paisley, a man of three and twenty. "Isabella was abandoned by you after you failed to seduce her, you blackguard! She told me all, and her story was confirmed by my friend here." He pointed to Mr. Thorpe.

Frederick snickered. "You name *that* man a friend? Then you are a bigger fool than I thought, even after agreeing to marry Miss Thorpe!"

Sir Robert's rage increased. "Why, you—"

"Enough!" roared Buford. "Gentlemen, as an apology from the challenged was deemed insufficient, we shall commence. Captain Tilney, the challenged, has the choice of weapons, and he has selected swords. Gentlemen, you shall hand your weapons to the other's second for inspection."

The seconds looked over the swords carefully as Buford continued. "The rules are these: the parties shall engage until one is well-blooded, disabled, or disarmed or until, after receiving a wound and blood being drawn, Sir Robert, as the challenger, begs pardon. Are the seconds satisfied with the weapons? Good. Please return them to the antagonists. Gentlemen, take your positions."

The two men raised their swords and reached forward until they touched. Buford drew his sword and placed the tip under the others. "Ready?" A moment later, he pulled up sharply, separating the two blades and starting the duel.

Frederick stepped back, twitching his sword lightly in the air, all the better to take his opponent's measure. As he expected, Sir Robert was angry and inexperienced. Frederick was an expert fencer, and while there was great danger here, he thought it likely he would triumph.

Sir Robert gritted his teeth. "Do you fight or dance, you coward?" He made a great slash at Frederick, who blocked the attack. Again and again, the Scot tried to get through the captain's defense to no avail.

Frederick grinned as he parried the last blow, causing Sir Robert almost to lose his footing. "Do you wish to continue, sir? You have proven your courage. Walk away and be satisfied; I shall not gainsay you."

"I will only be satisfied with your blood, you bastard!" Sir Robert cried as he mounted his fiercest attack. Frederick blocked, then in a blur counter-attacked. His blade moving too fast to see, he struck the inside of Sir Robert's sword arm. The Scot nobleman screamed in pain as his sword fell from his nerveless hand. A moment later, Sir Robert was on his knees, Frederick's blade over his heart.

In a calm voice, Frederick said, "I have drawn first blood. Do you yield, sir?"

The young man looked up from his wound, fear and resignation painted on his face. "I-I cannot fight; I am at your mercy. Do what you must."

"Frederick, do not—" Buford began to say as he stepped forward, but Frederick raised his free hand.

"You are a fool, Sir Robert, but a brave fool. Live and learn from this. Trust no woman." With that, he stepped back from his opponent, bowed with a flourish, a cocky smile dancing on his lips, and turned to walk away. "Do you see, George?" he said to his grinning second. "I told you there was no need for concern."

Blakeney's smile suddenly vanished. "Frederick, look out!"

Frederick whirled about, blade at the ready, to see an incensed Brian Paisley with a hand on the butt of the pistol in his belt. At the same time, Buford had drawn his own pistol and leveled it at the young Scotsman.

"Hold!" the colonel shouted in a voice of iron. "Touch that pistol and, by heaven, I'll drop you where you stand!"

Frederick blinked in astonishment at the tableaux before him. He realized that, but for Buford's actions, young Paisley would have shot him.

"Young masters, pray do not!" cried the doctor.

His face white, Buford slowly approached Mr. Paisley. "If you so much as twitch, you are a dead man," he snarled as he switched his pistol to his left hand. His eyes never leaving those of the terrified young man, Buford eased the gun from Paisley's waistband. He stepped back, hefted the weapon, and with a curse, threw it as far as he could into the river.

"No!" cried Mr. Paisley. "That belongs to my father!"

Buford spun on him. "Would you rather I shoot you, then? Are you ready to die? Is that what you want?" Buford jammed his pistol barrel under Mr. Paisley's chin. "If that is your wish, I will oblige you." Flaming blue eyes bore into the petrified man. "Do you know how I earned my title, boy? While you were still hunting frogs in your father's pond, I was fighting the King's enemies. I have killed scores of men better than you, Paisley. One more will not hurt my conscience."

"Y-You would not d-dare. My father—"

"Who is your father compared to mine?" Buford jabbed his pistol upwards. "Your ancestors chased sheep in the hills of Caledonia. Mine signed Magna Carta. You are nothing to me!"

"Sir John, mercy, I pray you!" pleaded the wounded Sir Robert. "My brother is full young and headstrong. He cannot be worth your wrath."

The colonel of cavalry took in a calming breath. "Very well, sir. But I charge you to keep this hothead in line, or he will not be so fortunate next time." Buford returned his attention to the sweating man before him. "Understand this, my fine young noble, stay out of my sight, for I would just as soon put a bullet in your head as not. Do you hear me?"

Young Paisley groaned pitifully, causing Buford to glance down. He lowered his pistol, and with a voice filled with disgust, continued. "I see you do. Leave now—and change your breeches, for heaven's sake."

By now, the doctor had begun treating Sir Robert. "The cut was deep yet struck no artery. I have stopped the bleeding. Sir Robert shall recover."

As Buford returned to his friends, Frederick had a comment for John Thorpe, who was already halfway to his coach. "I shall remember you, sirrah, and the part you played in this. Flee, you coward."

Buford turned to the others. "Let us leave this place."

IN FRUSTRATION, BUFORD THREW HIS HAT INTO THE FAR CORNER of the room he shared with Frederick during their visit to Oxford.

Frederick laughed. "Come, Buford, no cause for all that. I would say we had an excellent time here. Good food and wine, good friends"—he patted Blakeney on the back—"pretty girls with which to dance. Even a bit o' sport. Better than dreary old Bath, that is certain!"

"Sport?" Buford turned on Frederick. "You call this morning 'sport'?"

"Why, yes. You did not really think I was in any danger from that young buck, did you?"

"And what do you call his brother's actions? Good lord, Frederick, I was almost forced to shoot him! I nearly killed a boy because you cannot keep from behaving badly with women!"

Frederick, affronted, protested. "Buford, I did not—"

"Frederick, tell me the damn truth. All of it!"

Frederick compressed his lips and turned to the window. "I met Isabella Thorpe in Bath during the time my brother, Henry, was courting Catherine Morland. Miss Thorpe was attractive and welcoming. I danced with her and called on her several times."

He gestured. "Supposedly, she was engaged to Catherine's brother James at the time."

"Supposedly?"

"Very well, she *was* betrothed! But she did not behave as though she was! Gad, Buford, the chit threw herself at me. She did not break things off with James Morland because of my pretty face. No, it was because James was poor and I was heir to Northanger Abbey! If any attempted seduction was going on, it was on Miss Thorpe's part. She wanted to secure me by arranging a compromise. I was fortunate to extract myself. I believe James owes me a debt of gratitude."

Buford stared at his friend. "And now she has the young Sir Robert. He is wealthy enough. So why last night's performance?"

"I do not know. I cannot read the light-skirt's mind!"

George Blakeney, who had been standing silent witness to the discussion, finally spoke. "It is said 'hell hath no fury like a woman scorned.' Perhaps it is no more than that."

Frederick laughed. "I see you are not sleeping during your classes, George!"

"You may be right, Blakeney," said Buford slowly, "or perhaps Miss Thorpe was unsure of her position with Sir Robert and felt she needed assurance that he would have to honor his engagement." He raised an eyebrow.

"What? By fighting me?"

Buford nodded. "Of course. He would be more honor bound to her than ever if he had killed you."

Frederick's jaw dropped. The thought had never occurred to him. "That whore!"

"You now see where your actions have brought you?" Buford demanded.

"*My* actions? Oh, come now, Buford!"

"Yes, your actions! If you would stop flirting with every pretty woman in every room you walk into, you would not get into these scrapes. I am tired of coming to your rescue." At Frederick's incredulous look, Buford counted on his fingers. "Ellen Peabody,

Mary King, Lady Joanne Barksdale, Annabella Adams, Charlotte Davis—"

Frederick cut him off. "You do not have to name them all, Buford! Besides, you are no better."

Instead of laughing it off as Frederick expected, Buford grew even grimmer. "You are right, Frederick. I was as big a scoundrel as you —even worse. But no more. I have seen the errors of my ways. I have vowed to honor my father and my fallen comrades by being a gentleman. No more dallying. No more assignations. I have thrown off all of my unworthy acquaintances. I shall live honorably, and the next woman I bed shall be my wife."

Recalling their shared adventures of the past, Frederick was incredulous. "Bold words, my friend."

"You think this is a joke? Open your eyes, Frederick! Do you not see the path of unhappiness you are upon?" With a cry, Buford threw up his hands. "If you do not understand, then we have nothing else to say to each other."

"What do you mean?"

Intense blue eyes bore into him. "I said I have thrown off *all* my unworthy acquaintances. Until you reform your ways, Captain Tilney, we must part."

Frederick stepped back, hurt to the quick. Since entering the army together, the two had been inseparable. Now, one of his best friends was cutting all ties. The bile of betrayal rose in his throat. "As you wish, Sir John." Unable to help himself, he added, "Knighthood has surely changed my jolly companion."

Buford paused on the way to his room to pack. "Not knighthood, Captain, but war. Farewell." He softy closed the bedroom door behind him.

Frederick stared at the door, stunned by what had happened. Then he felt a hand on his shoulder. "Do not worry, Frederick," George said in an attempt to console him. "Buford is just angry. He is still upset over what happened with Paisley. Mark my words. He will apologize."

Frederick shook his head slowly. "No, he will not. In all the years I have known him, I have never seen John Buford take back his words. Never."

George patted his shoulder. "Err…let us get some breakfast, eh? I am a bit peckish."

Frederick sighed and, with a bit of false humor, said, "Zounds, but that is a capital idea, George. Lead the way."

They were having their second cup of coffee when Sir John stepped into the post carriage for London without taking his leave of them.

Woodston, Gloucestershire

A WEEK LATER FOUND FREDERICK TAKING TEA IN THE PARLOR OF the parsonage house at Woodston, home of his brother, Henry, and sister-in-law, Catherine.

"I tell you, Henry," Frederick complained, "Father is worse than ever! All the good feeling he shared at your and Eleanor's weddings has turned to mist! May the Devil take him!"

"Frederick!" Catherine scolded him.

Frederick shook his head. "You are truly an angel, Cathy, after the way he treated you."

It was not hyperbole. General Tilney was happy to have Miss Catherine Morland visit Northanger Abbey when he believed her an heiress. After learning that she was only the daughter of a clergy-man who, while respectable and comfortable, was far from rich, the furious general drove the poor girl from his home in the middle of the night. The grievous insult had led to a rupture between father and sons. Captain Tilney was outraged, but his anger paled to that of Henry. Relations between the Abbey and Woodston were only mildly mended upon Henry's marriage to Miss Morland.

Henry reached out and took Catherine's hand in easy affection. "Mrs. Tilney has taken to her role of parson's wife with full enthusiasm. But, truly, we have forgiven him. Have we not, my dear?" He kissed her hand as she nodded, a becoming blush rising to her cheeks. "That being said, we know how the general can be. Where are you to be sent now?"

"I am being transferred to the Royal Horse Guards Blue."

Henry sat up. "From the Twelfth Dragoons? That is unusual, is it not?"

"Damned right, it is! Oh, my apologies, Cathy. Worse than that, I am to be assigned to the Household Cavalry. Instead of being in a front-line regiment, I am to be a play-solider for His Majesty's amusement! And suffer the expense of buying all new blue uniforms!"

"I did not know Father had any influence left with the General Staff."

"Apparently, enough to effect the transfer but not enough to get a promotion without paying for it! All my good service with the Twelfth is as nothing, and in return, I earn the ill will of lieutenants looking forward to their captaincy. I am in a fine pickle!"

"Why would he do that?" Catherine asked.

"Matrimony, Cathy, matrimony. He believes being in London will help me secure a proper mistress for Northanger Abbey."

"Well, that is understandable, Frederick," replied his brother with a grin. "Both Eleanor and I have found the companions of our future lives while you, at eight-and-twenty, are well on your way to being labeled by the *ton* a confirmed bachelor."

Frederick blanched at his brother's teasing. "Hardly *that*, as you well know!"

Catherine shook her head. "I never know half the time of what you two are speaking."

"Never mind, dear. Frederick, it *is* time you settled down, you know."

"I suppose." Frederick allowed. "I expect all the good women are taken"—he toasted Catherine with his teacup—"but I should endeavor to try harder."

Henry looked at his brother for a moment and then turned to his wife. "My love, would you excuse us? I must speak to Frederick on family business."

Catherine had been married to Henry Tilney long enough to understand his meaning. He wished to be frank with his brother, and he would give a précis to her later in private. "Of course, Henry. I must see to the dinner. Enjoy your tea." A kiss on the cheek to both men and she was out of the room, closing the door behind her.

Henry began almost immediately. "I know how overbearing Father is, but you have dealt with him before without losing your good cheer. What is troubling you?"

"Besides that my path to advancement has been made longer?"

"The army was never your permanent profession."

"True. Do you have anything stronger than tea?"

Henry went to a sideboard and poured two sherries. Accepting his glass, Frederick said, "It is John Buford. I am afraid strong words have passed between us."

"Tell me."

Frederick gave his brother an accounting of his misadventures in Oxford. Henry considered the information before speaking.

"Sir John has been your good friend, and I am sorry this matter has come between you. What do you propose to do about it?"

"What can I do? If Buford will not see me, how can I make things right—if I was in the wrong."

"Do you not think you were in the wrong?"

Frederick glanced at Henry. "You would ask that question, Brother."

Henry's face was impassive. "Well?"

"I am not in the wrong—not entirely. Oh, I suppose I should not have flirted with Miss Thorpe, but as things turned out, it was for the best, or you may have been forced to call that chit your sister."

The clergyman sat back. "True. A more unpleasant prospect is hard to imagine. James is far better off without her. But do you think your actions did not cause pain and consternation?"

"I suppose they did—at the time," Frederick allowed.

"I was witness to it, Frederick. Catherine was most distressed for her brother's sake."

"If so, Cathy has forgiven me. And James is quite cordial."

"Yes, but that is because they are Morlands, and there is not an unforgiving bone in their bodies, but they do not forget. Do not be surprised if James keeps any lady dear to him away from your company."

Frederick blanched. "Does Cathy wish me away?"

"Of course not," Henry assured him. "She has accepted you and loves you as her brother. A troublesome brother, to sure, but we Tilneys are a troublesome lot." He paused. "Frederick, do you not see that by your actions, you lower your prospects of a happy marriage?"

Frederick snorted. "Who can realistically have such expectations?"

"Few can. Our mother certainly did not. However, you must admit that Eleanor is deliriously happy, and my own situation is not bad at all."

"Not bad? Now, there is an understatement if ever I heard one! Cathy is the best of women. One of the few, besides Eleanor, worthy of a man's affection and trust." At Henry's questioning look, Frederick added, "Oh, do not worry about that! I envy your situation, but I do not begrudge you your choice of wife." He took a sip from his glass. "I only wish I could be confidant of finding her like."

Henry softly smiled. "I do not think there are any more Catherines, but I am sure there is the right lady for you out there."

Frederick crossed his legs and played with the seam of his trousers. "If only I could be as sure as you, I would not rest until she is found."

"Are you certain you are looking in the right places? I found Catherine lost in the Pump Room in the middle of a crowd. Where do you seek your match?"

Frederick frowned. "I have the annoying feeling you agree with Buford."

Henry fought off a smile. "Wisdom is not limited to Holy Scripture."

"I will give the matter some consideration. Agreed?"

"If you find my words worthy of further thought, I am humbled."

Frederick let out a bark of a laugh. "Humble! If there is one thing you and I share, it is that we cannot be called humble." He finished off his drink. "We have too much of our father in us."

"We are put upon this Earth to overcome our weaknesses."

"I said I would think about it." Frederick stood up. "Now, if you will excuse me, I must reply to a letter from a Major Denny of Horse Guards."

Henry nodded. "Of course. And I must return to my sermon for Sunday. I shall see you at dinner."

Frederick could not stop from asking. "And what shall be the subject of your talk?" At Henry's wide grin, he knew before his brother answered.

"Humility."

Chapter 2

A clerk in the ministry of the Interior burst into the room. "He is here! Louis has entered Paris!"

The room exploded with noise as all the occupants of the office dropped their work and began to discuss and debate the effect this event would have on their livelihoods—all the occupants but one. An old bearded man, sitting in his alcove bent over his work, paid no attention to the clamor.

The clerk rushed to his side and shook him by his shoulder. "Lafarge, did you not hear? The King is in Paris!"

The old man threw the hand off his person in exasperation. "Yes, yes—the Count of Provence is now Louis XVIII. We knew this day was coming. Now, leave me to my work!"

The clerk did not take offence. "I hear that Louis is so stricken with the gout he must be wheeled about in a chair."

M. Lafarge's eyes never left his papers. "Have you nothing else to do but tell me gossip?"

Ignoring his cries, the clerk seized the papers and tossed them into the air. "A new world, Lafarge, and you will take no note of it? Idiot! This work means nothing as we will all be dismissed tomorrow!"

"Stop it! Leave him alone!"

The two turned to see a tall man in his early thirties standing near the entrance to the alcove. Though dressed in civilian clothes, his air was thoroughly military. He glared at the intimidated clerk who immediately slunk off to join the others. The old man crawled about on the floor on his hands and knees, retrieving his papers.

"Here, sir, let me help you." The tall man gathered the papers, placed them on the desk, and then helped M. Lafarge to his feet.

"*Merci*, monsieur. I do not know your name."

"My name is *Capitaine* Honoré Bourgeois, monsieur," he said with a slight bow.

"Ah, the new man. I thank you for your help. I am Monsieur Lafarge." He eyed Bourgeois as he resumed his seat behind his desk. "You do not join in the festivities or the lamentations?"

If anything, the man stood taller. "The army assigned me to this office to work. I must do my duty."

A crafty look grew in Lafarge's eyes. "To King, as you did to Emperor?"

"My duty is to France, whether empire or kingdom—France," Bourgeois said firmly.

M. Lafarge smiled. "Well said, *Capitaine*. Now, if you would excuse me." He gestured at the papers on his desk.

Bourgeois executed another small bow and took his leave. M. Lafarge returned to his labors but only after glancing at the officer's retreating back.

London

"How does it look?" Frederick Tilney asked his companion, tugging at his new dress-blue uniform coat. "Everything straight?"

George Blakeney snickered. "Lord, Frederick, you act as though you are being presented to the Queen!" They moved towards the door of the ballroom.

"I am not like you, George. It is not every day I meet the Prince Regent."

"Such are the benefits of having Prinny as one's godfather." George grinned as the door was opened by a pair of servants. A butler escorted them across the growing crowd to a corner. There, they found a fat man, dressed in the latest fashion, talking to a couple.

The butler bowed. "Your Grace, may I present Mr. Blakeney and Captain Tilney."

HRH George Augustus Frederick, the Prince Regent, smiled from ear to ear. "Georgie, my boy! Good to see you, good to see you. And where is that rascal father of yours?" He pulled George into as much of an embrace as his eighteen-stone frame would allow.

"He shall be here soon, Your Grace. Nothing would keep him away. Pray allow me to present my friend Captain Tilney."

Frederick made his leg. "Your Highness."

The Regent put up one fat hand. "None of that! 'Tis only the Duke of Cornwall tonight. The 'Regent' is still in the palace, thank goodness."

"Your Grace." Frederick bowed his head. It was not unusual for the Regent to use one of his lesser titles if only to do away with protocol on an informal evening.

The Regent eyed Frederick's uniform with approval and spoke to the man beside him. "I think this one may be one of yours, Uxbridge. The Blues, eh? Excellent, excellent!" Frederick turned to the couple next to the Regent as his liege continued. "Have you met Lord Uxbridge, Captain?"

"I have not yet the pleasure, sir. Captain Tilney, Household Cavalry, m'lord," Tilney said as he bowed to General Sir Henry William Paget, the Earl of Uxbridge.

Lord Uxbridge, in civilian clothes, flicked a smile in return as he spoke to the Regent. "I was with the Light Dragoons in the Peninsula, m'lord, not the heavies." He turned his attention to Frederick. "Tilney, eh? I thought you in the Twelfth."

Frederick colored slightly. "I was until recently, sir. I joined the Blues not three weeks ago." He bowed to the lady beside Lord Uxbridge.

"Ah, yes—my wife, gentlemen." Lady Uxbridge—the former Lady Charlotte Wellesley before her divorce five years prior from Sir Henry Wellesley, Wellington's brother—smiled slightly. The two gentlemen labored to keep any expression but delight from their faces. The scandal of Lord Uxbridge and Lady Wellesley had caused a sensation.

To make small talk, Frederick was about to inquire how the former general enjoyed the House of Lords when the Regent cried out, "At last!" He waved his arm. "Get over here, you lazy popinjay! Finally, someone amusing has arrived!"

Glancing at George and seeing the smile on his face, Frederick turned to see a tall, broad-shouldered man escorting two women and walking towards them, led by the butler. The man, about fifty, wore his grey hair cut in the Roman fashion. His bright blue eyes shone above the pair of spectacles balanced on his narrow, aristocratic nose. His clothes—lace-cuffed shirt, brightly colored vest, and tight pantaloon trousers—were of the latest fashion promoted by the now-disgraced Beau Brummell who had fallen out of favor with the Regent the year before. The woman to his right was of an age with her escort, but for a lady of fifty, she was lovely. Streaks of grey threaded through her well-coiffed hair, and her figure was that of a woman half her age.

But Frederick's eye was firmly captured by the young lady to the gentleman's left. Taller than the older lady, she moved with an effortless grace, and her lovely golden gown, while modest on the whole, did little to hide her womanly charms. The unblemished ivory of her youthful skin was shown to great advantage by the tiny white roses in her ebony hair. She was, in a word, breathtaking.

The butler bowed. "Your Grace—Sir Percy Blakeney, Lady Blakeney, and Miss Blakeney."

That...that cannot be little Violet! Frederick's mind protested.

Sir Percy Blakeney made his leg. "Your Grace," he drawled while bowing low enough almost to touch his knee. Rising, he grimaced. "Odd's fish, but that is harder than it used to be!"

Lady Marguerite Blakeney hid a giggle. Even a quarter century since abandoning the name Marguerite St. Just, she could still be amused at her husband's antics.

The Regent laughed. "Oh, Percy, you looked like a scarecrow! Finally some amusement! I am bored to death!" He remembered himself. "Oh! Pardon, Uxbridge—no offence intended, man."

"None taken, sir," Lord Uxbridge replied easily.

Sir Percy smiled. "Happy to have been of service, sir."

The Regent welcomed Marguerite and then turned to the young lady. "Is this little Violet Yvonne? My, how you have grown! You are quite a lady now."

Miss Blakeney, a dark-haired beauty of seventeen, smiled. "Thank you, Your Grace." Her deep blue eyes proved true to her name, Violet.

The Regent indicated the others. "Percy, do you know Uxbridge?"

"Only by reputation. A great pleasure, m'lord."

Marguerite almost sighed. Percy cared nothing for scandals, but he could not help teasing the earl just a little. Lord Uxbridge took the jest well; the look in his eye suggested he knew Sir Percy's reputation as well.

"I am pleased and honored to meet you, sir," the earl said.

"Honored? Gad, it don't take much to impress you, sir!"

Lady Uxbridge then spoke. "From what we have been told, we owe you and others a great deal, Sir Percival."

"Please, milady, call me Sir Percy. Zooks, and there are those who owe *me* a great deal. Most of them are found in the card room of my club." He turned to his son. "George! Do not just stand there. Why, one would think you were a statue. And…gad, is that Captain Tilney?"

The tall officer in blue bowed. "It is, Sir Percy. I am pleased to meet you and Lady Blakeney again."

"It has been what—three or four years since we saw you last at Richmond?"

"Closer to five, sir."

Sir Percy raised an eyebrow. "I didn't recognize you in blue. Not that it don't suit you—red is a ghastly color—but I thought you in the Twelfth."

Tilney softly sighed, but before he answered, the orchestra started, which caused George Blakeney to look about the room.

"Looking for someone, George?" teased Sir Percy.

"Umm…yes," he admitted.

His mother took mercy on him. "You will find the Wentworths

by the refreshments."

George grinned ear to ear. "Thank you, Mother. Godfather, please excuse me. Father—Mother—milord—milady—" By now, Blakeney was halfway across the floor. He turned and called out, "Dance with Violet, Frederick!"

"What was that about?" asked Prinny.

Sir Percy smirked. "That was about Miss Dorothy Wentworth, m'lord. Ah, he is there…he is asking…success! A true Blakeney!" Sure enough, George was escorting a very pretty girl to the line.

"Wentworth," mused the Regent, "that name is familiar."

"Is she related to the Captain Wentworth famous for his exploits aboard the *Laconia*?" asked Lord Uxbridge.

"A cousin, milord," answered Marguerite. "Captain Wentworth's father was a second son." She turned to Frederick. "I believe George made a request of you, sir."

Frederick smiled, which made the handsome blond-haired officer very pleasant to behold. "He did, but I would not be so presumptuous. Miss Blakeney," he said to Violet, "would you dance the first set with an old friend?"

Violet shyly smiled. "I would be pleased to, sir." Taking her hand gently, the officer led the young woman to join the others.

"Well," groused Prinny, "if there is to be dancing, I shall retire to the card room. Coming, Percy?"

"I shall join you anon, sir."

The Regent waddled off to a back room, the butler following in his wake. The two couples turned to watch the dancers.

"Ah, dancing. Wasted on the young, you know," Sir Percy said. Marguerite followed his eyes. He was keeping a close watch on his daughter.

"So, you will not dance, Sir Percy?" asked Lady Uxbridge.

"Faith, I might if you would so honor me. All but the waltz, I beg you."

Lord Uxbridge nodded. "A notorious dance, to be sure."

"Indeed, yes," Sir Percy said gravely. "Those who dare to attempt it should be horsewhipped—do you not agree, Lady Blakeney?"

"Indeed, sir." Marguerite's elegant gloved hand hid a smile.

Percy turned to the ladies. "Would you care for something, Lady Uxbridge?" Told a glass of punch would not be refused, Sir Percy and Lord Uxbridge went off to fulfill their ladies' desires.

Lady Uxbridge turned to Marguerite. "You are very kind, but do not feel you have to entertain us."

"Faith!" cried Marguerite. "'Tis not unpleasant unless you desire privacy, milady."

"I assure you, no. I have enjoyed our conversation. But…" She paused. "I would not have our presence keep you from your friends."

Marguerite turned, a serious look in her eyes. "They are no friends of mine if they object to any of my acquaintances, Lady Uxbridge. You will not find us such shallow folk. The hypocrisy of the *ton* is no stranger to me. I have suffered under its disapproval and wear my conquering of it as a badge of honor." She scanned the crowd. "You and I both know that half of the couples here enjoy their dalliances behind closed doors. Infidelity is their sport. If many were as honest as—" She glanced at her companion. "Well, the world would be a happier place, I think."

"Thank you, Lady Blakeney."

Marguerite laughed. "Gad, I sound a radical! Ah, there is someone I would have you meet! Ffoulkes! Suzanne! Come meet my friend!"

VIOLET BLAKENEY WAS ENJOYING HER DANCE WITH FREDERICK Tilney very much. She had met him when she was twelve, barely out of the schoolroom. He had visited Richmond as George's guest a handful of times before army duties took him away. Yet, Violet had developed an infatuation with the devastatingly handsome officer. It had been five years since she had last seen him, and he still remained chief in her fantasies. It was well that George had mentioned Captain Tilney was to join him tonight; otherwise, she would have grown quite distracted.

Frederick softened the military precision of his movements with a slight smile on his handsome face. He came close and said sternly, "I am very cross with your brother, Miss Blakeney."

She decided to tease. "Miss Blakeney? There was a time you knew me as Violet."

Frederick's eyes flashed. "Such is the difference five years make. You are now a young lady and deserve to be treated as such. I hope I may count Miss Blakeney as my friend as I did little Violet, George's sister."

Oh, but there was sweet danger in those eyes! Violet hoped she did not read too much into the dashing captain's expression. "Of course you are my friend, even though you did put a frog down my back."

"A thousand pardons! I have no idea why I did such a thing." A playful expression danced on his face.

She knew exactly why. She had been George's annoying little sister, who would not leave the two young men to practice fencing in peace. "You are forgiven, sir. But you say you are angry with George?"

He nodded gravely. "I am afraid so, madam. George has had the effrontery not to extend me an invitation to Richmond to see the beauties of Surrey again. I do not think I will ever forgive him!" He flashed a teasing smile.

Violet smiled softly. "And are the beauties of Surrey so famous that you would regret not returning?"

"Any man with eyes would. Fortunately, my loss has been recompensed tonight."

Violet flushed at the captain's flirtation. "Sir, you should not say such things," she whispered halfheartedly.

Frederick lost his smile. "Forgive me, Miss Blakeney, but I could not resist expressing my admiration of…the flowers in your hair."

Violet looked at him in surprise, her hand rising to her hair. "My flowers?"

"Yes," he said, his face softening. "I confess I enjoy white roses very much. I assume they are from the conservatory at Richmond, an impressive structure if I recall rightly."

The girl was confused and disappointed, for she had thought Frederick had been talking about her. A response was on her lips when she detected a mischievous glint in his eye. She tried to look displeased with him and failed.

"They are, sir. This is something new. I did not know your interests included a horticultural bent."

"Well"—he grinned—"I *am* heir to my family's estate, so I should know something about growing things. I must have some knowledge of agriculture. But who could not take note of such perfection?"

She nodded. "For my mother, I thank you."

"By the way, the flowers are pretty too." With that, the steps of the dance drew them too far apart for her response.

It was just as well, a blushing Violet considered, for she had to admit she enjoyed Frederick's outrageous flirting, and the short time away from him gave her the opportunity to swallow the rebuke she almost gave.

Let me see what he does next, now that he has outmaneuvered me. Perhaps I can give back some of his own.

Frederick drew close again, contrition on his face. "Miss Blakeney, forgive me. I should not have said what I did. I am afraid I have embarrassed you and have given you a very poor impression of me."

Violet did not smile, but her look was not at all unfriendly. "Captain Tilney, I accept your apology. I have recovered from embarrassment before; it will not be a lasting condition."

The dance drew them apart again for a moment. When he was close enough, she said in a low voice, "As for my opinion of you, time will tell whether it is poor or not." She smiled sweetly as she turned, earning a smile in return.

They continued the dance, exchanging more suitable conversation.

THE BLAKENEYS, UXBRIDGES, AND FFOULKESES STOOD AND OBserved the young people finish their dance. Marguerite's eye was upon George as he returned Miss Wentworth to her family. It seemed he was making good progress there, she noted, as he spoke with ease to the girl's relations. She glanced at her husband, intending to call his attention to their son, but she noticed that his eyes were fixed instead on their daughter.

"Percy?" she whispered.

"Hmm?" His attention never wavered as Captain Tilney walked

Violet to her brother and the Wentworths. Once Violet left the cavalryman's arm, Sir Percy turned to his wife. "Did you say something, m'dear?"

Marguerite shook her head, curious over her husband's unusual behavior. Since Violet's coming out a few months before, he had seen her dance many times and never batted an eye. She did not know what Percy was about. Surely, Captain Tilney was a man of good character, as were all of George's friends. She was about to remark about it when the musicians began to play a particular piece of music.

"Odd's fish, but that sounds a pretty jig!" cried Sir Percy. "What is your opinion, Lady Uxbridge?"

"Sir Percy, I declare that is a waltz," she said, amazed. "But, is it not early in the evening for such a dance?"

It was the usual practice for a waltz to be played late in the evening after those who would be scandalized by the decadent dance had already left for home. For it to be the second dance was unprecedented. No band of musicians would dare to play such a piece unless they had been well compensated. Marguerite narrowed her eyes at Sir Percy. He did not disappoint.

The baronet was grim. "Gad, I would say that you were right, m'lady. Very unfortunate. The players should have a very stern talking to. But, another punishment comes to mind." He held out his hand to his wife. "Lady Blakeney, would you oblige me?"

She curtsied. "If you wish, sir."

She placed her hand in his, and the two made their way to the dance floor. In moments, they were in each other's arms, swept along by the music. Out of the corner of her eye, Marguerite saw that George and Violet were among the small group of couples dancing. She leaned her head close to Sir Percy.

"I take it you bribed the musicians, my love?"

"Of course," he said. "Prinny will soon demand that I attend him in the card room, and that will be all the dancing for the evening, I am afraid. I would not disappoint you."

Marguerite smiled. "But, sir," she said, her eyes fluttering like a girl half her age, "did you not say those who dance the waltz should be horsewhipped?"

A tender look filled Sir Percy's eyes behind his spectacles—a look reserved only for *her*. "I should have made myself better understood. I reserve horsewhipping for anyone but me who attempts to dance the waltz with my Margot."

"Then, the backs of the gentlemen of England are forever safe," she answered with all the love in her heart, "for I shall never dance like this with anyone but you, *mon chéri*."

FREDERICK WATCHED AS GEORGE WALTZED WITH MISS BLAKENEY. A strange, unpleasant feeling settled in his breast.

This is ridiculous! One dance with her and I am jealous of her brother! Get a hold of yourself, man! She is but a child! A very pretty child, indeed, but a child nevertheless. I am ten years her senior at least!

He schooled his features to show disinterest, but he could not cease his thoughts. Violet Blakeney was a good-natured, intelligent girl and far from coy. No, she had seen his flirting for the diversion it was and had returned it measure for measure. But good Lord, she had grown uncommonly pretty!

Bah! She is a beautiful girl, I will grant that—but that is all. She is sister to my good friend, and I shall not dally with her. No, she is all that is good and lovely. I will not harm her. I will behave myself. She is safe from me.

But I will get an invitation to Richmond, by God.

Chapter 3

The Season was designed, among other things, to present young ladies making their debut into society. Once the required presentation to the Queen was accomplished, the real work began—finding husbands for the latest collection of would-be brides. There were many rules and customs to be followed; indeed, navigating this enterprise was as intricate as any dance in a ballroom.

Convention required that, after a debutante attended a ball, callers would descend upon her the next day. Some would be family and friends offering congratulations or sharing stories. Some would be female acquaintances of the *ton* seeking gossip. The most anticipated and dreaded were the calls of the gentlemen. A young lady had no power to choose her admirers. Only the most egregious rakes and scoundrels could be turned away without raising a fracas that would result in a few lines in the newspapers' society pages. It was, therefore, the sometimes-unpleasant duty of the young lady and her relations to suffer the attentions of the unworthy if the more welcome attendance of an agreeable gentleman was to be enjoyed without scandal.

The Blakeney estate in Richmond, outside of London in Surrey, was one of the most beautiful in the country, and only her family held a larger place in Lady Blakeney's heart. Yet, it was a mixed blessing. The inconvenience of being an hour or more from Town was felt every time Marguerite visited friends, went shopping, or attended an entertainment. Sir Percy, as attentive as he was rich, had purchased a house in Town, and it was mainly used as a staging point for their excursions. However, the family seldom spent more than two nights together in the place, so dear was the charm and seclusion of Richmond.

Privacy was vital to the success of the Blakeney marriage. At first, Marguerite understood the need for secrecy, because Percy's activities with the League of the Scarlet Pimpernel put his life, and those of his loved ones, in constant danger from the agents and admirers of the bloody French Revolution. Thus he had created his alter ego —the buffoonish Sir Percy, always dressed in the latest fashion and perhaps the greatest fool in the kingdom. So well had Percy played the part that even Marguerite was deceived for a time. It was hard for anyone not privy to the secret to take Sir Percy seriously, a fact that kept the dear man alive.

Almost twenty years had passed since the fall of Robespierre and his Reign of Terror. The League had been disbanded, and the Pimpernel descended into legend. Yet, Sir Percy lived on—less insipid, more rational, but still somewhat silly, though he was now considered more eccentric than idiotic. To Marguerite's continued bemusement, it was only at Richmond or their estate in Scotland that the foppish Sir Percy, clotheshorse and master of the fashionable drawing rooms of London and Bath, dropped his carefully crafted disguise and revealed himself to be simply Percy Blakeney—brave patriot, brilliant thinker, loyal friend, excellent father, fair master, and ardent lover and husband. Only behind closed doors could Marguerite enjoy the unconcealed nature of the man she adored. The children, knowing no other life, accepted this state of affairs and instinctively kept the family's secrets.

Yes, Richmond was important to Lady Blakeney's happiness, but now it served another function. Being close to London, Marguerite could retire to the Blakeney ancestral home and limit interruptions on the family's daily life by the *ton* without appearing to reject society.

To be honest, both Marguerite and Percy enjoyed the hustle and bustle of the Season, and it was not only the closeness of good friends and the stimulation of the attractions of Town that pleased them. Lifelong actors both, they were excessively diverted by the success of their twenty-year performance as the preening Sir Percy and his long-suffering wife.

The privacy that the relative remoteness of Richmond afforded proved to be an additional asset, for it limited the calls after a ball to those of the most loyal or most determined. It did have its drawbacks, however. After so long a trip, visitors tended to linger longer than the customary quarter hour.

Which was why Lady Blakeney and her daughter were suffering their thirtieth minute entertaining Mrs. Annabella Norris and Lady Victoria Uppercross in the sitting room at Richmond with no end in sight.

Mrs. Norris was holding court. "It was so pleasant to see so many of our friends at a party so late in the Season. Everyone will set off for the country or perhaps to the Continent now that the awful unpleasantness is over. London will be quite empty, I am sure. What a bore!"

Violet, with all good manners, asked the expected question. "And you, Mrs. Norris? Are you off to the country?"

"No, more's the pity. There was talk of removing to a cottage in Brighton, but Mr. Norris has business in Town that requires his presence, so we will not be going." She turned to Marguerite. "Now, with the Peace, do you not long to return home?"

Marguerite smiled politely. "Mrs. Norris, I am at home, as you see. We are soon to remove to Scotland, so there is much preparation to do."

"Oh, but I meant your *real* home. I understand you still have family in France," Mrs. Norris responded.

Insufferable woman! Marguerite thought. "I have cousins in Paris."

"Oh, Paris! I long to see it. Lady Victoria, you were in Paris during the last Peace, I believe."

Lady Victoria, whose eyes had not left Violet's person since she sat down for tea, said, "Indeed, it was all delightful." She took a sip of her tea.

Marguerite's acting skills served her well. She pretended rapt attention to Mrs. Norris's ramblings while taking the two ladies' measure. Mrs. Norris, who sought to advance her status among the members of the *ton*, was a tall, slim woman in her late twenties with the curious affliction of having a mouth slightly too large for her face. Or perhaps it only seemed that way since the lady seemed unable to keep it shut. She dressed to astound others with the extravagance of her wardrobe. How well her choice of dress suited her coloring and figure was a matter of debate behind the fans of the ladies of society. She was married to Mr. Norris, a gentleman whose fortune came from the sugar trade.

Lady Victoria Uppercross was another creature entirely. A darkly beautiful woman of thirty who looked at least five years younger than her true age, she was renowned for her grace, charm, and impeccable dress. It was all an act; she was as heartless as she was promiscuous, and there were rumors that she counted among her lovers some of the most dashing men of the fashionable set to which all the ladies present belonged.

Lady Victoria set her cup down. "Miss Blakeney, I noticed you were dancing with a handsome officer last night."

Violet was perplexed. "Do you refer to Captain Tilney?"

Both women reacted to the name. Mrs. Norris blanched while Lady Victoria's eyes flashed. Marguerite could only wonder at it.

"Captain Tilney of Northanger Abbey?" Lady Victoria tried to make her question sound offhanded and failed.

"Yes, do you know him?" A small frown creased Violet's forehead.

"A slight acquaintance." She turned to her companion. "But you know him better; do you not, my dear Annabella?"

"A bit." Mrs. Norris blushed. "Before my marriage," she added unnecessarily.

Marguerite watched Lady Victoria's cruel teasing of Mrs. Norris with dawning understanding. She was certain of the woman's malicious intent.

Lady Victoria wants Captain Tilney for herself and stakes her claim. And she insinuates that the captain had a romantic relationship with Mrs. Norris to discourage Violet. Certainly, the woman had some interest in the gentleman, but neither Lady Victoria nor Mrs. Norris knows that he is in the Blues now or that he was in Town. I do not think either knows the captain very well.

Marguerite decided to throw a few barbs of her own. "Captain Tilney is the *particular* friend of my son. We were very happy to renew his acquaintance—we have known him for several years —and wish him joy on his transfer. You did not recognize him in his new uniform, I am sure. Did you not speak to him?"

"No," Lady Victoria admitted.

It was as Marguerite had suspected. "Pity."

Lady Victoria was not done. "Speaking of acquaintances, I did not know you knew Lord and Lady Uxbridge."

"We met them last night. Charming people."

Mrs. Norris had finally recovered sufficiently to speak. "I am sure they are, your ladyship, although there are certain people—I shall not name them—who do not find their company so delightful." She twittered behind her hand.

Marguerite knew she was speaking of the Duke of Wellington and his brothers, Sir Henry Wellesley and Richard, Marquess Wellesley. Marguerite held no particular love for the Wellesleys. They were too much Tory for her taste although she did appreciate the marquess's support of Catholic Emancipation and the duke's defense of the kingdom.

Before she could say anything, Violet spoke. "Perhaps. The Regent finds their presence tolerable, and so do I."

Marguerite gave a nod of approval to her daughter, and the conversation died for a moment.

Marguerite knew many of the Blakeneys' acquaintances, both respectable and repugnant, were due to their deep friendship with the Regent. Publicly, Prince George was considered a libertine and wastrel, particularly by those who backed the monarch, George III. It was fashionable to be a Whig and, therefore, to oppose the Tory governments that had waged war on Imperial France.

Marguerite knew the other side of Prinny's character. He backed the Whigs over some matters, such as emancipation and Wilberforce's crusade, but broke with them over others. The Regent was a fierce opponent of both Republican France and Napoleon. He was a kind and generous friend. He was not a member of the League of the Scarlet Pimpernel, but his support and assistance had proven invaluable. Because of Prinny, Percy and hundreds of French nobles were alive. If for that alone, Marguerite loved the man and overlooked the Regent's proclivities and his more unsavory hangers-on.

Loyalty to Prinny had its limits, however. Marguerite suffered to entertain the unpleasant Mrs. Norris and the unsavory Lady Victoria, for they were fellow members of the exalted society of the Regent's friends. Three-quarters of an hour of Lady Blakeney's life had been granted, and that was more than enough. Mrs. Norris was in mid story about the latest fashions when Marguerite rose from her chair.

"Lady Victoria, Mrs. Norris, words cannot describe how much my daughter and I have been honored by your kindly visit." Interrupted, Mrs. Norris could only look stupidly at her host. Marguerite continued. "Unfortunately, my husband leaves for Scotland tomorrow, and I must oversee his packing. I am sure you understand."

The two visitors knew they were being dismissed, but they could not take too much offense. They had stayed beyond the usual time, and it would not do to insult one of the wealthiest families in the kingdom. The ladies took their leave cordially, full of false wishes for health and happiness, and were seen to the door in good time. Once the Blakeney women were alone, Violet gave a violent sigh.

"Faith, but I thought they would never leave! Mama, how is it you know such unpleasant people? And what was Lady Victoria about? She stared at me the entire time! Is my hair out of place?"

Marguerite hugged her daughter. "No, my love, you are as lovely as ever." It was her turn to sigh as the ladies returned to the parlor. "Our friendship with the Regent has a price. I am afraid you have just experienced a part of it. It would not do for Prinny's acquaintances to quarrel among themselves and place him in the regrettable position of choosing sides. That it happens cannot be denied, but it would be very bad of us to add to his burdens."

"And what of Lady Victoria? I believe she only looked to find fault."

Marguerite pursed her lips. "I must agree. She sees a young, graceful, rich, and beautiful woman entering society. You will undoubtedly attract admirers, some of which may be favorites of hers. You are competition, my love."

Violet's mouth dropped open in shock. "I would not want the attentions of any admirer of hers!"

"Violet," Marguerite said seriously, "a young lady has no power over whom she can count as her admirers. We can determine who is welcome to call, but that is all. We must endeavor to tolerate such attention and take care not to give encouragement, intended or not, to the unworthy."

"Yes, Mama," Violet said, resigned to her fate. She then brightened. "Now that the callers have gone, may I go riding?"

Her mother's eyebrows rose. "Violet, it is still early. There may yet be callers."

Violet begged, her eyes pleading in a fashion that had served before. "Mama, please let me go. I have dutifully waited on callers all Season. Surely, there will be no more today. Besides, I have ridden so little these last months that I am sure I will disgrace Papa when we go to Scotland. You would not have me shamed by all the Highland girls!"

Marguerite laughed. "Oh, very well! Off with you! We will not have it said that Miss Blakeney cannot ride."

Receiving a thank you and a kiss from her happy daughter, Marguerite watched Violet dash up the stairs to change just as the butler approached with a note. She quickly scanned the slip of paper.

"It seems George has brought a guest for tonight," she said half to herself. She ordered that a room be made available and left to find Sir Percy.

For the first time in years, Frederick Tilney walked the grounds of Richmond, and time had not diminished what he admired about the place.

The Blakeney estate had been built centuries before, and the family had not been disinclined over improvement to the house. The massive brick and stone edifice was softened by the number of windows that adorned the aspect as well as the trees planted nearby. The grounds were extensive and well cared for by an attentive hand. The stables were the finest Frederick had ever beheld, and he was jealous on behalf of the Blues own horses.

Frederick and George stood before the estate's stables, awaiting their mounts, and Frederick spent the time complimenting Richmond. His honest enthusiasm was slightly embarrassing for his friend.

"Thankee, Frederick." George blushed. "It is a fine place, I know, but 'tis just home to me, you see."

"You must be proud of it," Frederick insisted. "As I have said before, Northanger is nothing to it, nor is any other great house in which I have set foot."

"Oh, I am not sure about that! It is not a palace by any means. Do not mistake me," George clarified, "I do love the dear, old place, but one day it will be my responsibly. I can tell you, I own that the prospect of becoming the master is overwhelming."

Frederick's first consideration was to speak—to reassure his young friend and give empty words of empathy. He found his voice stuck in his throat, however, for he recalled that George's fears were his own. Indeed, Northanger Abbey was nothing to Richmond, but it was a sizable estate. There were duties and responsibilities that a sensible man would not leave to his steward.

However, General Tilney had insisted his firstborn and heir follow in his footsteps and had purchased Frederick's commission at the earliest age possible. For almost half his life, the army had been his passion, and he had excelled in his lessons of horse and sword and drill. Because of that, he knew almost nothing of accounts or finances or crop rotation, for that part of his education had been neglected.

Henry Tilney had been correct. The army was never to be his permanent profession. Frederick, for all his bluster, knew his abilities and his limitations. He feared no man with his sword in his hand, and he would obey an order to charge directly into Bonaparte's redoubtable Imperial Guard without hesitation. Asked to discuss the price of wheat against barley, however, and he was utterly at sea.

Frederick's thoughts flew through his mind in an instant, and George hardly noticed the hesitation. Before his guest could change the subject, fate did it for them.

"Violet!" cried George. "Will you join us on our ride?"

Frederick's eyes followed George's gaze to see the girl approaching from the house. Miss Blakeney had made quite an impression the night before, all in golden and white, in the best finery money could buy. Her outfit now was a revelation: good fabrics, made and chosen for riding rather than show, and tailored to show the rider to best advantage. Frederick knew instantly Miss Blakeney would look as comfortable and as lovely on a horse as she had in a ballroom, and for a man who lived in the out-of-doors and loved it, his admiration could only grow.

"Captain Tilney," Miss Blakeney said with a surprised smile as she curtsied in response to his bow, "I did not know you were to be here today." She glanced at her brother. "George did not tell us."

"I sent a note to Mama," George muttered.

"Your brother was kind enough to invite me to take in the beauties of Surrey on horseback."

"At your insistence!" cried George good-naturedly.

Frederick's smile grew. "I believe your attendance would only add to our enjoyment."

Miss Blakeney looked Frederick dead in the eye with a strength of character that belied her young age. "Indeed—the beauties of Surrey?" Her sweet voice was tinged with challenge and reproach, and Frederick was wise to consider his reply.

"Yes, Miss Blakeney, if you and your brother would be so kind as to show them to me."

The girl was visibly pleased with his polite and correct response. "It would be my pleasure, sir." She nodded and followed the groom to retrieve her horse.

The gentlemen mounted and awaited Violet. Frederick noticed that George eyed him with some agitation.

Blakeney said in a low voice, "Remember yourself. She is my sister."

Good God! Does George think me so base as to dally with Miss Blakeney? He swallowed his pride for the time being. "Of course, George. Never fear. I have nothing but the highest respect for all of your family."

Blakeney had the good grace to reply abashedly, "Sorry, old man. I should not have said that. I do not know what came over me." At that moment, Miss Blakeney emerged from the stable, her mare as fine an example of horseflesh as Frederick had ever seen. "Ah, Violet! Shall we set off?"

Captain Tilney was all gallantry. "After you, Miss Blakeney."

She acquiesced, and the three set off. It did not take Frederick long to see his blunder. From behind, he found it nearly impossible not to admire Violet Blakeney's seat.

MOST OF THE IMPROVEMENTS MADE TO BLAKENEY MANOR WERE to satisfy Lady Blakeney's desire for more light in the house. Scores of windows had been added or enlarged. Few great houses in England could boast of the Versailles-like walls of glass that adorned the home of Sir Percy. It was Marguerite's delight.

There was one area in the house that her improvements could not reach, and it was in the bowels of the keep. It was there that Lady Blakeney searched for her husband.

Opening a well-greased door in the basement, she quietly entered a long, dark room, the meager sunlight from the small, narrow bank of windows along one wall near the ceiling insufficient to the task of properly illuminating the space. Oil lamps and candles were employed to compensate, with middling results. It did not help that the cool, dank place—even the floor—was made entirely of stone. A few tapestries and war banners adorned the otherwise bare walls. At the far end, placed high in a spot of prominence, was a great seal with a red, five-petal flower at its center. Swords, muskets, and suits of armor were stored with great care in racks opposite the windows. A long table with chairs dominated one-half of the room, the other given totally to the sport of fencing.

Most of Blakeney Manor had been remade in the image of its mistress, but this place was not hers. This was the domain of the Pimpernel.

Marguerite's eyes were drawn to the far side of the long room, where a tall gentleman in his shirtsleeves practiced fencing. Slowly, deliberately, the man worked through the motions of defense and offense against a burlap-covered object in the shape of a human torso with several black targets painted on its surface. He stood sideways, right foot forward, his foil held as an extension of his arm. So engrossed was he in his labors, he appeared to have no knowledge that there was a witness to his exercises.

A quarter century before, the Parisian actress Marguerite St. Just had been captivated by the most beautiful man she had ever beheld. Since then, Lady Blakeney had made her husband her standard of perfection in a gentleman, and many a dashing courtier would be slighted by her as bearing no comparison to Sir Percy.

She stood silently, taking great pleasure in observing the play of the still-considerable muscles of his broad shoulders and back as they moved gracefully under his sweat-drenched, almost transparent shirt. A warm heat filled her belly as she recalled the countless times her fingertips had run along those same muscles while she joyfully made love to him. *Past fifty*, she thought, *and he can still turn my head.*

The idyllic moment was shattered when, with an oath, Sir Percy dropped his foil and gripped his sword-hand, the blade's metallic contact with the floor echoing throughout the hall.

"Percy!" Marguerite dashed to his side as quickly as her little feet would allow. Sir Percy watched her approach with a mixture of mortification and resignation on his damp face.

"Ah, 'tis nothing, m'dear," he drawled. He tried to hide his discomfort, but his wife could see the pain behind his eyes. Ignoring his protests, she tenderly inspected his right hand.

"Is it the rheumatism again?"

"It comes and goes," Sir Percy admitted. "I have been trying to work it out."

Marguerite gently but firmly pulled Sir Percy towards a bench. "Come, sit down. I will fetch the white willow bark." She noticed he walked to the bench with a decided limp.

It took but a moment once he was settled and easy. The local apothecary had concocted a tincture of white willow bark for just such an occasion, and a vial of it was stored in one of the cabinets in the room. A draught was produced, and Sir Percy choked it down.

The baronet coughed as he handed the glass to his wife. "Gad, but that is vile! Where is my brandy—or better yet, my good port?"

Marguerite's gaze was drawn to the pink, M-shaped scar on Sir Percy's left forearm—evidence of the Pimpernel's last battle of wits with their nemesis, the fiend Chauvelin. *May he burn in Hell!* She recalled how her fearless and clever husband had bribed a French veterinary to brand him with the mark of a convict, all the better to disguise himself and rescue Marguerite from certain death. She remembered all the chances and pains her beloved had undertaken as the Pimpernel to foil Chauvelin and his terrible master, Robespierre, and save countless Frenchmen from the guillotine—all, Sir Percy claimed, in the name of sport.

It was a lie, of course. Sir Percy may have enjoyed himself, but what drove him was love of his fellow man and an iron will to do what was right. Yet, the abuses he had suffered and the years that had passed conspired now to bring him low.

Marguerite kissed his brow. "Rest a moment, love. Recover, and we will have a glass together in your study."

"That would please me above all things," Sir Percy said as he kissed her fingers. "So, what brings you down here to my dark cave?"

"We have a guest tonight. George has brought home Captain Tilney. They are to return to London tomorrow."

"Tilney, eh? Good, I would like to further my acquaintance with the man. Ahh!" Sir Percy groaned as he got to his feet. "A bit of a sip then off to me bath. Must look our best for the good captain. Oh!" he gasped as he tried to walk. Marguerite was quick to support him.

"Here, Percy, lean on me."

"Now, leave off," Sir Percy complained. "I shall be as right as rain in a moment."

Marguerite knew what would appease him. She whispered in his ear, "I know, m'dear, but will you deny me the pleasure of standing so close to you?"

"Oh!" he laughed. "Well, if you put it that way, lead on, my lovely!"

Chapter 4

Sir Percy Blakeney, knight and baronet, came from an illustrious family. His great-great grandfather and namesake, Percy Blakeney, was known as Diogenes, the Laughing Cavalier of England's ally, Holland. Charles I of England made him a baronet for his deeds. This first Sir Percy had bestowed the gift—and curse—of the love of adventure to his descendants.

From a young age, Percy was estranged from his parents, Sir Algernon Blakeney and Lady Joan Dewhurst. Raised mostly by his mother's people, the Dewhursts, Percy lost his mother to madness at age ten and his father to a heart ailment five years later.

At school, Percy counted among his friends Andrew Ffoulkes and William Pitt (the Younger), the future prime minister. Pitt's admiration of William Wilberforce, his interest in Parliamentary reform, and his determination to confront France appealed to Sir Percy's moderate Whiggish leanings. The new baronet had no love for Charles James Fox—drunkard, gambler, philanderer, and defender of the French Revolution. As for George, the Prince of Wales (who was as notorious as Fox), Sir Percy formed a life-long intimacy with the future king over their preference for common entertainments over so-called "proper" amusements such as opera.

In 1789, during a period of peace between Britain and the French Republic, Sir Percy journeyed to Paris on an unofficial intelligence mission for Pitt and met the love of his life: the actress Marguerite St. Just. Sir Percy had already begun cultivating his persona as a dandy of the first order, the better to protect himself from a world that life had taught him to be cold and unfeeling. In Marguerite, he met a fellow creature, for she too hid her intelligence behind a façade of carelessness. She was as captivated by his six-foot-three-inches of masculinity as he was mesmerized by her incandescent dark beauty. By 1792, the pair married, the Terror had begun, and the League of the Scarlet Pimpernel was in full operation.

At first, Marguerite knew nothing of her husband's escapades. Sir Percy did not trust his bride, having been convinced she denounced innocents to the guillotine. Once he learned the truth, the couple's passion was reignited, and Marguerite became a full member of the League. For almost three years, Sir Percy and his band fought to save the lives of those who should have been the enemies of his country—the former aristocrats of the kingdom of France—from the whirlwind of the Terror. Finally, after the fall of Robespierre, the couple began the process of raising a family.

In 1795, George was born, followed two years later by Violet Yvonne. In that year, during one last scrimmage with the French, Sir Percy lost his beloved sailboat, the *Daydream*—sunk in battle —and almost his life. As a result, he heeded Marguerite's pleas to give up his life of adventure. Instead, he threw himself into the management of his estates, holdings, investments, and more importantly, his family.

Rumors abounded about the League, but Sir Percy's true exploits were known only to a select few; counted among them were Prince George and Pitt. Any reward his country could provide was his for the asking, but Sir Percy turned them all down. He once said to Prinny, "Lud, your highness, give me a medal for sport? Keep it for those poor fellows in uniform who deserve it! As for me, all I ask is another glass of this port!"

George Blakeney grew as tall as Sir Percy was although he was slim where his father was muscular. He was open and gregarious, loved the out-of-doors and activity, and did not suffer for friends in school. No fool, he was sharp-witted but lacked the incredible genius of his father.

Violet, shorter and delicate, was more of an amalgamation of her father and mother. Dark and lovely with a streak of independence, she preferred to listen and evaluate before speaking. Even her brother owned Violet was an excellent judge of character. She was highly educated, attended by tutors who knew how to teach young ladies more than to play and draw.

George and Violet knew that Sir Percy was the Scarlet Pimpernel, that gay, dashing master of disguise who so confounded the dastardly Chauvelin. The tales of his adventures were their bedtime stories. They longed to tell their acquaintances that their father, rather than being a foolish popinjay, was really one of England's greatest heroes. However, their parents taught from a young age to keep the family's secrets. No one was to know what their brave papa did against the godless revolutionaries. Consequently, they smiled and nodded as their friends openly gawked or laughed behind her hands at Sir Percy's clowning about. *They* knew the truth and were content.

Close friends of the Blakeneys might have wondered whether the couple spared any love for their children, given their total devotion to each other. It was a reasonable question, one that underestimated the determination of Percy and Marguerite that their children should not suffer as they did. George, when not at school, was his father's shadow at work and sport, while Violet spent countless hours at her mother's side. No playacting now, no masks for the *ton*—just father and son and mother and daughter. Dinner was the favorite time of day, when the little family could talk, laugh, and share in familial companionship.

Sometimes this loving cocoon was invaded by outsiders. Sir Andrew Ffoulkes and Lady Suzanne were frequent guests, and the Dewhursts were always welcomed. This night was a rarity; George's good friend, Captain Frederick Tilney, was to sup.

The great house in Richmond was sizeable, and the main dining room could seat a score or more in comfort. The family instead took its meals in a more intimate space, and informally too. Sir Percy sat at the head of the table, as was his due, but Lady Blakeney was often at his right rather than opposite him at the foot. Violet's place was next to her mother, while George, when he was at home, sat on his father's left. This night, he went lower at Sir Percy's request, and his place was usurped by Captain Tilney.

The better for Father's intended interrogation of Captain Tilney, thought Violet.

She knew well her adored father's ways. It was not in Sir Percy's nature to allow a man at his dinner table and not take a measure of his character. Any concern Violet might have had for the captain's sensibilities was dispelled by their guest's ease of manner. Captain Tilney knew what he was about, it seemed, so there was no need to worry.

Exactly *why* she was worried for the captain's sake was a thought for later contemplation in her bedroom after she retired.

Violet listened to the gentlemen's conversation while enjoying the soup.

"So," Sir Percy said with no trace of the dandy in his voice, "all your siblings are now married and settled, leaving your poor father to suffer all alone in the abbey."

Captain Tilney chuckled. "I do not think the general suffers, sir. Indeed, that my brother and sister are so agreeably situated is a source of great satisfaction."

"And yourself, sir?" the baronet asked as he ate.

"I do not quite take your meaning. I am presently employed in safeguarding our sovereign."

"A vital mission, to be sure. You are new to the Blues, I believe."

"You are correct. Less than a month ago, I served in the Twelfth Dragoons."

"And now you are in the Royal Horse Guards. A much more pleasant posting, allowing one to enjoy all the joys of Town and society."

"There is truth in that if one were desirous of such things. To some, such distractions are a burden."

Sir Percy smiled but eyed the young officer closely. "I suppose it would take time away from the spit and polish York expects."

"It would not do to so disappoint His Grace," Captain Tilney drily returned.

"Not to mention disrupting your fencing practice," George Blakeney added as the servants came to remove the soup bowls and serve the main course.

Captain Tilney grinned and leaned toward his friend. "Now *that* is a diversion to be desired."

Sir Percy nodded. "My son tells me you have continued your study of the blade. It seems you are quite the master."

"I am competent enough."

Violet found that, while Captain Tilney's words were properly humble, his demeanor was not. She hid a smile. *He is proud of his accomplishments, and it is not at all disagreeable in my eyes. His confidence only makes him handsomer. Oh, my!*

"You are too modest, Frederick! Father, he has been the champion of the club these past two years."

"Congratulations." Sir Percy raised his glass to the captain. "Perhaps I will have the opportunity of witnessing your proficiency one day."

"I would be honored, Sir Percy."

Violet noted her father's hand shook slightly, and the roast beef on his plate had been cut up in the kitchen. *Oh, dear! Papa's rheumatism has returned.*

She glanced at her mother, only to find that, rather than attending to Sir Percy, she was watching Captain Tilney closely. Violet had seen that look before; she too weighed the content of the captain's character.

Lady Blakeney asked, "Is fencing the only diversion you enjoy, Captain Tilney?"

The captain took a moment to answer. "Generally, I prefer to be out-of-doors, your ladyship. Riding, shooting, and fishing are among my interests."

"Handy for a soldier," said Sir Percy dryly.

"It is a happy coincidence, sir. To return to your ladyship's question, I must say there is much to be enjoyed inside as well. I never pass up a concert when I have the chance, and"—with a glance at Violet—"dancing can be very agreeable."

Violet felt a blush on her cheeks and was mortified to see both Captain Tilney and Lady Blakeney witness it. *Insufferable man!*

Her amused mother asked, "What is your opinion of the theatre?"

"Not high, I am afraid. Oh, it is enjoyable enough, but all the dashing about and long speeches can become tiresome. One has to pay such close attention. It is more work than pleasure sometimes. Shakespeare is the worst."

"Here, here," Sir Percy interjected with a thump on the table.

Violet cried, "So, you are of Papa's opinion that entertainment should be relaxing rather than stimulating?"

Captain Tilney smiled. "My other pursuits are stimulating enough, Miss Blakeney. Surely, you cannot condemn me for occasionally preferring the entertainment that comes to me rather than the one that insists I go to it?"

"Comes to you?" Violet repeated.

"Yes. At a concert, I can sit back and let the music flow over my senses like water in a stream flows over the stones and rocks."

"And a play is the opposite?"

"Exactly."

"Hah!" cried the baronet. "I will have to remember that one the next time Prinny berates me."

Violet was not ready to quit the battlefield. "But, sir! Shakespeare—the great genius of literature! How can you disparage him?" She did not note how the others sat back and observed the battle of wits.

Captain Tilney shook his head playfully. "You misunderstand me, Miss Blakeney. I have the greatest admiration for the Bard of Avon. I have read his histories and comedies many a time with undiminished enjoyment."

"And the tragedies?

"I cannot like the tragedies. As great as they are, they are…too tragic." He grinned. "The romances are tolerable, but the sonnets are a particular joy." With that, he looked up above her head and recited a few lines from Sonnet 18:

"Shall I compare thee to a summer's day?
Thou art more lovely and more temperate:
Rough winds do shake the darling buds of May,
And summer's lease hath all too short a date."

Violet held in a gasp. There was no doubt that the sonnet was a daring flirtation—and right at table!

Frederick Tilney stared at Violet. "No, I shall never disparage Shakespeare's words." He then turned to Sir Percy. "But, sir, would you not agree the actors who dare to recite his lines on stage are ofttimes unworthy of them?"

Sir Percy looked knowingly at Captain Tilney but answered his question. "I cannot. Words are words, and one is like another. They leave the tongue and flit away into nothingness." He turned to his right. "Lady Blakeney disagrees, however."

The former actress narrowed her eyes. "Very true, sir. It is my observation that words hold great power, some more than others. That is why I prefer reserving the Bard's lines for the *professionals.*" Her slight accent on the last word was a warning, Violet knew, and Captain Tilney did not miss it.

"I am of your thinking, Lady Blakeney." Captain Tilney added with a smile, "And I believe that supports my estimation of the matter. My poor recitation is ample evidence that quoting Shakespeare should be avoided at all costs!"

The captain's jest could not be ignored, the table erupted in good-natured laughter, and the dinner continued in pleasant fellowship.

THE SEPARATION AFTER DINNER WAS SHORT, AND THE GENTLEMEN carried their brandy into the music room to hear the ladies play. Once the delightful performances had concluded, the host begged to be excused, given his planned departure the next morning. The young gentlemen concurred as Mr. Blakeney was to journey to Oxford after depositing his friend in Town, and everyone retired to their rooms for the night.

Frederick dismissed the provided servant, for as a solider of middling rank, he was accustomed to fending for himself. The bed proved as comfortable as it was inviting, and in his shirtsleeves, the captain—on his back, hands behind his head—mulled over the events of the day.

Richmond had proven as beautiful as he remembered, but thinking back, Frederick thought he might have missed some of the sights as Violet Blakeney had proven to be a most distracting guide. She had grown to be charming and lovely. Certainly, she filled her riding costume most agreeably, an ability that ranked high in Frederick's estimation of an accomplished lady. She was an expert horsewoman —another happy discovery.

The little ebony-haired terror of five years ago was gone for good, and he could not regret it.

During the ride, Miss Blakeney had proven to be well informed as to the workings of the estate. In fact, she knew almost as much about Richmond as George did—certainly more than Frederick knew about Northanger Abbey. This was disconcerting.

How is it, Frederick considered, *that a young lady should be conversant about crops and cattle, and I am not? I should know these things! Bah—it is Father's fault. He could not be troubled to teach me what I need to know. Should anything happen to the general, how shall I get on? George worries over his preparations, but damn me, even his sister knows more about estate management than I do!*

His thoughts brought him back to Violet Blakeney, and he smiled. Her dress at dinner was quite becoming, and she was a vision as she sang and played. Good Lord, she was pretty! And the way her eyes flashed as he teased her at dinner was all delightful.

Lady Blakeney's rebuff was recalled as well, and Frederick grew uneasy. Had he spoken too freely—again? Had he truly offended Miss Blakeney this time? The very thought of Violet thinking ill of him was exceedingly troubling.

Why the devil should I care?

Fool! She is the sister of your friend, his conscience admonished him. *Not only is she a sweet and innocent child, you cannot have it said that you go about abusing the relations of your fellows! It is simply not done!*

I wonder whether her lips are as soft as her voice...

Frederick shot up in bed, his eyes wide. *Good God! That I should have such thoughts of Violet—I mean, Miss Blakeney!*

Frederick stared out into the soft gloom of his room, his mind awhirl. Finally, he rose and began undressing.

No, she is Violet to me.

IN HER ROOM, VIOLET BLAKENEY SAT AT HER DRESSING TABLE AS her maid brushed out her hair before braiding it for the night. Her thoughts were of her brother's handsome friend and her mixed feelings for the tall, blonde officer.

She had enjoyed her ride about the estate immensely. Captain Tilney was an excellent rider, and he had expressed no condemnation at her jumping a few rails as other gentlemen had done before, shocked at what they had deemed unladylike behavior. No, his only comments were of admiration. Frederick was a jolly, agreeable companion and very gentlemanly.

Until dinner.

Violet's frown was misunderstood by her abigail, and it took her a moment to assure the girl that she had not roughly pulled her hair. As the maid returned to her task, Violet reflected on the conversation at table earlier.

Zounds, Frederick Tilney is a tease and no mistake. I thought my face would burst into flame when he recited that sonnet! I could have died from mortification!

But he looked so sweetly at me even after Momma was so sharp with him. Does he fancy me?

Oh, what a silly girl I am! He is but George's mischievous friend. I am sure Frederick meant nothing but to have some sport at my expense. I must remember Lady Uppercross's words. She all but called him a rake of the worst order!

"There, miss," said the maid, breaking into her thoughts, "is that not pretty?"

Violet thanked the girl and dismissed her. After climbing into bed and snuggling under the sheets, she renewed her deliberation.

But Momma defended Frederick. She said Lady Uppercross was warning me off because she wants the captain for her lover! Odd's life, how wicked! Would Frederick reject her overtures? Is he an honorable man? Momma believes so, and so does George.

If Frederick is a gentleman, why does he tease me? Perhaps he was not teasing...but flirting! Was he flirting?

A vision came to her of being in Frederick Tilney's arms—of being embraced in the same way her father held her mother when he thought no one could see. Violet could feel a flush run down her whole body. She bit her lip.

I am such a fool! One dance and a few flirtatious remarks do not love and devotion make! He is a handsome and charming man, as much as any man can be. I like his company, and that is all. I must remember I know nothing of his true character.

But if the opportunity to know him better arises, I will not forsake it. Oh...but he is exceedingly handsome! I do hope his character is as fine as his looks! That would be most agreeable!

MARGUERITE, IN A PALE NIGHTGOWN AND ROBE, OPENED THE door to the parlor that connected the mistress's rooms to the master's. She saw Sir Percy in a robe of deepest blue, pouring his usual two glasses of sherry and placing them on a side table next to the small settee. Hearing her steps, he turned and flashed that private smile reserved for her alone and guided her to take her seat.

"You did not spend much time in your study with the gentlemen," she observed as her husband handed her a glass.

Sir Percy took his own sherry. "No, it was more desirable to spend time with you and Violet than to discuss foreign affairs."

"What think you now of Captain Tilney?"

Sir Percy pondered this briefly. "He has grown a bit in the last few years: still charming and outgoing, well-spoken, and now not lacking in brains. He paid us every courtesy, even as he flirted shamelessly with our daughter."

"I noticed that too."

He chuckled. "By gad, you did, and no sweeter set down was ever administered! I must admit he was exceedingly civil in accepting your correction and endeavored to act in a more suitable manner afterwards." He took a sip. "Still, he should not have done it."

"He is young, it was playfully done, and Violet was not harmed. To be honest, I believe she was pleased by his wit, although it is doubtful she would admit it."

"Violet likes him?" Sir Percy frowned slightly.

"I will go no further than to say she does not *dislike* him. Can you blame her? He is perhaps the only agreeable young man we have met this Season—handsome, dashing, available, and not after her money."

Sir Percy's expression darkened further. "Odd's fish, we have surely met more than our share of demmed fortune-hunters; that is certain." He turned to his wife. "What makes you think Tilney is not mercenary?"

"It is in the way he carries himself. Others, when they come to Richmond, spend half the time gawking at the rooms when they are not trying to get into *your* best books, m'dear, in hopes of securing an ally in their quest for Violet's dowry. Captain Tilney is different. He has never done that. He is perfectly easy and pays no one particular attention. One would think he has spent a great deal of time in grand estates. As George tells me he has not, I must conclude our home impresses him little if at all."

"Perhaps we have been deceived as to the grandeur of Northanger Abbey."

His wife laughed. "Zooks—in Gloucestershire? I doubt it." In a more serious tone, she added, "His name was mentioned by Lady Uppercross and Mrs. Norris during a visit today."

Sir Percy was outraged. "Lady Uppercross? Margot, that demmed harlot talks of Tilney, and you yet defend him?"

"You would as well if you had heard her words," Marguerite patiently explained. "Apparently, she was rather put out that the good captain had managed to avoid her bed all this time. She was trying to dissuade Violet from forming an attachment to the man."

Sir Percy was confused. "I do not understand. She was trying to warn Violet off? Why would she want to do that?"

Marguerite sighed. Sometimes her clever and darling husband was insensible to what was obvious to any woman. "To reserve him for herself. Love, why would a fallen woman fear a virtuous one? Because to a good, steadfast man, there is no contest. That is as favorable a sign as any as to Captain Tilney's true self." She affectionately ran her fingertips across his cheek. "Percy, we have raised George well. He is an excellent judge of character. I trust his choice of friends."

"You make a good point. I will tell you now I was concerned when George first brought Colonel Buford—Sir John, now—to Richmond. Sink me, the stories I have heard! Yet, there is no doubt Buford is a new man. That pompous fool, Matlock, thinks the world of him, and while I do not see eye-to-eye with the earl on most things, he's far too upright and proud to befriend a scoundrel. So I will say I was wrong about Sir John, and I am willing to give Captain Tilney the benefit of the doubt." He sighed and finished his glass. "Any other suitors for Violet you wish to discuss before I take myself to the wilds of Scotland?"

Marguerite set her half-empty glass upon the table and leaned her head on Percy's shoulder. "Ah, I dread tomorrow. I hate it when you leave."

"It cannot be helped. The steward has been requesting my presence for a fortnight." He wrapped his strong arm about her.

"How is your hand, love?"

Sir Percy flexed the fingers of his right hand. "La, as you see! I had my man dose me with more of the white willow bark, and begad—it did the trick and no mistake." Marguerite caressed his hand, and Percy seized her fingers and kissed them. "May I come to you tonight, sweetheart?"

"With us to part for one month complete? I would have you nowhere but in my bed, *mon chéri*."

The whole house arose at sunup for breakfast and departure. The morning shadows were still long as Sir Percy's carriage and George's gig were loaded with trunks. Frederick took his leave of his hosts as they waited outside the house.

"Happy to have met you again, Captain," said Sir Percy with a handshake. "George has praised your fencing abilities to the skies. Perhaps one day you will oblige me with a demonstration of your skill."

"You honor me, sir. I hope it shall be soon and that I do not disappoint."

"Ah, hmm…we shall see."

Frederick was certain that the baronet was talking about more than sport.

Lady Blakeney was more gracious. "As you enjoy music more than the theatre, perhaps you would like to join us at a recital next week?"

Frederick smiled widely and could not help glancing at Violet as he answered. "You are very kind. I would be happy to attend."

"I will send a card around. Until next Wednesday, Captain."

Violet smiled softy when Frederick bowed over her hand. "I hope that a recital is not too much of a disappointment to such an admirer of the stage."

She looked through her lashes. "I will endeavor to persevere for your sake, Captain."

Frederick felt something new: a gurgling excitement in his belly as he comprehended her teasing. The lady did not think ill of him, which made him very happy.

He said in a softer tone, "Adieu, Miss Blakeney."

He reluctantly released her hand and straightened. He noticed that Sir Percy had been distracted by a conversation with George, but Lady Blakeney had watched his interaction with her daughter most closely. Frederick felt he had been caught tasting the pie before dinner and stiffly bowed to the lady. She only smiled in an enigmatic manner and nodded.

George joined him, and both climbed into the gig. There, they were witness to Sir Percy's leave-taking. Violet gave her father a hug and kissed him on both cheeks in the French manner before she stepped back and released him to her mother.

Frederick watched as the two held hands and talked softly in French. He was vaguely uncomfortable, feeling as though he were intruding on a very personal moment. His fears were soon validated, for in the next instant, Lady Blakeney threw her arms about Sir Percy's neck, and the two shared a passionate kiss.

Frederick glanced at Blakeney and was amazed that his friend showed no astonishment at the sight. Before Frederick could turn his head away, the interlude was over. Sir Percy released his wife, stepped backwards to give her a courtly bow, and leapt through the open door into his coach.

The carriage set off, and George urged his own team to follow. Lady Blakeney wiped tears from her eyes as she waved goodbye to them all.

George cleared his throat. "I, umm…hope you enjoyed your visit, Frederick."

"I did indeed," he assured his friend. "I thank you again for the invitation."

Blakeney was somewhat distracted. "Happy to do it…no trouble at all." He sighed and turned to Frederick, his countenance serious. "Pardon me, but I must ask. What are your intentions? Towards Violet, I mean. What are your intentions regarding my sister?"

Frederick was utterly taken aback. "George, I do not know that I have any. I mean, I…" He took a moment to collect his thoughts. "George, for heaven's sake, she is the sister of my good friend! I knew her as a child. I will not say I have not noted Miss Blakeney has grown to be a handsome young woman. I am not blind! I do not know what to think. It is all quite disconcerting!"

"It is disconcerting to me also."

"Have I acted in an ungentlemanly manner?"

Blakeney pursed his lips. "I shall speak plainly. You have been flirting with her."

"Flirting? No! I tease her because I like her!" he explained. "You cannot suspect my motives!"

"Sometimes it is hard to tell when you are teasing and when you are flirting. I have observed you in the past, and that is why you have been misconstrued by others."

"Good Lord, George, you know me!"

Frederick's outburst earned him a hard look. "Yes, I do."

"Do you not trust me?" A sudden pain flared in Frederick's chest. What if Blakeney cast off his friendship as Buford had.

His young friend stared at the reins in his hands. "I do. Yes, I trust you."

The reluctance in his voice struck at Frederick. He placed a hand on George's shoulder. "I shall not abuse your faith, my friend. I honor you and your family too much to act in any way less than as a gentleman with any of your relations, much less your sister. You have nothing to fear. I shall treat her with the same respect I hold for my own dear sister, Eleanor. You have my word."

George nodded and then turned to him. "Have a care, Frederick," he beseeched. "Violet is young, and her heart is tender. I would not have her hurt, even unintentionally."

"Better me than her," Frederick declared. "If I fail you, you shall have the first blow!"

"Very well, then." In a lighter tone, Blakeney added, "I hope you enjoy the concert next week."

"I expect I shall. Music and good friends—what could be better?"

"Winning a fencing match against you, I think." Blakeney wore a wry grin.

Frederick laughed and clapped his hand on his friend's shoulder again. "One day you shall if you keep practicing."

The two talked of sport as they turned off the main road to go into London, and Sir Percy's carriage rolled northwards toward Scotland.

Chapter 5

A t the appointed hour, Frederick exited a hackney and made his way through the sparse crowd entering the performance hall. He had wrestled with his considerable vanity over the choice of attire and had settled on his dress uniform. He thought the scarlet and gold braid against the navy blue of the jacket would allow him to stand out from the rest of the gentlemen, and he was proven correct almost immediately. The Blakeney ladies had already arrived and stood with another couple, and Lady Blakeney saw him soon after he entered the lobby. She smiled in welcome and called her daughter's attention to him as he approached. Violet's open delight was a welcome sight.

A few steps more and Frederick made a very correct bow. "Lady Blakeney, Miss Blakeney, good evening. I thank you for including me in your entertainment and trust I find you in good health."

Lady Blakeney's welcome was all warmth and ease. "Captain Tilney, you are welcomed indeed. We are very well, thank you."

Violet blushed prettily. "Good evening, Captain Tilney."

Once again, Frederick was struck by how much Violet Blakeney had grown in five years. From her father, she had inherited height; she was a half head taller than her mother. Her dark good looks were clearly from Lady Blakeney. French heritage was apparent in her dress and deportment. She was aware that she was beautiful and saw no need to adorn herself with needless embellishment. The dress was exquisite in its simplicity of cut and fabric. Her luxuriant black hair was pulled away from her lovely face and held in place with diamond hairpins. Long gloves and a single diamond dangling from a thin gold necklace completed the ensemble.

Unlike the numerous English roses who filled the room, there was nothing coy in this half-French beauty. Violet's gaze was open and frank with a hint of interest. It was similar to the penetrating look often seen in Sir Percy's eyes. This was no simpering miss but a woman-in-waiting: mature and intelligent beyond her years. Her full lips smiled in honest approval—approval of *him*.

A strong stirring filled Frederick's being. It was more than simple desire. He *needed* this girl to think well of him.

"May I introduce you to my friends?" Lady Blakeney indicated the others. "Sir Andrew, Lady Suzanne, allow me to introduce Captain Tilney of the Blues and George's good friend. Captain Tilney, may I present Sir Andrew Ffoulkes and Lady Ffoulkes, our dearest friends in the world."

Frederick forced himself to exchange pleasantries with the couple, resolute in his intent to be all that was polite and gentlemanly, inwardly frustrated that he could not spend all his time monopolizing the attentions of the lovely Violet Blakeney. He paid particular notice to Lady Ffoulkes as she pointed out some of their fellow attendees.

"I say, my dear," she said in a low voice to Sir Andrew as she gestured with her fan, "do you recognize that striking lady in pale blue by the statue there? The party of four? I declare I have seen her before."

Frederick turned and was startled to behold Sir John Buford standing at the far side of the room with a gentleman and two ladies, the scarlet sash of a Companion of the Bath standing in sharp contrast against his white shirt and black jacket. Buford was facing his direction, and the two locked eyes for a moment.

"Ah," Sir Andrew said, "that is Mrs. Bingley if I am not mistaken. She is Mrs. Darcy's sister."

Almost unconsciously, Frederick made a slight motion with his hand—a small wave of welcome. Sir John frowned slightly and, to Frederick's intense mortification, turned away.

Frederick was shaken to his core. *By God, Buford cut me!*

For years, John Buford had been one of his closest companions. They had trained together, eaten together, and drank to excess together. In their youth, before Buford went to Portugal, each took turns extricating the other out of trouble. They enjoyed all the pleasures the young and wealthy pursued. Now, he was rejected by a man he once called a brother. Frederick could feel the blood rush from his face. The pain was like a knife in his belly.

The others seemed not to notice. "Faith, she is a lovely one," said Lady Blakeney. "The attentive gentleman next to her must be Mr. Bingley."

"He is," said Sir Andrew, "and the lady in green is Miss Bingley. But I do not know the second gentleman."

White as a sheet, Frederick attempted to speak as impassively as possible. "That is Sir John Buford, a colonel in His Majesty's Light Dragoons." He hoped his voice was tolerably even.

"A fellow officer, Captain Tilney? Do you know him?" Without waiting for an answer, Sir Andrew turned to Lady Blakeney. "Perhaps we can have the captain make the introductions and ask them to join us for the concert."

Frederick fought to hide his horror at the idea. *Buford just snubbed me, and I am to walk over there and demand his attention, so he may insult me publicly? What am I to do? How do I explain myself?*

His agonized thoughts were interrupted by the sound of Violet's voice. "We are acquainted with Sir John, Godfather, but there is the bell for the performance. I think we must go in." In a soft voice, she asked, "Are you well, Captain?"

Frederick's eyes glanced at the girl. The open concern on her face told the tale. She had seen the interaction between himself and Sir John and pitied him. Yet she kept her observations to herself and acted in a manner to protect his dignity. Frederick was both thankful and humiliated by her extraordinary kindness. His regard for her grew tenfold. With Herculean effort, a humbled Frederick schooled his features and spoke in his usual, unperturbed manner.

"Never better, Miss Blakeney. May I?" He extended an arm to each of the Blakeney ladies and escorted them into the hall.

When the concert was over, Violet and Lady Blakeney exited the hall, escorted by Captain Tilney. The music of Mozart was as pleasing as ever, but Violet's attention was too divided to enjoy the performance fully, drawn as she was by Captain Tilney's nervousness. She had indeed seen that Sir John had cut the captain, and while she longed to know the reason behind it, her first thought was to protect her friend from further harm.

The worst time came during the intermission, and she babbled some nonsense to keep Sir Andrew occupied and away from the Bingley party. Violet sensed that Captain Tilney's anxiety had lessened afterwards, and she became convinced that *he* knew that *she* knew of his discomfort.

When it was time to leave, Violet leisurely arranged her wrap, thereby assuring their party was among the last to leave. It served, and by the time they reached the streets, the Bingley party was nowhere in evidence.

As they waited for their carriages, Violet took the opportunity to study the captain. He was more at ease than before but withdrawn, talking only when someone engaged him in conversation. Violet assumed he was distressed by the encounter with Sir John, and she longed to find a way to comfort him. She also saw that her mother was watching them and suspected that a long conversation at home was in her future.

Carriages were brought up to the pavement for the patrons, and young men held the horses' bridles as the guests boarded. A large party was moving to a coach when the team of horses, startled by another carriage passing by, reared up, tossing the post boy to the ground. The driver on the box was unable to control the upset team, and the youth was in jeopardy of being trampled.

Violet screamed.

The next instant, Captain Tilney appeared at the head of the two-horse team, reached up, seized the bridles, and pulled firmly. Violet's heart was in her mouth as she watched her friend stand between the flailing hooves and the frightened boy, dirt flying all about. The horses fought him, but the intrepid captain was undeterred and would not loosen his grip, all the time speaking to the panicky animals in a low, soothing voice. His efforts allowed the boy to quickly crawl away safely out of danger. By the time other men rushed forward to help, the team had grown calm. Only then did Violet start to breathe again.

Footmen from the coach relieved Captain Tilney, his once pristine uniform now filthy, splotched with dirt. His queue undone, his blond hair fell about his shoulders. The captain's friends moved to him in time to hear the overweight owner of the coach loudly complain to the supervisor of the unfortunate post boy.

"I have never been so badly treated in my life! My wife was frightened half out of her wits! What did that scoundrel do to my horses? I shall complain to the management!"

The heroic officer stepped up. "Captain Tilney at your service, sir. Is your good lady well?"

The rotund gentleman, his face red from wine and anger, was taken aback at the tall, intimidating soldier. "I...err...yes. I must thank you, sir, for your quick action."

"I am pleased to have been of assistance." The smile on Captain Tilney's lips was not reflected in his eyes. With his queue undone, he looked quite savage.

"Yes, but I am very put out by this entire matter." The gentleman turned to the supervisor. "I insist that something be done about this young menace!"

"What?" Captain Tilney interrupted. "You mean this fine lad here? Why, he risked his neck trying to keep your team under control. You should be thankful he was not trampled."

"It would serve him right, the clumsy fool!"

"I see," Captain Tilney said in a low voice, all good humor done away. He loomed over the churlish fool. "Your coach is ready and the team calmed, so I am certain you can leave in safety now. I wish you and your lady good night...*sir*." The captain pierced the man with a glare.

The fat gentleman backed away from the tall, dangerous-looking officer and, with an oath, climbed into his coach. Captain Tilney did not watch it leave; instead, he walked over to the frightened youth.

"How are you faring, my lad?" He ruffled the young man's hair. "Quite the scare, what?"

The boy nodded. "Yes, sir. Thankee, sir. You...you saved me life, you did."

"What is your name?"

"Nate, sir."

Captain Tilney grinned and passed the boy a coin. "You would have done the same for me, Nate."

The boy could hardly believe his good fortune. "Yes, sir. Thank you, sir!"

Captain Tilney turned to the supervisor. "You know that was an accident, do you not, and Nate was not at fault?"

"Aye," the man answered. "I will remember, sir."

"See that you do," added Sir Andrew, who gave the man some money. He turned to the officer. "I am afraid your uniform is the worse for wear, Captain."

Tilney grimaced as he looked down and dusted off his coat. "My man will be beside himself cleaning this lot, but there is nothing for it." He turned to the ladies. "I hope you did not take fright."

Lady Blakeney answered for them all. "We are perfectly well and thankful you were not harmed. It was a very brave thing you did, Captain."

Violet was surprised to see Captain Tilney shrug. "Think nothing of it, my lady. I am well acquainted with horses. We are old friends." He then took his leave of them, and Violet noticed her mother whispering something in the captain's ear. He smiled, bowed over her hand, and turned to Violet.

"Miss Blakeney, until we meet again."

Violet's emotions were already quite high, and Captain Tilney's intense look did nothing to calm her. Indeed, the effect was quite the opposite. Seeing his hair undone and face red with exertion, she became well aware of the man beneath the gentleman before her. Echoes of a primitive yearning for strength and safety and security rang through her mind. It was both disturbing and attractive. Still, she was able to bid him farewell with tolerable composure.

A few minutes later in the Blakeney carriage, her mother sighed. "Not the best way to end an evening, is it, Violet?"

"No, Mama. It is very fortunate Captain Tilney was able to help that poor boy."

"Yes. He is brave and quick thinking. And he was very kind to young Nate. I believe the boy's position is safe." Violet felt her mother's inquisitive glance. "You were very sly tonight, Violet. It did not escape my notice that Captain Tilney was out of sorts during the concert, and you—you were acting very strangely. Why?"

Violet, coloring, told her mother what she saw between Captain Tilney and Sir John. Even in the darkness, she knew her mother was frowning.

"I am distressed to hear that some quarrel has arisen between Captain Tilney and Sir John." She was silent for some moments. "Were you trying to protect him from embarrassment?"

"Yes, Mama."

"You have become good friends with Captain Tilney," her mother observed.

"Yes, Mama." Unsure of the depths of her feelings, she added, "He is George's friend, and he is ours."

"Mmm-hmm," was Lady Blakeney's only answer, and so the subject was exhausted, much to Violet's relief.

Chapter 6

A few days later, Lady Blakeney awaited Captain Tilney in the parlor of Blakeney House. She wished to have private words with the young man, so the invitation to tea coincided with Violet's music lesson.

Marguerite studied Captain Tilney closely when he was shown in by the butler. The man was clearly surprised to find her alone, but recovered quickly and made his bow without evidence of unease. Once the usual civilities were exchanged, the captain asked about Miss Blakeney.

"She is well and is practicing her instrument. She will join us shortly," her mother told him, the soft notes of a pianoforte floating in the background. "I must say again how impressed I was last Wednesday. Your quick action averted a tragedy."

"Say nothing of that," he answered. "I am happy the only harm received was to my uniform."

As Captain Tilney spoke, he looked only at his hostess, showing little interest in the furnishings or objects d'art scattered about the room. *Unless he is very good at hiding his scrutiny*, Marguerite considered while pouring the tea, *my initial assessment is correct. He cares little for our wealth.*

"I hope you found the concert enjoyable."

"I did, and I cannot thank you enough for the invitation."

"You are very welcome," Marguerite replied as she handed him his cup. "I must own I was worried, for you seemed out of sorts before we parted afterwards. Was it because of someone in the audience?" She watched for his reaction. *Where there is smoke, there is fire, and disagreements often are forewarnings of scandal. I must know whether anything untoward will affect my family.*

Captain Tilney paled, looked her in the eye, and seemed to struggle a bit before setting down the cup in a decidedly resigned manner. "Disguise is impossible, I believe." The captain looked up. "There is a quarrel between Sir John Buford and me, I regret to say, and you witnessed a very unfortunate moment. I hope you were not made uncomfortable."

"Not at all," Marguerite assured him. "A falling out is a very sad business. I hope you will soon resolve your differences, if only for George's sake."

Captain Tilney sat up straight, his countenance haughty and proud. "I share your hope, my lady, but the matter is entirely in Sir John's hands."

"I see. I hope he does not, then, remain intractable, lest you have an irrevocable break."

"It would not be of my making, Lady Blakeney."

Marguerite studied him for a moment.

A very proud man. He is upset about the quarrel and wishes it gone but does not feel any responsibility for it.

She wondered whether the man was just stubborn or whether this was a flaw in his character. *Such stubbornness can be overcome by appealing to a man's sense of justice. But if he truly believes himself to be a man without fault, then I pity the woman who marries him.*

Is this consistent with a gentleman who confronts danger without hesitation to save a servant? Who are you, Captain?

She put aside her musings for the moment. "Forgive me for bringing up such a painful matter. Indeed, on a more pleasant note, I believe I have recently met some other friends of yours."

The captain's face relaxed. "I am glad to hear it. Of whom are you speaking?" He reached for the cup.

Lady Blakeney almost felt sorry for the man. "Mrs. Norris and

Lady Uppercross."

Later, Marguerite would marvel that Captain Tilney did not drop the teacup into his lap. He sat stock-still with a face of stone, and his eyes grew wide, first with surprise, then anger, and finally...she was not certain. Fear? Dismay? A combination of both?

"I do not understand the point of this conversation, madam," the officer managed coldly after a few moments.

Marguerite dropped all disguise. "Odd's fish, do you not? Do you think I do not wish to be well acquainted with young men who call on my daughter, sir? Do you think me so bereft of parental affection and common sense?"

The verbal slap stunned the man out of his controlled composure. "Of...of course not! Forgive me, but—" He paused for a breath. "I must beg your pardon, Lady Blakeney. I am not used to people questioning my motives or character. You certainly have the right," he was quick to add. "This is your house, but I am afraid you are misinformed."

"Indeed?" Marguerite tilted her head. "In what way?"

Captain Tilney was firm. "*Friend* is a term I would not use in conjunction with the two ladies you mentioned."

Eyes narrowed, Marguerite pointed out, "Your list of former friends grows long, Captain."

"Lady Blakeney, I must protest!"

Marguerite was not enjoying herself. In spite of everything, she liked the courageous captain, and she was persuaded there was a good man beneath his charm and conceit. Under any other circumstance, she would further the acquaintance and judge his true character based upon the evidence over time. But that option was no longer available, for she suspected Violet's heart was in danger. Better to have things out now, break through Captain Tilney's pride, and risk alienating him than have her daughter suffer a greater heartbreak later. *Answer me truthfully, sir!* she silently urged. *Be open; earn my trust!* She steeled herself to be firm.

"You do wish to call on Miss Blakeney, do you not?"

His eyes said yes before his lips did.

Lady Blakeney glanced at the clock on the mantle. "We have thirty minutes before Violet is done with her lesson, Captain. I think you have time to tell me about Mrs. Norris and Lady Uppercross."

Never had Violet wished more for a music lesson to end! Captain Tilney was to come for tea, and she had selected a particularly pretty frock for the occasion. She hoped to settle herself and gain mastery of her emotions before he came. There was no doubt the handsome officer was making inroads into her favor.

Once she was dismissed, Violet hurried to the parlor as quickly as propriety allowed. Her surprise was complete when, upon entering the room, she beheld the gentleman already here, standing behind a chair, face drained, while her mother attended him from the sofa. She hardly knew the picture she presented standing frozen at the doorway—eyes wide, cheeks scarlet, bosom heaving.

"Violet, is your lesson done?" her mother asked innocently. "Well, come in, dear."

Violet knew instantly that she had been intentionally deceived —that Mama wanted her away while she spoke to Captain Tilney. About what, she had only suspicions.

A serious Captain Tilney bowed. "Good afternoon, Miss Blakeney." He quickly glanced at her mother as if seeking permission. "You look very well today."

Violet wore a small frown as she thanked him for the compliment. All she could think was that Mama had abused the young man for some reason, and she felt distressed for his sake. She turned to her mother, trying to think of some way to ask what had happened, when she was astonished again.

"Violet," Lady Blakeney observed in a strange voice, "you look quite flushed. Does she not, Captain Tilney?" She turned to the officer who, after a moment's delay, nodded. Lady Blakeney turned back to her daughter. "My love, you should refresh yourself with a stroll in the gardens before tea. Will you attend her, Captain?"

Violet wondered for a fleeting moment whether her mother had gone mad. Captain Tilney hesitated and looked at Lady Blakeney again. He received only a blank look.

"It would be an honor."

"I think Violet would be *very* interested in the subject of our conversation, Captain," Lady Blakeney said, causing Captain Tilney to stiffen.

The man took a deep breath before extending his arm. "Miss Blakeney, shall we?"

As the weather was warm, Violet had no need of a spencer. She paused only to retrieve her bonnet and gloves, and soon the pair was walking in the rose garden behind the house. The flowers were in full bloom, but the beauty of the display held scant interest for her. Violet longed to know what Captain Tilney was to say, for she was certain this scheme of her mother's was a device for the two to have a bit of private conversation.

Properly, they were not unchaperoned, for the gardener was toiling in the rosebushes—proper indeed but unfortunate. As necessary as his task of working manure into the ground was to the flowers, it would not do for the gardener to overhear their conversation!

The captain, eyes widened at the sight of the gardener, seemed to agree with Violet's assessment. With a determined air, he guided her to the garden bench. Violet sat at Captain Tilney's request, but the gentleman remained on his feet and silent, glancing at the gardener, obviously aggrieved at the man's presence. A solution needed to be discovered.

Think, Violet, think! Surely, an educated lady can devise a solution for this situation! The thought of education gave Violet inspiration.

"Parlez-vous français?" Violet asked her companion.

Startled, Captain Tilney replied, *"Oui, je parle français."*

With a soft smile, Violet continued in French. "Will you tell me what you were speaking of with my mother?"

Captain Tilney stared at her for a moment. The light of realization lit his eyes, but there was no amusement at her cleverness. No, the man was nervous and grim. In halting French, he spoke.

"First, mademoiselle, I must thank you for saving me from

great embarrassment Wednesday evening. Would I be wrong to conclude you witnessed the unhappy exchange between Sir John Buford and me?"

Violet blushed. "I did see Sir John's rude actions; that is so. Think nothing of it, *Capitaine*. I could not have you suffer further mortification."

"That is very kind. You see, Sir John and I have quarreled. I would not have it so, but there it is."

"Is there nothing to be done that would end the quarrel?"

"I am afraid not. It is not by my doing or desire. We are no longer friends until Sir John wishes it otherwise."

"That is unfortunate. I am sorry for you."

Captain Tilney nodded, but his expression grew even more grave, and he began to pace. He was clearly struggling with his thoughts. Violet grew anxious on his behalf.

The officer stopped and turned to her. "Your mother requested —nay, demanded—that I tell you…explain to you my…acquaintance with Lady Uppercross and Mme. Norris."

Violet's eyes grew wide. That she was full curious about the matter, she would not deny, but she became apprehensive at his anxiety. She wondered whether this was news she really wanted to know.

"Several Seasons ago, I made the acquaintance of Mme. Norris when she was still Mlle. Adams. We encountered each other at parties and dances. I do not believe I paid her any particular attention though we danced and shared the usual inane conversation one has at such occasions. I felt no danger for her reputation, for it was common knowledge she had accepted the courtship of M. Norris, a gentleman of some fortune."

The captain paused and looked at the gardener. Violet understood his meaning.

"*Capitaine* Tilney, do not fear. Old MacDaniel is from Scotland and certainly does not understand French." She smiled. "I am afraid he barely speaks the King's English."

The side of his mouth twitched at her jest, but he became serious again. "I suppose I should tell you that I enjoy teasing. It gives me pleasure to please young ladies, to see their blushes and smiles."

"I have noticed," she replied drily. Violet wondered whether this was meant for her.

Captain Tilney grimaced. "It is all meant in harmless fun, but sometimes, my intentions have been…misunderstood." He glanced at the trees above her head. "More than once."

Violet willed herself to be calm, to hear him out. "Are you saying that such a misunderstanding arose between you and Mlle. Adams?"

"*Oui*. Fortunately it was cleared up quickly, but I have no doubt it was as uncomfortable for her as it was for me."

"I am sure." Anger rose in Violet's breast. "Am I to understand, *Capitaine* Tilney, that you toyed with the feelings of a young lady while she was being courted by another man?"

"Mademoiselle, please allow me to explain."

Violet rose. "I doubt any explanation would be satisfactory!" The rising voices caught the attention of the gardener, and he looked at the daughter of his employer as if wondering whether his assistance was needed.

Tilney pleaded. "I beg of you—give me a chance! Trust me!"

Fighting her resentment, she forced herself to look into Tilney's eyes. He was sincere and…something else. Afraid? Despondent? She was not sure, but his unexpected vulnerability gave her pause.

"Very well, *Capitaine*. I will hear you out." She sat back down and gestured to the gardener that all was well. For his part, the servant rocked back on his heels, but kept his eyes on the pair.

Captain Tilney thanked her for her patience. "It is a failing of mine, I know, that I let loose my tongue far too often. I do not always realize until too late that what I mean to be harmless amusement is not received in that manner. Empty flattery is sometimes taken to be sincere expressions of something more." Tilney frowned at his feet. "I must share some of the responsibility for this state of affairs."

"Only some, *Capitaine?*"

He looked up at her, and there was righteous anger in his face. "*Oui*. In the case of Mlle. Adams, I teased her, yes, but I already knew she had accepted the courtship of M. Norris. I perceived it as two friends harmlessly amusing themselves. Imagine my distress when her teasing turned to flirtation. Is it right for a lady to flirt with men other than her intended? If she allowed her feelings to waver, to regret her choice, should she not bear some of the fault?"

Violet frowned. "She flirted with you? She regretted her choice?"

He nodded. "*Je vous prie de m'excuser*—it is unseemly of me to say, but I must defend myself. Not only did she most shamelessly flirt with me, she let me know she would be willing to transfer her affections." He snorted. "I assure you, I cared nothing for her or she for me. Her interest was in Northanger Abbey. But once she learned that my expectations were not as grand as her intended's, she offered a very different and irregular arrangement."

Some of Violet's anger gave way to disgust. "Irregular? You do not mean—? I-I cannot say it."

"It happens often enough among the *ton*, mademoiselle." His meaningful look changed to one of pride. "I refused her, of course."

His answer failed to satisfy, and in her disappointment, Violet said what normally she would not. She knew enough of the world to realize that an officer, particularly a charmingly handsome one, might not have been chaste. "Is it because she was not pretty enough?"

"Mlle. Blakeney, I would never agree to *that* type of arrangement with any lady, no matter how beautiful."

A bit of hope for his character still burned in Violet's heart, but it was almost extinguished by his admission that he was not serious about her. She bit her lip. "Please forgive my unseemly question, but I own that I am glad to hear your disavowal of that sort of behavior. And what of Lady Uppercross? Does she harbor the same hopes you dashed in her friend?"

The captain seemed to relax a bit. "I believe she does. Lady Uppercross is a very singular creature. She does not feel mortification over my rejection of her, unlike her friend. No, her resolve is only redoubled." He thought for a moment. "There are gentlemen who revel in the hunt—not for the sport of the activity or to be able to enjoy the fruits of their labor on the dinner table but to cover the walls of their studies with trophies rather than books. To show to their fellows they are more…manly, if you will, than other men. They are braggarts in my opinion."

"I know of such men, and I believe you are correct. But what does that have to do—" Violet saw his meaning, and could not resist a small grin. "So, you are to be one of the 'trophies' on Lady Uppercross's wall?"

"Precisely."

"And what are her chances for success?"

"None at all."

Violet sighed. She was happy to have much of Captain Tilney's behavior exonerated—to a point. He had admitted he sometimes said things he did not mean, and it had led to misunderstandings as to his intentions. And the two ladies in question had been proven not to be ladies at all. Still, it was painful to realize that her hopes for the handsome captain were only girlish fantasies. She rose from the bench, attempting to hide her hurt.

"I thank you for this interview, *Capitaine,* as unpleasant as it surely was for you. Shall we go in to tea?" She stopped, for she felt Captain Tilney's hand on her arm.

"Mlle. Blakeney, I am a very private man. Do you have any curiosity to know why I agreed, with your mother's approval, to open my private affairs to such an extent for your perusal?"

She lifted her eyes to see that strange, longing expression again. She tried to hold down the excitement that threatened to bloom in her breast. Many thoughts came to her, but she could not speak for the world.

"Ah, you choose to be silent," he observed. "But I have gone too far not to speak." He stared at her, his throat working. "Mlle. Blakeney, I have told you these things, and I am willing to share all my private concerns with you, because it is the price your generous mother has demanded of me. I must place my trust in you."

"Trust? What?" In her surprise, Violet had slipped back into English.

Captain Tilney, his countenance intense, answered her in kind. "Miss Blakeney, pray believe that I have *not* been toying with you."

"Oh!" was all that Violet could say.

He slowly took her hands in his. "I know we have been reacquainted for a very short time, but I have come to realize you are quite unlike any young lady I have ever met. You challenge me. You make me want to be a better man. I would like to know you—not as George's little sister, but for yourself. I wish us to be friends. With your permission, I would very much like to continue to call on you while you remain in Town."

Violet's hopes rose like a phoenix from the ashes. "Yes. If my mother agrees, yes." She returned his smile. "I should like that too."

Captain Tilney finally smiled. "And will I be forgiven if a few pretty compliments slip through my lips?"

Violet raised an eyebrow. "Perhaps." Her eyes twinkled. "It depends on how pretty they are."

"Harrumph!"

The two turned to see the gardener with one eyebrow raised. "Here now, that'll be enough o'that, laddie. Ya two best be gettin' inside, I'm thinkin', or the misses'll be lookin' fur ya. Now, go on."

Violet blushed intensely, but Captain Tilney only grinned. He bowed to the gardener, offered his arm to Violet, and the two walked inside with lighter hearts than before.

Captain Tilney stayed only a short time after the pair returned to the sitting room. His leave-taking was all that was correct, but Marguerite did not miss the special look he reserved for Violet or her daughter's blushing response.

Her inquiry began upon the shutting of the front door. "So, has the good captain explained himself to your satisfaction?"

Violet lifted her chin. "He has, and we have agreed to be friends. I gave him permission to call again."

Marguerite pursed her full lips. "You know I shall not keep this from your father."

"Mama, there is nothing to keep from him. As I said, Captain Tilney is my friend as well as George's. His company is very agreeable, and I look forward to his visits."

There was no use in inquiring further, Marguerite knew. Time would tell whether this acquaintance grew serious. "Very well. I owe your father a letter in any case. Shall you enclose a note?"

"I shall write one directly." Violet rose. "By the way, Mama, do you think Sir Andrew could arrange a viewing of the Changing of the Guard for me?"

"I am certain he could." Marguerite gave her daughter an arch look. "This is a new interest."

Violet shrugged. "It has occurred to me that I have never witnessed it. I am sure it is very interesting."

"No doubt. Particularly if the Blues are involved?"

She raised an eyebrow. "Blue always was my favorite color."

Chapter 7

June

Major Archibald Denny thought it was unusual to escort a baronet and his goddaughter through the halls of Horse Guards, the headquarters of the British Army. These were unusual guests too, he had been informed. Sir Andrew Ffoulkes, friend to HRH the Prince Regent, was acknowledged to have given good service to the king in the past, and Miss Blakeney belonged to a wealthy family that was particularly close to the Regent.

Do your duty and do not show your annoyance, Major Denny told himself. He had learned that lesson while he was still in the——shire militia, and that credo had served him well once he bought his lieutenancy in the Regulars. Denny had to earn his promotion to captain, for he had no funds to buy his commission. His current rank was due to a death vacancy. He had worked hard to get where he was, and if his superiors ordered him to escort civilians to a choice spot to view the Changing of the Life Guard, who was he to complain? At least it was a change from shuffling papers or acting as a glorified errand boy for his lordship.

Escort a pretty lady and watch horses go by. What could be more pleasant?

Major Denny's outlook changed considerably once the small party entered the designated viewing room. He had reason enough to come smartly to attention when Major-General Sir William Ponsonby, Commander of the Royal Dragoons, immaculate in his scarlet uniform, entered the room. However, it was the *other* occupant who commanded his focus.

"Ffoulkes! Miss Violet! Good morning, good morning!" cried the Regent. "Fine day to view a parade, what?"

"Indeed, Your Royal Highness," Ffoulkes said as he bowed. Miss Blakeney offered a deep curtsey.

"You are just in time, Miss Blakeney," reported Sir William, gesturing to the open windows. The Changing of the Life Guards starts promptly at eleven. I think you will find the Dragoons in excellent form."

The Regent laughed. "I suppose she would, Ponsonby, if she notices them, which I doubt. I hear the lady has a predisposition for *blue*. Do you not, m'dear?" He laughed again at Miss Blakeney's blushes.

Major Denny noticed that the major-general gave him an expectant look. It recalled him to his duty. "Ah…Your Royal Highness, Miss Blakeney, sirs—may I offer you any refreshments?"

All but Miss Blakeney refused a glass of wine, and he had just handed her a glass when a trumpet sounded the Royal Salute. The ceremony had begun.

The group took their places at the windows overlooking the vast Horse Guards Parade grounds. To their right, on the north side of the grounds, ten men in the scarlet and black of the Royal Dragoons waited for their relief. Riding toward them from the park was an equal number of riders in navy blue tunics with white breaches. Leading the detachment from the Royal Horse Guards Blue was a tall man with blond hair under his helmet. Major Denny noted the young lady clasped her hands together at her lips, hiding a delighted smile at the sight of the officer.

The Regent whispered to Sir Andrew, "I take it she has seen Captain Tilney."

The age-old ceremony continued. The Blues rode past the Dragoons before forming up opposite about two dozen feet from each other. Captain Tilney shouted a few commands, and several of the Blues rode with him into Horse Guards.

"First, relief of the old guard," explained Sir William. Within a few minutes, Captain Tilney returned with the relieved Dragoons who joined their comrades. The two officers met at the middle of the formation, saluted each other, and the trumpeter of the Blues played as the Dragoons retired. Once the field was theirs, the Blues moved en mass into the interior of Horse Guards.

The group walked away from the window as the major-general continued. "They will be on duty until tomorrow, when the Dragoons return. Of course, the guard is dismounted at night."

"Of course," said Miss Blakeney. "And this ceremony happens each day, no matter the weather?"

"Yes," said the Regent, "even in the rain or snow. I feel for the poor buggers. Oh, pardon me, Miss Blakeney. Did your Captain Tilney look smart enough?"

Miss Blakeney smiled. "They all looked very fine. Thank you, sir, for your hospitality."

"Happy to do it," said Prinny. "We have time for you to take your ease before you go." He glanced at Miss Blakeney. "Excuse me, my dear. Must have a word with Ponsonby." The Regent walked over to the far side of the room, and Major Denny followed at Sir William's gesture.

"Sir William," said the Regent in a low voice, "I know you are with the Dragoons, but please pass the word to the Blues that we would consider it a personal favor if Captain Tilney is shown every possible consideration"—he looked over at Miss Blakeney, sitting and talking with Sir Andrew—"when it comes to duty."

The major-general bowed his head. "As you wish, sir. See to it, Major."

Major Denny bowed his head. "Yes, sir."

The Regent grinned. "Ladies must have their dancing partners, you know."

My dearest Percy,

I was delighted to receive your letter and to read that all is well in Scotland. I, too, miss your presence deeply and long for our reunion. July cannot come soon enough! But there are modistes to visit and shopping to be done before your loved ones quit Town.

You write of your concerns over Violet's courtship with the captain. Let me allay your fears with this brief note. There is no formal courtship. It would be impossible without your consent. Indeed, Violet agrees she does not know the gentleman well enough to consider a formal and serious attachment.

The captain and I have come to an understanding, and I have given T permission to call, and Violet is happy to spend time with him. Often they walk or ride in the park nearby, escorted by your largest footman. You see, as always, I anticipate your desires, my love. The captain comes for tea as often as he may and has had dinner with us twice. Violet enjoys his company, as do I. He is polite, charming, and often amusing.

Our removal northwards will tell the tale. If their attachment can weather the time and distance only Scotland can offer, then we may consider T in a new light.

I shall close now, my love, as there is the bell. Cook has set out refreshments, and T is surely here. I will write again later. Until then, know that I am and shall always be,

Your very dear wife,
MARGOT

Captain F. Tilney
Royal Horse Guards Blue, London

Dear Sir,

My friends in Town have written to me of your conquest. Allow me to congratulate you! The daughter of Sir Percival Blakeney, Bart., is a prize I should never have imagined you would obtain when I affected your transfer into the Blues! I had to call in several favors to do it, and here is our reward. Miss Blakeney must be worth fifty thousand at least! What an addition to Northanger Abbey! Of course, Sir Percy is a damnable Whig, but what of it? My son, you have done the Tilney name proud!

However, how is it you have become so sly? There is not a mention of it in your letters, save your account of your visit to Richmond with young Blakeney. I suppose you have been too involved with your courting.

Well then, carry on. I expect I shall soon see the lady in Gloucestershire.

Yours, etc.
GENERAL TILNEY

In disgust, Frederick tossed the general's letter on the writing table in his room. He wondered for a moment who might be his money-grubbing father's spy before dismissing the thought. It did not matter. His attentions to Violet were openly discussed in the mess, and if his personal business was the subject of jealous conversation in the barracks, surely it was all over town.

He cursed. It was a new feeling, this anger and resentment on Violet's behalf. Usually, it was his own pride he jealously guarded. For a moment, Frederick allowed he might be somewhat responsible —after all, it was not as though he kept his admiration for Violet secret—but the thought was soon quashed, replaced by antipathy for London society and his fellow officers.

His musings were interrupted by a knock on his door. "Enter," he called. Upon seeing who his visitor was, he leapt to his feet.

"Captain Tilney," said Major Denny, "your presence is requested in the duty office."

Frederick frowned as he followed the major. Once there, he saw the colonel of the regiment sitting behind his desk, a stack of papers before him. He barely acknowledged Frederick before addressing him.

"Captain, I have before me the schedule for next week."

"Yes, Colonel, I have seen it."

"Not *this* one, sir," he growled. "There is a change. You have night duty on Friday rather than Wednesday."

"Oh." Frederick was surprised at the man's annoyance. "Very good, sir."

The colonel placed his hands together and leaned over the papers on his desk. "There is a ball at Almack's Wednesday night, is there not?"

Frederick searched his memory. "I believe you are correct, sir."

"Well?" the man barked.

"I do not understand your question, Colonel."

"Do you or do you not want a pass for Wednesday night?"

"I do not recall asking for one, sir. After all, I was scheduled for duty—"

"Damn you, sir! Do not play the fool with me!" With that, the colonel tossed the pass at him.

Frederick watched as it flitted to the floor at his feet. Surprise turned into anger. "Sir, I do not understand. Have I done something wrong?"

The colonel rose. "Captain Tilney, I know the Blues is regarded as a plum assignment for officers interested in making their way into London society. We do not have the hardest duty of those who wear the King's uniform. But by God, sir, I do not appreciate an officer who uses high connections to make certain his official duties do not adversely affect his social engagements! Your conduct has been noted!"

Frederick was astonished. "Permission to speak frankly, sir."

"Granted."

"Colonel, I know nothing about this. I have not, now or ever, used any so-called 'connections' to avoid my duties or to rearrange my responsibilities to suit my fancy. Furthermore, I have not asked anyone to do anything like this." He gestured at the pass, still on the floor. "If someone has, I ask you to tell me his name."

The colonel sat down, his eyes still filled with resentment. "This request came from the regiment."

"His lordship? But...but why?"

"I hoped you would tell me." The two locked eyes for a moment before the colonel turned away. "Perhaps I was mistaken. I apologize, Captain." He turned back to face Frederick again. "Enjoy the ball."

Frederick's eyes drifted down to the scrap of paper. Offended by the colonel's insinuation, his first inclination was to leave it, but a vision of dancing with Violet came to him, and with a small smile, he retrieved the pass.

"You are dismissed, Tilney." The colonel waved him away. Frederick bowed his head, turned sharply, and left the room.

The Colonel of the Blues was still sitting, dissatisfied, when there was another knock on his door.

"I thought I would see whether you were in as I was visiting Ponsonby," said a man in his thirties in civilian clothes.

"Brandon!" cried the colonel. "Come in, come in."

Colonel Christopher Brandon shook hands with his old friend and took a seat at the desk. "I heard a bit of that," he said as he jerked a thumb over his shoulder. "What was it all about?"

"Ahh, another pleasure-seeking officer looking to marry into the peerage," his companion said. "Do you know Captain Tilney?"

Colonel Brandon nodded. "I know of him. Good man. I thought he was in the Twelfth. Is he in the Blues now?"

"Yes, and he did not waste any time making friends in high places."

"How high?"

"Let us see—he is courting the daughter of Sir Percy Blakeney, who is the particular friend of the Regent. High enough for you?" His eyebrows rose.

Colonel Brandon whistled. "Ah, I see how that would make things difficult for you."

"Yes. Damn, when Tilney first showed up, I had hopes for him. Good seat, knew his business. But now I get requests from on high, and they always seem to involve Tilney. Making sure his is the most convenient schedule when it comes to dances and parties. The other officers are livid about it."

"Strange. From what Buford has told about Captain Tilney, he would not use connections to place himself above his fellows. Too smart for that nonsense."

"That is what Tilney said." The colonel brooded. "It could be the Blakeneys. They are close to the Regent. And it is not hard to believe that Prinny would throw his considerable weight around." The man snorted. "Ahh…come Brandon, do you expect me to believe Tilney knows nothing of this? That people are pulling strings behind his back? Hah! Bonaparte has a better chance of escaping from Elba! Enough of this! Let us get something to eat. I am famished."

It was only a day later that Captain Tilney called on the Blakeneys, and Marguerite was surprised by his early arrival.

"Captain! You are very welcome, but you are a bit before your usual time. Violet is still above stairs," she teased. "She will be but a moment."

"Thank you, madam, but I came a-purpose, for I have business with you." The captain was grave, an unusual occurrence.

Marguerite was taken aback. "Business with me! How singular! Pray, speak at once."

The tall officer passed a hand across his forehead. "Oh, my lady, please excuse my words. It is only that I have had the most uncomfortable interview with my commanding officer. Certain matters are now better understood, but I fear I must ask you a very impertinent question if only to settle my mind."

Mollified, Marguerite gestured to a chair. "Captain, we are your friends. Please be seated, and I will answer any question you ask to the best of my ability." She, in turn, returned to the sofa.

"Thank you, Lady Blakeney. I cannot tell you what your words mean to me." He paused as he took a seat. "My colonel informs me that certain officials—certain *high* officials—have expressed interest in my concerns. He does not say *who*, but I believe you cannot mistake his inference."

Marguerite frowned. "No, indeed. Pray continue."

"My colonel has insinuated that these same officials have made it their business to make sure my activities are arranged so that I am available for your convenience."

It had been some time since Marguerite was shocked. "Odd's life! And I suppose your question is whether such a report is accurate?"

Tilney stared at his shoes. "Yes, madam. It pains me to ask, and I truly regret the necessity of this action, but my character demands it."

Marguerite spoke slowly and firmly. "Captain Tilney, let me assure you that I have not made any such request and that *my* character forbids me from even considering such a thing."

She knew, however, that not all of her acquaintance would hesitate to use whatever influence they owned for their amusement and that one in particular wielded great power indeed.

Captain Tilney nodded. "Thank you, my lady. I am mortified that it was necessary to put such a question to you."

"It is quite forgotten. You said something about 'certain matters.' Have you had any difficulties, sir?"

Captain Tilney glanced away. "No, just a better understanding of the behavior of some in the mess room." He turned to her. "Now that I know the cause, I am content. I have not been harmed. I apologize for distressing you."

"Say nothing of that. As I said, you are our friend, and it is natural that we should be concerned for your welfare."

Her expression was warm and open, but Marguerite's mind was troubled. She knew the Prince Regent well enough to believe him capable of such an act, and she knew enough of Prinny's fondness for Violet to guess the motivation. That he had become aware of Violet's growing admiration for Captain Tilney was no great surprise as the gossips of the *ton* were more effective at gathering information than the King's intelligence service. Her only concern was what to do about it. Prinny could be stubborn as a mule, and if he had decided to interfere with Captain Tilney's career, she feared she could do little to stop him.

Captain Tilney smiled for the first time since coming into the room. "Then I have another question, and it is a far more pleasant one. Are you and Miss Blakeney by any chance planning to attend the next ball at Almack's?"

My dear Ffoulkes,

First, let me assure you and Suzanne of my continued good heath, even though I find myself imprisoned in the wilds of Scotland.

I must own I am troubled over the attentions shown by Captain Tilney toward Violet, for I know too little of the gentleman. If I were in residence, I could better take this man's measure. But alas, in Scotland I must remain.

My inquiries about Captain Tilney have resulted in a mixed bag of opinions about the man. In his profession, he is generally admired. He is known as a hardworking and honorable officer, loyal to the Crown and his fellows. He carries out his duties with dash and zeal, but he does not demonstrate any particular initiative or ambition. Faith, his courage cannot be denied, given Margot's story of the concert.

However, in Town his reputation is not so set, though nothing too scandalous has been attached to him. There are those who say his behavior has been, at times, questionable, particularly towards the ladies. But, just as many excuse his teasing remarks as nothing out of the ordinary and perfectly acceptable, particularly when weighed against the actions of the more notorious denizens of the ton. Odd's fish, surely nothing as bad as you and I have witnessed in Lady Jersey's house.

I have heard enough to be troubled, and I would have acted but for remembrance of my misjudgment of Sir John Buford. That gentleman's behavior was far more scandalous than Captain Tilney's, but there are none now who would denounce him. You know I do not get on with Wellington, but his partiality for Buford cannot be ignored. The Iron Duke is too particular and unforgiving to tolerate a rogue.

My dear Ffoulkes, if I was wrong about Buford, can I be wrong about Tilney? I know he is George's particular friend, but I cannot overlook my son's youth and inexperience. Margot, too, likes and defends the man.

I should be content, and I will be if you would do me a great service. Please look into the character of Captain Tilney. Should you find anything untoward, I trust you will let me know by post.

Zounds, I now feel foolish about making such a request of Violet's devoted godfather. Pray forgive your old friend. I know you would do nothing less, and your silence to date should give me comfort.

Yours, etc.

BLAKENEY

Chapter 8

The month of June flew by for Violet Blakeney. There were teas in the sitting room, rides in the park, dinners with Lady Blakeney's friends, balls at Almack's, and excursions to Vauxhall Gardens—all in the delightful company of Captain Frederick Tilney. Whenever the handsome officer could be excused from his duties—which, happily, seemed to be often—he could be depended upon to call at Blakeney House and to pay particular attention to *her*.

She discovered many things about Captain Tilney. He liked mushrooms but despised kidneys, he enjoyed art and music more than politics, and he was a confident horseman but hesitant in other matters. His self-assured ways were a mask, hiding his doubts and inadequacies from the world.

As time passed, Captain Tilney appeared easier in Violet's company and in her mother's. He would admit his failings, speak of losing his dear mother, and share his disappointment at his lack of advancement in the army. Violet learned by bits and pieces that the captain was beholden to his exacting father for his present position, and that was a source of vexation to the gentleman. Violet, who had known nothing but love and kindness from her parents, could only pity him.

Yet, Captain Tilney was not a gloomy companion. Added to his strikingly handsome features and lovely deep voice, he was gallant, gregarious, and generous. He was perfectly polite and affable to Lady Blakeney and always solicitous about Violet's comfort. Perhaps it was empty courtesy, but he gave every impression that he enjoyed shopping as much as riding, if simply to be in the company of the ladies from Blakeney House and, particularly, in hers. He showed absolutely no interest in her family's fortune or connections.

Violet had formed a deep attachment to her dear captain, but all things come to an end. It was now July, and Violet's time in London was drawing to a close.

On the day before her removal to Scotland, Violet spent more time than usual at her mirror. Captain Tilney was to visit the Blakeney ladies one last time, and she was determined to appear at her best. Upon the captain's arrival, Tilney was led to the parlor where Violet greeted him with outstretched hands.

"I am afraid you must suffer my company without Mama for now, Captain." Violet smiled as Tilney bowed over her hand. "A dispute of a domestic nature has arisen, and my mother must attend to it. She will join us soon."

The captain grinned as he took in her appearance. "I shall endeavor to persevere, Miss Blakeney."

Violet blushed at Captain Tilney's recollection of her impertinent remarks at Richmond as well as his clear admiration. He had begun to ask after Lady Blakeney's health when the sound of voices raised in argument could be heard.

Violet was mortified. "Captain, I feel an inclination to take a stroll in the rose gardens. Would you care to join me?"

Captain Tilney nodded in kind understanding. "Of course, Miss Blakeney. Nothing would suit me better."

Moments later, Violet and her admirer were outside, taking in the afternoon sun and the fragrance of the flowers. Violet was so relieved to remove her guest from overhearing the disagreement occurring within that it was some time before she realized they were quite alone without.

"Oh, dear! Mr. MacDaniel does not tend to the garden today."

Captain Tilney looked around. "Shall we return indoors?"

"No!" Weighed against witnessing the Blakeney's household crisis, the impropriety of walking for a few minutes alone with a friend of the family seemed insignificant. "I believe I shall sit on the bench in the shade and take in this fine day."

The bench was in full view of the house. Violet took her seat, but Captain Tilney did not. Instead, he stood nearby in an increasingly nervous manner.

"Captain, are you well?"

"Never better." He looked back towards the door. "You quit Town tomorrow for Scotland, do you not?"

"Yes. We journey to Oxford to retrieve George before continuing onward."

"It will be very agreeable to be with your brother and father, I have no doubt." His eyes seemed to be everywhere but on her.

"Of course. We are very close and have missed each other exceedingly."

"Naturally. Your stay in Scotland will be of some duration?"

She frowned. Why did Captain Tilney not sit beside her? What could cause his strange behavior? "George will, of course, return to Oxford for the next term, and my father seldom leaves his house in Scotland before the first of October—certainly before the first snows."

"Very wise of him." The officer paused. "Would you object if I called upon you after you return to Richmond?"

Suddenly, everything was clear. "No! I-I mean…Captain Tilney, I would be honored and happy if you would call on my family. I look forward to it."

Captain Tilney turned his gaze to her, and Violet felt her heart in her throat. His blue eyes had grown dark and intense. "I would not have you to mistake my meaning. The matter of my calling on Richmond is entirely up to you, as you would be the object of my visit. Your words alone will keep me from Richmond or draw me hence."

"Oh!" was her startled reaction. The captain suggested he did not come to Richmond as a family friend, but as her ardent admirer!

"Miss Blakeney, our acquaintance is yet new, but I must tell you that I have developed a most earnest and tender friendship for you. It is my wish to continue that friendship, even deepen it, if that should be agreeable to you, and I will do everything that is expected of an honorable gentleman. But, madam, I can no longer go on as I have. I can no longer accept the kindness of your mother or hope to speak to your father if my presence is uncomfortable to *you*. I would never wish to give you pain, including the mortification of an unwanted courtship."

Violet grew quite lightheaded at Captain Tilney's declaration. She had dared to hope for admiration from him, even some affection, but *this*—a near avowal of love! It took her breath away.

Captain Tilney sat on the bench. "Will you allow me to continue to call on you when you return?"

Through her happiness, she forced herself to speak. "Yes!" She smiled. "Yes, Captain Tilney, I would be delighted to receive you."

"And perhaps...may I speak then to your father? To ask his permission to formally pay court to you, if we come to an understanding?"

She could not look at him for all the world. "I have no objection if you speak to my father."

Without knowing how it came to pass, Violet's small, soft hands were encased in his large, rough ones. "Oh, Miss Blakeney—my dear Miss Blakeney, I am very happy to hear it."

Captain Tilney wore a joyful, relived smile. Before Violet could wonder *why* she was so relieved, she found her lips very close to his. "Miss Blakeney..." His throat was working.

Violet could not stop herself from closing the distance between them any more than she could stop breathing. The kiss was tentative and soft, very sweet, and altogether too short—a very agreeable first kiss.

"Forgive me," an unremorseful Captain Tilney said gently. "I should not have done that."

Violet looked down and smiled. He was not sorry in the least and neither was she, but she was happy for his gentlemanly words and for taking the blame for *her* forwardness. "You are forgiven, Captain."

"My name is Frederick."

What he was asking was enormous and agreeable. "You are forgiven, *Frederick*."

Frederick—he was now and forever *Frederick* to her, and Frederick's smile grew open and wide. He let out a relieved breath and lightly kissed her brow. "Thank you, my dear Miss Blakeney."

"Zounds, sir! There seems to be an inequality in how we refer to each other." She ran a finger on his cheek. "You may use my name, if you wish"

Again, he kissed her forehead. "Nothing would give me greater joy, *Violet*." He sat back and sighed happily.

Though very happy, Violet was still puzzled by his behavior. "You act as though a great weight has been lifted from your shoulders. Was the thought of asking me so overwhelming?"

"You have no idea," he said carelessly before flushing. "Oh, forgive my silly words, but I own I was concerned. I wanted to be sure of my reception before you went away."

"Before? Why is this? Surely, you did not doubt our friendship?"

"Doubt you? Never! I wanted you to be sure of me. I could not take the chance of some young nobleman working his way into your heart and have you thinking I care nothing for you. You are very beautiful, and there are many who would desire your company."

Violet's mouth twisted. "Desire my dowry is more likely."

An instant later, Frederick had released her hands and shot to his feet, obviously disturbed.

"Frederick, what is it?"

The man paced, his strong fingers running through his long blond hair, almost pulling it out of its queue. "Talk of your dowry brings something to mind," he said in a dejected voice. "I should tell you now that my expectations may not be agreeable to you or your father."

His face was hard as he looked at her. "I am but a captain in his Majesty's Dragoons. Fourteen shillings seven pence a day. Two hundred sixty-six pounds, less uniform and horse. Two hundred sixty-six a year—half that if I am tossed aside during the Peace.

"Oh, I have higher expectations, madam. Once my father departs from this earth, I shall be the master of Northanger Abbey. As you know, I am deficient in matters of estate management, but I know all too well that the lands bring in just a little more than two thousand a year."

His expression became soft and anguished. "And you, Miss Blakeney? A baronet's daughter. A fair lady whose father owns property in Richmond and Scotland and is the particular friend of the Prince Regent." He smiled a painful, ironic smile. "Somehow, I do not think your good father will be pleased."

The blood had drained from Violet's face during his recital. She knew well the economics of the marriage market, but until today, it had been abstract, something for the future. Frederick made it real and current. She also knew her family's character. She stood with a cool countenance.

"How very singular, Captain Tilney! Your expectations are the same as mine. I see no difficulties."

Frederick's jaw dropped. "Two thousand a year? I may not have been the cleverest boy at school, but I do know my figures. You have just admitted that you are worth forty thousand pounds! How can you say there are no difficulties?"

"I am not a fool, Frederick. I know this issue is an important one. But you should know something." She took a step closer to him. "My mother came to my very wealthy father with nothing but the clothes on her back. One of the richest men in England had brought home an actress from the Paris stage. An *actress*, sir! It was a scandal, of course, but my parents cared not two straws about it. I dare say their union has been a happy one." She smiled. "Do you think my father would wish less for his children?"

Frederick was serious. "Violet, you should know I care nothing for your money."

"I know that, and so too, I expect, does Mama."

A look of wonder overspread Frederick's countenance. "You believe me. You trust me."

"How can I not trust my dear friend?" *And the owner of my heart?*

Their bodies collided in a violent embrace. This kiss was all the first was not: selfish and selfless. They gave and took pleasure from each other. Violet felt Frederick's strong hands on her back, crushing her torso against his broad chest. Her arms wound about his neck, pulling her body even closer. Her nipples were hard against her corset, and a new type of hardness jabbed her belly. Desire intoxicated her mind.

Frederick was the first to recover. "My dearest, we *must* stop!"

Violet was proud of his control and ashamed at her lack of it. She allowed herself to be escorted to the bench. This time he readily sat next to her and, after repairing his queue, took her hand again.

"You cannot know what it means for you to trust me," he said, brushing his lips along her knuckles.

Violet fought the shiver coursing through her body. "Frederick, what is it?"

He sighed. "Many years ago, I met a young lady, the daughter of one of my mother's friends. After my mother passed, the family came to pay their respects, and I became acquainted with this lady. We grew to like each other, but I could not court her as I was still in mourning. She promised to wait the required six months for me. But before four months had past, I read in the papers that my friend was betrothed to a viscount."

He frowned. "We met a year later at a party in London. I suppose she could read the hurt on my face. She told me her father, an untitled gentleman from Lancaster, had expectations of increasing his influence and had reconciled her to the match. She was content in her choice. Besides, she claimed no guarantee from me that I would keep to my promise—that I would not forget her. She did not trust me."

Violet was not best pleased to hear of a lost love from Frederick's past, but she tried to comfort him. "She was unworthy of your faith, Frederick, or her feelings were false."

"Perhaps. I own that my heart had grown hard." He gazed at her. "But you have changed that. You trust me. And I trust in you."

Violet was in danger of losing herself to her feelings, so touched was she by her lover's confession. However, she was saved from acting in a disgraceful manner again when the door opened and Lady Blakeney stepped out.

"Ah, Violet, Captain Tilney, there you are!" By then, the two young people's hands were properly by their sides, even though they were sitting a little too close for propriety's sake. "It is a beautiful day, is it not?"

Frederick stood. "Indeed, madam. Miss Blakeney wanted to enjoy the air, and I could not deny her the pleasure."

Violet hoped the sunlight hid her flushed face. Lady Blakeney glanced quickly at the two, her eyes dancing.

"I see. But I must end this charming interlude as tea is ready in the parlor. Will you not come inside?"

THAT EVENING, A SMILING FREDERICK STRETCHED HIS LONG FRAME across his cot, his jacket undone and his hands behind his head. This certainly had been one of the best days in his life.

I took the risk, and it served! I was open, and Violet was open with me. She loves me; I am certain of it! Damn, I will have to wait until October at the earliest before I have my dearest in my arms again. Oh, these next four months will seem an eternity! Darling Violet, how I shall miss you!

He felt a stirring in his breeches. *How I shall dream of you, my sweet Violet!*

MARGUERITE HAD POSTPONED TALKING TO VIOLET UNTIL THE next day when they were well on their way to Oxford. Once on the road, she began.

"My love, please tell me about your walk in the garden yesterday with Captain Tilney."

As she expected, Violet blushed. "What do you wish to know, Mama?"

"If I am not mistaken, I believe you and the good captain shared more than fine weather, my dear."

"Mama, Captain Tilney asked to call on me again when I come back from Scotland. We have no official understanding, but I believe he wants to go to Papa, and he was only waiting for my permission. He likes me very much, and I like him." She gave her mother a very earnest look. "He is a good man, Mama, and very honorable. He cares nothing for my dowry—believe me, for we spoke of it. He thought I would reject him because of it!"

"You spoke of many serous things, then! You trust Captain Tilney?"

"Yes. Oh, that is another thing. Captain Tilney has been mis-used most unjustly by a lady in the past. It is a source of great pain for him."

Marguerite was taken aback. "He shared this with you? Please, tell me all." Violet relayed the captain's story, and at the end of it, Marguerite sat back.

"Well, my dear, I do not know whether it was entirely proper for the captain to share all of this with you, but I must admit I like him better for it. I begin to understand him. He has suffered great pain, and ofttimes a man who has been hurt behaves in a careless fashion."

"I do not understand."

"A man is as different from a woman as the sun from the moon. When a lady is hurt, she shares it with her friends but hides from society at large. A man does just the opposite—he talks to no one but attempts to set aside his hurt by improper behavior, often in public." She nodded, happy with her own conclusions. "That Captain Tilney was willing to tell you these things proves that he was freeing himself from the chains of mortification. He sees that he has been profligate and wishes to make amends. He shows his trust in others by sharing things that would shame any man. Good for him!

"But, my dear, as much as you like Captain Tilney and as much as he likes you, we must be careful. Allow everything to happen in its own time, let the proprieties be observed, and all will be well." She took her daughter's hand. "We must talk to your father."

Violet bit her lip, tears in her eyes. "Yes, Mama."

Marguerite hugged her youngest to her breast. "Trust us, my love." She laughed. "I like him too."

Chapter 9

I t was a rainy day, and *Capitaine* Honoré Bourgeois hated rainy days. He sat at his desk in the offices of the Ministry of the Interior and rubbed his aching thigh. It was on days like these that his wound gave him the most trouble.

Capitaine Bourgeois had commanded a company of infantry in Spain, trying to subdue the guerrillas that had infested the Catalonian countryside. It had been a frustrating two years of chasing the phantoms through villages and farms, knowing the rebels were receiving arms and supplies from the British.

In the spring of 1813, the true enemy arrived in force. The British, with their Portuguese and Spanish allies, raised an army over 100,000 strong. Led by General the Marquess Wellington, it moved against a French force half its strength under "King" Joseph Bonaparte and his pet marshal, Jean-Baptiste Jourdan. There was no help from Paris; *l'Empereur* was limping back from his failed invasion of Russia.

Marshal Jourdan had not won a battle in ten years, and it showed. The French did all they could to avoid battle, but maneuver after maneuver failed.

On June 21, the hammer fell at Vitoria. Wellington decisively defeated Joseph and Jourdan, who both barely escaped capture. Bourgeois's company tried to hold their position, Bourgeois ignoring the blow his leg received from a British hussar. But loyal subordinates saw he could no longer stand. Heedless of his cries, they threw down their weapons and carried their commander off the field to safety.

Weeks later, Bourgeois was across the Pyrenees in a hospital in Toulouse. The surgeons managed to save the leg, and he begged to return to his command. But the army had other plans for the *capitaine* and sent him to Paris—just in time for the surrender.

Bourgeois had no idea what was to become of him. The half-crippled captain of infantry pledged loyalty to the Crown and awaited his fate. His misery was brightened by a small bit of good fortune. His courage in the field impressed his new masters, and he was posted to the Ministry of the Interior. He was to watch for spies and traitors—traitors to the Crown, not the Empire.

To Bourgeois it meant little. The army was his home and France his lover. He would serve the *drapeau blanc* as ardently as he had served the *drapeau tricolore.*

Now he spent hour upon hour scanning lists of names, looking for possible intelligence agents among the diplomats. It was a frustrating enterprise, for were not all diplomats spies? Bourgeois filled his days searching for needles in haystacks.

No, he thought, *rather needles in stacks of needles.*

He made marks against a few names and brought the list to his immediate supervisor, M. Lafarge. The old, bearded man made no comment on his approach. Bourgeois placed the list on top of the stack of documents on the desk.

"Not many, monsieur."

M. Lafarge picked up the list and held it close to his eyes, running a long forefinger across the page. He made no comment before dropping the list back on the desk. Bourgeois retrieved the paper and turned to walk back to his desk.

M. Lafarge's voice interrupted his progress. "You are limping, *Capitaine.* Are you well?"

Bourgeois was reluctant to discuss his aliment. "A gift from an English hussar." He gestured at the windows. "The rain, it makes it worse."

M. Lafarge's eyes took on a strange look. "*Excusez-moi.* Have a seat, *Capitaine,* and rest your leg." After a brief pause, Bourgeois sat himself in a chair by M. Lafarge's desk. "You have a good reason to hate the English, *oui*?"

"I have no reason to love them." Bourgeois felt slightly uncomfortable as the old man studied him.

"Forgive me, *Capitaine,* for not taking the opportunity to get to know you before now. Where are you from?"

"Orléans. My father worked in the Loiret departmental government."

"Your family, they still live there?"

"*Non.* My father and mother, they are dead. My only brother died in Prussia, serving the Empire."

"My sympathies. I understand the army assigned you to the Ministry. Do you enjoy your work?"

Bourgeois hesitated. Truth to be told, as a man of action, he found the work dull and repetitive, but with his wound, he was fortunate the army had not pensioned him off. He prevaricated. "At times such as these, a man should be thankful for employment."

M. Lafarge smirked. "Judiciously said." He looked out at the row of empty desks. "You see what the changes in government have wrought. Almost all who served in this room were dismissed. The king's ministers saw no need for the emperor's fawning bureaucrats. They can find their own and soon will. We few were retained to keep this place open until our replacements are chosen." He smiled. "But I will not be replaced, *non.* They know I have served both the Republic and the Empire with equal enthusiasm, and they know I will do the same for the Kingdom. What of you, Bourgeois?"

"I serve France, whether on the battlefield or off."

"Do you wish to stay here?"

"I must eat."

M. Lafarge frowned. "I thought you a patriot. I have misjudged you."

The *capitaine* realized his blunder. For all his complaining, Bourgeois needed this job to fill his belly and keep a roof over his head.

It would not do to offend Lafarge, for he might be more influential than Bourgeois thought. This old man might be the difference between starving or not.

"You misunderstand me, monsieur. I love France, and I will serve her until I die, but I am a man used to the barracks and the battlefield. For such a man, how valuable is my service here?"

M. Lafarge appeared to examine his very soul. "More valuable than you know, *Capitaine*." The man looked around, eyed the two clerks on the far side of the office, and lowered his voice. "The work we do here—that I do here—keeps France safe from her enemies."

Bourgeois thought about that. "We have enemies still, that is so—"

M. Lafarge interrupted him. "Who are they? Who are our enemies?" he demanded.

"The Prussians, the Dutch—"

"Bah! They are nothing! We have but one enemy—our age-old enemy. You know who they are by what they have done to you."

Bourgeois touched his thigh. "The English."

"*Oui*. Those bastards from across the sea have invaded us time and time again. They have stolen our colonies and disrupted our trade. The English, and the English alone, are our eternal foe."

"Forgive me, monsieur, but the court disagrees with you. The English have put Louis on the throne. As far as Paris is concerned, the English are our friends."

"Fools! Yes, the English installed the Bourbon, but not for France's sake. It was only because it suited them. Do not think they will now be our loving friends. Can you not see what is happening? Soon, the future of all Europe will be determined at the Congress of Vienna. Our participation was not thought to be needed or desired. It was only at the last moment that the other powers allowed a delegation from France to attend. Did you hear what I said? *Allowed!* The greatest nation in the world must now beg to attend their little conference."

"It is an insult, I agree, but at least we will be there."

"*Oui*. The self-styled Great Powers are weak. They did not carry through on excluding us from the talks, but our delegation will have no voice, no vote. They are observers as our fate is decided by foreigners. The English, they are behind this."

Bourgeois shrugged. "Can you blame them? We lost the war. Besides, what can this congress do to us? We will still be France."

"You think so? Then you do not see the danger— danger only we can stop."

"What danger?"

"The final destruction of France—by Frenchmen."

Bourgeois began to think Lafarge was mad. "What do you mean? Who are these traitors? Why have they not been denounced?"

"They are not here yet, but they soon will be. Thousands of them, once their training is complete."

"Where are they?"

"England."

Bourgeois was taken aback. "What French traitors are in England? I have not heard of any great desertion of French troops to England."

"You are correct. These traitors have been in England for many years, since you were just a babe."

"What? This is nonsense."

"I can prove it." M. Lafarge whispered, "Have you heard of *Le Mouron Rouge?*"

Bourgeois was now certain Lafarge was mad. "Fairy tales to frighten children."

The old man shook his head slowly, smiling all the time. "I have the records."

"Records?" Bourgeois took a moment to digest that one word. "You mean to say that *Le Mouron Rouge* was real?"

"Keep your voice down! *Oui*, I have the records of one Armand Chauvelin, formally chief agent of the *Comité de salut public. Le Mouron Rouge* was indeed real."

His thoughts completely jumbled, Bourgeois could only say, "But how does this affect us now?"

"This is the source of the traitors—the *aristos Le Mouron Rouge* transported to England. Do you think they refrained from breeding? Do you believe these exiled sons of France do not thirst for revenge and resettlement?"

As a boy raised to love France as much as his own family, Bourgeois saw the logic. Of course, French émigré aristocrats would want to return. Who would not? Moreover, it would be natural that they would want their lands and holdings back.

"You can prove this?"

"I said I have Chauvelin's records. I can prove it, *oui.*"

"Then we must warn the government!"

"*Non*, not now. They would not believe me. The government is too indebted to the English to *want* to believe me. It is too soon to go to them."

"Then what are we to do if this story is true?"

M. Lafarge pursed his lips. Bourgeois was certain he was displeased at his continued doubt. The old man sat straight in his chair. "We must remain vigilant. Look here." He pulled a packet of papers from a desk drawer. "Here is a list of the names of the *aristos* who fled to England. I can keep track of them if they dare try to enter the country legally. That is why I labor so hard to remain in the Ministry. I am the first line of defense."

Bourgeois glanced at the writing on the top page. The first name on the list was not French.

"Sir Percival Blakeney, Baronet? Who is he?"

A sly look graced M. Lafarge's worn features as he returned the papers to the drawer. "I have said enough for today. I have been using my eyes and wits to safeguard France these twenty years, and I will continue to do so. I shall not leave this desk until the threat is past." He sat up straight. "Go back to your work, Bourgeois, while you can. If, however, you wish to remain in the Ministry and help me with my mission, I have much more to show you. Good day, monsieur."

A confused *Capitaine* Bourgeois made his way back to his desk. *Surely, M. Lafarge is zealous in his desire to protect France,* he told himself, *but this! An invasion by thousands of Frenchmen. Boogeymen. Secret files from twenty years in the past. Lafarge is obsessed. It cannot be real. It cannot.*

Try as he might, Bourgeois could not shake the fear that, perhaps, M. Lafarge was right.

London

Having never been in love before, Frederick had to own himself astonished at how much he missed Violet's company as he relayed his melancholy feelings to a friend at his club.

"I tell you, Tom, I never thought I would be one to pine so for a lady," he said to his companions in a soft voice as they sat at a corner table. "This last month has seemed a year. I feel like a fool."

Instead of laughing, Thomas Bertram, heir to Mansfield Park, simply patted Frederick on the shoulder. "Perhaps there is more to this than you thought. It has happened to odder fellows."

Frederick was confused. Had another of his jolly companions joined the serious and respectable? At one time, Tom Bertram could be counted on to raise a little hell. Since a serious illness a few years ago, however, he had changed his ways. Now, the man who haunted the streets of London in his youth barely stirred from Northamptonshire. *Is there something in the ale these days?*

"Hah!" laughed the Hon. John Yates, Bertram's brother-in-law. "I would say forty thousand pounds would change many a man's thinking." At a stern glance from Bertram, he soberly added, "Not that all men think that way, of course. There is something to be said for affection."

Frederick could tell Bertram was not well pleased with the comment made by his sister's husband. There were several reasons for that. It was whispered that Mr. Yates had married the former Julia Bertram for her connections. Also, no one could forget Maria Rushworth's disgrace. Money and marriage was not a welcomed subject of conversation for the Bertrams.

Before Frederick could change the subject, however, they were approached by an acquaintance.

"Bertram! I have not seen you in an age!" the newcomer cried. "And you, Tilney. I heard you were in Town these days."

Frederick stood and took the man's outstretched hand.

"Manwaring, it has been a long time. In from Langford, are you? Have you met Mr. Yates?"

The gentlemen were introduced. "I am having a bit of a party at my house in Town tomorrow evening. Nothing much—just the old crowd. I think you will find it amusing. Say you will come. You, too, Mr. Yates."

Frederick answered before any of the others could speak. "Thank you, Manwaring. We will be glad to come." He turned to his companions. "Will we not?"

To his surprise, Bertram's face was rather closed. Still, after taking a breath, he said, "I will be there." He turned to Frederick. "Sorry to rush off, Frederick, but Yates and I have an appointment with our agent."

"Nothing serious, I trust?" Mr. Manwaring inquired.

"Of course not," Bertram responded coolly. "Until tomorrow then." Bertram and Mr. Yates took their leave.

Mr. Manwaring shook his head. "You know, if I did not know Bertram better, I would think he had exchanged places with his brother, the minister. What a severe look he wore! He is probably just worried over his allowance from the baronet!"

Frederick did not think so, but he kept his thoughts to himself. "I must be to Horse Guards, Manwaring. Thank you again for the invitation."

"It will be a jolly time, Tilney, I assure you."

Scotland

"I AM SORRY YOU HAVE TO RUN OFF FOR LONDON, FATHER," GEORGE said as the Blakeneys sat down for dinner,

"Pish posh! There is nothing for it! The banker writes, and I must attend. A new investment has come up. I will not be long. I should be back in a fortnight."

"Mr. Watts's invention again, sir?"

Sir Percy waved his hand. "Yes. There is this fellow who thinks he can make a steam locomotive like that Puffing Billy in Northumberland. Maybe move people along with the contraption."

"Nasty, noisy beasts from what I have read," said Marguerite. "Who would ride on such a thing?"

Sir Percy laughed. "Lud, I am certain the man is touched, m'dear, but even madmen can be clever. If I can make a few pounds, that would not be such a bad thing—would it, George?"

"No, sir. Already steam is used in boats. If it works on land, then I will say nothing evil about it."

"Faith, you will never get me onto one of those steam-powered boats," Marguerite said darkly, "or loco-motive, either. My phaeton suits me very well, thank you."

Sir Percy turned to his daughter. "And you, Violet? Are you an adventurer like your brother, or shall you keep Mama company in her carriage?"

A rare smile, seen far too seldom in the last few weeks, graced her lips. "I believe I can do both. The world is changing, and we must change with it. Now that we have peace, many things will change." Violet took her mother's hand, "But, I shall never abandon you for a machine, Mama."

"Well said, my dear," Sir Percy said, in a serious voice few outside the family ever heard. In his more usual comportment, he cried, "And where is the soup? Odd's fish, shall I die of starvation before it gets here, do you think?"

At that instant, the maid came in with the tureen. Used to Sir Percy's ways, she took no offence. "Ooch, Sir Percy, and here it tis. You shan't waste away, m'lord. Lady Blakeney, may I serve?"

Chapter 10

Frederick, Bertram, and Mr. Yates arrived in good time for the party at Mr. Manwaring's lodgings. As they expected, Mrs. Manwaring was not in attendance; all of London knew the couple were estranged. There was a surprise, however. While Lady Susan Martin could always be expected somewhere in Mr. Manwaring's vicinity, the attendance of her husband, Sir James Martin, could only be viewed as extraordinary.

Lady Susan was an extraordinarily attractive, exceptionally charming, dark-haired woman in her forties—as beautiful as a statue, sharp as a knife, and false as the day was long. She had been described in Frederick's hearing as "the most accomplished coquette in England." Her younger, wealthy husband was a very different creature: light haired, portly, gregarious, rather silly, and a bit of a rattle. The foolish Sir James made himself agreeable to Mr. Manwaring's guests while his wife stood by his side silently, her dark, calculating eyes taking in everything about her. Frederick found nothing in her worthy of his respect.

The group invited was small, though other guests were expected later. Mr. and Mrs. Willoughby were acquaintances, but Frederick knew Mr. and Mrs. Robert Ferrars only by reputation, which he found repugnant. Henry Tilney was a friend of the Rev. Edward Ferrars, and Frederick had learned of the infamous manner in which that fine man had been treated by his family. The elder Mrs. Ferrars, an acquaintance of the general, had disowned the reverend in favor of her younger son. Robert Ferrars expressed no dismay at the injustice but reveled in his good fortune.

The purpose of the party was to provide the usual entertainments for Mr. Manwaring. The gentlemen were to play cards while the women amused themselves in the parlor, a pianoforte established there for that purpose. The men withdrew to the study, where a great table had been set up. Bertram begged off playing, so it was Frederick at table with Mr. Manwaring, Mr. Willoughby, Sir James, Mr. Yates, and Mr. Ferrars. The stakes were set—a little high for polite society but not enough to concern Frederick.

Frederick looked about the table as the cards were dealt. He was across the table from Mr. Manwaring. To Frederick's left was Mr. Yates; to his right was Mr. Willoughby.

John and Sophia Willoughby skated along the periphery of Lady Jersey's set, laboring to gain full access to that most fashionable branch of the *ton*. It was whispered that Mr. Willoughby had an eye for the ladies, but he was kept on a short leash by his wife. He was a pleasant enough fellow, well known as a breeder of hounds, a decent shot, and not particularly gifted with intelligent conversation unless the subject was sport. He did not gamble to excess and could hold his liquor.

The snobbish and gossipy Mr. Ferrars, who sat on the other side of Mr. Yates, was the opposite of Mr. Willoughby. The man was known to favor high-stakes games in his club and elsewhere, gambling the funds that rightly should have been his brother's. That Mr. Ferrars had not yet frittered away his fortune meant either that he was more clever than he appeared or that he used other means for his success at the gaming table. The man would bear watching.

The jovial Sir James sat between Mr. Ferrars and Mr. Manwaring. Frederick could not understand how Sir James could be on rather amiable terms with his host. It was known that the lovely Lady Susan had a particularly close friendship with Mr. Manwaring, and it was said that relationship was one reason for the rift in the

Manwaring household. How *close* a friendship was the subject of gossip. Frederick could well believe Sir James was a cuckold, and the man who put the horns on him was sitting next to him.

Frederick considered himself a tolerant man, and he maintained acquaintances with men he did not particularly like or trust. If a fellow cheated on his wife or drank too much, what was that to him? If the man was amusing and paid his own way, Frederick could look the other way.

Ladies, of course, were different. An untrustworthy temptress could lead a man astray. Thus, his particular dislike of Lady Susan.

As Frederick collected his cards and put money in the pot, he wondered why he maintained an acquaintance with Mr. Manwaring. Liberal minded though he considered himself to be, Frederick was no fool. When he first met the man, he respected him as Mr. Manwaring confidently navigated his way through society, seeming to give no consideration to what people thought. True, John Buford never liked him, but now that Frederick thought about it, Buford always had a slight puritan streak.

As Frederick grew to know Mr. Manwaring better, he respected him less. Too many slights against the man's character had been made in Frederick's hearing for him not to take notice. There was a ruthlessness about the man that Frederick could not abide, as evidenced tonight. Mr. Manwaring not only invited his lover's husband to his house but played cards with him. Frederick suspected there was a method to it.

It was not many hands later that Frederick saw Mr. Manwaring's purpose. Due to many years in the barracks and tents, Frederick was as good a card player as any. He was holding his own, as was Mr. Willoughby, but Mr. Yates was not faring as well. However, Mr. Manwaring and Mr. Ferrars were doing *extremely* well and at Sir James's expense.

During a shuffling of the cards, Bertram caught Frederick's eyes and sent a look. It seemed he agreed with the perception that things were going far too well for Mr. Manwaring.

Frederick was sure that Mr. Manwaring was cheating, but for

the life of him, he could not detect how. He thought on all he had learned from his fellows of cheating at cards.

Only the most foolish and reckless of cardsharps would try to cheat the whole table. It would be obvious to his playing partners that something was amiss. Better to choose one victim—someone trusting and rich—and take all his money.

He glanced at Sir James. Frederick also noted that a bottle of brandy was at the gentleman's elbow rather than wine. A gentleman should never drink heavy spirits when playing cards if he wished to keep his wits about him. Sir James did not keep to that dictum.

Stretching, Frederick took a cautious look about the room, only to be disappointed. There were no strategically placed windows or mirrors. The only man in the room not playing was Bertram, and Frederick was certain he was not in Mr. Manwaring's confidence. Mr. Manwaring could not see Sir James's cards.

Very well—the cards are marked. But how?

He studied the backs of his cards as Yates dealt. The pattern was intricate, and he could see nothing that would indicate what he had. This would require further study.

As the game progressed, Mr. Yates, whose pockets were lighter by twenty pounds, retired; Bertram took his place. Sir James had lost far more, and Frederick looked at his own small winnings with concern. He was up by five pounds, but most of it had come from Sir James. Frederick's stomach turned. He felt he had benefited from chicanery.

To make this plan work, the other players would be allowed to win their share of hands, even the occasional large pot. Manwaring would also need a confederate to share the "luck" so his cheating would go undetected. Mr. Willoughby is winning far too little. Besides, his location at the table could not assist Manwaring. Sir James is between Manwaring and Mr. Ferrars, who is doing well. Is he the partner in this?

It was Sir James's turn to deal, and he remarked that he hoped his luck would soon change. Frederick suspected it would not, and a strange look shared between Mr. Manwaring and Mr. Ferrars only strengthened that expectation. They were somehow working in concert, he was persuaded.

Another hand and Sir James lost another few pounds. It was Mr. Manwaring's deal, and Frederick paid close attention. Finally, *there it was*—a slight fumble as Mr. Manwaring dealt a card to Sir James. The card had come from the bottom of the deck. Frederick glanced about quickly, but it was apparent that no one else saw it.

Frederick gave only passing attention to his cards, desperately thinking of some way to extricate himself from the game. It would be the height of bad manners to leave now while he was winning, and an accusation of cheating without proof would destroy him among the *ton* if not have him meeting Mr. Manwaring on a field of honor. Manwaring would have choice of weapons, and he was known as a dead shot with pistols.

How do I get Bertram and Mr. Yates away from here? I cannot stand and denounce Manwaring as I have no proof. I cannot see how the cards are marked.

I could pretend illness. That would serve to extract my friends and me from this place. But what of Mr. Willoughby and Sir James? Can I, in good conscience, leave them in the lion's den?

Salvation takes strange forms, and at that moment, two men walked in. In an instant, Frederick and Bertram were on their feet in anger.

"Thorpe!?"

"Crawford!?"

John Thorpe and Henry Crawford, who had been chatting as they entered, stopped dead in their tracks. Mr. Crawford, the partner in Mrs. Rushworth's disgrace, was stunned to see the brother of his former paramour and attempted to recover.

"Good evening, Mr. Bertram. Manwaring, sorry we are late—"

Bertram struggled to control himself, and Mr. Yates came to his aid, taking his arm.

"Gentlemen, I believe it is best that my brother and I take our leave of you." Mr. Yates glared furiously at his former friend.

"Do not leave on my account," Mr. Crawford said dryly, causing Thorpe to giggle. Bertram made an incoherent sound and tried to throw off Mr. Yates's arm. Frederick stepped forward between the men. At nearly a head taller than Mr. Crawford, Frederick loomed over him.

"I have heard of you, Mr. Crawford," he growled. "You mock my friends at your peril."

Mr. Crawford tried to bluster. "What have I done to you to deserve such treatment? Manwaring, what is this?"

Frederick's eyes flicked over to a white-faced Thorpe. "Well, for one thing, you have made a friend of my enemy. That alone puts you in my bad books." He turned to the trembling man behind Mr. Crawford and snarled his name.

"I-I have done nothing!" the fool cried. "I am an invited guest!"

Frederick gritted his teeth. "Do not be concerned, Thorpe. This time you have done me good service. For if *you* are welcomed in this house, I know *I* shall never darken its doors again. Thank you for enlightening me."

Thorpe, confused, could only mumble.

Frederick turned to Bertram and Mr. Yates, and was happy to see Bertram had gained control of himself. "Tom, I believe it was a poor idea of mine to come. Forgive me."

A corner of Bertram's lip rose. "You have had better ideas, Frederick. Let us leave this place."

"Of course." Frederick glanced about the room. Mr. Willoughby was standing, surprised and concerned, as was Mr. Ferrars. Mr. Manwaring simply sat and stewed.

Ruined your little game, did we? thought Frederick.

Frederick wondered whether he should do something for the stunned Sir James. An idea came to him. He crossed over to Mr. Manwaring to shake his hand.

"Farewell, Manwaring. Do not bother to call, *old friend*." He smiled without humor.

As he turned, Frederick "tripped" and fell over Sir James, knocking over his brandy glass. As he tried to disentangle himself, he also caused the suspect deck of cards to spill onto the wet carpet, soaking them and rendering them useless.

Apologizing profusely, Frederick helped Sir James to his feet and made to leave, collecting his own winnings. As he passed Thorpe, he said in a low voice, "I have not forgotten my vow, Thorpe. Beware my face."

The three men left the house with Mr. Manwaring on their heels, protesting loudly.

The carriage of Sir Andrew Ffoulkes rolled through the narrow, nighttime streets of the city. Ffoulkes would not usually find himself in such a place at that time of day, but Lady Suzanne loved the theatre, and this was the quickest route back to their lodgings in Town. Having two loaded pistols under the seat and two burly footmen outside assuaged any fears.

That is, until there was a ruckus outside their window. His wife could not help but look out.

"Odd's life, Suzanne, do be careful!" the baronet cried as he retrieved a weapon.

"All is well, Andrew," said his wife. "There are some men arguing in the doorway of a house. They seem to be gentlemen."

Ffoulkes looked for himself. "I say, is that not Captain Tilney?"

"Faith, I believe you are correct."

The driver finally seemed to realize what was about, for the carriage shot forward, leaving the angry men in its wake.

Ffoulkes shook his head. "Bad business, m'dear. That was Mr. Manwaring's house. A very unsavory character, I am afraid."

"Then what was a nice gentleman like Captain Tilney doing there?"

Ffoulkes said nothing and sat, deeply unhappy. Sir Percy would have to be told, and he did not look forward to having to do it.

Chapter 11

August

From a London newspaper:

This newspaper can confirm the account of a fracas outside the house of the well-known Mr. M of— Street two nights ago. According to reliable sources, we can confidently report that among the gentlemen involved in the mêlée must be counted the dashing Captain of Horse that has so charmed the daughter of a most illustrious friend of HRH.

PAPERWORK WAS WHAT FREDERICK LIKED LEAST ABOUT BEING AN officer. Reports, correspondence, even budgets—it was all mind-numbing, hand-cramping, and spirit-killing. He preferred a twenty-mile forced march, or even standing guard, to doing figures. He sighed and labored to balance his numbers one more time when Major Denny arrived at his tiny office.

"Captain Tilney, you have a guest in the duty office."

Frederick smiled at the reprieve from his torture. He thanked the major and followed him eagerly to the office. Great was his surprise at learning his guest's identity.

"Sir Percy!"

The baronet, splendid in a bottle-green coat, patterned vest, and buff breeches rose from a chair. "Ah, Captain Tilney, I hope you do not mind an old man stopping by for a few moments."

Frederick smiled and moved quickly to take Sir Percy's hand. "Indeed, you are most welcome, sir! I am happy to see you in such good health." The two exchanged pleasantries.

"Major Denny," said Sir Percy, "do you recall my second request?"

The major nodded and escorted the two into the regimental colonel's office. "The colonel is out of the office today, but I am sure he would be happy to offer you hospitality. You shall not be disturbed." With that, Denny closed the door to the outer office.

"Sit down, sit down, Captain," said Sir Percy as he took a seat behind the desk. A nonplussed Frederick did as he was bid. "I hope I am not taking you from your duties."

"Oh, no sir! I am very glad to see you." Frederick laughed. "In fact, your visit takes me away from much tedious paperwork, for which my tired pen thanks you."

Sir Percy peered over his spectacles at him. "Lud, that can be so tiresome, to be sure," he said dryly.

"I had not expected you in London for some months yet."

"I had some business in Town."

"And you took the time to see me? I am honored." Frederick had not planned to ask Sir Percy's permission so soon, but surely, his presence here was providential. *He must approve of me to show such consideration. Perhaps Violet has already talked to him.* He felt he should strike while the iron was hot.

"Sir Percy, pray allow me to take advantage of this happy occurrence to speak to you about a matter of great importance."

Sir Percy's eyebrows rose. "Great importance, is it? Gad, sir, speak on."

Frederick fought the nervousness he felt. "It should come as no great surprise that I hold your family in the highest regard. Your son, George, has been my friend for many years, and I appreciate the hospitality you have always shown me when I visited Richmond." Sir Percy nodded. "You know, I hope, that Lady Blakeney was so kind as to permit my visits while she and Miss Blakeney were in Town in June."

"I am aware of it, yes."

"Then you should know, sir, that my friendship with your daughter has blossomed into something far deeper than mere acquaintance." He stood. "I am a gentleman's son and an officer in the king's army. My attentions to your daughter have been all that is honorable. I love your daughter and believe she has a tender regard towards me. Sir Percy, I formally ask that you grant me the high honor to pay court to Miss Blakeney when she returns from the North."

To Frederick's consternation, Sir Percy said nothing. He only sat back, his hands together, studying him with an intense gaze. Frederick stood at attention, his concern becoming more and more evident on his face as beads of sweat grew on his forehead. Finally, Sir Percy rocked forward.

"You ask to court my daughter?"

"Yes, sir, I do."

Instead of answering, the baronet reached into his coat pocket, extracted a small piece of paper, and deposited it on top of a stack of forms where Frederick could clearly see it. Frederick glanced at it and gasped. It was the report from the papers about the night at Manwaring's.

Frederick had seen the story, of course, but thought little of it. He assumed no one would be able to identify him as being one of the men discussed. He now realized he had been very wrong.

"Sir Percy, allow me to explain."

"Explain what, Captain?" Sir Percy asked easily. "That you attended a soirée at the home of one of the most notorious characters in London? What is there to explain? You like cards, you like drink, and you like the company of disreputable people. I quite understand. I have several friends very much like you. *One* name shall go unmentioned. I am sure you understand." He winked.

Frederick knew he was speaking of the Regent. "Sir, those are not my usual pursuits."

"I am glad to hear it. You *are* admitting you are the officer mentioned, are you not?"

"Yes, sir."

"I see. Zounds, I believe you had a question for me. Now, what was it?"

"I was asking permission to court your daughter."

"Oh, yes." Sir Percy paused, smiling. "The answer is no."

Frederick felt his gut fall to his feet. "Sir, I beg you to reconsider. You should know that I do not gamble or drink to intoxication. The evening at Mr. Manwaring's was a mistake, I admit. I left as soon as I realized—"

"Hmm, thus the altercation in the middle of ___ Street?"

"Yes. Mr. Manwaring took exception to the manner of my leave-taking."

"Oh, so it was Mr. Manwaring's fault?"

Frederick felt he was on dangerous ground. "Yes, sir."

"Dear me! I am glad for your escape! To think that Mr. Manwaring could kidnap an officer in the king's own Hussars! What is this world coming to? Tell me, did he have help? Did he use swords or pistols to convince you to enter his house?"

The seemingly lighthearted comment felt like a slap in the face. "I—a few friends and I were invited there."

"Oh. So you went willingly?"

Frederick bowed his head. "Yes, sir. As I said, attending this party was a mistake, and my friends and I left as soon as possible."

"Yes. Mr. Bertram and Mr. Yates, was it not?" Frederick's jaw dropped. Sir Percy's tone became serious. "Mr. Bertram's reputation is not the best."

"Sir, Mr. Bertram is an honorable gentleman." At Sir Percy's glare, he added, "I admit his reputation was not good in the past, but he has changed his ways."

Right before Frederick's eyes, the foppish Sir Percy became someone else. His facial expression, his voice, his posture—all spoke of strength and intelligence. A serious, powerful, even dangerous presence. Not a man to be taken lightly.

"It seems most of your acquaintances are rogues, reformed or not, Captain Tilney. Why is that?"

Frederick had no answer.

"And why should I risk my daughter's reputation being sullied by closer acquaintance with you?"

"Sir! I—"

"Do not think I am without my sources, sir. I have looked into the matter, and I regret to report I am disappointed with the accounts I have received in regards to your character." He held up his hand when Frederick tried to speak. "I have talked with my daughter and my wife. I have listened to their defense of you. I was almost convinced you had left your past behavior in the past. But this episode proves we were deceived."

"Sir, I beg you to trust me! I know I made a mistake, but you must not paint me with the same brush you use for the others. Give me another chance, and I will prove myself to you." He gulped. "Sir, allow me to continue to call upon your family, I pray you."

Sir Percy looked sadly at him. "Odd's fish, I almost wish I could, Captain. You are a likeable young man, and I have enjoyed your company. But Violet's reputation is precious and cannot be threatened. You may continue your acquaintance with George for now, but I am sure you can understand the female members of my family will have to keep their distance."

Frederick, in desperation, cried, "Sir, this is not my fault!"

Sir Percy cried, "Not your fault? Sink me, then whose is it?" The baronet's words unrelentingly hammered Frederick's soul. "Is someone else to blame for your attendance at Mr. Manwaring's? Is it my wife's fault that you behaved in an overly familiar manner with my daughter? Is it Violet's plotting that led you to this 'not-quite-an-understanding' between you? Were all the ladies you have had difficulties with in the past out to snare you? Is it the king's fault that you have been in *four duels in the last six years*?" Sir Percy rose. "Tell me, sir, in all of your years, have you been responsible for *anything*?"

Frederick felt six inches tall.

"*You* told my wife that you knew of your reputation, and you promised her you would henceforth act in a responsible manner. *You* told my daughter that she makes you want to be a better man.

Oh, yes," he said at Frederick's shocked look, "Violet told me every-thing. Well sir, is *this*," he slapped the scrap of newsprint, "evidence of your reformation? Is *this* how you keep your word?"

Frederick, his world collapsing about him, could say nothing.

"Captain Tilney, it pains me to say this, but you are not good enough for my daughter. You will desist in your attentions to her. You will not call at my home. Do I make myself clear?"

Frederick fell back into his training, and he assumed a stance of attention. "Perfectly clear, sir."

"Good. If you would excuse me, I have business elsewhere. Goodbye, Captain."

Frederick stepped back to allow Sir Percy to exit the office. The baronet had his hand on the doorknob when he turned.

"I wish you good fortune in the future, sir. Truly, I believe there is a man somewhere in that uniform. It will be a happy day indeed if you find him." With that, he opened the door and left.

Frederick had not enjoyed a happy childhood, suffering a tyrant for a father and a weakling for a mother. Even with the affectionate attentions of his siblings, he was often lonely and sad. His mother's death had robbed him of the only unconditional love from a woman he had ever known, and that blow was felt more acutely as the years went by.

But at this moment, standing in his commander's office in the midst of the wreckage of all his hopes, Frederick had never before felt so alone and abandoned.

Scotland

"How could you, Papa?" cried Violet.

Sir Percy, upon his return from London, had requested a private conversation with Violet and Lady Blakeney. His countenance had given Violet no clue as to the purpose of the discussion, so his edict against contact with Captain Tilney was a shock, and his reasons gave Violet no consolation.

"Violet," Sir Percy said, "you must not speak to me in such a manner."

"I am sorry," she said, not meaning a word of it, "but I beg you to reconsider and allow Captain Tilney to continue to call. Let him prove he is the gentleman I know him to be! For my sake, do not bar him from Richmond!"

Sir Percy shook his head. "No, he is not to enter my house. I am sorry, my dear, but that is my firm decision."

"Percy—" began Lady Blakeney, but she was cut off.

"No." Sir Percy lightly slapped the table. "My mind is fixed; I shall not be moved."

Violet, desperate, could only say, "But Papa, I *love* him!"

Her father's face could have been made of stone. "What do you know of love? You are too young—"

"I know more than you! You have forgotten what love is!"

The room was still as her words rang in the air. Her father glared at her, and Violet, now ashamed of her outburst, covered her mouth and dashed from the study. She did not stop until she had raced up the stairs, slammed the door to her room behind her, and thrown herself on the bed. There she let loose all the tears her grief and disappointment demanded.

How long she wept, she knew not. She did not realize she was no longer alone until she felt the bed shift as another sat upon it, close to her.

"Oh, Violet..." Her mother's words were soft—as soft as the fingers with which she caressed her daughter's hair.

Violet turned her tear-streaked face from the pillow. "Mama, oh, Mama...why? Why is Papa so cruel?"

"He does not mean to be cruel, dearest. He is only concerned for your welfare."

She looked at her mother. "But, Mama, you know—"

"Hush, dear. He is doing what he thinks is right. We talked after you left." Lady Blakeney's voice grew firmer. "You kept some things from me. I did not know you and Captain Tilney had progressed into a courtship. Both of you were very wrong to keep it from me."

Unhappy over her mother's censure, Violet turned over on her back and tried to explain. "He was to wait to talk to Papa until I returned to London. Everything then would have been open, I swear."

Lady Blakeney sighed. "His actions in Town reflect badly on him."

"He attended a party—that is all!"

"The people there were very disreputable."

Violet could not understand why her mother was being so unfeeling. "Were they any worse than those who frequent Lady Jersey's?"

Lady Blakeney sat up straight, biting her lip. Violet once again regretted her angry, loose tongue, but she could form no apology. She considered herself in the right, no matter how much that hurt her mother.

"There are things you do not understand," Lady Blakeney said in a tone she had never used before in speaking to her—cold, insistent, and harsh. "Your father and I associate with many people in the first circles, not all of whom we approve or respect. I know as well as anyone what goes on in certain sets of the *ton*.

"However, your father is the particular friend of the Prince Regent. We owe His Royal Highness much more than you realize, and our gratitude knows no bounds. Indeed, it would not be too much to say that, without his friendship and patronage, your father and I would no longer be alive."

Lady Blakeney paused to let her words be understood, and it served. Violet, shocked and frightened, paid the closest attention to her mother.

"I will tell you that your father and I do not approve of Prinny's private affairs. We all know of Mrs. Fitzherbert, Countess Jersey, and the Marchioness Hertford. The Regent married poorly for state reasons. I have met Princess Caroline, and I well understand Prinny's aversion. The arrogant woman will not bathe! I understand she has left Britain for Brunswick and Italy, and we are all the better for her leaving, no matter how popular she is with the masses. They only support her because of the general condemnation of the Regent's conduct.

"That does not mean we condone infidelity. We have never had any of Prinny's favorites here in our home, and we never shall. The prince understands this and does not resent your father for it. In this, we are fortunate, for your father is close to Prinny."

Violet paid little attention to her mother's explanation, so stunned was she by Lady Blakeney's extraordinary claim. "Mama, you said you and Papa owe your lives to the Prince Regent?"

Lady Blakeney nodded. "It was during the time of the Pimpernel. If not for the prince's support and his influence with the government, your father would not have had all the resources he needed to successfully carry out his mission of saving the people threatened by the French Revolution. He would not have rescued as many as he did, I can assure you of that. There were several times when either your father or I were in the clutches of that vile man Chauvelin, and Prinny's timely assistance in providing boats and other things made all the difference."

Violet was ashamed. "I am sorry. I did not know."

"We did not want to frighten you or your brother with the dangers the League overcame."

Violet was mortified by the words she used to justify her conduct, yet she was ready to defend Frederick again. "I still believe Papa is being unreasonable about Captain Tilney."

"And you were very wrong to deceive us as to the depth of your attachment," Lady Blakeney returned. "You know I would not have given you as much freedom in Town had I known. I am disappointed."

"But, Mama, I love him!"

Lady Blakeney raised an eyebrow. "Do you, dear?"

"Yes! Frederick is everything kind and gentlemanly. He loves me for myself and not for my money. I can think of no other man who so suits me in character and disposition as well as he does." She took her mother's hands in hers. "Mama, make Papa give him another chance!"

Lady Blakeney squeezed her hands and said with a small smile, "I agree about Captain Tilney's appearance, for he is handsome, witty, and agreeable. It is his character that is in dispute."

"Mama, he is no fortune hunter!"

"Perhaps not, but there are other qualities upon which to judge a man's character, such as honesty, integrity, responsibility, and determination. Captain Tilney does not recommend himself to your father or to me by his actions." Her smile left her face. "It was his duty to speak to me forthrightly about you, and he did not. He made promises he did not keep, he has shown recklessness in his choice of companions and pursuits, and he has not shown the industry or ambition necessary to improve himself. Most worrisome is that he takes little credit for his culpability in his misfortunes. He needs to assume responsibility for his life and future."

Violet wanted to defend her sweetheart, but the truth of her mother's words weighed heavily on her. She dropped her head. "He said he would change, and I still believe him."

"I hope you are right." Lady Blakeney paused. "Will you apologize to your father?"

"I-I cannot face him right now. I will tomorrow." She turned to her mother. "Will you talk to Papa?"

"I make no promises. It is your father's decision, and I will support him in whatever he decrees." Lady Blakeney softened. "The only person that can improve Captain Tilney in your father's eyes is Captain Tilney himself. That will be neither an easy task nor a quick one. The evidence of time will be the proof of improvement —nothing else."

"Then I will wait for him," Violet stubbornly declared. "Frederick will prove Papa wrong; you will see."

Lady Blakeney only bowed her head, kissed Violet on the forehead, and left the room. Once the door shut, Violet gave way to the flood of tears she had quelled.

MARGUERITE FOUND HER HUSBAND STILL ENSCONCED IN HIS STUDY. His chair was turned towards the window, and Marguerite knew he was gazing at the rocks and trees without in earnest contemplation, as was his wont when he was troubled. She approached him, her slippers soft on the carpet, and put a hand on his shoulder.

"Percy, I have spoken to Violet."

Sir Percy patted her hand once in acknowledgement, but stared resolutely outside where a man on horseback was riding away. "What did she have to say for herself?"

"She is very upset and unhappy. She remains above stairs. She is sorry for what she said to you and will apologize, but she will need a little time."

"La, both my children are angry with me," Sir Percy said with resignation as he gestured at the window. "George and I argued, and he stormed out. He is riding off his displeasure, I have no doubt."

Marguerite sighed.

Sir Percy turned his head slightly and looked up at her, his spectacles balanced at the end of his nose. "And you, m'dear? Are you to give me the devil for my actions?"

"No, Percy." She gave his shoulder a squeeze and left his side to take a seat on the sofa. "Will you speak with me?"

Sir Percy scowled but rose from the chair and joined his wife on the sofa.

Marguerite thought carefully before she spoke. "I quite agree with your perception of Violet's situation. She and Captain Tilney should have been open about their attachment and should have approached me in London with a full account of their feelings. Their concealment was unworthy of them. I own that I am disappointed in Violet."

"And Tilney?" Sir Percy thundered. "Surely, Violet bears some fault, but she is but seventeen. To be young is to be foolish. But, by gad, *he* has not the excuse of age—far from it."

"All very true. The greater part of the blame must rest with the captain." She paused. "Violet's heart is broken, dear. I believe her affection for the captain is real, and I think he returns her feelings." Sir Percy made to speak, but she overrode his rejoinder. "You did not see them together. Their friendship and admiration were evident. He treated her very well and took no advantage of her, as other young men of our acquaintance might have done."

"Odd's life, perhaps not of her person, but he certainly took full advantage of our connections!"

"What do you mean?"

Sir Percy glowered. "I have heard stories of how Captain Tilney was quite the favorite of the regiment, getting all the plum assignments and arranging things so he was available for entertainment."

Marguerite shook her head. "Oh, Percy, that was not Captain Tilney's doing! That was Prinny!" She told him the captain had talked to her about the rumors. Sir Percy scowled as he listened.

"Well, perhaps it *was* Prinny, but Tilney could have spoken up about it. He took advantage of the situation in any case. It was badly done and no mistake."

Marguerite knew this line of argument would not serve to soften Percy's heart, so she tried to be direct. "It would have taken an extraordinary man to do as you suggest, but that is neither here nor there. I ask whether you truly mean to bar Captain Tilney from Richmond and our house in London."

"I do. Do you have another opinion, madam?" Sir Percy said in his lord-of-the-manor voice.

"I do, sir!" she shot back in the same manner before assuming a more reasonable tone. "Percy, I believe it would do well for us to show some mercy in this case. Captain Tilney, for all his abilities, is in need of guidance." She gave her husband a knowing look. "You are not alone in having sources. Violet has told me much of what passed between her and the captain—though not as much as she should have—and my informants have given me a good picture of the captain's home life.

"His father, General Tilney, is a grasping, unpleasant man. He has been unkind to his children, and he controls the captain's career. He cares for nothing but promoting his family's prestige."

Sir Percy nodded gravely. "Your account corresponds to what I have learned about the general. And you wish to have such a man as a relation?"

"I believe Captain Tilney has all the makings of a good man. Imagine what he could be if he had an excellent example to guide him?"

She could see her husband eye her speculatively before huffing. "Balderdash! I thank you for the pretty compliment, m'dear, but I was placed on this earth to raise my own children and no one else's. Captain Tilney must see to himself. I am sorry for Violet and for Tilney too, as he is an agreeable and entertaining fellow, but as I told George, Tilney is not good enough to court my daughter. I cannot take the chance that Violet's reputation might be irreversibly damaged by close association with Captain Tilney. I must ask that my wishes in the matter be observed."

Marguerite admitted defeat. "It shall be as you wish." A moment later, she felt his hand on hers.

"And you, Margot? Are you angry with me as well?"

She took his hand and squeezed it. "No, Percy. I am disappointed in how things have come to pass." At his urging, she was soon leaning against him. "I wish it were different."

Softly, Sir Percy sighed in her ear, "So do I, m'love."

Chapter 12

O ver breakfast, Violet apologized to her father for the way she had spoken to him the day before but held fast to her affection and attachment to Frederick Tilney. She was convinced her sweetheart would be able to prove his worthiness as her suitor, and she fully expected the captain would be welcomed to Richmond by December.

She spent the remainder of her time in Scotland enjoying the countryside, often by herself. George had returned to Oxford, and while she missed her brother exceedingly, he wrote to her regularly. By previous agreement, his letters were full of news of Frederick. His service, acting as a go-between for his sister and friend, brought no small measure of relief to Violet. If she could not be with her lover, at least she had news of him.

London

FREDERICK WAS DEVASTATED BY THE DEMOLITION OF HIS HOPES AT the hands of Sir Percy. Not to see or to hold his dear Violet again was an intolerable notion. Frederick had opened his heart, only to have it smashed. For weeks, he had no idea how to get along.

George Blakeney—thank the Lord—had not abandoned him and had written his apologies and commiserations. He begged Frederick not to give up hope. Violet, in her brother's estimation, would stay true to her admirer. He urged Frederick to do whatever was necessary to prove his worthiness to Sir Percy and gain the baronet's consent to court Violet.

The satisfaction Frederick felt in knowing of Violet's continued regard and George's unshaken support faded in the face of the avalanche of trials that descended upon him. News of his banishment from Richmond had traveled abroad.

He would remember the next months as the "bad time"; it was as close to hell as he had ever known in his personal and professional life. The latest letter from General Tilney was one example:

You, sir, had the opportunity to establish the Tilney name in the highest reaches of the First Circles. Your failure in not securing a connection with the Blakeneys will harm more than yourself. Your entire family will suffer because of your incompetence. I am most seriously displeased that my expenditure of influence and funds should be so wasted by my heir. It is a happy circumstance for you, sir, that the law of this country does not allow for the amendment of lawful entailment; otherwise, the future of Northanger Abbey would be entrusted to other, more worthy hands.

Concerns within his regiment quite overwhelmed the captain of cavalry. Word of his dressing down by Sir Percy had spread about the mess room like wildfire. Officers he had respected snickered at him behind his back. It was one thing to draw sabers and charge starving rioters while he was in the Twelfth Dragoons, but to lose the respect of his fellow officers was intolerable.

Worse still was the loss of his mysterious patron's favor. Frederick had been popular with the men in his company, mainly because they shared in his favorable treatment. Now, all shared in his fall. Whenever a dance was in the offing, the company was sure to be on duty. Inspections became frequent and thorough, and more than one man saw his meager pay reduced by fines. Lastly, the unpleasant task of training new recruits fell to them. As the new men's mistakes were counted against the company as a whole, leave was sharply reduced.

His colonel took some delight in informing Frederick of his downfall. "Fortune has changed, Captain Tilney," he had said with a sneer as Frederick read with dismay the new duty calendar. "A shame about all the dancing you will miss, but such is fate."

"Sir, as I did not ask for favorable assignments, I feel such treatment is unfair," Frederick said, indicating the paper. "I speak not for myself—I am an officer and will do my duty—but for my men. It is my company that will suffer."

"You should have thought about that before you played the game of influence. Dismissed."

Many in the company grumbled about the treatment, a few openly blaming their captain. As for his two lieutenants, they were a mixed bag. Mr. Remington had a temper, and it was not improved when his request for transfer was denied by the regiment.

The Hon. Mr. Brookings was a different sort. He carried out his responsibilities and kept his squad in line with nary a word of discontent. The third son of a viscount, Brookings could have expected better treatment, but he asked for nothing. One evening while guarding Horse Guards, Frederick called his lieutenant into the duty office and asked about his attitude. Lt. Brookings shrugged.

"I am in the army, sir, and it is not my place to question my orders. If I may say so, you have been a good and fair commander. We have had pleasant luck and may do so again. Fate is fate, sir. I have no complaints."

Frederick was impressed with the lieutenant. "If you do not mind my asking, why are you a lieutenant? Surely the son of a viscount would be at least a captain, if not higher."

The man shrugged. "Creditors before sons, sir. It will serve," he added at Frederick's attempted apology. "I have gotten quite used to it."

Another blow came weeks later when Frederick learned Major Denny was leaving Horse Guards for the General Staff. Frederick had grown to like the hardworking and sympathetic officer and felt he was losing his last ally in the duty office.

"Allow me to congratulate you on your transfer, Major," Frederick told him as he visited with Denny for the last time. "I am sorry to see you go. I have enjoyed serving with you. You will do well; I have no doubt. General Staff is a quick route to higher rank. Your family must be generous."

Major Denny stopped his packing and gave Frederick a queer look. "I am the son of a vicar, Captain Tilney. My family is neither rich nor influential."

Frederick felt the blood rush from his face. "By gad, I feel a fool! Forgive me, sir."

"It is quite all right, Captain. It is an understandable mistake. Mine has not been the usual route to promotion. I started in the militia, and my family scraped together the funds to buy a lieutenant's commission in the Regulars. I was fortunate to earn a competency promotion to captain, and Major Worthing's untimely death created a vacancy I was honored to fill."

Frederick was taken aback. He had heard of competency promotions, but Major Denny was the first recipient he had ever met. "Then, let me atone for my inexcusable bumbling by wishing you renewed joy at your transfer, for you surely deserve it." This time, Major Denny shook his hand. "I am very sorry to lose you, sir." Frederick sighed. "I feel sometimes you are the only friend I have here."

Major Denny eyed Frederick for a moment. He lowered his voice. "Stand your ground, Tilney. I have had my eye on you. You are a good officer, and you have treated your men well. You do not deserve your circumstance; it is not of your making." He glanced at the colonel's office. "It is unworthy of others to take joy in your misfortune."

"Thank you, sir," said Frederick, touched. "I wish I knew how to undo all this."

Major Denny's eyebrow rose. "You mean you do not know? Tilney, the forces behind this are *very high*. Indeed, there are few higher if you catch my meaning."

Frederick was puzzled until he remembered the name of George Blakeney's godfather. "Good God! You do not mean—"

"You have made enemies of the friends of your friends."

It was all so clear now. The Prince Regent, as a favor to the daughter of his friend, had decided to involve himself in Frederick's career. The prince's brother, the Duke of York, was commander-in-chief of the army. Now that Frederick was rejected as a suitor, Prinny and the Duke's protection had been lifted with the expected results. Frederick wondered how he could have been so blind.

"But what can I do?" he said in despair. "I have no influence at court."

"Neither do I," Major Denny said. "There is but one course open to you now. You must be the best."

"The best, sir?"

"Yes, the best officer in the regiment. Your company must be outstanding. You do that and keep out of trouble, and their lordships will see your worth. This scandal will pass; they all do." He shook Frederick's hand. "Good luck, Tilney. I shall follow your career with interest."

With that, Frederick returned to his office. Glancing at the stack of hated paperwork, he recalled Major Denny's advice as well as Sir Percy's parting retort:

"Truly, I believe there is a man somewhere in that uniform. It will be a happy day indeed if you find him."

With a sigh, Frederick got down to work. *Well, my lad, if you wish to make a man of yourself, it would be wise to start with this lot.*

October: Paris

THE DAYS GREW SHORTER AS THE YEAR DREW NEAR ITS END, AND the growing darkness of evening found *Capitaine* Bourgeois stepping out of a hired carriage onto a street near the ruins of what used to be *la Bastille*. As the coach continued on its way, Bourgeois pulled a scrap of paper from his coat and peered closely in the dim light at the address written upon it. His location confirmed, the *capitaine* took a moment to survey the dilapidated neighborhood.

This section of Paris had been run down even before the momentous events of July 14, 1789. Who but the most wretched would live near a prison? The deterioration of the neighborhood had only accelerated in the decades since the revolution. Most of the buildings were two or three stories. Few, if any, boasted oil lamps by the doors, and the stench of poor drainage only added to the gloom and ugliness of the place.

M. Lafarge's address was a narrow, four-story building in the middle of the row of structures. It appeared to Bourgeois to house a series of flats. He walked resolutely to the single door, where a sign indicated that M. Lafarge's lodgings were on the top floor. Bourgeois eyed the rickety staircase, hoping the height away from the stink of the streets was worth risking his neck on stairs of questionable condition. Carefully, he began his journey upwards.

For weeks, Bourgeois had considered and reconsidered his bizarre August conversation with M. Lafarge. Try as he might, he could not dismiss the old man's claims. Finally, two days ago, he confronted the man, demanding to see the proof he claimed to have in his possession. M. Lafarge then invited Bourgeois to his house, where he kept the papers—thus, the reason for his journey tonight.

Bourgeois reached the top floor landing to discover a single door. Apparently, M. Lafarge's lodgings occupied the entire top of the building. Bourgeois's knock was swiftly answered, and Lafarge bid him enter.

As the owner locked the door behind him, Bourgeois quickly looked about the room. He walked directly into a large space with three large windows to his right that overlooked the street below. A quick sniff proved Bourgeois's conjecture correct; the rooms were high enough above the stench outside to make the air in the room tolerable. A desk and chair were set before the bank of windows.

There were several closed doors to his left that led to other areas of the apartment, the one to a tiny kitchen left open. In the center of the room was a dining table with chairs. A fireplace was directly before him, graced by a single wing chair. The furniture was of good quality if a bit threadbare. There was no art on the walls. The few bookcases were full to overflowing, and the desk and table were covered in papers. There was a large chest next to the table. Oil lamps and candles provided what light the fireplace did not.

"Welcome to my humble abode, *Capitaine*," M. Lafarge said in a patronizing voice. "Make yourself comfortable while I retrieve refreshments."

Bourgeois sat at the dinner table, glancing at the papers for a few moments before Lafarge returned with a plate of various cheeses and bread. He put the platter on the table, right on top of the papers, and moved to a sideboard near the door. He poured two glasses of red wine from a decanter.

"Try this, *Capitaine*," he said as he handed Bourgeois his glass.

The *capitaine* was astonished by the quality of the vintage. "This is excellent, monsieur. *Merci beaucoup*."

"You are surprised, *Capitaine?*" M. Lafarge said with a smirk.

Bourgeois decided the old man was trying to bait him for reasons of his own and ignored the jibe. "You claimed you have records that can prove the existence of *Le Mouron Rouge*."

"You wish to get right down to business? A man of action, I see."

Bourgeois had no patience for whatever games Lafarge had in mind. "I have come to see the records if they exist, monsieur."

"Oh, they do." M. Lafarge reached down and opened the chest with a flourish. It was filled to the top with handwritten papers and journals. "Behold!" Lafarge reached in and extracted a journal. "This is one of the private journals of the late *Citoyen* Armand Chauvelin," he said as he held the object aloft, "along with correspondence, records, and reports to and from *Citoyen* Maximilien Robespierre and others of the *Comité de salut public.* I think you will find it interesting." He tossed the book to Bourgeois, and it landed on the table with a thump.

Bourgeois looked at his host with suspicion. "I have looked into this man Chauvelin. He was executed in 1794 in the wake of Thermidor for treason and murder."

Lafarge raised his eyebrows. "Treason? Yes, I suppose they had to call it something. You will see here that, instead of a traitor, Chauvelin was a patriot, laboring to save *la Révolution* from the *aristos*, and that executing true traitors is not murder."

Bourgeois picked up the journal. "And this will prove the existence of *Le Mouron Rouge?*"

M. Lafarge smiled widely. "See for yourself."

Two hours and two bottles of wine later, Bourgeois was convinced. "*Mon Dieu*, all the stories were true!" he said as he placed a letter from Robespierre on the table.

M. Lafarge patted the papers with what seemed like affection. "*Oui.* This man, Blakeney, this so-called Pimpernel, has been a great danger to the state for many years."

Bourgeois looked his host in the eye. "Is he still? The purge of the *aristos* ended with the fall of Robespierre."

M. Lafarge snorted, "*Ne soyez pas un imbécile*! Did you not see?" He quickly sorted through the papers from the chest and extracted one sheet. "Look here! In April of 1798, four years after Thermidor, Blakeney's yacht, the *Daydream*, armed as a man-of-war, was seen prowling the coast with the intent to raid our ports. Two French frigates engaged her and holed the raider, but the pirate Blakeney succeeded in escaping. His accursed luck stayed true, but not for his boat! Such was the damage the *Daydream* suffered that the boat sank before it reached the safety of an English harbor. Several of the crew were lost, but Blakeney was recovered by an English frigate commanded by none other than Admiral Lord Nelson."

Bourgeois thought about that. "We were still at war with the English. But is Blakeney still active? The sinking of the *Daydream* was sixteen years ago. He must be an old man now. Is he still a threat?"

M. Lafarge drew himself up, sitting in the rickety chair as straight as a statue. "Do you not thirst for justice, Bourgeois? The man is a criminal!"

Bourgeois waved off his argument. "War is criminal, monsieur. If we punished all men who took up arms, I would be among those in the dock. What you speak of is for God's justice, not man's. I ask again. Is this man Blakeney a threat to France now?"

M. Lafarge's stare was intense as he seemed to consider Bourgeois's question for almost a minute. "Sir Percy Blakeney is a man of considerable influence for a mere baronet. He counts among his acquaintances the cream of the English aristocracy. We know he is close to the Crown; princes and prime ministers call him friend. Look here." He pointed to a paper. "Robespierre and Chauvelin thought him an agent in the service of Pitt and the English king. He attacks France, and when he is on the verge of drowning, who should save him but England's greatest sailor. Coincidence? I think not!

"Consider! Percy Blakeney has proven himself a man of extraordinary skills and intelligence. For several years, he singlehandedly made a fool of our entire country! Then, in 1798, at the height of his influence and powers, he retired from the fight and spent the next fifteen years playing the dandy for the amusement of the Prince of Wales—while his country was at war! Does this make sense to you?"

"I must admit it does not."

M. Lafarge grinned. "I believe Sir Percy has changed his occupation. He is no longer the Scarlet Pimpernel, for he has a higher title. It is my firm belief that Sir Percy is the head of the English intelligence service!"

Bourgeois's jaw dropped. "But...but Paris always thought that office was in their Admiralty—the Royal Navy."

His host let loose a bark of laughter. "You see how clever these mongrels are? They make it seems as though England's spy network is managed by their navy; all the while, it is the purview of the Prince Regent and his chief agent, Sir Percy Blakeney. And why not? Did not *Le Mouron Rouge* create a vast network of spies and traitors in France? What could be easier than to utilize an existing web of informers, all of whom answer to one man—Blakeney!"

Bourgeois sat back, working through the haze of wine in his head to comprehend M. Lafarge's logic. He could find no flaw in the premise. Like a thunderbolt, it all made perfect sense to him. The godforsaken English were far more insidious than he had imagined!

"*Mon Dieu!* What shall we do?"

M. Lafarge cursed. "Nothing, *Capitaine,* nothing. England is our friend now! Bah!" He took a swig of wine. "But, now that *I* know and *you* know how things are, we can better protect France.

Hah! Blakeney thinks he is safe from us, and he is right, but only as long as he remains in England. Should he come to France—well, that is another matter!"

Bourgeois turned to him in surprise. "Why would Blakeney come to France?"

"Because of his wife—*la salope*!" Lafarge spat.

Bourgeois, his mind clouded by Bordeaux, did not take offence at M. Lafarge's crudity. "What do you mean—his wife?"

The old bearded man leaned across the table and leered. "Blakeney did not only take French *aristos* to England, he took a Frenchwoman for himself. He married an actress by the name of Marguerite St. Just, the belle of the Parisian stage." He belched. "I am surprised he actually married the harlot rather than simply installing her as his mistress. I suppose she refused him her bed until he said his vows before the priest—or minister, or whatever those heretical bastards call their holy men.

"In any case, the St. Just woman still has relatives in France. A cousin, M. Pierre St. Just, is a jeweler of high regard in Paris. He does well because he is careful not to take any political stand. He sells to the new Bourbon royalty and their hangers-on just as readily as he did to the former Empress Josephine's old favorites."

M. Lafarge sat back and said with arrogant confidence, "All we have to do is have the St. Just family watched. Eventually, Lady Blakeney will want to return to France with her besotted husband by her side. Then we will have him!"

"Have him, monsieur? For what? What will we do with him?"

M. Lafarge smiled the smile of a fanatic. "Justice, *Capitaine*. You will help me." It was not a question.

"*Oui*, monsieur," vowed *Capitaine* Bourgeois.

Chapter 13

The months had crawled by for Violet. Notwithstanding the letters from George assuring her of Frederick's devotion, Sir Percy's intractability with regard to his opinion of the wayward captain was a great source of unhappiness for her. She had made little headway in softening his heart. Begging, cajoling, even varying attempts at reasoning and resorting to silence had all proved ineffectual. Papa had decided, and there was nothing Violet could do about it.

Her time in Scotland had finally come to a close, and Violet rode in the Blakeney carriage with excited anticipation. Somewhere in her girlish fantasies, she half expected that Frederick, dashing in his best blue uniform, would soon call upon Richmond—damning all decrees and banishments, demand an audience with Papa, and browbeat him into sanctioning their courtship. How lovely and romantic that would be!

Of course, it did not happen. Girlish fantasies seldom do.

The Season was months away, but Richmond was the Blakeneys' seat, and there Sir Percy would spend the winter. There were parties enough to anticipate as the time of Advent was upon them, but mostly it was a period of intimate dinners and card parties and, therefore, little opportunity to meet Frederick by chance or by design at some function, if she dared.

The Yuletide was a joyous time at Richmond, and Lady Blakeney insisted that Violet assist her in seeing to the festive decorations. It was a testament to her daughter's low spirits that the normally cheerful girl went about her duties with little enthusiasm. When her mother inquired after her, more often than not, Violet responded with a soft, "I am as well as can be expected."

As November turned into December, Violet found herself ensconced in her room one afternoon, seated on the wide windowsill that served as the lid of a box. She watched a few snowflakes fall in the gathering gloom, feeling each one was a little piece of her heart. As had happened so many times during autumn, she felt tears wet upon her cheeks. She missed Frederick exceedingly.

Her eye caught some movement, and her sorrow temporarily forgotten, Violet gave the two figures emerging from the house her full attention.

It was Mama and Papa, bundled up against the cold, taking a stroll about the bare and brown gardens that slept in anticipation of spring's sweet kiss. She watched their open easiness and affection with a mixture of happiness and envy. Violet's mind drew a picture of herself with Frederick enjoying such a moment of domestic bliss. She could not help but smile at the sight.

Violet sat back, a thought that had sat dormant in the back of her mind suddenly coming forward. Such scenes of marital pleasure were rare among their family's acquaintances. From an early age, Violet knew the love her parents shared was exceptional and special. To have that kind of relationship with another was her dearest dream. She now remembered it was her parents' dream, as well.

How selfish I have been! I do believe Papa is wrong about Frederick, but I have forgotten he only wants the best for me. I am not yet eighteen, and I have not experienced one jot of what Papa and Mama have gone through in their lives—for themselves, for George and me, and for Britain.

How many times has Papa warned me to guard my heart? How many times has Mama told me of the tricks fortune hunters would use to get their hands on my dowry? Did not my first Season teach me anything?

How many insipid viscounts and vainglorious gentlemen had Papa sent packing, no matter how good their prospects? Papa is fair and right to be suspicious. I must be patient and trust Frederick will continue to try to change Papa's opinion of him and not give up.

Violet sighed. *Will Frederick keep trying? I know George tells me not to lose hope, but how can I expect that Frederick, after being treated so unfairly, will not give me up as bad business? No man can be expected to so humble himself. Have I lost him? I do not know.*

I have thought myself worldly and knowledgeable in the ways of the heart. How foolish! I have been nothing but a spoilt child these many months. This is a tragedy and no one person's fault. I have not treated Papa as I should—or Mama, either. I am ashamed. Until this moment, I did not know myself.

Violet looked up through the glass at the snow clouds above the trees. *I pray that Your will be done, Lord, and I ask You to give me the wisdom to see Your purpose in all things. Amen.*

London: December

In the months that followed, Frederick lost himself in his work and duties and spent little time bemoaning his fate. His reports were now the first to be delivered to his superiors rather than the last. Always a fastidious man, Frederick's uniforms now gleamed with renewed splendor. His deportment and tone of voice were correct at all times. He was every inch the ideal officer.

Frederick also worked industriously to improve his company. He insisted the kits of his men be as immaculate as his own. The company conducted drill after drill, perfecting each minute motion of their ceremonial duties. No detail escaped his notice. His company, stung at first by his increased attention to spit and polish, soon took great pride in their comportment, especially as they began to win accolades from the regiment. Tilney's company was no longer considered "lucky," given underserved precedence because of favoritism. They were as good a unit as any in the Horse Guards and better than most. Instead of suffering the derision of their comrades because of their captain's disgrace, they again enjoyed the envious congratulations of their fellows, this time for winning honest competition in drill.

The respect he earned from his fellows in the officer's mess—some most grudgingly offered—gave Frederick a sense of pride and accomplishment both for himself and his company. It was not a complete victory. There were those he had not won over—particularly Lt. Remington and his commanding colonel—but they kept their ill opinion of Captain Tilney to themselves now, and for that, Frederick had to be satisfied.

The company's duty schedule had not changed, which accounted for part of the reason for Remington's continued animosity. The most inconvenient tasks and duties still fell to them. However, the majority of the company accepted their lot with better humor, and it was often heard from his people, responding to teasing, "Well, if you want something done right, best send for Tilney's boys."

His labors proved an unexpected balm to Frederick's wounded pride. While working, he did not have time to think of Violet. Only at night did his thoughts return to what he had lost. He had increased his correspondence with his brother, Henry, and George's letters kept coming. Rather than drinking and carousing, Frederick read more now, particularly poetry and Shakespeare.

He forced himself to read the tragedies. It was painful, for he saw parallels in his own life, especially in *Hamlet*. The gloomy Dane was a victim of his unscrupulous uncle and weak mother, but Hamlet was a greater victim of his own indecisiveness. The prince's vacillation and recklessness helped lead to his lover Ophelia's madness and self-destruction. Hamlet was grief-stricken, but did he ever realize his culpability in Ophelia's death? Did Hamlet ever really show his love for his beloved, as Romeo had for Juliet?

Frederick considered his regard for Violet. He was certain he loved her, but he was unsure he was worthy of her. Had he behaved as an officer and a gentleman ought? He knew he should have made no promises and taken no liberties until he had secured an understanding with her father. Months of soul-searching had resulted in Frederick's firmly blaming himself for this personal disaster.

He knew his reputation had suffered because of his association with dishonorable men but thought nothing of it until it was too late. Buford had been right. He had sown the seeds of his own destruction. Had he truly made a break from his past, he would be spending this Christmastide as a constant visitor to Richmond, basking in the friendship of the Blakeneys and the affection of dear Violet.

What a fool I have been! I knew nothing of love! I knew only of passion and desire before. But you, Violet, with your sweet smiles and delightful company—your conversation and accomplishments are everything I have ever desired in a lady. I see us now, residing happily at Northanger Abbey in perfect harmony and contentment.

What a lovely dream—a dream that shall never come true, thanks to a stupidity that rivaled that of Prince Hamlet.

To bury these mortifying thoughts, he sought physical action. When not on duty or in his quarters, Frederick could be found at his fencing club. Always an excellent fencer, he now committed himself to achieving perfection in dueling. He spent hours practicing and had become nigh unbeatable. Many in the club would not fight him for fear of swift and crushing defeat. It was left to the instructors to serve as his opponents, and watching their matches with Frederick became a favored occupation of the other members.

On one December day at the fencing club, Frederick was happy to find George Blakeney, just returned from Oxford, waiting for him. A match was soon agreed upon, and Frederick quickly won the first two passes.

"Lud, Frederick," panted his friend, "you *have* been practicing!"

"A bit," Frederick allowed, "but you are doing well." At George's disparaging scoff, his friend continued. "No, it is true. Your footwork is much improved—look." To the disappointment of their impromptu audience, Frederick stopped the match, and he and George compared the position of their feet and knees. An instructor came forward, and soon the three were working out combinations of counterattack.

"You see?" Frederick asked George. "Keep your knee well flexed as you prepare for the counter-riposte." He demonstrated, keeping his weight balanced on the balls of his feet, his foil moving through the air faster than could be seen.

"Well done," came a deep voice from behind. "But you may want to better disguise the second intention, or the counter-riposte will fail."

Frederick froze at the sound of that voice, as well known as his own. It fell to George to cry out, "Buford! By Jove, it is good to see you!"

Frederick removed his fencing helmet and turned around. Standing nearby was Sir John Buford dressed in civilian clothes, arms crossed over his chest. He wore a neutral expression, but his blue eyes showed a hint of nervousness, as though he were uncertain of his reception.

As well he should be, thought Frederick, remembering the cut his estranged comrade delivered six months ago at the concert. Still, years of friendship could not be put aside, and his next thought was a hope Buford had come to apologize, unlikely as that was. In all the time he had known John Buford, the fellow had apologized for nothing.

The tall, dark-haired man stood quietly, expectantly. It occurred to Frederick that Buford was giving him a choice: acknowledge him or ignore him. For a fleeting instant, Frederick knew he had been given the chance to repay Buford with his own coin. This was impossible, of course. Their former camaraderie was too strong.

"Sir John." Frederick was cautious.

"Captain Tilney," returned Buford, replying in kind. Frederick did not know what to say next, but George saved the day.

"What brings you here? Looking for a bit of practice?"

"No," the colonel said. "I was in the neighborhood and thought to stop by for a drink."

George turned to Frederick, the question clear on his face. Frederick nodded and said, "Capital idea, Colonel. Give us half a minute, I pray you."

Frederick quickly dismissed the instructor, put away his equipment, and towel around his neck, joined Buford and George at one of the small tables used by the club members for refreshment between and after bouts. The club served no strong spirits, but a bottle of wine appeared moments after the men took their seats. George poured for all three as Frederick and Buford silently looked at each other.

George lifted his glass. "Well, this calls for a toast—"

Frederick cut him off. "Let me, George. To Colonel Sir John Buford on the occasion of his betrothal. May he and his intended have much joy, contentment, and peace."

Buford finally smiled. "Thankee, Tilney."

The three drank while Frederick considered. *Hmm, from Captain Tilney to just Tilney. Still, not the more familiar Frederick. Do I have leave to address him as I once did? I had best be wary.*

"Yes," George said, "we saw the banns in the newspaper. Miss Bingley is a fortunate lady!"

Frederick decided to take a chance. "Perhaps, perhaps not." He grinned to lighten his teasing.

Buford's blue eyes shot to his, considering. Then, the man relaxed and laughed, "Too true, too true. She is definitely getting the lesser part of the bargain. I am the one who is fortunate."

Frederick relaxed as well. "The Bingleys are related to the Darcys by marriage, I believe. So, how do you feel about being Mr. Darcy's relation?"

Buford smirked. "Darcy is not a bad chap once you get to know him. Reserved in public, even to those in the First Circles. I befriended him long ago through Colonel Fitzwilliam, and Darcy is perfectly easy and often amusing in private."

"Ah, ha! So the scarecrow does have a personality? I had wondered."

Buford shook his head. "Spend five minutes with *Mrs.* Darcy, and you would learn that! She is one who does not suffer those who are pompous or imprudent. A matched pair, they are. His gravity is offset by her openness, but both are loyal and generous."

Frederick grunted. "I heard a man should take care not to spend *too* much time with Mrs. Darcy, or he will receive Mr. Darcy's dreaded glare of doom."

Buford laughed. "True, he is a protective sort, but he is not alone in possessiveness. If any lady of the *ton* wishes not to suffer Mrs. Darcy's displeasure, she should not flirt with her husband. Not that Mrs. Darcy would make a scene, but her wit can be deadly. Besides, one word to Lady Matlock can destroy someone in society."

George changed the subject. "Thank you for the invitation to the wedding, Buford, but I am afraid I will be unable to attend. I am sorry, but family obligations—"

"Say nothing of that, George: I understand," Buford said. He then turned his eyes to Frederick.

All the easiness Frederick had felt had fled at the mention of Buford's wedding day. He had not received an invitation and did not expect one. Still, it was damned uncomfortable to be reminded of it. George belatedly realized his blunder and looked at his friend in mortification, saying nothing lest he make a bad situation worse.

For his part, Buford dropped his eyes to the table before him. Slowly, he reached into his jacket pocket and removed an envelope. Made of fine paper, it had Frederick's name written across its surface. Buford carefully placed the envelope face up on the table, just under his fingers, and raised his head.

With a jerk, Frederick's attention returned to Buford's face. The colonel sat there resolutely, his face impassive. George, for his part, sat stunned. He knew this was a moment of significance. Frederick opened his mouth to question him but shut it with a snap.

Why is he delivering it personally? Does he think I would just tear it up without an answer? Of course, I would not. He knows that. So, what is he about? Why is he doing this publicly?

Publicly—of course!

He looked again at the envelope and then at his former friend. Frederick stared into Buford's eyes and nodded. Slowly, deliberately, he extended his hand to cover the envelope. With a small smile, he pulled it across the table to himself. A warm feeling of relief and happiness filled him for the first time in many months. He did not have to look around to know that every eye in the room was fixed upon this little tableau.

"Thank you, *Buford*," he said a little louder than necessary as he put the envelope into his pocket. "The mail at the barracks can be so undependable."

Buford's face relaxed into a small smile. He said quietly, "I remember, *Frederick*. I wanted to make sure you got this. I earnestly hope you can attend."

Frederick returned the smile. "My schedule is not mine to make. Trust me to be there if I am able."

Buford nodded. "I understand. Well, gentlemen," he said in a normal voice as he rose, "I am sorry our time together is so short, but I have an important appointment I must not miss."

"Tea with your intended?" Frederick guessed.

Buford's smile widened. "It has been good to see you, Frederick. *Very* good to see you." They shook hands before the colonel took his leave of George. The two watched as Buford made his way out of the club. The other members, seeing that the show was over, went about their business.

George whispered to Frederick, "Well, *that* was an unexpected pleasure. I thought you said Buford never apologizes. What have you to say now?"

"George, my lad," he said as he clapped the younger man on the back, "I have been very wrong for a long time about a great many things. I am just coming to realize how much in the wrong I have been. This, however, is the first of my mistakes that I have lived to enjoy."

Chapter 14

I t was a bright, relatively moderate winter's day, perfect for a wedding. At least, it was in the eyes of Mrs. Bingley. The numerous guests for the wedding breakfast in honor of Sir John and the new Lady Buford would not be tromping in snow to mar the hard-won splendor of Jane Bingley's floors, of that one could be sure.

The rooms were festooned in the colors of the Buford coat-of-arms, and the bride was lovely in light blue. The staff of Bingley House had gone out of their way to provide the best food that could be gotten in January. After all, Bingley House could look forward to no other weddings until a day far in the future when Mr. Bingley would give away his little daughter, Susan.

Due to the weather, the receiving line was contained within, allowing the guests to enjoy the warmth and hospitality of their hosts. Therefore, Frederick Tilney had plenty of time to shake off the cold before congratulating the happy couple.

"Frederick, my friend," said a smiling Sir John Buford. "How good of you to come!"

"It is I who should thank you," replied Frederick. "It is good to see you and wish you joy on your wedding day."

"May I present Lady Buford? My dear, this is Captain Tilney of Northanger Abbey."

Frederick eyed the tall, slim, dark-haired woman, a cameo of carnelian shell resting on her slight bosom, a small smile adorning her attractive face. He had heard of the former Caroline Bingley, and he was surprised that Buford, who had so loudly proclaimed he was done with the fast set of the *ton,* would align himself for life with a notorious social sycophant. But lately, he had heard of changes in her character—that the Darcys had quite accepted the lady who had publicly set her cap on Pemberley. The gracious and sincere welcome he received from Lady Buford seemed to indicate that more than his old friend had reformed.

Once Frederick made his way from the reception line, he soon found himself in conversation with Colonel Brandon and his young wife. At their invitation, he shared the breakfast with them and the Earl and Countess of Matlock. The earl held court.

"It is fortunate we were in Town," he declared. "I so despise traveling in winter—a nasty business."

"I certainly agree, milord."

"I see you are in the Blues. Is that how you met this fellow?" Lord Matlock gestured at Colonel Brandon.

"I do not spend much time with the Life Guards, sir," said Colonel Brandon. "I am inactive, you see. But I knew of Tilney from Buford and his service with the Twelfth Dragoons."

"Aha. Captain Tilney, are you acquainted with my son, Colonel Fitzwilliam?"

Frederick shook his head. "By reputation only." He turned to the countess. "Which is excellent, I may report, milady."

Lady Matlock laughed. "Which may or may not be accurate. I know well my rapscallion son, sir."

The earl eyed the young captain. "Your father—General Tilney of Northanger Abbey?"

"Yes, sir."

Frederick could see that, whatever the earl's personal opinion of the general might be, he kept it to himself. "Hmm…Gloucestershire is no small distance from Town, eh? Quite different from the city."

Frederick took a chance. "As different as Derbyshire, I think you would agree."

"Hmm, what? Oh! Oh, yes, quite right." A smile flashed across the earl's lips. "You are a quick one, Captain. You remind me of my nephew's wife."

"Thank you, sir. Mrs. Darcy is a remarkable lady."

Lord Matlock laughed. "She caught Darcy, did she not?" He glanced with affection at a far table, where Mr. and Mrs. Darcy were conversing with Miss Darcy. "I do not mind saying she is a worthy addition to the family."

Mrs. Brandon smiled. "As a friend of Mrs. Darcy, I will not say different."

The earl turned back to Frederick. "Still, now that you are in the Blues, you must meet with a different set of people, Captain."

"Indeed, sir."

Lady Matlock looked up. "Did I not see you with the Blakeneys at a soirée last summer, Captain?"

The earl harrumphed. "Blakeney? Blakeney? You mean that nincompoop Sir Percy?"

Frederick gritted his teeth. "I have had the honor of meeting them, milord." He may have had his differences with Sir Percy, but Frederick had grown to admire the baronet. In the months since their confrontation, Frederick had come to realize that his difficulties had been of his own making.

"There are those who say Sir Percy Blakeney has done great things for the Crown," added Colonel Brandon.

Lord Matlock turned to the colonel. "You mean that business with the Frenchies? What was it—Popernail—Purplenell?"

"Pimpernel, sir," said Colonel Brandon.

"Oh, yes—Pimpernel! I do not know about that. No one is exactly sure what happened back then. Some master of disguise saving thousands from the guillotine? How likely is that?"

Mrs. Brandon said evenly, "About as likely as Sir Francis Drake against the Armada, my lord?"

"Hmm? Oh, yes…I see." The earl smiled. "Good point, Mrs. Brandon." He turned to the colonel. "I see Darcy and I are not the only ones with clever wives." He patted Lady Matlock's hand with fondness. "Let that be a lesson to you, Captain Tilney. Marry a smart woman!

"Still, I cannot see Blakeney risking his life for a bunch of Frogs, even if his wife is one. Ffoulkes and Dewhurst? Perhaps. But *Blakeney*—the only man to give Brummell a run for his money? More likely, he financed whatever was going on. He could certainly afford it. Richer than Croesus, I am told."

"That still makes him one of the heroes, dear, even if they only saved a score," said the countess.

"True—if only he was not such a dandy! I cannot stand the fellow. He is part of Lady Jersey's set, you know. I do not like his politics, either."

"As a baronet, he is not in the House of Lords," Colonel Brandon pointed out.

"Of course. But he is a damnable Whig just like all of the Regent's friends."

"Hugh, your language?"

"Sorry, m'dear. Well, I was with them on the slavery issue —Wilberforce was right about that. But too many of them refused to see the danger that Corsican pretender presented. Why, they admired the little tyrant! Half of them are outright Jacobins, you know."

"I can assure you, sir, that Sir Percy has no love for Bonaparte, and I would never call him a radical," Frederick stated.

"Well, perhaps he has some sense even though he is in the Regent's circle," Lord Matlock allowed.

"Whatever else we may think about the Regent, he is no fool. That may be the reason he keeps appointing Tory governments," added Colonel Brandon.

"Yes," agreed the earl, "and they have proper deference for the Crown. Which is why this whole business of emancipation is nonsense! You simply cannot give the vote to a bunch of Papists whose first loyalty is to the Bishop of Rome! That would be giving the henhouse key to the foxes! All you have to do is look at the Irish, sir, and you see the problem."

To Frederick's surprise, Colonel Brandon nodded. "There are many who agree with you, sir."

Lady Matlock touched her husband's hand. "Hugh, may we speak of something other than politics?"

Chastised, the earl began recounting his last foray to his hunting lodge in Scotland, but Fredrick hardly attended. He was lost in his ruminations.

Well, milord, forgive me if I do not agree with you about emancipation! Sir Percy's motivations were pure. Lady Blakeney had certainly been Catholic and might still be. And Frederick remembered John Buford's relations on his mother's side were all French Catholics, and he knew of no greater defender of king and country than Buford. Even though his brother was an Anglican clergyman, Frederick did not think it right that a man who fought for his country was not allowed to vote because of his religion.

Frederick suddenly realized this line of thinking was very different than his father's or even his brother's. *Zounds!* he thought. *Am I turning republican?*

AFTER THE WEDDING BREAKFAST, FREDERICK WAS PLEASANTLY surprised that Sir John sought him out. Frederick received another hearty handshake from his formerly estranged friend.

"Frederick, I must thank you again for coming," Buford said with a smile.

"It is I who must thank you for the invitation. It was as unexpected as it was undeserved—for me, that is."

Buford glanced away in embarrassment. "I must beg your pardon, Frederick. I would take back my words in Oxford. I feel such a hypocrite!"

Frederick placed his hand on the colonel's arm. "I have come to realize you were justified in what you said. You have made me think, and a painful experience it was, I can tell you." He sighed. "My actions have not served me well. You warned me, and I should have attended."

Buford eyed him with compassion. "I heard something about

Miss Blakeney."

Frederick grunted. "It is all over Town! Yes, I have been a fool, and it has cost me greatly."

"Have faith, Frederick. It will all turn out right in the end." Buford glanced at his new wife, deep in conversation with Mrs. Bingley and Mrs. Darcy. "If things are meant to be, they will be. Live your life well from here on out, and good things will be your reward. I am proof of that."

And so is your wife, thought Frederick, again surprised at the cordiality between Lady Buford and Mrs. Darcy. "So, you are for Vienna, I hear."

"Yes, to serve at Wellington's beck and call." Buford grinned. "Dealing with foreigners without either sword or pistol in hand will be a new experience. But I expect it will be just as vexing!"

"I am sure of it!" Frederick said, laughing. "Does Lady Buford travel with you?"

"Yes," said Buford, a strange, softening expression on his face. Frederick noted it with disguised amusement.

"Well, my friend, I know the time for leaving is upon us," Frederick said, shaking Buford's hand. "Good fortune in Vienna. Do not allow the Iron Duke to work you too hard!"

"I shall keep that in mind. Farewell, Frederick."

For some reason, Frederick added, "Take care, Buford."

Sir John responded with a puzzled look. "Of course. Until we meet again."

As Frederick left Bingley House, he felt strangely unsettled. *Why should I be concerned? What can happen to Buford in Vienna?*

Richmond

Marguerite engaged in small talk with her brother's wife, Marie St. Just, as the maid placed the tea service on the table. Sir Percy was discussing drainage with Armand St. Just while George and Violet talked with the Ffoulkeses. The ladies then poured the tea, which gave Marguerite's brother the opportunity to change the subject.

"You know," he stated after trying his tea, "I have been in correspondence with my cousins in Paris. You remember, Margot —Cousin Pierre, the jeweler. He said Mme. St. Just had written to Violet." Armand turned to his niece.

Violet smiled. "She has, Uncle, several times, and has invited me to visit."

"She did?" Armand cried. "Well, you must go then!"

Marguerite's eyebrows rose in response to her brother's outburst. Even though he was now a respectable barrister, Armand was still known for his impetuous impulses.

Sir Percy smiled. "My dear Armand, Violet is but seventeen. She cannot go to Paris."

"Father, you know I turn eighteen next month!"

"Seventeen, eighteen—still too young to go by yourself."

"I am sure George would go with her," Armand responded. "What do you say, George? Fancy a trip to France?"

"Nothing would give me greater joy, Uncle, but I must return to Oxford."

Armand snorted. "Book learning—bah! You need to experience real life, my boy." George simply smiled and shrugged as Armand continued. "But it matters not as I now have a mind to escort Violet myself—myself and Marie, that is."

"Armand!" cried his wife. "You astonish me. Visit Paris?"

"Certainly, my dear. I have nothing pending that I cannot put off for a few weeks." He turned to Violet. "What say you, my dear niece? Will you come to Paris?"

Violet smiled uncertainly. "You are not joking, Uncle?" Told he was not, she answered, "I…it is for my father to decide." She turned to an unusually silent Sir Percy.

Marguerite had no doubt as to her husband's thinking. In the four and twenty years of their marriage, she had learned Sir Percy's mind. They held the same opinion of Armand: he was jolly, loyal, brave, and generous, but not always the deepest thinker.

Sir Percy had never told Marguerite the full details of the rescue of Armand in 1794. She knew her brother had rushed to Paris in a fit of stupid gallantry to save the actress Jeanne Lange from the guillotine while the rest of the League labored to deliver the Dauphin from the Revolution. As it turned out, nothing came of Armand's grand gesture. Mlle. Lange fell in love with an English viscount while Armand would eventully marry Marie, the lovely and steadfast daughter of a judge.

Marguerite knew *something* had passed between her husband and brother, for since that day, Armand would never challenge Percy's thoughts, actions, or opinions. How unlike the headstrong boy he was before and still was to the rest of the world! What debt did Armand owe to Percy? Marguerite had asked, of course. What wife would not? But neither would speak of it.

Sir Andrew Ffoulkes, silent until then, said, "I understand from Dewhurst that Paris is quite lovely these days." He earned a stern look from Sir Percy.

Armand laughed. "Paris in springtime—nothing lovelier!" He turned to his brother-in-law, and in a tone of deference said, "It is up to you to give Violet permission, of course."

Sir Percy glanced at Ffoulkes and Armand in irritation before saying to Violet, "We will see, m'dear."

THAT NIGHT, WITH THE CONNECTING DOOR TO THE MASTER'S SUITE left open, Marguerite's maid brushed her mistress's hair. Without a word, Sir Percy in his robe walked over and retrieved the brush from the unsurprised maid, an abigail of many years and accustomed to the unorthodox goings-on in Richmond. With a curtsy, she made her way out of the room.

Sir Percy ran the brush through Marguerite's still-luxuriant ebony hair, now sprinkled with lines of grey, his eyes glued to the image of his wife in the mirror. Marguerite enjoyed his attentions in silence for a while.

"What think you of Armand's idea, Percy?"

"La—what do I usually think of Armand's ideas?"

"I thought so." The brush pulled at a tangle. "Violet remains unhappy."

"That will pass soon enough."

"It has been over six months! She needs diversion."

Sir Percy said nothing at first. "Perhaps a trip might be just the thing."

"It would be good for her to meet more of my family—see more of my old home."

Sir Percy frowned. "Do you wish to go?"

"No!" his wife said at once. "I am done with France. My memories are still far too painful. 'Tis my old home, nothing more—not my *real* home." She stared at her husband in the mirror. "I have but one home now."

His lip twitched. "And where is that?"

"Wherever my husband is."

With a groan, Sir Percy dropped the brush on the dressing table. Marguerite rose and turned into his arms. "Oh, Margot—*ma chérie* —my dearest," he managed before her lips claimed his.

Chapter 15

For not one minute did Violet doubt that Lady Blakeney would fail to convince Sir Percy to permit her to go to Paris. She had seen *that* look in Mama's eyes before, and Papa was defenseless against her.

Would Frederick be so defenseless against me? Oh, how I wish Frederick was coming with me.

Violet quickly chastised herself. It was foolish to continue pining over Captain Tilney. True, she had pledged undying devotion, and in the six months of their forced estrangement, her heart had not wavered. She loved Frederick as much in January as she did the previous summer.

But what of Frederick? George insisted he remained true to her, but was it really so? There were so many temptations in Town. There were so many lovely ladies and so many fathers who would welcome an alliance with the heir to Northanger Abbey. How long could Frederick resist? Could his love survive such a test? She believed Frederick was all that was good and faithful—but six months! It had been an eternity to her. How much worse could it be for him?

It is useless. Papa will never relent. My love is selfish. If indeed I love Frederick, I should release him.

Her joy turned to tears, and as she had done countless times since September, she gave way to weeping for all she had lost.

London

THE SHOP WAS WELL KNOWN FOR THE QUALITY OF THE LADIES' fineries sold there. As their wares were of exceptional craftsmanship and exquisite detail, the proprietors could reasonably expect a handsome price for them. "Discriminating" would best describe the patrons who frequented this establishment, and as Frederick Tilney had always thought himself a man of excellent taste, there could be no other shop in London for his patronage, especially for this particular shopping expedition.

The event was his dear sister's birthday. Eleanor spent the majority of her winters at her viscount's estate in the north. Yorkshire was a brutal place at this time of year, Frederick knew. *But perhaps less brutal than Northanger Abbey when Father is in one of his rages.*

Frederick forced his attention back to today's mission. He needed a birthday gift for Eleanor, and a warm pair of gloves would be the very thing. The clerk had been most helpful, and Frederick readily approved of his choice of winter leather gloves lined in beaver. The price was dear—far more than Frederick had intended to spend —and he was weighing the purchase when the bell of the front door rang.

Instinctively, he turned and was astonished to see Violet Blakeney walking in with Lady Blakeney and two other ladies.

Violet was clearly surprised, and the lovers stared at one another. The door shut behind the ladies, and the only sound in the shop besides the slight echo of the bell was Lady Ffoulkes's slight gasp. Lady Blakeney's dark eyes pierced the young officer. Other than the clerk, the only one in the shop who was unaware of the drama unfolding was the third lady.

Lady Blakeney broke the pregnant silence. "Good afternoon, Captain Tilney."

Frederick found his voice. "Good afternoon, my lady. Lady Ffoulkes, Miss Blakeney, I hope I find you all in good health." His eyes were glued to Violet.

Violet's gaze was locked on him. "We are very well, thank you." Automatically, Violet introduced her aunt Marie St. Just to Frederick.

"We are doing a bit of shopping in preparation for my niece's visit to Paris," Mrs. St. Just informed him.

Frederick had never played cards to excess with his fellows in the barracks, but when he did, he won more than his share, having the talent to hide his emotions. This ability served him well now. Outwardly calm, he showed only light surprise when, in reality, Frederick's emotions were roiling.

Violet is going to Paris? Why did George not warn me? Are the Blakeneys sending her away from me? Frederick tried not to panic.

Mrs. St. Just glanced at what Frederick was holding. "Those gloves are lovely! For a special lady, I suppose?"

"Ah." Frederick looked at the box of gloves. "My sister's birthday is next month." He turned to Violet again, his expression troubled. "It is very cold in Yorkshire."

Violet's concerned eyes never left his face. "A very thoughtful gift, Captain. She is fortunate in such a caring brother."

Frederick laughed. "Ha! Perhaps in one of her brothers, Miss Blakeney, but I shall not claim such a distinction." He swallowed. "I was undecided, actually. I could use a lady's opinion."

Violet smiled slightly. "I would be happy to assist you, sir."

He took a step towards her and was pleased to see that she met him halfway. He handed her the box without another word. He simply drank in her beloved features.

Violet made a show of admiring the proposed present. "My aunt is correct." She ran her fingers over the fur. "They are lovely, yet practical too. From what you have told me of your sister, Eleanor, she will be very thankful—the perfect gift from an affectionate brother."

She glanced at her mother, who frowned at their encounter. She then turned fully to Frederick, placing herself between him and Lady Blakeney, and looked at Frederick with all the love she had for him.

Noting her reaction, Frederick felt that warm glow he had experienced only in her presence return to his heart. "Thank you, Miss Blakeney."

"Violet!" Lady Blakeney's voice was sharper than usual. "Come along. There is nothing for us here."

Violet's eyes slammed shut. "Yes, Mama," she whispered as she handed the gloves back to Frederick.

He took the opportunity to steal a quick caress of her wrist as he retrieved the box and felt a jolt of response from Violet. Frederick tried to say all he felt with his eyes.

Violet, I love you! If you believe in me at all, believe this: even if you are across an ocean, I will be true!

"Violet." Her mother's voice was softer this time.

"I must go, Captain." Her voice trembled.

Frederick glared at the other ladies present for an instant. *Who is my enemy? Is it you, Lady Blakeney?* By the time his gaze returned to Violet, he was tolerably composed.

"I wish you a safe journey, Miss Blakeney." She nodded and turned to the door. On impulse, he added, "God bless you."

Violet stopped for an instant and turned her face to his, her lips parting to speak, but no words came. Only a tear.

Lady Blakeney tenderly stroked her daughter's arm. "Come, my love." As Violet walked through the door, her mother remained. "I wish you good day, Captain Tilney. You have my best wishes… and my prayers."

Frederick could not mistake Lady Blakeney's look of kind understanding. He felt ashamed of his earlier feelings. This lady was no enemy. This situation was not of her making. "It was good to see you again, milady."

Lady Blakeney wore a sad smile. "And you, sir. God bless you as well."

Frederick stood where he was after the ladies departed—for how long, he did not know.

"Sir," said the clerk irritably, as though sure the officer had chased off several good customers, "shall I wrap that for you?"

Brought back to the present, Frederick quickly completed his purchase and took leave of the unhappy clerk. Once on the street, he looked about the milling crowd but did not see the Blakeney party. Just as he was about to give up, he noticed a movement in the window of the shop across the street. Narrowing his eyes, he could see Violet standing next to a dress display, staring at him.

Frederick could do nothing but gaze back as the passersby made their way around him. Unable to do as he wished—to rush into the shop and take Violet in his arms—he stood in impotent frustration until he realized the ridiculousness of his position.

Fool! Had you behaved better, you never would have given Sir Percy reason to mistrust you. You could even now be escorting Violet on her shopping, earning her smiles and touches. You do not deserve her.

Frederick slowly touched the rim of his hat, bowed slightly, and began his walk back to Horse Guards, wondering whether he would ever see Violet Blakeney again.

VIOLET COULD NOT KNOW FOR CERTAIN WHAT WAS GOING THROUGH Frederick's mind, but as long as he stood there, staring at the window of the dress shop from across the street, she would keep her vigil. Mama, thankfully, allowed her this consideration.

The upcoming trip to Paris required new dresses and other items. This shop was a particular favorite of Lady Blakeney, and the four ladies were interested to learn what fashions the owners suggested for spring. Frederick was never far from Violet's thoughts; however, she never expected to see him in a ladies' establishment in the most exclusive part of London!

Violet saw pain and desperation in his eyes. She knew he wished to speak to her, but it was impossible for the present.

I will wait for you, my beloved Frederick!

Her mother spoke. "Violet, we have some dresses we would like you to consider. Will you attend?"

Violet saw Frederick walk away and turned away from the window. "Yes, Mama."

As the modiste exhibited the best fabrics her shop stocked, Violet's thoughts remained with the young cavalryman.

Frederick looked so sad and dejected. I wanted to comfort him, but I could not. Now I am to leave for France and shall not return for months. I must speak with him, but Mama and Papa will not relent!

The girl grew angry. *What has Frederick done that was so bad?*

Leave the house of a disreputable person? Do not Mama and Papa attend soirees at Lady Jersey's? Do they not attend dinners with Prinny's mistresses?

Yes, we owe much to the Regent, but Papa is so unfair! He excuses Prinny, but he will not listen to Frederick's explanations. George believes him and so do I!

I have tried to write, but George will not forward my letters. There must be a way I can send an unmistakable message to Frederick!

She looked about the shop, and her eyes fell on the glass display case.

"Violet!" her mother hissed. "Your attention, if you please."

A plan in her mind, Violet grew calm and content. "Of course, Mama."

SEVERAL DAYS LATER, FREDERICK WALKED INTO A PUB ABOUT A mile from his quarters, George Blakeney's note in his pocket. The message was succinct: *Meet me at two o'clock. I have a message for you.*

Frederick had no idea of the message's contents. Why could George not forward it? Curiosity burning within him, he searched the room with his eyes until they fell upon a familiar form at a table near the back. In moments, he was seated across from his friend.

"All right, George, I am here at the appointed hour. Now, what are you about? I did not know you were in Town from Oxford."

George Blakeney frowned at the tabletop. "This is against my better judgment, but I gave my word."

Frederick's gut clenched. "If you are unsure of your assessment, should you carry it out?"

George looked up from the table. "*You* would certainly want me to."

"I would never ask you do something dishonorable!"

At last, a smile appeared on his friend's face, albeit a small one. He said nothing. He only placed a small envelope between them. Unlike the one John Buford offered in December, this one had no writing on it.

Puzzled, Frederick opened it. Inside was not a letter, but a tiny glass locket, containing a few strands of hair. His fingers trembled.

There was only one person who would send him such a thing!

"You see why I delivered this personally?" George mumbled. "I could not have this fall into the grubby hands of your fellow officers."

"Of course, I understand!" Frederick's voice choked. "I-I cannot thank you enough, or her, either." He closed his fist about the treasure. "This is a true balm to my soul. But wait! I must get word to—"

"Quiet!" George demanded. "Keep your voice down, or you overthrow all my precautions! *I* shall send word to—" He looked pointedly at Frederick's fist.

"Thankee, George. You are a true friend."

"This is all I can do, Frederick. I have agreed to be an intermediary between"—he glanced again—"and you. But no letters! Any messages will come through me." He grinned. "There will be no mischief between the two of you. Consider me your chaperone."

A desperate Frederick instantly agreed. Reassured of Violet's affections, his wit returned. "You will be a troublesome chaperone, I wager."

"I will do my best."

As Frederick began to speak again, George held up a hand. "Think carefully what you wish to say, Frederick. It is best you write me. She leaves within the week."

Reality set in. "How long will she be gone?"

"Not long. Two months—three at most."

Relieved, Frederick asked, "How long are you in Town?"

"I leave in the morning, but send no messages to Blakeney House. Rather, write me in Oxford. Have no fear—I will send a short note to her with your thanks."

"And my love, sir!"

George grinned. "That goes without saying."

Chapter 16

The journey across the English Channel passed quickly, thanks to a calm sea and westerly winds, and Violet arrived at Calais in the morning after a full day on the ship. Armand St. Just was quick to secure transportation to Paris. The little group took a pause in their journey at a small inn along the way, enabling M. Pierre St. Just to meet the travelers when the coach pulled into the Paris station.

"Bonjour! Bonjour! *Bienvenus à Paris!*" a short, thin, well-dressed man cried, waving his hat. M. Pierre St. Just's posture was not good, having developed a permanent stoop from his many hours at his jeweler's bench. However, his eyes twinkled behind his glasses, and with a large smile, he embraced and kissed them all on both cheeks in the French fashion.

Traveling trunks were quickly stored in Pierre's carriage, and once their owners were more comfortably secured in the vehicle, Pierre gave the driver the order to make for his house.

Armand eyed the two guards riding at the rear of the carriage. "Your business is doing well, Pierre?"

Their host followed Armand's gaze. "Ah, you refer to my two enormous friends? They are a necessity these days." He lowered his voice. "The Restoration has brought peace—and many unemployed soldiers too, looking to feed their bellies. There was not so much crime during the Empire, but the price was constant conflict." He shrugged. "I can afford them."

Violet regarded her balding and wrinkled cousin. As Cousin Pierre was ten years younger than Mama, she could only account for his aging to the stress of living during war and revolution. Armand had told her during the voyage that Pierre was not involved with the League's activities; in fact, Pierre was totally ignorant of the Scarlet Pimpernel. He and his immediate family had lived hand-to-mouth during the worst of the Terror, keeping to themselves and hoping they would escape denouncement to the authorities.

Pierre St. Just was a gregarious man, proud of his city and happy to take his guests on a short tour before arriving at his house. The conversation turned to the sights around them. Violet sat enthralled, looking through the carriage windows as Cousin Pierre pointed out the Tuileries Palace, the Arc du Carrousel, and most poignant of all, the Place de la Concorde.

"A very sad place, this, when it was the Place de la Révolution. Very sad." Pierre shook his head.

Violet could only agree. Many times, she had heard stories of the huge square where the revolutionary dictatorship had erected the guillotine. In her mind's eye, she could see the scene: a large raised platform, ringed by soldiers—the stage for the National Razor. The tumbrels filled with the offerings to the Revolution —the rich and poor, the pious and criminal, the young and old —all to meet the same quick and gruesome end. The hordes of *sansculottes* cheering madly as the Infernal Machine dispatched one victim after another to the sound of rolling drums. Thousands had died here during the thirteen months of the Reign of Terror. It was a place of ghosts.

Across the Seine, the Palais Bourbon could be seen. Further up the river, the party passed by the two islands in the river, the Île Saint-Louis and the Île de la Cité, home to the Hôtel-Dieu and Notre Dame de Paris.

"Ah," sighed Pierre as he crossed himself, "what those criminal

Hébertistes did to Notre Dame! All the treasures—stolen! *Culte de la Raison,* indeed! Chaumette[4], I spit on your grave!"

The carriage moved deeper into the lanes of La Rive Droite, and it was not long before it stopped before a shop in a fashionable district of the city. It was a small storefront on a pleasant lane, well kept, with a sign emblazoned with "M. ST. JUST" affixed to the plaster. A footman opened the carriage door, and Pierre helped them all down, welcoming his guests to his house.

The childless St. Justs lived in apartments above the store, and it was there Violet was introduced to her cousin's wife, who greeted them most cordially. Camille St. Just was as plump as her husband was thin, and Violet could hardly keep from laughing, reminded as she was of the old nursery rhyme. Her dress was plain, yet of good materials and workmanship. Adorning her neck and fingers was exquisite jewelry of gold and semi-precious stones.

"All for sale, alas!" she said laughingly. "My husband uses me as a living display case."

Once the luggage was placed in their rooms on the third floor and the travelers refreshed themselves, the party removed to the dining room where Camille proved she had talents comparable to her husband, but hers were in the kitchen. Violet had eaten *coq au vin* many a time, as her mother hired only French cooks. Perhaps it was the wine or the company or Paris itself, but never had she enjoyed the fragrant chicken stew more than that night.

The time after dinner passed in pleasant talk, initially dominated by Armand and Pierre catching up on twenty years of family history and Violet listening intently. Only once or twice did her uncle refer to incidents that, while seemingly innocent, obliquely concerned the activities of the League. Each time, Armand caught himself and,

---

4 Pierre Gaspard "Anaxagoras" Chaumette was one of the ultra-radical firebrands of the French Revolution. With fellow extremist atheist, Jacques Hébert, he founded the *Culte de la Raison* (Cult of Reason) in an attempt to replace Christianity. This was in direct opposition to Maximilien Robespierre's *Culte de l'Être supreme* (Cult of the Supreme Being). Robespierre had his two rivals and their followers executed on April 13, 1794. Robespierre himself would suffer the guillotine three months later.

JACK CALDWELL

with an apologetic glance to his niece, changed the subject. Violet hid her frown. She was aware of his lapses, thanks to her superior knowledge of the particulars, and she had been trained from an early age never to talk of the Pimpernel. She could only wonder at her uncle's carelessness.

Thankfully, their hosts seemed to be ignorant of Armand's insinuations. It fell to Aunt St. Just to move the discussion to the party's plans for the visit, and Pierre declared that he would act as a guide as often as his business would allow.

Violet retired to her rooms, her enthusiasm blemished by a bit of melancholy. She had resolved to enjoy herself and not think of Frederick during her trip, but that was a hopeless resolution. Once she had spied the uniformed guards about Tuileries Palace, she could not help being reminded of her lover's profession. *How wonderful it would have been to have Frederick by my side today*, she thought. Paris was a city for lovers, it was said, but hers was still in London.

I must not fret, she reminded herself as she laid her head on the pillow. *I will be back at Richmond before June, and surely by then, Frederick will be ready to appeal to Papa again. George writes that Frederick has been diligently applying himself. Surely, Papa will be reasonable. I will be happy in Paris and pray that this summer in London will be even happier.*

CAPITAINE BOURGEOIS LOOKED UP FROM THE PAPER IN HIS HAND, an oath escaping his lips. Finally, all his months of study had shown results! Immediately, he made his way across the office to M. Lafarge's desk and shoved the paper under the old man's nose.

"Read this, monsieur," he ordered with barely disguised anticipation.

M. Lafarge made no attempt to hide his dissatisfaction with Bourgeois's demand, but he took the offered sheet and scanned what was written there. As Bourgeois expected, M. Lafarge froze halfway down the page.

"You see?" Bourgeois said excitedly. "St. Just—one of the names

172

we were looking for. Do you know the man?"

"Armand St. Just…" M. Lafarge mumbled. "That name—could it be?" He quickly opened the drawer that contained his list, withdrew the document, and studied it. "*Oui*! It is the brother! But the wife—" His attention returned to Bourgeois's paper. "Not Jeanne Lange? I had thought…" The man appeared to be lost in thought.

"Thought what, monsieur?"

M. Lafarge seemed to recover. "Nothing, it is nothing. So, Armand St. Just has returned! Excellent work, Bourgeois! Finally, we are making progress. Let us see…he is here with his wife and niece. Her name is…*Mon Dieu!*"

Bourgeois watched as the man literally shook. "Monsieur! Are you well?"

"*Blakeney*," M. Lafarge breathed. He trained blazing eyes on his compatriot. "Idiot! Why did you not inform me about this immediately?"

Bourgeois was confused. "Blakeney? Where? I did not notice. May I see?" M. Lafarge handed him the page and pointed out the name. "*Je vous prie de m'excuser,* monsieur. I did not take the time to read this part. Once I saw the name St. Just, I hurried to call it to your attention."

M. Lafarge snatched the paper from Bourgeois's hands and read it again. "Blakeney, Violet Yvonne, niece. Nothing else. I wonder…" He read more. "*Merde!* This says they landed at Calais over a week ago! Where are they going?"

"It says their destination is Paris."

"I can read that, you imbecile!" M. Lafarge seemed to catch himself and looked around. Sure enough, others in the office had heard his outburst and were looking at the two. In a quieter tone, M. Lafarge continued, "*Mes excuses, Capitaine.* You have done very good work. It is not your fault we have morons working the ports."

Bourgeois accepted the apology with a nod.

"Paris," M. Lafarge mused. "They could be at M. Pierre St. Just's house. But why have I not received any reports?" He turned to Bourgeois again. "Are the St. Justs under surveillance?"

"Not continuously, monsieur. We have not the funds to pay for it. I have someone check on them about once a week."

M. Lafarge cursed again. "This must change." He sighed. "Do not concern yourself with surveillance any longer, *Capitaine*. I shall see to it. I can acquire the funds and the men. Instead, find out more about this Mlle. Blakeney. I must know who she is."

London

IT WAS A LOVELY WINTER'S AFTERNOON, CLEAR AND CRISP. FREDerick tried to concentrate as he worked on yet another report. But every time his eye strayed from the task before him to the window, his thoughts drifted to Violet and her activities in France at that very moment. His hand rose to his chest to feel the small locket under his shirt.

Secure in his conviction that he had won Violet's affections and satisfied his ladylove would return to England, Frederick now had a firm goal. He would continue his reformation and approach Sir Percy again before Violet's return. Frederick did not expect a total victory, but if he were allowed simply to call on the Blakeneys, he would be satisfied. He would be patient, for he knew Violet was a prize worth the effort.

Frederick sighed as he set down his pen. He needed to complete his report, but to do so he had to have those of his lieutenants, and he had not yet received them. He rose from his desk and went into the outer offices. There he found Lt. Remington busily scribbling on paper and, to his astonishment, Lt. Brookings scrutinizing the *Times*.

"Mr. Brookings!" Frederick snapped in his best command voice. "May I inquire as to the meaning of this?"

Lt. Brookings jumped so smartly out of his chair that it was nearly overturned. "Captain Tilney! Allow me to explain."

"I certainly hope you can, sir." Frederick's voice dripped with sarcasm. "If you find your duties so little taxing that you can enjoy the newspaper at your desk, I can find something for you to do!"

"Sir, I am reading reports from Paris in an attempt to keep abreast of their state of affairs. I believe it is of the greatest importance that we know what is happening in France."

Frederick frowned. "By reading the newspaper?"

"Yes, sir. The stories are very informative—much more than the reports we receive from Whitehall."

"Well, what do you expect?" snorted Lt. Remington. "We are at peace with the Frogs. All *that* rubbish"—he indicated the papers —"is simply gossip."

"Mr. Remington," Frederick said icily, "I believe *I* was questioning Mr. Brookings." He turned to the man. "Continue, Lieutenant."

"Sir, as we have been at war with France for a hundred years, off and on, I believe this is a worthy endeavor."

Frederick nodded. "Your point is taken. Would you care to share your insights?"

"Sir, it is my opinion that the reign of King Louis is unpopular. He has failed to keep his promises and thereby squandered the people's good will. His minister of finance, Baron Louis, has retained the detested taxes on tobacco, wine, and salt rather than abolishing them. There is resentment over the émigrés returning to France and their demands for restoration of land and property. There has been rioting in Bordeaux."

Frederick could not help but be interested. "I have heard of these disturbances. What has that to do with us? Remember, we have our own bread riots, yet the Crown is not endangered. Is Louis in jeopardy of falling victim to a new revolution?"

"I would remind you that instability in France inevitably concerns our foreign affairs, sir."

"True, but Bonaparte is exiled to Elba. To whom can the malcontents turn?"

Lt. Brookings smiled. "I did not say the Bourbon would fall, sir. I only described the present conditions in France."

Frederick was unsettled, knowing Violet was in Paris. A vision of his sweetheart caught up in a riot sent shivers down his spine.

Lt. Brookings continued. "Also, troubles in France would hurt our trade."

"You speak like a shopkeeper, Brookings!" Lt. Remington mocked him.

"Laugh all you like, Remington, but had Bonaparte not been so set on destroying British trade, he might well be still sitting in Paris as Emperor of the French instead of rotting by the seaside in Elba."

"That is an interesting conjecture, Mr. Brookings," Frederick observed. "I would like to hear your reasoning."

"Oh, the lecture will begin now," groaned Lt. Remington. Frederick ignored him.

"Sir, until Austerlitz, Bonaparte was unbeatable. Our only victories over the French were at sea. In 1805, he made peace with all the members of the Coalition except England. He could have ignored us, for we lacked the men and munitions to attack him by ourselves, but he did not. He hated us and set to starve us out. Bonaparte set up his trade blockade, the so-called Continental System, and demanded the countries that had signed peace treaties with him observe it.

"Portugal refused, and Bonaparte sent his army to punish them in 1808. He had to go through his ally Spain to get at them, and the Spaniards were outraged by what they considered an invasion. They forced the abdication of the Corsican's puppet, King Charles, in favor of the heir, Ferdinand. Bonaparte responded by orchestrating the overthrow of Ferdinand and installing Joseph Bonaparte as king.

"This led to a full uprising in Spain, and we took advantage of it, landing on the Peninsula and bringing the Spanish Army over to our side. Bonaparte was forced to spend precious blood and gold to hold Spain. Thousands of Frenchmen died, and many thousands more were pinned down by us and our Spanish and Portuguese allies. They were men Bonaparte could have used in Russia in 1812 or to stop the Coalition in 1814. But by then, France had been bled dry and victory was ours.

"So trade is important and not just to our shopkeepers." Brookings smiled at Remington. "Had Bonaparte ignored Portugal's refusal to join the Continental System, or better yet, not tried to starve

England, he might still have France."

Frederick nodded, impressed with his subordinate's reasoning. "Fascinating, Mr. Brookings. You very well might be right." Frederick changed the subject. "However, there are reports to be done, and I have yet to receive yours—or yours, Mr. Remington."

Lt. Brookings had the good grace to be embarrassed. "I beg your pardon, sir. My report is done, but I have neglected to give it to you." He handed Frederick the required papers. "It will not happen again."

"I do not expect it will, Lieutenant," he said with a small smile to lessen the reprimand. "And yours, Mr. Remington?"

The other officer picked up his pen. "I am just finishing it now, sir."

"Excellent. Carry on." Frederick turned to leave but over his shoulder said, "Oh, and Mr. Brookings, I suggest you save your investigation of French affairs for your own time. I believe the stables could stand a surprise inspection. Do you not think so?"

"At once, sir."

"Good man. Mr. Remington, that report within thirty minutes, if you please."

Frederick returned to his office with Brookings's report and began to work on his, vowing to read his own newspaper with more care from now on.

Paris

BOURGEOIS SAT BEFORE A DESK IN M. LAFARGE'S APARTMENTS. THE old man explained it was best to keep their activities secret from the rest of the ministry until they gathered sufficient evidence to convince the government of the righteousness of their accusations. Bourgeois saw no reason to argue otherwise. Besides, it gave him the opportunity to sample more of the old man's excellent wine collection, which he did while M. Lafarge read his report.

The *capitaine* was admiring the wine's color in the candlelight when his contemplations were interrupted by a thump. Looking at his host, he saw M. Lafarge had set the report down on the desk and was straining to see through the window into the darkness of the Parisian night. He could hear Lafarge mumbling to himself but could only make out the word "daughter."

Abruptly, M. Lafarge turned back into the room. "You have done very well, *Capitaine*. I could not expect more or better work. So, Sir Percy Blakeney's daughter is in Paris! Let us consider our next move."

"I would imagine we would keep her under close observation."

"*Non*, that is not enough! We do not need the daughter of *Le Mouron Rouge*—we need *Le Mouron Rouge* himself! I must think of a way..."

"Why is she here?" Bourgeois mused. "Is she part of Blakeney's activities?"

M. Lafarge looked up. "Hmm? Oh, *oui*, she could be, or she could be innocent and only being used to obscure her uncle's activities." M. Lafarge stopped and laughed. "*Non*, Armand St. Just is a fool. He is not capable of spying on a cow, much less a country." He glanced at Bourgeois. "Ah, but Blakeney! He is just clever enough to use his daughter to deliver documents or carry reports back to England."

"Ingenious. But why now? Why is Blakeney active in France now? What has changed?"

M. Lafarge frowned. "Do you doubt me?"

"*Non,* monsieur." Still, Bourgeois's question was written plain on his face.

"Bah! It could be for any number of reasons. For example, England has replaced Castlereagh as the head of the English delegation at the Congress of Vienna with Wellington because Castlereagh was considered too friendly with the French. Hah, as though any Englishman would look out for France's interests! I am certain Blakeney is acting in concert with Wellington." He looked at Bourgeois. "The Iron Duke has no love for us."

Bourgeois could not stop his hand from rubbing his thigh. "*Oui*, I know that."

M. Lafarge bit his thumbnail. "I *should* have the girl arrested, but the government would never permit it! *Merde!* They are women —no courage at all. They still believe England can be our friend. Bah!" M. Lafarge seemed lost in thought for a moment. "For all his faults, the Emperor was not so blind. If *he* were still in the Tuileries—"

"Take care, monsieur. Even to speak of Bonaparte can be considered treason."

M. Lafarge eyed Bourgeois narrowly but said nothing. Finally, he rose from his chair, ending the meeting.

"Merci, *Capitaine*, for your excellent work. We will continue to watch Mlle. Blakeney closely. Without doubt, an opportunity will present itself."

March 1: Golfe-Juan, France

The battered brig, *L'Incostant*, painted in false English colors, pulled alongside the dock of the little town on the rocky coast of the Cap d'Antibes, the Tricolor waving proudly from its mainmast. A xebec[5] named *L'Étoile* prepared to heave-to, while the schooner *Saint-Esprit* maneuvered close by. Immediately, sailors set themselves to transport the passengers from the little fleet to dry land, especially one man. A few other small ships kept lookout during the landing.

This special passenger, the former Emperor of Elba, had entertained admirers from England, impressing upon them his stated intention of remaining in his island kingdom. He showed them, Whig politicians and English admirals alike, that he was a lion without claws. On the evening before his departure, he had attended a Carnival ball as though nothing out of the ordinary was about to occur.

When he and his people boarded their ships, the Allied blockade squadron was not on station. The little Elban fleet had sailed for three days, the lookouts constantly scanning the horizon for the English Navy. They did not arrive, proving that efforts to lull the jailers of Elba to sleep had been successful.

Now, thanks to lies on his part, criminal negligence on the part of others, and ships filled with chests of gold and eleven hundred

5 A xebec, a small, three-masted ship having an overhanging bow and stern with both square and lateen sails once common in the Mediterranean.

soldiers, the one-time Emperor of the French walked the sands of the Côte d'Azur, intending to retake his rightful place in the Palace of Tuileries.

Napoleon Bonaparte had returned, and France would be his again.

Chapter 17

A fter several weeks of enjoying Paris, Pierre St. Just declared that Violet must see some of the treasures in the French countryside. So in late February, M. St. Just closed his shop and everyone boarded a carriage. After two days of pleasant travel, they arrived in the heart of the Loire Valley and the home of one of his customers, the Dupin family.

The Château de Chenonceau was a castle of tan stone with black tiles topping the roofs and spires of the keep. In that, it was not particularly noteworthy, save it had escaped the sacking suffered by so many other châteaux in the area. It boasted an enormous formal garden, laid out in four triangles—again, not unique. What set Chenonceau apart from its sisters was the arched bridge and three-story grand gallery spanning the width of the River Cher.

Violet could not believe her eyes. She had seen many castles and fine country estates next to a river, but never had she seen one *in* a river, or rather, over one. The great house was something out of a fairy tale.

The party stayed at a small county estate outside of the nearby village of Chenonceaux belonging to a friend of Pierre. They used it as a base for further ventures into the heart of the Loire. It was too early in the year for anyone besides farmers to be in the region, so Violet attended no parties or dinners. She spent hours seeing the sights, riding, writing letters, and reading. There was no news of the outside world, so the little party had no idea that everything had turned upside down.

Paris

It would be days before news of the momentous event from the south would reach the capital, but once it did, the effect was electric. All over the city, speculation centered on whether the emperor would succeed in retaking the throne or whether Louis's armies would finally put an end to the Corsican. The majority of the people were undecided. The king's rule was unpopular, but the emperor's return could ignite new hostilities with the rest of Europe. Too many of France's sons slept in graves stretching from Moscow to Lisbon for his welcome to be sure.

All depended on the army, and it was a blow when it was learned that the Fifth and Seventh Regiments, instead of arresting Napoleon, had joined forces with him en mass. It was the talk of a rapidly panicking city, except in the nearly empty Ministry of the Interior. There, another subject occupied the attention of two of its employees.

"What do you mean, they are gone?"

Bourgeois winced at M. Lafarge's question. "I am sorry, monsieur—"

M. Lafarge was livid. "How could this have happened?"

"The men you hired were not there when Mlle. Blakeney and the St. Justs left." Bourgeois managed to say this without insubordination.

"Merde!"

"But I know where they are, monsieur! A neighbor informed me they went on holiday to Chenonceaux. They are expected back in a week or so."

M. Lafarge fell back into his chair, and Bourgeois was thankful there was no one else in the office to witness this scene. "Those bastards I hired stole my money!" He looked up at Bourgeois. "You are certain this intelligence is accurate?"

Bourgeois nodded.

M. Lafarge cursed again. "They must be found—they must! You must track them down, Bourgeois!"

"But monsieur, my duties—"

"Never mind that!" M. Lafarge indicated the vacant office. "Do you see anyone else here? The emperor's return has thrown Paris into chaos. Everyone is waiting to see whether there will be civil war."

"There will be no civil war," Bourgeois said with conviction. "The soldiers will not fight the emperor. The king and his ministers have treated the veterans badly."

"What of Ney? He boasted he will bring Napoleon back in an iron cage."

Bourgeois sneered. "*Le Brave des Braves* can say whatever he wants. His men will flock to the emperor's banner just like the others, and Marshal Ney will find himself in his own cage if he tries to stop them. The soldiers will install Napoleon back in Tuileries."

"Then, it is of the essence that we find Mlle. Blakeney! This is our chance." M. Lafarge rose to his feet. "Leave for the Loire immediately. I will answer for you if anyone asks. Take no action for now; just send word of your progress. Once you find the St. Justs, follow them."

"And you, monsieur?"

"I have much work to do. I must find men who are more dependable, and there are other preparations to be made. Go now!"

Richmond

"My God!" Marguerite placed a hand over her lips, her involuntary plea to the Almighty echoing through the dining room.

Her husband still held the morning newspaper in his hands. "By gad, m'dear, you are right to call out to our Maker," Sir Percy growled. "This is bad news and no mistake. Boney back in France and our girl there!" He crumpled up the paper and tossed it with great violence across the room. "God damn them! The Navy was supposed to keep Bonaparte on Elba! Where were our blasted ships?"

Percy's obscenity frightened Marguerite as much as the terrifying news from France. Percy *never* cursed except in extreme matters. And this *was* extreme. Napoleon Bonaparte, the destroyer of mankind, was back in France! What would King Louis do? Would he flee or fight? Would there be war? And would their darling daughter be caught up in the middle of it?

Sir Percy stood. "Forgive me, m'dear, for my outburst and for leaving you to breakfast alone, but I must to St. James's and see the Regent as soon as may be."

Marguerite rose and rushed to him as he was leaving. "Do not let me detain you a moment, my love! I know you will do everything you can to recover Violet. Only take care on your ride to London. I…I could not bear it if you were injured."

Sir Percy pulled his weeping wife to his breast. "Never fear, Margot. I must inform Prinny that Violet is with Armand and his wife in Paris. He will see to it that our diplomats extend their protection to them. The government will help us. We will see our girl back to England soon. I swear it."

London

A NEW SENSE OF URGENCY SPREAD ALL OVER HORSE GUARDS UPON learning the news from the Continent. Bonaparte's return was a clear signal that war could resume, and it could not have come at a worse time.

"If it is war, lads," Frederick told his lieutenants, "we are in a pickle. Too many of our experienced troops are across the Atlantic because of the American war, and it will take months to get them all back here. We will have to fight with what we have, and the army will be sure to call us into service."

Lt. Remington stood bug-eyed, his throat working, apparently trying to take in all he had heard. For his part, Lt. Brookings paled but said in a level voice, "What are your orders, sir?"

"Until we hear otherwise from Whitehall, we should continue our duties. However, I want this company to be ready to deploy to the Continent if the word comes. Go to your commands and make sure every trooper's kit is properly prepared. Redouble the training for the recruits. Use your veterans. They should know what they are about, and their experience will be invaluable. Keep to the spit-and-polish. The men need the discipline." Frederick relaxed a bit. "Do not lose your heads, gentlemen. It is not certain Bonaparte will retake the crown. The French might just slap him in irons, and all this will be for naught."

"I do not think so, sir," said Lt. Brookings softly.

Frederick grinned. "Your studies of French politics again, Mr. Brookings? As I have said, you just might be right. All the more reason to get ready, what?" The two subordinates nodded. "Carry on." The lieutenants left Frederick's office.

Frederick sat back and allowed his mind to return to his concern for Violet. What he had feared for weeks had come to pass, and his beloved was caught up in the middle of it. Her locket burned a hole in his chest.

Deuce take it! Violet is in danger, and I can do nothing! What is the use of being a soldier if I cannot protect my loved ones?

He tried to calm down. *Sir Percy must be aware of this. He is close to the crown. Surely, he can urge the government to do something. Of course—he can have Prinny or the prime minister write to our ambassador in Paris. Violet would be safe in our embassy, surely.*

I must concentrate on my duties. If only I could stop worrying!

However, try as he might, thoughts of Violet and her safety stayed foremost in his mind. With a sigh, he surrendered to his uncertainties. He simply *had* to know what was being done to recover his beloved.

He pulled out a sheet and wrote an express to George Blakeney.

Chenonceaux

PIERRE ST. JUST BURST INTO THE PARLOR OF THE GUESTHOUSE, shouting, "Napoleon! Napoleon has returned! He is marching even now from the south towards Paris!"

The seriousness of the situation was obvious, and the party prepared to depart Chenonceaux immediately. The women supervised the packing while the men discussed the next course of action. When

Violet and the other ladies joined the gentlemen in the study, they learned a plan had been set in place. They all would return to Paris as quickly as could be, and then the visitors would push on to the coast in hope of finding transport across the channel.

The plan did not last a single day. Marie St. Just failed to navigate the ramshackle stairs at the inn where the travelers ended their journey that evening. The result of her tumble was an injury to her ankle, and the local apothecary was quickly summoned. Better suited to mixing drafts than mending limbs, he said he *thought* the joint was sound and recommended tincture of laudanum for the pain. An upset Uncle Armand demanded that his wife be seen by a surgeon or, better yet, a physician. Therefore, the party decided to stop in Paris so that Marie would receive proper medical care.

No one in the party noticed the tall man in a traveling cloak, sitting by himself in the public room of the inn, or how he started when Aunt St. Just cried out in English as she fell. As they took their supper above stairs in the rooms, they could not know that the man had questioned the owner about the travelers. And when Violet and the St. Justs left in the morning, they never noticed they were being followed.

Paris

Bourgeois reported to M. Lafarge at the old man's house the evening he returned.

"I was fortunate," he admitted as he took a swig of ale. "By the time I arrived in Chenonceaux, the St. Justs had left. I gambled that they had heard the news of the emperor and were headed for Paris, so I made my way back, checking at all the inns. Last night as I was eating my supper at a place just north of Orléans, I heard a woman cry out in English after she fell on the stairs. There were two couples and a young lady in very fine traveling clothes. I questioned the owner, showing him my ministry identification, and he confirmed that two rooms had been taken by M. St. Just. I followed them back to the city today and hurried to tell you."

"But where are they now?"

"They have returned to M. St. Just's house. I assume it is being watched?"

M. Lafarge nodded. "*Oui*. I have hired new men. If anyone leaves, they will inform me immediately. So, Mme. St. Just is injured? Good—that should keep them in Paris for a few days. It will give me time to prepare everything."

"Any news of the emperor?"

"No, except that he has yet to be stopped. Oh, and the Congress of Vienna has declared him an outlaw and pledged to unite against him. If Napoleon returns, we will be at war again."

Bourgeois raised an eyebrow. "You seem untroubled, monsieur."

"Why should I be troubled? This turmoil plays into our hands, particularly if the Bourbon flees and the Corsican recovers the throne."

"How is that?"

"Chaos, Bourgeois! The spies will not be able to seek sanctuary with the diplomats. You have done good work. You have proven to be a man of exceptional talents. I did not know you spoke English."

"I do not speak English, monsieur," Bourgeois admitted. At Lafarge's questioning look, he added, "I heard enough of it in Spain to recognize it."

M. Lafarge shrugged. "Here is bread and cheese. Fill your belly and get yourself home to bed. You have deserved your rest, *mon ami*."

Richmond

Marguerite and Sir Percy were taking tea in the parlor when George strode into the room.

"Odd's fish, George!" cried his father. "Why are you not at Oxford?"

"You could not expect me to stay away while Violet is in danger, sir!" George bent to kiss his mother's cheek quickly. "What is to be done, Father?"

Sir Percy's face was grim. "Nothing, so you might as well go back."

"Nothing? But, Papa, I must—"

Sir Percy raised his hand. "The Crown has informed our ambassador in Paris of Violet's presence and has instructed him to safeguard her. Unfortunately, your uncle has taken her to the country. I received a letter from your uncle several days ago. He, your aunt, and your sister are in the Loire Valley looking at fine houses. He makes no mention of the crisis, so I assume things are quiet there. I have shared this with the government, and an express pouch has been sent to Paris. The embassy is looking for them, and our people will soon find Violet if they have not already."

George frowned. "But she has not been found yet."

"We do not know that," Percy replied as he handed his cup to Marguerite for a refill. "Lud, since you are here, you might as well take tea."

"Take tea! But Papa—"

This time Marguerite interrupted him. "There is nothing for it, George. Do remember your manners and sit down. We are happy to see you, my dear."

George stared at both his parents before plopping onto the couch with a grunt. "So, we are expected to just sit and wait?"

"Try the cake," Sir Percy said as Marguerite handed back his cup. "Cook did a particularly fine job today."

"I must say you are placing a lot of trust in the embassy staff. I do not understand how you can be so calm about the matter!"

Sir Percy glared at his son. "It is because I have no choice!" As George made to interrupt, Sir Percy continued. "I have been told in no uncertain words to stay away. The Crown has no use for —how did the Duke of York put it? — 'A broken-down old man gallivanting about the French countryside without a care in the world while the country goes to hell.' The demmed Duke can turn a phrase, what? By gad, after everything I have done."

He turned towards the window, and Marguerite could tell Percy was trying to rein in his temper. "The matter has been taken out of my hands. The government will make every effort to find, protect, and recover your sister and your aunt and uncle."

An astonished George glanced at his mother before speaking to Sir Percy again. "But what of the League?"

Sir Percy turned. "The League? What of the League?"

"Papa, why not reassemble the League and go get her?"

Sir Percy looked around, but there were no servants about. "George, are you mad? The League is no more! The members who are still alive are in worse shape than I." He turned to Marguerite. "Odd's fish, but can you just see Dewhurst trying to ride about the Loire Valley? He can barely climb into his coach!"

George was insistent. "Then we will go in your stead!"

"We? Who are *we*?"

"The sons of the League! Young Dewhurst, Percy Ffoulkes, and I."

Sir Percy laughed. "Zounds, but that is a joke! You are all young and untrained! Percy Ffoulkes is still at boarding school! Besides, there are not enough of you." He patted George on the shoulder. "I am proud of your offer, Son, but you must see it is impossible."

George stubbornly continued. "Papa, I am full earnest. If we are too few and too young, we can get help. My friend, Captain Tilney, for instance—"

"Tilney?" Sir Percy said.

"We have been corresponding. He knows Violet is in France, and he is very concerned. He is clever and brave and knows the ways of war."

"No, Captain Tilney cannot help us even if the League is re-formed. His duty is to King and Parliament. I know you think highly of the man, and I hope he has taken the opportunity to improve himself, but our family is none of his concern.

"It would not make any difference in any case," Sir Percy continued, "You see, the League was more than Ffoulkes, Dewhurst, and the others. We had scores of informers and helpers all over France —noblemen and farm hands and smugglers. They were our eyes and ears. Without them, we would have been arrested and guillotined the first time we stepped foot in France. That network is long gone. It is as dead as the League."

Sir Percy's features took on a bleak look as he manipulated his right hand. It was but an instant, but Marguerite saw it and shared in her husband's melancholy, for she knew his rheumatism had returned. Sir Percy then composed himself and smiled sadly at his son.

"We must be realistic. We can do nothing but put our trust in the government. Do not worry. Our diplomats will find and protect Violet."

An agonized Marguerite hoped their faith was not ill placed. She certainly agreed with her husband about George. The last thing she wanted was for her son to imitate the Pimpernel and put himself in harm's way. No, the only proper thing to do was to be patient, place her trust in the abilities of the king's diplomats, and pray.

Paris

UPON THE PARTY'S RETURN TO PIERRE'S HOUSE, A PHYSICIAN WAS summoned to examine Marie's ankle. The man declared the joint was sound and diagnosed the injury to be a bad sprain. He advised Armand that his wife should walk as little as possible and be restricted to bed for at least a week.

Therefore, the plans for Violet and her relations changed, and the party decided to delay their flight to Calais. Armand sent a letter to Richmond, assuring Violet's parents of their health, relative safety, and their expected return. In the meantime, Violet and Camille St. Just took turns waiting upon Marie.

From the window of the house that faced the street, Violet was witness to the increasing tension in the city. Every day brought dozens of rumors, most of them contradictory: Napoleon was dead, the king's ministers had worked out a bargain with the usurper, the emperor had fled to America, the Prussians had invaded, and the king had been imprisoned.

So when it was shouted in the streets that the king had fled to the United Netherlands, it was initially dismissed as just another false report. Within hours, however, the truth became apparent: The Tricolor began replacing the White Flag of the Bourbons.

Armand declared he would depart Paris with his wife and niece as soon as possible, dismissing Pierre's warnings that the country roads would surely be dangerous. Violet did not wait to listen to the arguments but rushed to see to the packing. In an hour, all was ready to be loaded into the carriage. Pierre had relented to Armand's scheme but insisted his guards accompany them.

As Violet was taking leave of her cousins, there was a pounding on the stairs. The next instant the door flew open and a frightened manservant half-stumbled into the room followed by several soldiers.

"*Mille pardons, monsieur*, but I could not stop them!" the servant cried, his hand clutching Pierre's lapels. For his part, the jeweler gawked in terrified silence.

"What is the meaning of this?" cried Armand, taking a step to shield his wife and niece.

One of the soldiers, an officer by his uniform, pulled out a paper. "Are you M. Armand St. Just?" he demanded in a loud voice.

"I am, and who are you?"

"I am *Capitaine* Honoré Bourgeois of the Ministry of the Interior. In the name of the emperor, I place you and your party under arrest."

Chapter 18

Violet felt shock as the next half-hour flew by in a daze. Later, she would have vague memories of men shouting, her aunt being carried down the stairs by two soldiers, and herself jammed into a too-small carriage between her furious uncle and terrified aunt.

By the time Violet fought her way out of her fog of confusion, the carriage was rolling through the dark, rough, narrow streets of Paris. After trying to comfort her sobbing aunt clutching her sleeve, Violet's eyes locked on the two rough-looking guards seated across from them. Both were filthy, their uniforms ill fitting. One was bored, not showing the least interest in his charges; the other did not disguise his hunger to taste Violet's charms. A sting of fear caused her to move even closer into her aunt's embrace.

The journey ended before a tall building fronting a narrow street. The prisoners were herded into the lobby and brought before two more soldiers seated behind a table. They indicated the group should continue to the stairs. Once again, Marie St. Just was carried while the others followed. Four flights up, the party walked through the only door off the landing into a large, dimly lit room. The soldiers placed Marie on the single sofa, and the tall officer spoke—*Capitaine* Bourgeois, she recalled.

"These will be your quarters. Make yourselves comfortable. Your belongings will be delivered shortly." He looked at each of the party carefully, his eyes resting on Violet the longest. She began to fear her virtue was in danger from any and all of her captors.

"We are British citizens," Armand cried. "I again demand to see the British ambassador! You have no right to hold us."

"There is no British ambassador," *Capitaine* Bourgeois said contemptuously. "All those cowards have fled the capital. Besides, you have no rights as you are under arrest for suspicion of espionage."

Armand was incredulous. "Espionage? I am no spy!"

"That remains to be seen, monsieur."

"I tell you I am no spy! There has been a great mistake made here!"

Capitaine Bourgeois ignored him. "Bread, cheese, and wine will be brought up soon. The bedrooms are over there." He pointed to the doors across the room. "The kitchen is over there. Do not trouble yourselves looking for knives or forks. They have been removed for your protection. You will have to make do with spoons.

"There will be a guard posted at all times on the landing, so do not attempt anything foolish. I suggest you do not stand too close to the windows," he added with a small ironic smile. "You are four stories up, and it is a rather long fall."

He grew serious again. "You will be fed twice a day, and a maidservant will empty the chamber pots in the morning. Understand these privileges will be taken away if there are any violations of the following rules.

"You will not talk to any servant or guard who comes into the room. We will knock on the door before anyone enters, and you will take a seat in the nearest chair when you hear that knock. You will cooperate with all orders immediately. You will not cause any damage or make any noise. You will not attempt to gain the attention of anyone outside of this building—no waving, no calling out, no messages. Do not try to escape. Violations will be severely punished. Do you understand these rules?"

Armand took a step forward. "What of the safety of my wife and niece?"

Capitaine Bourgeois looked affronted. "No one will be mistreated as long as the rules are followed. My men do not harm women."

"And we are supposed to take your word?"

"*Oui!* My word as a French officer—no harm will come to these ladies."

Violet found her voice. "And how will you assure that, *Capitaine?*"

Captain Bourgeois turned to her, his surprise that she had spoken clear on his face. Violet wondered whether she had angered him when his expression softened a bit.

"Mlle. Blakeney, I swear on the grave of my father that if any man so much as touches you or Mme. St. Just, I will kill him. Satisfied?"

Violet was stunned at the softly spoken, violent declaration and was only able to answer him with a single nod of her head. The *capitaine* turned again to Armand.

"Understand, monsieur, I guarantee the *safety* of your ladies, not their *comfort.* Do nothing foolish. Cooperation would be wise. I will see you again in the morning." With that, *Capitaine* Bourgeois and his men left the room, the sound of the turning lock echoing in their wake.

"Armand! *Je suis*—" cried Marie, but her husband raised his hand, cutting her off.

"Speak English, my dear," he said in a low and urgent voice. "There is a chance these fellows do not understand it."

"What are we going to do, Armand? I am so frightened!"

He took the terrified woman into his arms and looked about the room. "I think we are going to be guests here for a time, so it might be best if you and Violet see to the accommodations. I believe there are two bedrooms. Choose between them—find one with a bed that will not hurt my poor back, if that is possible." He smiled at his silliness.

Marie hugged him tighter.

His grin disappeared. "I would sooner have you and Violet out of the main room when the guards return with the luggage and food. I do not trust them, no matter what *Capitaine* Bourgeois says."

Violet shuddered.

Her aunt asked the question that was foremost in all their minds. "How are we to return home?"

"We have committed no crime, my dear, so they cannot hold us. There are laws here," assured her barrister husband. "We must be patient until matters are settled."

Violet thought her uncle's words were condescending. There was nothing normal about their circumstances. Surely, these men were acting above the law, whether British or French, but she saw the wisdom of placating her aunt.

"How are we to get word back home?" she asked.

"That is going to prove difficult to accomplish." Her uncle wrinkled his brow. "The soldiers did not arrest Pierre. We must trust he will do what we cannot. We must pray that Cousin Pierre writes to Richmond."

The next morning, two soldiers came after breakfast to collect Armand. Never before had Violet been as frightened as when her uncle was marched out of the room to an uncertain fate. Her sobbing aunt was beside herself, and it fell to Violet to offer what consolation she could.

For an hour, they sat in abject misery, Violet restraining her tears for her Marie's sake. Great was their relief when Armand was returned to them, apparently unharmed.

"Odd's life, but I was fearful when those brutes came for me," he admitted once he received his ladies' kisses of welcome and seated himself on the sofa. "But they only led me to a room on the third floor, directly below us. It was dark—they had drawn the curtains —and there was but a single candle on the desk where I was seated. *Capitaine* Bourgeois questioned me while another man stood in the shadows, observing the entire interview."

Marie could say nothing. She simply clung to her husband's arm, sniffing and wiping away an occasional tear.

Violet asked, "What were they asking about?"

Armand shook his head. "Contacts—plans. They still believe I am some sort of spy!" He stared hard at Violet. "They asked many questions about your father, my dear," he continued in a lower voice. "They seem to think he is some sort of mastermind, managing a great intelligence network in France."

Violet caught her breath. Her aunt exclaimed, "Is he, Armand? Are we in danger?"

"Of course not! Percy is exactly what he appears to be—a landed member of the gentry! He is no gay adventurer!"

Violet could read his thoughts. *Not anymore.*

"What do we do?" Marie said. "How do we prove our innocence?"

"I have no idea, save tell the truth and hope these men are not completely mad."

Capitaine Bourgeois opened the heavy drapes, allowing the morning air into the stuffy room. He turned to his companion. "What do you think?"

M. Lafarge sipped his coffee, black and oily. "It is as I expected. Armand St. Just is an idiot. He is not in his brother-in-law's employ. Indeed, I would have been shocked to learn otherwise. He is as impetuous and emotional as ever. Very bad for a spy or courier."

Bourgeois frowned. "How do you know him so well?"

M. Lafarge looked up. "It is all in Chauvelin's papers. I have read them over and over again these twenty years. I know these people as well as anyone. *Non*, M. St. Just is not part of Blakeney's enterprise," he said darkly, "but I believe the girl is. We need to question her."

"Monsieur, I must return to the ministry."

M. Lafarge rose. "Of course. One of us must be here at all times while the other is at the ministry. I do not completely trust the guards. The ladies upstairs are tempting, are they not?"

"I gave them my word nothing would happen to them."

"And nothing shall."

Bourgeois reached for his hat. "I have been meaning to ask you. How did you manage to take over this entire apartment building?"

M. Lafarge smiled. "I had the landlord evict the other tenants."

"That must have cost him some money. By what means did you convince him to do as you wished?"

"No means at all. In fact, it was his idea." M. Lafarge grinned at Bourgeois's perplexed expression. "*I* am the landlord."

"You! You own this building? On a bureaucrat's salary? How could you afford it?"

"Chauvelin left me more than papers. He left me a small fortune as well. I have invested it wisely. Buying this place is an example. My needs are few. Therefore, I have the funds to see us through this quest."

Bourgeois remembered the excellent food and wine he had shared with his mentor. "Is that how you can afford the guards?"

"Leave all that to me. You concentrate on securing the ports. No one must enter the country without our notice. *Au revoir,* Bourgeois. I will see you in the morning."

Chapter 19

London

With word of Bonaparte's return to the throne, Britain prepared to renew the war. The Royal Navy moved quickly to blockade French ports. This was a necessary action, but it reduced the ships available to transport veteran troops from Canada and the Caribbean. The Seventh Coalition could not wait in any case.

The Rhine and the mountains would slow any French movement against Austria, so the only way Bonaparte could attack quickly was through the Low Countries. Wellington and the Prussians needed to block the open north door from France, as to give the Austrians and Russians time to mobilize on the eastern frontier. It was imperative that troops be dispatched quickly, so the British were forced to use what they had on hand.

Frederick had every expectation that his company would be called up, but the orders he ultimately received were a shock.

"I do not understand," he complained to his colonel. "Lord Somerset is forming the Household Brigade with the Blues, the Life Guards, and the Dragoon Guards, but my company stays here?"

"Yes, yes," said his irritated commanding officer, seated at his desk, his attention on the papers before him. "Just because there is a war does not mean there are no longer threats against the king or his ministers. Or have you forgotten Perceval?"

"No, sir, I have not." Spencer Perceval, the Prime Minister, had been shot dead in the lobby of the House of Commons in 1812 by a disgruntled merchant named John Bellingham. "I see the need to maintain the guard, but I must protest my orders."

At that, the colonel looked up. "Why? Do you think you are too good for them?"

"With all due respect, yes, sir. My company is the best in the regiment. I insist we be among those sent abroad."

The colonel leapt to his feet. "*You* insist? Just who the devil do you think you are?"

Frederick kept his eyes trained on a spot two inches above his commander's head. "The captain of the finest company in the regiment, sir."

"Listen here, you son-of-a-bitch," the colonel growled, stepping around the desk until he was only a few inches from Frederick's face, "you have lost all of your influence. I told you that you would pay for playing your games."

"Sir, I was not responsible for—"

"Enough! I do not like you, Tilney. I do not trust you. I would not have you if you were the last bloody unit available. You are staying home, and that is an order! Now get out of here before I have you brought before a court-martial!"

Frederick bowed, turned on his heel, and exited the office without a word. Frustrated with the unending hostility shown by his commander, Frederick decided to go over the man's head and take his case to Lord Somerset himself. It might mean the end of his career, but he cared not. He had to find a way to be useful.

He sought out Major Denny, only to find him with two other officers.

"Tilney!" said Colonel Brandon. "General, this is Captain Tilney of the Blues."

"General," said Frederick as he bowed to Major-General Sir William Ponsonby, commander of the Royal Dragoon Guards.

"Tilney—I have heard of you," said the general.

Frederick showed no expression. "Yes, sir."

Sir William chuckled. "Oh, no worries, man, only good reports. My companies should be as sharp."

"Tilney," said Colonel Brandon, "we shall be finished with Denny in a moment."

"Oh, go ahead, Captain," offered Sir William. "I suppose you have much to do before you embark for Belgium."

"That is the point, sir," said Frederick. "I have been informed that my company is not slated to go to the Continent, and I beg to speak with Lord Somerset."

"Not going?" cried Colonel Brandon. "What is this?"

"The major-general is not available," Major Denny informed him. "To be honest, Tilney, I am not sure he will have the time for an interview."

Frederick felt the bitterest frustration while a grave Sir William seemed to be in thought. "Gentlemen, let us repair to my office." In a few moments, the four officers were behind closed doors.

"Tilney," began Sir William, "it should come as no surprise that you have made enemies at Whitehall. I wish I could say petty jealousy has no place in the army, but that would be a lie. Just between us," he lowered his voice, "I have heard more than one man speak out against Uxbridge commanding the Cavalry Corps. I will not share my opinion of his lordship's personal affairs. However," he said in a louder voice, "if Wellington wants him, that is good enough for me.

"I wish I could do something for you, Tilney. The reports I have seen of your command have been excellent, but I have my hands full just trying to keep my own command in one piece. The name Union Brigade sounds noble, does it not? English, Irish, and Scottish cavalry regiments, fighting together for King and Country. Hah, it is a recipe for disaster! The Royals, the Inniskillings, and the Scots Greys can barely stand each other.

"My job is to turn them into a unified fighting force. I am certain that Somerset's assignment will be just as taxing. We do not need further dissension in the ranks. If your colonel has seen fit to leave you behind, then there is nothing for it."

Frederick closed his eyes in disillusionment. "Yes, sir."

"I am sorry for your disappointment, Tilney," offered Colonel Brandon.

"Thank you, sir. My men have worked hard. It is not right that they should be punished."

"War is not a game or a reward."

"Well said, Brandon," said Sir William. "Tilney, your assignment here is important. The honor of the regiment falls on your shoulders."

Frederick sighed. "Yes, sir. We will uphold the reputation of the Blues."

"Good man." The finality of the general's words was a clear dismissal. Frederick bowed and left the room. Sir William had been generous with his praise, and Frederick should have been satisfied, but he was not. Instead, he nursed a smoldering rage.

Bonaparte was back, his Violet was in danger, and he was able to do nothing.

Paris

WHEN THE TIME CAME FOR VIOLET'S INTERROGATION, SHE WAS escorted alone to the floor below by *Capitaine* Bourgeois. She had few expectations, but to her mind, the *capitaine* treated her very gently for a prisoner. Unlike her uncle's situation, the room was not dark, for light streamed in through the open drapes. Waiting for her at a desk stood an old man, bearded and wearing spectacles. He politely waited until she was seated before taking a chair himself. *Capitaine* Bourgeois moved to stand behind the old man with his arms crossed.

Violet griped her hands below the table in an effort to control her nervousness. Her eyes darted about the room but found nothing of interest, save the man seated across from her. For his part, he seemed content to simply stare at her and say nothing.

The silence dragged on for several minutes. Violet fought the impulse to speak, if for no other reason than to break the uncomfortable atmosphere, and she was mortified to feel her hands shake. Finally, the old man cleared his throat.

"So, you are the daughter of Sir Percy Blakeney, *oui*?" the old man spit out.

"Yes, he is my father," Violet answered in English. She was outraged at the treatment afforded to herself and her relations. She might have to answer this man's questions, but she was not going to make it easy for him.

The old man said in English, "I speak your mongrel tongue quite well, young lady. We will continue as you choose if your French is not—how do you say?—not up to snuff."

Staring intently at the insulting man opposite, Violet was taken aback by the hard look of hatred in his eyes. "Why are you holding my relations and me prisoner?"

"I ask the questions here, miss, not you. What brings you to France?"

"I am visiting my cousins in—"

The old man cut her off. "Who are your contacts?"

"I do not take your meaning."

"Who have you met with since coming to Paris?"

Violet grew brave at the old man's rude tone. "Who are you to ask me such questions? In my country, ladies are not treated in this manner." Her eyes flashed. "By whose authority do you hold us against our will?"

The old man smirked. "You have spirit, I see. I should have known. I am M. Lafarge. This is my associate, *Capitaine* Bourgeois. We are with the Ministry of the Interior, and you are being held for suspicion of espionage." He leaned closer. "Spying, young lady. It would do well for you to cooperate with us, for it will end badly for you if you do not."

"I am a British citizen. I demand to speak to the ambassador."

"The English have all fled like the cowards they are. Besides," he glanced at a paper before him, "your mother is Marguerite St. Just, yes?"

"That is my mother's maiden name."

"You know she was an actress on the Parisian stage?"

Violet felt the slur in M. Lafarge's tone, but did not rise to the bait. "My mother has been Lady Blakeney these four and twenty years. To what do these questions pertain?"

"Your mother is a Frenchwoman and so are you. I can charge you with treason, and the penalty is *not* imprisonment."

Violet used her anger to control her fear. "You are mistaken, sir. I am an Englishwoman, the daughter of a baronet, and proud of it. You threaten like a brute. You are no gentleman."

"*Gentleman?*" M. Lafarge sneered. "There are no *gentlemen* in France—no damned *aristos*—only patriots. You will tell me what you know, or you will pay the penalty." He shoved a paper at her. "Do you know these people?"

Violet could not help but glance at the paper. It was a list of names, some familiar to her: *Suzanne de Tournay de Basserive* and *Jeanne Lange*. Others were not. She suddenly realized that this was a list of people rescued by the League of the Scarlet Pimpernel. With horror, she realized this man, Lafarge, knew her father was at least connected with the League if not the Pimpernel himself!

All her life, Violet had been taught to keep the family's secrets. She could lie bald-faced to the Archbishop of Canterbury if needed and at the same time appear so innocent that butter could not melt in her mouth. She needed to call on that ability now.

"I know Lady Suzanne Ffoulkes, née de Tournay. The others, I do not know. Who are they?"

M. Lafarge frowned. "Look closer. Are you certain?"

"Perfectly certain."

"These are the *ci-divant aristos* who escaped just punishment for their crimes against France, thanks to the help of the English agent, *Le Mouron Rouge*. You call him The Scarlet Pimpernel."

Violet smiled. "A fairy story."

"You lie. He is real, and you know this. The Scarlet Pimpernel is an English baronet by the name of Sir Percy Blakeney." He smiled again. "Your father."

Violet forced herself to laugh. "My father, the Scarlet Pimpernel? You are mistaken. I love my father dearly, but really! If the Pimpernel did indeed exist, the last man he could be is Sir Percy Blakeney!" She tried another gambit, hoping she did not overplay her hand. "*Capitaine* Bourgeois, certainly you do not believe this!" She hoped to raise dissension between her captors.

Her ploy failed. The officer looked blankly at Violet, confirming he did not speak or understand English.

M. Lafarge shouted, "Enough! You will tell me whether you know any of these people!" He jabbed at the paper with one boney finger. "What has happened to these people, for instance?"

Violet looked and saw the names: *Fleurette and Amédé Colombe.* She shook her head and said quite honestly, "I have told you I do not know them."

"Monsieur…" said Bourgeois nervously.

M. Lafarge whipped his face towards the officer. Whatever he saw there seemed to calm him. He turned back to Violet, his dark eyes no longer blazing.

"We have spoken enough today, madam. The *capitaine* will escort you back to your rooms. However," he added as she rose, "we are not done with the interrogation. You will be questioned again. You will tell us what you know. You will tell us with whom you have met during your stay. I beg you; do not force us to resort to more… unpleasant methods to assure your cooperation."

Violet willed her hands not to shake. "You would not dare."

"Oh, I make no threats against you, madam," M. Lafarge said with a small smile. "You are valuable. It is a shame the same cannot be said for your aunt and uncle."

Violet's stomach dropped. "I was wrong to call you a brute. You are a monster."

"Their fate is in your hands. Consider this until we speak again. Good day." M. Lafarge turned and ordered Bourgeois to take her back to the rooms upstairs.

Capitaine Bourgeois guided her out of the room and up the staircase. He reached to hold Violet's arm, but she jerked it out of his hand. "Do not touch me!"

Capitaine Bourgeois shook his head. *"Je ne parle pas l'anglais,* mademoiselle. Forgive me, I meant no disrespect. The stairs, they are treacherous."

Violet spat in French, "Much like the men in Paris. I shall manage on my own."

The two continued to the top floor, *Capitaine* Bourgeois visibly troubled. "Mademoiselle," he urged quietly, "I beg you to cooperate. This is a serious business. It is a matter of State. Help us, and no harm will come to you or your relations."

Violet would not look at him. "Your words are softer but no less offensive! We are innocent guests in your country, yet you treat us like criminals. You are despicable."

The officer flinched. "It is not you or your friends who are the criminals but others. We must end their threat against the empire."

"*Oui*, your little emperor is back on the throne, ready to wage war against Europe once again. Mark it—we will stand against him as we have done before. And we will defeat him as before. You are fools!" Violet turned to him, furious. "Will you return to the army, *Capitaine*? Will you fight beside your precious emperor?"

"I will do my duty."

"Then you will die, and I hope it is my Frederick who sends you to the Devil!"

With that, she entered through the door into the flat without a backwards glance. Because of that, Violet did not see how her last words had affected *Capitaine* Bourgeois. He rubbed his chin, frowned, and turned to descend the stairs.

April: London

FREDERICK STOOD AT A WINDOW, WATCHING THE LAST OF THE Blues leave for the ships that would carry them to Antwerp. In a way, he was second in command of the detachment left behind. An inactive colonel had been appointed to manage Frederick's company and the company of Life Guards that would share the responsibility of protecting the government.

Frederick had to admit that, on paper, this was an important assignment, and by being close to Whitehall, he was sure to catch the eye of a superior. Advancement was possible, especially as there were sure to be casualties if battle was joined in the Low Countries.

It was the circumstance that rankled the most. Advancement

was important in the army, but Frederick's dream was to earn it by skill and sword. It would not do to receive promotion by being safe in England while others fell on distant battlefields. No matter what words of encouragement Major Denny had given him before embarking, Frederick felt he was being left behind.

Of course, General Tilney had a different opinion of the matter and expressed it in a letter.

This is a great opportunity for you. You remain in Horse Guards where you may impress great men who can do great things for you. There will be less competition for the ladies. Make the most of this!

Frederick was disgusted by his father's words. He was a soldier, not a courtier. He was trained to fight, not to play lackey to pompous windbags. He felt useless. He opened his shirt, careful not to disturb his cravat, and pulled out the locket of Violet's hair. He gazed at it with helpless anger.

I remain playing ceremonial soldier while the others go to face the foe. The same foe that keeps my dear Violet prisoner! Even Buford has been recalled to his regiment! I cannot bear it! I must do something!

Tucking his treasure back into his shirt, he turned back to his desk and picked up a letter from George Blakeney. It was an invitation to dinner at a pub near Horse Guards. He wanted to speak to Frederick about a secret enterprise, but he would give no more details. Frederick had no idea what his friend planned, but that did not matter. If this meant action, Frederick was of a mind to listen.

Chapter 20

The old, battered *Mary-Anne* slowly made its way through the moonless night towards the French coast. The schooner resembled a fishing vessel, which pleased its owner and master, who had spent no little time making it appear so. In fact, when business was slow, the ship's hold actually contained the riches of the sea.

That was the exception to the rule. In point of fact, the *Mary-Anne* was designed for the secret transport of the riches of men. It was a smuggler, and its captain proudly owned a heart as greedy and cold as any pirate who sailed the fabled Spanish Main. Gold was his true love, and if the price was right, Captain Hughes would sell his own mother. But he would never part with his dear *Mary-Anne*, his mistress and instrument. It was too valuable. With this tiny, leaking tub, he aimed to earn his fortune and retire to a comfortable country house.

A tall hatless man, his queue of yellow hair flapping in the breeze, leaned over the gunwale of the creaking sloop, staring out into the murk. Another man, shorter in stature, stood next to him, both mindless of the crew dressed in rags milling about the deck, attending to their task of sailing the ship. The fine black cloth of their coats instantly identified the passengers as gentlemen. The only similarity between these two and the crew was their dark clothing.

The tall man's companion quietly spoke. "Do you see anything, Frederick?"

"No, nothing, George," answered Captain Tilney.

"Ya won't see much, good masters," came a thick brogue from behind, "but we're close t' shore, t' be sure. I know these waters like the back of me hand." Captain Hughes was a middle-aged man, gray hair sticking out every way under his stained tricorn hat. He grinned in a reassuring manner, clearly showing the gaps in his yellowed teeth. The money George Blakeney had paid him for this trip had earned the gentlemen the captain's good will. "I ain't run aground yet in this here life, and I don't means t' do so t'night."

He ordered one of the crew forward to the bow. The scrawny man scrambled like a monkey between the bowsprit and cathead. He wrapped one arm through the shrouds and began tossing a weighted line overboard.

"Eighteen fathoms, by the deep," the leadsman called out softly.

The captain moved back to the helmsman at the wheel. "Steady as she goes."

Frederick and George stood impatiently for the next half hour, watching the leadsman methodically toss the heavy lead out before the slowly moving ship, the line running through his hands. The only sounds breaking the silence were the creaking of the ship, the soft splash of the weight, and the gentle call of the depth.

"Seventeen fathoms, mark … Fifteen, by the deep … Twelve, by the mark …"

A fortnight ago, Frederick had met with George in the private room of a local inn, and his friend had raised an extraordinary proposal. George's intention was to "reconstitute an intelligence network" in the Channel coastal region of France. They would gather the information necessary to attempt a recovery of Violet and her relations.

As he explained his plans, Frederick realized he was talking about something that had existed in the past. Recalling his conversations at Buford's wedding in January, Frederick had blurted out, "George, I must ask you where this knowledge of networks comes from. I have heard some rumors."

"I suppose you have. This is something used before—twenty years before, in fact. I mean to bring it back."

"Twenty years? Are you speaking of—"

"Yes. The League of the Scarlet Pimpernel."

Frederick was stunned to learn the League was real. George refused to go into greater detail except to state that no one would confirm either the true identity of the Pimpernel or even whether he was one man. Instead, he described how the League used scores of French informers to learn the movements and intentions of the opposition. It was due to this intelligence that the League was successful in rescuing people from the Terror.

His friend admitted the political climate in France had changed since the Revolution. Frenchmen who had been all too happy to help the enemies of the Committee of Public Safety would never betray France after Robespierre's fall. However, the coast was filled with pockets of royal loyalists, and he hoped they would be angry with Bonaparte for usurping Louis's throne.

"If we can find a few fellows, perhaps relations of those who had helped the League before, we can gather the information we need to rescue Violet. Are you with me?"

So there Frederick was: an officer in the king's army on ten days' official leave graciously given by his new commander, standing on the deck of what some would call a pirate ship off the coast of an enemy nation in the dead of night, planning to go ashore on a secret mission with a friend still a student at Oxford to rendezvous with suspected traitors with only his pistol, his sword, and his wits to protect him.

He was either mad or in love, he thought, and contemplated whether they were not indeed one and the same.

The lookout cried in a loud whisper, "Land, ho!" At the same time the leadsmen called out, "By the mark—seven fathoms. Hard bottom."

"Heave to!" ordered Captain Hughes. "Drop anchor—easy, mind ye, or you'll be beached when we get home."

Once the *Mary-Anne* was anchored, the captain climbed into a long boat with Frederick and George. "This should not take long," he said to the first mate. "Keep ye a weather eye on us and prepare t' raise anchor once ye spy us returning." The captain made himself comfortable as the boat was lowered to the water. With practiced movements, he freed the little craft from the hooks and seized the tiller.

"Avast there," he said to his companions with a chuckle. "There be no gentlemen aboard this here craft. Slap a hand on them oars and give a pull. Smooth now—like ye were crewing on the Isis."

Long minutes later, Frederick heard the scraping of sand along the bottom of the launch. Captain Hughes proved to be more nimble than his rotund figure would indicate, and he sprang smoothly from the long boat with a line and fastened it to a rocky outcropping. Frederick and George dragged the boat higher aground at the captain's direction.

"Stay here with the boat, an' make not a sound, mind," Captain Hughes growled in a low voice. "I'll be back in a trice. Listen for the whistle." Without waiting for a response, the man vanished into the gloom.

Frederick and George sat by the rocks, taking care to keep their heads out of sight. George was nervous, and Frederick was about to admonish his friend for fiddling with his pistol when they heard a low whistle. Taking no chances, both men drew their guns, only replacing them when they saw the captain with another man who carried a dark lantern.

"Well, sirs," said the captain, "here be a man who might be a help t' ye."

The newcomer spoke French. "Bonsoir, messieurs. My friend says you bring gold—not for wine but for information." He was dressed as much in rags as any member of the *Mary-Anne's* crew.

"*Oui*," said George in a strong English accent. "We will pay you well if you answer our questions."

The man looked at the captain. "It will not bring trouble, will it?" He returned his gaze to the gentlemen. "Money has been hard to get since the Peace. We do not see much profit. The fishing barely fills our bellies. *Le percepteurs des impôts* are crawling all over. We must take care."

George withdrew from his coat pocket a folded piece of paper. Once opened, Frederick saw it was a drawing of a red, five-petaled flower. "Does this mean anything to you?" George asked the man.

The smuggler shook his head. "*Non,* monsieur. What is it?"

Before George could respond, there was a commotion from inland. "*ARRÊTEZ! HALTE!* IN THE NAME OF THE EMPEROR, I ORDER YOU TO SURRENDER!"

"*Merde!*" the Frenchman cried in fear, dousing the dark lantern. "*Le percepteur*! We must flee!"

Both Captain Hughes and George drew their pistols, but Frederick quickly assessed the odds from the sound of numerous feet on the sand. "No! Put those away! There are too many!"

The French smuggler seemed to agree, and he took to his heels, scrambling over the rocks. The Englishmen ran for the long boat while the captain made for the boat line tied to the outcropping. All the time, the shouting tax collectors were drawing closer.

"*Arrêtez ou nous tirons!*" [6]

"Drag the boat out to the surf!" the captain cried as he worked the knot. "Smartly, lads—"

Suddenly, the air was torn with the flashes and crashes of gunfire. The captain fell to the rocky sand like a limp doll. Frederick dashed to help, but a moment's glance showed that Captain Hughes had taken a ball to the head. Frederick had seen death before, and it was never pretty. He freed the line and ran back to the boat.

George's eyes were wide. "What happened?"

"He is dead! Come on, George—push! Put your back into it, or they will get us too!"

Bullets were now splashing all about as they desperately dragged the boat into the surf. As George scrambled over the side, he screamed, "Ahh! I have been shot!"

Sick with fear and anger, Frederick pulled himself into the long boat. "George! Can you row?"

Receiving only a moan for an answer, Frederick took both oars

---

6 "Stop or we shoot!"

and pulled with all his might away from the beach of death. He faced backwards and saw numerous figures among the rocks reloading their muskets. He prayed that distance and darkness would shield them from a lucky shot. The French tax collectors starting firing again, and Frederick redoubled his efforts. Soon the long boat was out of range.

Now Frederick had a new worry. He had to make it back to the *Mary-Anne* by himself in the dark.

"A…a little more to the right. No…my right, Frederick."

Frederick was overjoyed at the sound of his friend's voice. George was neither dead nor incapacitated.

"Courage, George! Keep me straight to the ship." Frederick pulled on the oars as hard as he could. "Just like crewing on the Isis, remember?"

"Damn this leg! It hurts, Frederick."

"I am sure it does. Where is the ship?"

"You…you are doing well. Is the captain dead?"

Frederick kept rowing. "I am afraid so. Keep your eye on the ship."

"I will. Am…am I going to die too, Frederick?"

Frederick gritted his teeth. "No, by God, not if I have anything to say about it! Keep your head, George, and guide me!" He strained at the oars, trusting that George's direction was true.

Suddenly he heard a shout from shore that chilled him. The French tax collectors were launching their own boat.

Almost in a panic, Frederick redoubled his efforts. Long moments passed…

"What boat is that?"

Finally, the welcomed call from the *Mary-Anne*! Frederick turned and saw that George had slumped in the bow.

"Do not shoot! It is us! Help me—my friend has been shot!" He noticed that the crew was in the process of raising the anchor.

"Where's Cap'n Hughes?"

"The guards got him! Help me!"

"You just left 'im?"

"No, no—he was shot dead! I went back for him, but there was nothing for it! I am sorry!"

After a moment, a line was tossed, and Frederick was told to tie it to a cleat in the bow. Once the long boat was pulled along the ship's side, several men climbed down a rope ladder and prepared the craft to be raised. Frederick was told to stay where he was, so he turned his attention to George.

His friend was still conscious but very weak from shock. Blood was seeping from an ugly wound in his thigh. Frederick urged the men to hurry as he used his cravat to stem the bleeding. No sound was sweeter than the creak of the pulleys as the long boat was hoisted out of the sea.

Once the launch was fully raised, Frederick climbed out onto the deck. Observing the hostile looks of the crew, he knew he was still in dangerous waters and not just because of the French.

"Will no one help me lift Mr. Blakeney from the boat?"

The first mate spoke for the crew. "What 'appened on shore? What 'appened to the cap'n?"

As much as he wanted to rail at the men before him, Frederick knew it was no time for anger. George needed care, lest he bleed to death.

"We had met with a friend of Captain Hughes on the beach as was planned. We then were set upon by armed men—soldiers or government men. There was shooting. The captain was hit and my friend, too. We were fortunate to escape. Sir, my friend needs medical attention."

Several of the crew muttered. Frederick could make out "revenue agents" and "tax collectors."

"How do ye know the cap'n were dead?" demanded the mate.

"When I went to help him, I saw he received a musket ball through the back of his head." Frederick paused to let that sink in. "My sympathies. He must have been a close friend."

The mate ran a hand through his greasy hair. "He be my brother-in-law." He sighed. "I don't fancy tellin' Nancy the news, that's fur certain. She'll more than likely move back in wif me. Well, the *Mary-Anne*'s mine now, I'm to be thinkin'."

"Sir, my friend is hurt."

The new master of the *Mary-Anne* cocked an eyebrow. "Now, why should I be worryin' 'bout that?"

A loud boom interrupted Frederick's response. "Look!" cried one of the crew, "they're shootin' the cannons!"

Everyone on board looked out to see the flash of cannon fire from the small port town nearby. "Heave to!" screamed the new captain. "All hands—make ta come about! Move your arses, ye bloody lubbers!" He gave Frederick a cold look, his hand on a pistol handle sticking out of his waistband. "Give me one reason why I shouldn't throw ye and that bleedin' baggage right into the sea, Mister."

Frederick restrained himself from drawing his own weapon. These smugglers were as dangerous as any pirate. He would have to be careful. "You have been well paid for your services."

"Ye paid me brother-in-law, not me. Ye got more money?"

Frederick showed his teeth. "If you do not want to end your days swinging from a yardarm in Dover, you will make sure my friend gets back to England alive. If he does not, there is no place on Earth where you can hide from the retribution that will be brought against you."

The man laughed as he pulled the pistol. "Who are ye ta talk, seeing as you're 'ere too?"

"It is not my vengeance that concerns you, but the Crown's."

"Eh? What's that?" The man's eyes narrowed as he gestured at the boat with the gun barrel. "Who's he, then?"

"The Regent's godson."

The man's face paled. "You're lyin'."

"Do you wish to wager your life on that?"

Frederick could see the man's little brain working over the idea. With a curse, he turned and yelled, "Some of ye lazy bastards come lend a hand, an' get that gentleman out of th' boat! Move!"

Four of the crew gently lifted a senseless George out of the long boat, blood slowly dripping on the deck. "Take 'im to the cabin!" cried the new captain. "Gently, ye whore-sons!"

Chapter 21

rederick dipped a cloth into the basin of water, wrung it tightly, and reapplied it to George's brow. His friend lay in the bed of a Dover inn, the ceiling so low that Frederick had to take care not to strike his head on the rafters. Thankful that a dreaded fever had not taken hold of his comrade, Frederick sat back in the rough, uncomfortable chair, a candle burning fitfully next to his unfinished dinner.

Bone-weary, he rubbed his eyes. The apothecary advised him to rest hours ago, but he would not surrender his post by his friend's side. Not until the Blakeneys arrived.

The last two days had been a nightmare. No ship had pursued the *Mary-Anne*, but it took a full day and night before they raised Dover. Frederick was almost frantic for a surgeon. What passed for a surgeon on board the smuggler had been a Royal Navy loblolly boy, beached five years before. At least the filthy man could administer laudanum to ease George's suffering. It fell to Frederick to check his friend's bandages every few hours. The bleeding was not too bad, and if a proper surgeon could extract the musket ball, George could survive. Every hour counted.

No sooner had the *Mary-Anne* come along the quay than Frederick leapt from the ship, demanding where a surgeon could be found from everyone he saw. The local apothecary oversaw George's removal to the inn and sent for a retired naval surgeon who lived nearby. The dining room table served as an operating room. Between the ample light and the two men of medicine, the ball was quickly extracted. The wound had been sewn shut, George had been made comfortable in the room Frederick had secured, and a letter had been dispatched to Richmond. All that remained for Frederick was to wait for George's relations.

He was determined to stay awake until they arrived. He fought off entreaties from the apothecary and even his own exhausted body, but it would not do to take his rest until George was safely delivered to his family. Frederick leaned back in the chair, his head against the wall. Perhaps if he shut his eyes for a moment—

A loud crash brought Frederick back to his senses. *The French! They have followed us! Where is my sword?*

Frederick shook his head, clearing his thoughts. They were safe in England. That was an English voice. Sir Percy—it was Sir Percy!

He staggered to his feet, finally making out the tall gentleman in traveling clothes standing in the open doorway. Frederick realized he must have fallen asleep, and the noise that had awakened him was the bedroom door violently opened.

"Sir…Percy," he managed from his sleep-drugged tongue. "You are very welcomed, sir." He saw another face behind the gentleman. "Lady Blakeney—"

"How does my son fare?" the baronet demanded, his face pale and his blue eyes flashing behind his spectacles. The man's broad shoulders were tense in agitation.

"He is as well as can be expected. There is no fever, and his leg has stopped bleeding. He is not in danger."

"Oh, thank God!" cried Lady Blakeney, who flew to George's side. Sir Percy seemed to deflate a little, and stepped fully into the room, minding his head, his gaze never leaving the bed.

Frederick moved aside to give the family privacy. "I shall fetch the apothecary. He can more fully apprise you as to George's condition."

"A moment, sir." Sir Percy turned. "Surely, the innkeeper can be entrusted with such a mission. I would speak with you."

Frederick unconsciously ran the tip of his tongue across his dried lips. The letter he sent to Richmond had been succinct: *Pray hurry to Dover at the address below as soon as may be. George is ill. He is receiving the best of care. You may depend upon my diligence and care for him until your arrival.*

He had not explained the nature of George's injury although he suspected they could guess. George was on a mission for his father, after all. Still, it would be unpleasant to review the entire debacle.

"Certainly," he told the baronet. "Give me a moment to talk to the innkeeper and secure a private room." Sir Percy gave him a single nod and returned his attention to his son.

Minutes later, Frederick and Sir Percy were seated at a table in a small anteroom, glasses of wine before them.

"Zounds, Captain Tilney," Sir Percy said after the serving girl had left them, "I must wonder at these circumstances. Could I impose upon you to satisfy an old man's curiosity and tell me why I find my son injured in a dockside inn in Dover?" The man's drawl was casual. Frederick grew confused.

"Sir Percy," he said quietly, "I regret to report that our mission was unsuccessful. As we made contact with an informer, we were set upon by local officials. There were shots fired, the captain of our boat was killed, and George received a wound in the leg. We did what we could aboard ship, and a surgeon here in Dover removed the ball. I wrote as soon as I could. You made excellent time, sir."

Sir Percy blinked. "Sink me, you sound as though you have had quite the adventure, sir. Am I to understand that my son was shot?"

"Yes, sir."

"By local officials, you said?"

"Yes, sir. The French have apparently redoubled their efforts to stop smuggling."

"The French," Sir Percy breathed. "George was shot by French officials. I assume this was in France?"

"Of course. Where else would they be?"

"*What* were you doing in *France?*" Sir Percy's voice, while low, cut like a whip.

Understanding dawned on Frederick. "Sir, I thought you knew!"

"I know *nothing*, Captain," Sir Percy snapped. "What was my son doing in France?"

In a barely audible voice, Frederick explained their objective of rebuilding the intelligence network used by the League of the Scarlet Pimpernel so many years ago. As he spoke, he realized what had sounded sensible in a London pub appeared much less so in Dover. Sir Percy interrupted the tale only once.

"What did George tell you of the League?" he hissed.

"Not much—only that it had existed and that you knew some of the men who were in it. We hoped to gather enough information for the League to rescue Miss Blakeney." Frederick thought he heard Sir Percy sigh, but he was not certain. Once Frederick finished his tale, he faced Sir Percy's dark glare.

"You thought I knew of this madness?"

Frederick could recognize anger and instinctively fell back to his army training. "It was my understanding that this operation received your blessing if not your involvement, sir."

"Operation? You call this scheme a well-planned operation? Are the lords of Whitehall so incompetent that you would see *this* as an acceptable plan?"

Frederick had no answer.

"Odd's life, Captain, but I must wonder at your capacities. You are supposed to be a trained soldier. How could you approve of such insanity, much less involve yourself in it? Did it not occur to you to contact me directly to learn for yourself whether I concurred with this stupidity?"

Frederick stared at a point above Sir Percy's head. "No, sir, it did not."

"Good God, sir! You are an officer in the king's army. George is but a boy—a boy still in university. What does he know of intrigue and espionage and such matters? Why did you not stop him like an intelligent man?"

This verbal assault was far more painful than the one Sir Percy administered last year. "I-I was worried about Vio—Miss Blakeney."

"Yes, and so you risked the life of my other child. How thoughtful of you!"

"Sir, I—"

"I had hoped you would heed my words and make something of yourself. I see I was mistaken. George was foolish, but his youth, inexperience, and concern for his sister must be his excuse. *You* have no such excuse. You, sir, are a fool of the first order. Not only are you thoughtless, you are reckless. You have endangered my family for the last time.

"Stay away from my son. Stay away from my family. Stay away from my house, or by God, you will answer for it. Do you understand me?"

Dully, Frederick said, "Yes, sir."

"Did you pay for these rooms? For the apothecary and surgeon?"

"Yes."

"How much?"

Defeated, Frederick could at least resist Sir Percy in this. "Do not concern yourself. It is done."

"The devil it is!" Sir Percy slammed some notes on the table. "I will not be beholden to the likes of you. Our acquaintance is at an end." He rose. "I must speak to the apothecary. I am sure you can find your way out." Without another word, the baronet left the room.

Frederick eyed the money. He estimated there was at least twenty pounds there. It did not matter; he would not touch it even if it were a hundred times as much. Utterly crushed, he slowly rose from the table, straightened his coat, reached for his hat, and solemnly walked out of the inn towards the station for the post to London.

The Blakeney carriage moved at a very slow pace through the countryside of Kent. Most would say it was mad to travel at night, but Sir Percy was adamant that George be brought to Richmond without delay. The Dover apothecary, cowed by the Blakeney name and the influence attached to it, voiced no objection to the baronet's demand.

Marguerite was content to have her son's head on her lap while they traveled. Her halfhearted protests against moving George were gently but firmly rejected by her husband. It was just as well. George's wound had been sewn closed, laudanum kept him asleep, and Marguerite knew she would find no rest until he was in his own bed.

Her eyes traveled from the pale, peaceful face of her son to the troubled countenance of her husband. Percy stared out the window, seemingly lost in thought, one hand near an ornate box Marguerite knew to contain a brace of pistols. It was a wise precaution, for nighttime was the domain of highwaymen. However, she suspected the possibility of robbery was not uppermost in Percy's mind.

"My love," she said in a whisper, taking no chance her voice would waken George, "what are your thoughts?"

Percy's eyes darted to hers. "I am contemplating the wreckage of my life. My daughter is being held prisoner with your brother and sister-in-law in Paris for some godforsaken reason, and my son tried to get himself killed in her service. What sin have I committed, I wonder, to bring such pain to you?"

"Sin? Of what are you speaking?"

"Is this God's punishment upon me? It must be. You have done nothing to deserve this. Why should it be that you and the children suffer?" He bowed his head. "I must set this to rights."

"Percy, pray do not give in to despair! George is alive and will be well again. You will see." Her voice rose. "Surely, you are not planning to do anything foolish?"

Percy turned back to the window in answer.

"Percy, no! Do not go back to France! It will be your death!"

"I cannot leave Violet there. George, for all his foolishness, saw his duty to his sister. This task must fall to its rightful place. The responsibility of safeguarding my family is given to me. I will not forsake it or our daughter."

Marguerite, overwrought, could no longer hold back her tears. So violent was her weeping that Percy was soon on his knees on the floor of the carriage, begging to offer relief.

"Margot, pray do not cry! I cannot bear it!"

"No! No! You will go away and die, and I will be left all alone!

I cannot live without you!"

After some minutes of pleading, Percy said the only words that would placate her. "Margot, you win. I shall not go. I shall stay here with you for now."

Sniffling, she asked, "What do you mean, 'for now'?"

"I will bring you and George home and see that the best physicians attend him. He shall be made well. Meanwhile, I must begin steps to learn what is happening with Violet. I will go mad if I do not."

"You still plan to go to France."

"I promise you, only if it is absolutely necessary. And then only after I have made every preparation." There was a flash of his younger appearance. "Just like before."

"You were nearly killed last time."

Percy said nothing for a time. "I will see Violet home if it is the last thing I do. I *must* do this, Margot."

Chapter 22

apitaine Bourgeois shared dinner with M. Lafarge. Once again, the food and wine were excellent.

"The emperor is raising an army," Bourgeois said as he ate a bit of bread. "I may be recalled."

M. Lafarge lifted his wine glass. "I have taken care of that. You will remain with the ministry."

"What have you done?" Bourgeois exclaimed. "My duty—"

"—is with the ministry," M. Lafarge finished. "There is no use complaining. The deed is done." He shoved a forkful of stew into his mouth.

Bourgeois wondered again about his mentor. How did he earn such influence? How much money did he have? For not the first time, Bourgeois felt he was in a little boat in the fog without a paddle and at the mercy of forces beyond his control and understanding.

"What are the reports from the coast?" asked M. Lafarge.

"It has been quiet, save for an incident near Calais last week. *Les percepteurs des impôts* have been very active in stopping illegal trading." At M. Lafarge's questioning look, he elaborated. "An English smuggler was shot fleeing from arrest."

"Good riddance." M. Lafarge helped himself to more wine. "I have decided to stir the pot a bit."

It took a moment for Bourgeois to realize he was not taking about the stew. "How will you do that?"

"I have let *Le Mouron Rouge* sit wondering for a month. It is now time to season the trap. I will send the St. Justs back to England."

Bourgeois gasped. "Is that wise, monsieur? M. St. Just may yet prove valuable."

"*Non, mon capitaine.* He is nothing but the escort of Mlle. Blakeney. She is the bait that will bring *Le Mouron Rouge* into our hands." He threw back the remains of his glass. "Begin making preparations to transport the St. Justs to England. I want them to leave in the next two weeks."

Bourgeois rose. "I will begin at once, monsieur."

"No hurry, Bourgeois," M. Lafarge said. "Sit down, relax. It will wait for tomorrow. We still have this bottle to finish."

Bourgeois grinned. "It would be a sin to waste such wine."

"Indeed. Blakeney will be in our hands soon enough. It is the end of April, is it not? I would say…no later than the first week of June."

Woodston, Gloucestershire

FREDERICK LOWERED HIS GLASS WITH A SCOWL. "MY WORD, Henry, this is truly ghastly port!"

His brother frowned. "Where are your manners, Frederick? When did you begin to berate a man for the quality of the libations he serves his guests, particularly in his own study? You have never complained before."

Frederick sighed. "Forgive me. I am in a beastly mood."

Henry Tilney eyed his brother. "You have been a perfect boor these last three days. The only reason I have not thrown you out is that you have not mistreated Cathy," he teased before turning serious. "She is concerned for you, as am I. Will you not talk to me about it?"

"What good will that do?"

"At the least, it might amuse me." Henry smiled. "Consider it payment for our hospitality."

Frederick rocked forward and rested his arms on his knees, holding his glass in his hands. He stared at the amber wine. "Is Cathy offended by my presence?"

"Good Lord, no, Frederick! Of course not! We only wish to help."

Frederick sat quietly for a moment, considering. Then slowly, he told his brother about his courtship of Violet Blakeney, his estrangement from Sir Percy, his frustration with the army, and his fears for Violet in Paris. Henry said nothing until the tale of his adventure off the French coast with George Blakeney.

"Lord, preserve us! That was a close call, Frederick! How does Mr. Blakeney?"

"I have no idea as Sir Percy has forbidden me to write."

Henry said nothing and only refilled their glasses. After a sip, he said, "I must say that I think Sir Percy was rather hard on you. This...escapade was of Mr. Blakeney's making, was it not?"

Frederick rubbed his forehead. "It was a foolish idea. I should have stopped him."

"What if Cathy was in a like situation? I would have stopped at nothing. Would you have helped me?"

Frederick raised his head. "You would not have tried to sail for France."

"Oh? Then what would I have done?"

"I do not know. I would have thought of something."

Henry smiled. "*You* would have thought of something?"

"Of course. I—" Frederick saw his brother's point. "Well, I would have—"

"You are the soldier, not I. My area of expertise is the pulpit; yours is the battlefield. You would have taken all the planning on yourself, as you should. I think what is bothering you is that you believe Sir Percy was correct when he said you did not act like a soldier. Tell me, would you have planned this trip as your friend did?"

"No, I would have not."

"Then, what are you going to do?"

"Do? What can I do? Sir Percy has made it clear that he does not want my help."

"Then have you decided to walk away?"

"No! I mean—damnation, Henry, I love her!"

"Then what are you going to do?"

"I do not know!" Frederick tossed back the rest of his port in one swallow. "I have to change his mind somehow."

"Yes, I imagine so."

Frederick glared at his brother. "You know, Henry, one day I will grow tired of your manipulative ways."

Henry grinned. "Yes, I imagine so."

Frederick huffed and sat back in his chair. "Very well, since you are full of advice, how do you propose I do that?"

"I have not the least idea. You know the baronet, not I."

"That is not at all helpful!"

Henry shrugged. "Who else knows Sir Percy? Who might intercede for you?"

Frederick thought about that. *Not Lady Blakeney. Even if she were predisposed towards me, I am forbidden to contact her. Who else?*

Henry smiled at Frederick. "Well, you have some thinking to do. Put it off until tomorrow; it will keep you occupied on your trip back to London. You leave in the morning, do you not?"

"Yes. My leave from the Blues ends in two days."

Henry rose. "Well, let us return to Cathy. She has a new piece she has been practicing." He paused. "Frederick, that story about the League of the Scarlet Pimpernel—that it really existed—do you believe it to be true?"

Frederick remembered the drawing George showed the man in France—the drawing of a five-petaled flower. *A scarlet pimpernel.*

"Yes, I do."

May: Richmond

Marguerite Blakeney dearly loved her son. His concerns were hers. Much attention was given to George's education and accomplishments. She approved of his attentions to Miss Dorothy Wentworth and took great pains to further their acquaintance. A pretty, ginger-haired, round-faced girl with large, blue eyes, plump lips, and an unfashionably pert little nose, Miss Wentworth owned a deposition as charming as her character and as generous as her dowry. While Mrs. Wentworth was a bit of a trial—not disagreeable, only simple and ill read—Marguerite looked forward to the possibility she would one day embrace sweet Miss Wentworth as a daughter.

When the Wentworths learned George had been injured, they instantly wrote of their distress and begged to visit the invalid as soon as practicable. Therefore, a week after the Blakeney's personal physician declared both George's health and leg out of danger, the female members of the Wentworths of London came to spend a day at Richmond. In anticipation of the visit, George had been carefully moved to a sitting room off the family quarters and had been made as presentable as possible. George's low spirits rallied, and he greeted the Wentworths with as much pleasure as an active young man condemned to bed rest for at least six weeks could muster.

Marguerite was content to sit and watch her son gaze lovingly at the charming young woman softly reciting poetry for his entertainment. Mrs. Wentworth, thankfully, had brought a sampler, and she was satisfied to work on it rather than acquaint Lady Blakeney with the latest gossip from Town. As much as a marriage between George and Miss Wentworth would answer all her prayers for the happiness of her son, Marguerite dearly wished the two invaders away, for Percy was soon to arrive home from Town and his meeting with Armand.

Marguerite had been shocked when news reached Richmond of Armand's return to England, and she almost fainted when she understood that only Marie accompanied him. Violet was still imprisoned by those evil ruffians in Paris. An angry Percy had rushed to London to question his brother-in-law, and only George's care had prevented Marguerite from accompanying her husband. Thus, impatient for Percy's return and report, only Lady Blakeney's good breeding prevented her from behaving in an uncivil manner towards her guests.

Still, after nearly three hours, Marguerite's well of graciousness had drawn dry. Pursing her lips and wringing her hands, she was almost at the point of *thinking* of asking the ladies to depart when the butler appeared at the door.

"Begging your pardon, madam, but the master has returned and wishes your attendance in his study presently."

Marguerite leapt to her feet without thinking. She inwardly berated herself for her breach of decorum while she thanked the butler. She turned to her guests, forming her excuse, when she noted how Miss Wentworth's eyes darted to George's. An unseen message passed between them, and Miss Wentworth nodded and rose.

"Lady Blakeney, I must thank you for your forbearance in allowing our visit today. I fear we have overstayed, and we beg to excuse ourselves. Mother, it is time we returned home."

"Oh, is it?" said Mrs. Wentworth stupidly.

"Yes. We must be off, or we will not get home before dark."

"Oh, Dorothy!" she cried as she struggled to her feet. "What is the time? Why did you not say so before? You know how much I dislike traveling in the dark! The gypsies may be about!"

Marguerite was taken aback at this. "Allow me to see you out."

"No need, Lady Blakeney," the girl replied as she gave George her hand in farewell for a moment. "I am sure your business with Sir Percy is important. The butler can show us out."

Marguerite narrowed her eyes, a suspicion taking root, but she escorted her guests to the door and took leave of them with perfect graciousness. "I wish you a safe trip and hope we may meet again very soon."

Mrs. Wentworth thanked her profusely, invited her to tea next time she was in Town, and assured her the postmen would protect the carriage from the gypsies. Miss Wentworth gripped Marguerite's hands tightly and, with an earnest look, said, "God bless and keep you."

The ladies left, and Marguerite turned to her son. "What was *that*?" she demanded.

George had the grace not to dissemble. "Dorothy is aware of our troubles."

Marguerite cocked an eyebrow. "'Dorothy,' is it? Do you have anything to tell us?"

George managed a small grin. "Were I not still at Oxford, I would."

"How much have you told her?"

"Not everything yet. She knows Violet is a prisoner in France, and I got this"—he patted his leg—"trying to help her. Besides that, nothing more."

"When did you find time to do this?"

George colored but answered in a defiant voice, "Dorothy and I have been corresponding since the New Year."

"You have *written* to her? George, do you know what you have done?"

"Of course. Dorothy is well aware of my intentions and welcomes my suit." He paused. "Mama, I tell you now that I will tell her everything before I propose. She deserves nothing less."

A chill ran up Marguerite's spine. "*Everything*, George?" At his nod, she added, "Even if your father forbids it?"

George's countenance was flinty. "By gad, I will not ask Dorothy to join this family with lies and secrets between us. I am determined."

To Marguerite's ears, he sounded remarkably like Sir Percy. In that instant, she realized George was a boy no longer. Pride and loss battled in her breast. "I cannot approve of your methods, but I do approve of your choice. I must to your father now. Rest, my dear."

Moments later, Marguerite let herself into Percy's study. She found her husband at the side table, a decanter of brandy in his hand. "Ah, m'dear, may I pour you a glass?"

Marguerite noted his distracted voice and forgot all she wanted to say of George's indiscretion. "Do I need one, Percy?"

Sir Percy handed her a snifter. "It shall not hurt." He raised his own glass. "By gad, I love you."

"Percy! Dear lord, has something happened to Violet?"

Percy blanched. "No—no!" He took her free hand. "I am sorry, love. It was not my intention to frighten you. It is just that this matter is beyond my understanding. I cannot make heads or tails of it, and neither can Ffoulkes. He was with me when I met with our brother."

They sat and Percy quickly spoke of the meeting with Armand.

"So, the French government holds Violet because they think you a spy?" Marguerite cried. "That is madness! Are you certain

Armand is not confused?"

"You know our brother well, Margot," Percy observed. "Apparently, so do the French. They sent him with this." He handed her a letter in French.

Département de l'intérieur

Sir Percival Blakeney, Bart.
Richmond

Monsieur,

We regret to inform you that there are serious allegations that French laws have been violated. These unfortunate circumstances have necessitated the detention of your daughter, Mlle. Violet Blakeney, until our investigation is complete. Mlle. Blakeney is in a comfortable and secure location.

We foresee that we will require your deposition at some point before Mlle. Blakeney can be released. It is hoped the tensions between our two nations will not prevent you from participating in our investigation. You will be informed as to the time and place for your interview.

M. LAFARGE
Paris

"Dear God!" Marguerite breathed. "They think you some sort of spy! It cannot be true, can it?" As soon as she said it, she regretted her words. Percy, however, took no offence.

"No, Margot. I promised you years ago that I would give all that up, and I have. But apparently not everyone believes me." He frowned. "Who the devil is this Lafarge?"

"Does no one at St. James's Palace know?"

"Ffoulkes is looking into it."

"What of Whitehall? Captain Tilney can certainly help there." Percy turned to her. "No! Not Tilney."

"Percy, you are too hard on Captain Tilney. You heard what

George confessed. He practically lied to the captain to assure his cooperation. And if it was not for his cool head and quick action, George might still be in France, wounded or worse."

Percy stared at the far bookcase. "George never would have gone to France in the first place had Tilney used this head you so admire. I hold to my opinion of the man."

"Odd's life, but you are stubborn!" Marguerite cried. "Why do you dislike him so? Is it because you do not want to lose Violet to him?"

"He is reckless, foolhardy—"

"And so were you!" Marguerite shouted. "Have you forgotten what *I* lived through while you played gay adventurer? How I feared I had seen your face for the last time every time you left this house? How I died each time you set sail for France? I assure you, Percy, I have not!"

"I had to."

"Yes, keep telling yourself that! Keep pretending you were indispensable! You thought more of strangers than of your own wife!"

Marguerite broke down, weeping uncontrollably, and tried to fight off Percy when he moved to comfort her. He would not be denied, and soon Marguerite could speak again.

"Percy, forgive me—"

"No, m'dear, you have no need to ask forgiveness. I will never forget the pain I put you through. You deserved better. You never should have loved me."

"Do you not understand? I cannot live without you! I was made for you and you alone. I was born to love you."

"Margot, my own!"

"Percy, listen to me. You must give over this hatred of Captain Tilney. It is wrong."

"I do not hate him, but he is not good enough for Violet."

"If you are successful and Violet comes home, what will you do if she still wants him? Will you deny the wishes of her heart?"

"She *will* come home, and we will make a decision then."

Marguerite meant to continue her point when there was a knock on the door of the study.

"I beg pardon. Lord Anthony Dewhurst is here to see the master," said the butler.

Marguerite knew she must withdraw but vowed this was not her last word on the subject.

Chapter 23

iolet sat before the small pianoforte in the main room while the maid moved about, cleaning the flat. Since her aunt and uncle's release, Violet's captors had promoted Claudette to companion as well as maid. Having another woman share her imprisonment was a comfort, however minuscule.

Violet's initial worries had changed into a mixture of anger and boredom. It was easier to escape the monotony of captivity and find diversion when her aunt and uncle were still in residence. Now that they were gone and Violet's agonizing fears caused by their removal had receded, the tedium of imprisonment could only be borne by as much activity as possible. Violet took to walking about the room for a half hour twice a day. She requested needle and thread for embroidery. The instrument that had been provided was a welcomed surprise.

M. Lafarge's second and last interrogation had been less threatening. He seemed unconcerned with her answers. Violet found the man's behavior baffling, unlike that of his second-in-command. It was obvious that *Capitaine* Bourgeois was interested in her—to what end was a concern. Having Claudette about lessened Violet's apprehensions. Surely, M. Lafarge or *Capitaine* Bourgeois would not have provided her a companion had they meant any mischief.

At first reserved and quiet, Claudette slowly responded to Violet's attentions. The maid would not speak of her employment, but on matters of her own personal situation, she was open and easy. She would compliment Violet on her embroidery or her playing, always in a low tone. Violet was certain that fraternization was frowned upon by M. Lafarge, and Claudette seemed unwilling to endanger her position.

It was late afternoon, and Violet was working her way through a new piece of music she had recently received from *Capitaine* Bourgeois. She put aside her curiosity over the officer's intentions and lost herself in thoughts of Richmond. Her parents would be having tea now, she supposed, and she wondered how they were bearing up. Were Uncle Armand's reports comforting or not?

Violet was startled by the front door slamming shut. Her uncertainty increased at the sight of her visitor: one of the guards was standing at the now-closed door, a bottle in his hand. He was one of the men from the carriage ride—the one who had ogled her. He glanced in her direction, took a swig from the bottle, and pointed at the approaching Claudette.

"You—get out," he demanded. When Claudette declared she would do no such thing, the guard took her roughly by the arm and forced her out of the room. He then turned back to stare at Violet.

A chill ran down Violet's spine as she regarded the man's feral look, but she steeled herself to show no fear. As regally as she could manage, she stood, chin up, looking down her nose at the ruffian.

"You're a proud one, aren't you?" he leered. "Been lonely too, I'll wager."

"I am a guest of the state. You have no business here. Be gone."

"I mean you no harm, mademoiselle. I bring you comfort and companionship." He began to walk towards her. "*Une jolie fille* like you shouldn't have to be alone."

Fear threatened to choke her voice. "I am content with my maid for companionship. It is my wish that she return."

"Bah! You're a prisoner. I make the rules, not you!"

Violet started to edge back toward her bedroom. "Leave this room at once, or I shall report your behavior to *Capitaine* Bourgeois!"

"Ah, but you're a fiery one! I thought so in the carriage." Violet turned to flee, but the guard was too quick. Dropping the bottle, he moved like lighting, pinning her against the wall. He seized her arms and pulled her into an embrace. "Stop fighting, *petite fille* —it'll be so much nicer."

Violet struggled as he tried to kiss her. "Stop it! Unhand me!"

"Stop your screaming. It'll do you no good. No one will hear." He tightened his grip. "We can make this easy, or we can make this hard." He grinned. "Unless you like it rough. I've heard that about you *aristos*."

Violet nearly gagged at the stench of alcohol on the guard's breath. The man forced her hands above her head, and when she turned her face away from his, he slobbered on her neck. In her rising panic, she remembered something her father had taught her. Taking a deep breath, she rammed her knee as high as she could between the guard's legs. The man screamed, released her, and stumbled away, holding his groin.

He gasped. "*Merde!* You whore! You'll pay for that!"

Violet ran to the bedroom and shut the door, only to find there was no lock. Desperate, she leaned against it to hold it shut. Within moments, the guard was there, shouting curses as he tried to force his way in. Violet shut her eyes, focusing only on withstanding the onslaught. To her horror, she knew she was losing. The guard was too strong, and the door was slowing opening. She tried to think of what to do next.

There was a shout, and then the door shut as if the force on the other side had magically disappeared. Violet, panting, could not understand the noises from the other room at first. Slowly, she realized that it was the sounds of a man receiving a beating from many fists. Her fear was too great to open the door and see for certain, however.

"Mademoiselle, are you well?"

With a start, Violet realized it was *Capitaine* Bourgeois's voice. "*Oui*! Help me!" she screamed at the door.

"Everything is in hand! Stay where you are!" the officer cried.

In direct opposition to *Capitaine* Bourgeois's command, Violet slowly opened the door. She beheld the *capitaine* and two other guards standing over the figure of her attacker lying limp on the floor. From the man's battered face and her rescuers' bloody fists, she surmised her assailant had been beaten senseless.

Capitaine Bourgeois snarled, "Did this *salaud* hurt you?" He had a wild look in his eyes.

Violet shook her head, and the *capitaine* relaxed.

"Dieu merci!" He turned to the others. "Take Bernard downstairs, and do not bother being gentle about it! I will deal with him there." The guards boldly dragged their comrade out the door, and for the first time, Violet saw Claudette was standing next to it, her hands to her face.

Capitaine Bourgeois noticed what drew Violet's attention. "I walked into the front door of the building to hear your maid demand the guard come to your assistance. *She* had done her duty," he nodded at the woman, "but as for the rest, I must apologize—"

"For what, monsieur?" Violet cried, yielding to her outrage. "For making me a prisoner or for hiring brutes to guard me? I have committed no crime, yet I am being held, and I nearly lost my virtue. You are sorry? Then free me, *Capitaine*, and save your empty words for someone who wishes to hear them!"

With that, Violet retreated into the bedroom, slammed the door, fell on the bed, and allowed her hopeless tears to flow.

BOURGEOIS COULD EASILY SEE THAT M. LAFARGE WAS UNHAPPY AS he entered his apartment. He had apparently left the ministry as soon as he received Bourgeois's note.

"Tell me what happened!" he barked.

Resorting to his military training, Bourgeois gave a concise report of the incident in Mlle. Blakeney's rooms. M. Lafarge said not a word, but his murderous glare spoke volumes.

"Where is Bernard?"

"Downstairs, under guard, awaiting your judgment."

"Useless, all of them!" M. Lafarge growled as he rose from

his chair. "Bourgeois, I will require two men. I will deal with this *salaud*."

Bourgeois turned to obey, but a troubling thought stayed him. "Do you wish for my assistance?"

"*Non.* Stay here and guard the mademoiselle."

"Monsieur, I must say that I am unhappy with the character of the men you have hired. Allow me to find proper soldiers."

"*Non, Capitaine.* Not only is that unnecessary, it is impossible. The emperor is filling his armies. We will use what we have." He smiled a hard smile. "Never fear. This shall not happen again. Bernard shall be an example."

M. Lafarge swept out of the room, leaving an uneasy Bourgeois in his wake.

An hour later, in a small, ill-lit room off a stable on the other side of Paris, M. Lafarge stood face-to-face with another man. Bound in a chair behind M. Lafarge was the guard Bernard, bloody and barely conscious from the beating he had taken. Two other guards stood watch on either side of the man. The place smelled of wet straw and manure. If one looked hard, rats could be seen scrambling about the corners.

Before M. Lafarge stood a short, fat man, his fine clothes quite out of place amid the room's squalor. Surrounding him were a half-dozen large, dangerous-looking men in rags.

"Is this the kind of men my money buys, Robineaux?' He spat as he gestured behind him. "I am seriously displeased. You should know better than to try to cheat me."

The other man glowered quietly as he was berated by M. Lafarge. M. Robineaux was well known among the criminal element of Paris, and he did not take kindly to the dressing-down. "I would take care, M. Lafarge, lest your words be misinterpreted."

"Do not threaten me, monsieur! You know what I have done to keep the authorities away from your organization. You owe your livelihood to me."

M. Robineaux ground his teeth. "Spies can be replaced."

"But not the records I have secreted," M. Lafarge answered back with a sneer. "*Oui,* monsieur, I have taken every precaution. Should anything happen to me, those papers will be sent to the proper authorities."

"Now, *mon ami*, why such talk?" M. Robineaux returned in an offended tone. "You have been paid well. I believe you no longer trust me."

"Why should I when you send me men like Bernard?"

The man narrowed his eyes. "A mistake, monsieur, nothing more."

"I want him replaced with two others, and you will pay the cost, *mon ami*." M. Lafarge demanded in a mocking tone.

M. Robineaux glanced at the bound man in the chair. "And poor Pascal?"

Lafarge's voice was as cold as ice. "You deal with him. He knows too much."

The criminal cocked his head. "What is it you are doing? I do not think you have told me."

"I am protecting France, Robineaux. There is no money involved. Surely, that is no concern of yours."

"You wound me, M. Lafarge. I am as patriotic as the next man."

"Then see to it. And I want those two new men by the morning." Without waiting for a response, M. Lafarge turned and left the building, his two guards trailing behind, leaving Bernard to the mercy of his fellows.

M. Robineaux approached the nearly senseless man, shaking his head. "Ah, Pascal. You disappoint me. You were told to keep *ta verge* in your pants. Now you have cost me money. Such a waste." He turned to the men behind him. "See to it. I do not want him found." M. Robineaux left the room.

Pascal Bernard was a thief like his father and grandfather before him. Being a thief did not always pay well, which is why he accepted the invitation to join M. Robineaux and his "organization." Robineaux was known in the Parisian underworld as a careful and dangerous man, one who demanded total loyalty and obedience. Failure was punished with the most severe of penalties.

It took Pascal Bernard a long time to die.

London

Sir Andrew Ffoulkes was surprised when his butler announced that Captain Frederick Tilney was at his front door, requesting an audience. He was even more astonished at the captain's story. He was frankly flabbergasted to hear his petition.

"Gad, sir, you do not ask for little!" he said kindly. "Sir Percy is the dearest friend in my life. It would be unsupportable to go against his wishes."

Captain Tilney dropped his head. "I understand, sir. Forgive me for taking up your time."

"Now, none of that! I am glad you have come to tell me your tale. If it means anything to you, lad, I appreciate what you tried to do for Violet. And I thank you for saving George's life, for you certainly did. You should know that George will keep his leg, and it is expected he will fully recover."

Frederick smiled slightly. "I thank you for telling me, sir."

"I make you no promises, Captain, but I hope, once Violet is returned, that we may clear up this misunderstanding."

"Can you tell me what is being done to recover her?"

Sir Andrew stared at his desk. "The government is involved. That is all I can say."

Captain Tilney sighed. "I suppose that is all I can ask." He rose and extended his hand. "Sir Andrew, thank you for taking the time to see me."

Sir Andrew gave him a hearty handshake. "I wish you all the best, Captain." He watched his butler escort the officer out of his study before he collapsed into his chair.

Oh, this is a muddle and no mistake!

Sir Andrew realized his culpability in the fiasco. He knew that Prinny had extended his favor on behalf of the captain and that the regent had withdrawn it when Tilney and Percy had a falling out. He should have said something to Prinny about his actions and had not. He did ill by his goddaughter and felt guilty over the captain's difficulties.

He also was concerned over Percy's plans. *Odd's fish, Percy pretends it is 1794 all over again! We need help, and* that *man*, he glanced at his window, *would be just the one!*

But there is no turning Percy when he is determined. In thirty years, I have never gotten Percy to change his mind.

Sir Andrew smiled. He knew who would be able to, if anyone could.

He pulled out paper and began to write.

Chapter 24

The knock at the door caused Violet to flinch. It had been over a week since the attack, and while the guards had been unfailingly polite since, if not subservient, the memory of the assault lingered in Violet's mind.

Composing herself, she nodded at the now ever-present Claudette and set the book she was reading on the table next to the sofa. The maid moved to stand behind the sofa, and Violet waited one more moment before calling out, in accordance with the new procedure, "*Vous pouvez entrer.*"

Capitaine Bourgeois walked in and offered a short bow. "I hope I find you well, mademoiselle."

"*Je vais passablement bien, Capitaine.* To what do we owe your visit today?" She noted he had papers in his hand.

The officer looked about the room, his hands now behind his back. "Do you find the new arrangements satisfactory?"

Violet noted Claudette had moved off to continue her work. "As well as can be expected. If I must remain here, it is comforting to know Claudette will act as my companion."

"Have the guards and others followed the new regimen of requesting your leave before entering these rooms?"

"*Oui*, thank you for that." She looked at the officer. "May I know what has been done with…him?"

Steel glinted in *Capitaine* Bourgeois's eyes. "That one shall not trouble you again, I assure you."

"No one else would speak of it," Violet answered. "I assume he has been dismissed?"

"*Oui*, mademoiselle."

Violet knew she would get nothing more from the man. "*Merci*. Was there anything else?"

Capitaine Bourgeois hesitated for a moment before he withdrew one hand from behind his back and presented the papers. "These are for you."

"Music?"

"I thought while you were here, you would enjoy it," he said. "I like hearing you play."

Violet narrowed her eyes. "You expect me to play for your entertainment?"

Capitaine Bourgeois was taken aback. "*Non*, for your own! I mean, I enjoy it, but only if you wish it—to play, that is."

"And if I do not wish to play?"

He threw up his hands. "Then do not play! You are not my servant."

"Only your prisoner."

"I must do my duty, mademoiselle." *Capitaine* Bourgeois looked deflated. "I am sorry to have displeased you. If you will excuse me." He turned to leave the room.

Truth be told, Violet was confused. Unhappy as she was over her confinement, she was pleased at the gift, for she loved music. And thanks to *Capitaine* Bourgeois's timely rescue, she felt perversely safe in his presence. She later would reason it was her intense loneliness that caused her to cry out.

"Pray, *Capitaine*, will you not stay? I would enjoy some company."

Capitaine Bourgeois's dark expression lightened. He took a seat in a chair near the sofa. "I noticed you were reading a book. Do you like it?"

"*Oui*. I have read it in English, but this is the first time I have seen it in French." She picked up the volume and handed it to him. "Have you read it?"

Capitaine Bourgeois glanced at the title. "*Candide*? *Non*, I have not. I am not a great reader. I am surprised you read Voltaire." He handed the book back. "He is a great Frenchman and one of the inspirations of *la Révolution*."

Violet smiled. "M. Voltaire lived for a time in England and has many admirers there."

"Do English ladies read such things?"

Violet was offended. "I will not say that Voltaire is a favorite among the ladies of society, but to my mind, an accomplished lady should read other things besides novels and the Bible."

"*Pardonnez-moi.* I am stumbling all over my tongue. I am certain you are considered a very—how you say? A very accomplished lady."

"*Merci, Capitaine.*"

"What else do you enjoy?"

Violet spoke of dancing, playing, and riding. "I remember one time when I was riding on my father's estate with Frederick. I was a little naughty and jumped a fence three rails high!"

"Frederick? This is your brother?"

Violet's smile disappeared, replaced by a blush. "*Non.* He is a…a very good friend."

"A very good friend. Is this the man in the army?" His tone revealed jealousy.

Violet raised her chin. "*Oui. Capitaine* Frederick Tilney of the Blues—a cavalry regiment."

"I see. Your lover?"

"You forget yourself, *Capitaine!*"

"*Mes excuses.* I did not mean to offend you." His hard face said otherwise as he stood. "I must return to my duties." He paused. "Perhaps we may talk a little more tomorrow."

"As you wish," Violet said carefully. She was concerned over the *capitaine's* behavior, and she did not want another enemy in this place.

"Until then. I ask but one thing."

"And what is that?"

"That you call me by my name—Honoré."

Violet was taken aback. "You ask too much, monsieur. In my country, such a request is reserved for families and close friends."

Capitaine Bourgeois half smiled. "Would it not be more pleasant if we were friends, mademoiselle?"

"Do friends keep their friends prisoner?" Violet shot back.

"If I had my choice, you would not be a *prisoner*," he said, his voice full of meaning.

Violet knew she was playing with fire. "That is nice to know. Good night, *Capitaine*."

"Good night, mademoiselle."

Capitaine Bourgeois left, and Violet feared she had made a bad situation worse.

Honoré Bourgeois paused outside the door to take a great breath. He was a fool, he knew, but he could not help himself.

In the last weeks, he had grown to greatly admire Mlle. Blakeney. But wooing was new to him, and he had no idea how to show his approval of the young Englishwoman. Girls enjoyed gifts, he had always been told, which was why he had spent what little money he had on sheet music. She would play the music, and they would become friends. Simple.

Except it was not. It was obvious to him the girl resented her situation so much that she almost turned down his offering. Was it always this hard to compliment a girl? Never having a sweetheart before, he had no frame of reference.

The awkwardness of their situation was not completely lost on him: she was a prisoner, and he was her jailer. But his heart overrode his mind. He wanted—needed—to be her friend.

Now there was a further complication. Mlle. Blakeney had just confirmed a relationship with this damned Frederick. The favoritism that man enjoyed from the lady was enough to insure Bourgeois's hatred. That he was an English cavalryman—a comrade of the devil who had sliced open his leg in Spain—only increased his loathing of the man.

Still, Bourgeois was no brute. He would not take what she would not give. She was here, and this Frederick was not.

Time, he considered, was on his side.

Chapter 25

rederick exercised his sword arm, his foil whizzing through the air as his fencing master announced, "We shall practice the *doublé*, sir." The man took his place, waving his own foil. "I shall attack, and you use the counter-parry."

In a slow, deliberate motion, the master extended his arm and thrust forward. Frederick moved his own blade in a circular motion, deflecting the other foil.

"Excellent, sir," said his teacher. "Now, again."

Once more the instructor moved to attack, but this time Frederick's counter-parry was defeated when the other foil moved in the same direction but just slightly faster—the counter-disengage. Frederick found the foil at his chest while his own weapon was pointed towards the floor.

At the instructor's command, they changed positions. Now it was Frederick who attacked and defeated the counter-parry with the counter-disengage. Again and again, they practiced the move, the foils moving faster and faster.

Finally, the instructor called for a halt. "Now, we shall explore the ways of utilizing your second intention after a successful *doublé*."

For a few minutes, the two battled, Frederick's parries proving successful about half of the time. Sweat poured down Frederick's face, and after a particularly painful riposte by the master, he decided on an all-or-nothing response.

The two returned to the en garde position, and Frederick moved to attack. However, this time after the *doublé,* Frederick used the *flèche.* He leaned forward and, pushing off with his front right foot, leapt toward his opponent, bringing his left foot forward for the landing. Frederick made his hit on the man's torso in the air before his left foot landed and continued to run fully past the instructor. "Hit!" he cried.

The instructor tore off his helmet, a mixture of aggravation and admiration on his face. "A hit! I acknowledge it, sir," he panted.

The instructor's assistant declared in admiration, "As pretty a *flèche* as I have ever seen."

"Well done, sir. Shall we again?" The instructor's foil made tiny circles beside his leg.

Frederick had a mind to agree and give the man the opportunity to inflict some revenge, but his time was short. "Thank you, no. I must be off soon. You shall get your chance next week." The instructor smiled, nodded, and wished him good day.

As Frederick walked toward the changing rooms, a servant approached with a small tray. "Captain Tilney, this gentleman expresses his compliments and wishes a few moments of your time."

Frederick glanced at the card and stopped breathing. *Sir Percival Blakeney, Bart.*

Jerking his head up and searching the room, he saw Sir Percy. Dressed in a green coat with a striped vest, the baronet locked eyes with him, touching the rim of his top hat. Frederick nodded automatically.

"My compliments, and inform Sir Percy I will attend him directly," he told the servant. With that, Frederick hurried to change.

A FEW MINUTES LATER, FREDERICK FOUND SIR PERCY SEATED AT an out-of-the-way corner table. "Ah, I am happy you could join me," the man drawled in his usual careless manner as he stood to greet him.

Frederick could not but wonder at Sir Percy's presence. "I am honored by your visit, sir." He cautiously bowed and remained standing as the older man returned to his chair, recalling the unpleasantness of their last two interviews. "How may I serve you?"

"It is I who wish to serve you. First, this wine of questionable quality that stands at the table. Second, my apology for my words in Dover. I have wronged you, sir."

Frederick was stunned. "I thank you, Sir Percy," he managed.

"Sit down, Captain, and share a glass with an old man."

Frederick took a chair. "I would be happy to, but one glass only. I must tell you I am due soon at my post."

Sir Percy poured as he spoke. "Then I shall not waste your time. George has spoken to me of the deceitful manner he used to secure your assistance for his late adventure. I would take back some of my words. You had every reason to think I had blessed that enterprise."

Frederick thought for a moment before he spoke. "George's concerns over Miss Blakeney must be his excuse as well as mine. I will admit it did not take much persuasion to guarantee my participation. I am very concerned for your daughter, sir."

"Hmm." The two said nothing more as they sipped. "Zounds, I came here to give you a chance to try me on the mat, but what I just witnessed made me think the better of it! You have great skill, sir."

Frederick made to thank him, but something occurred to him. "You knew I was here?"

Sir Percy wore a knowing glint behind his glasses. "You are here every Wednesday, are you not?"

Frederick pursed his lips. "It seems your investigation into my habits is quite complete, Sir Percy." He began to grow angry. "Are there any matters I can clarify for you?"

Sir Percy cocked an eyebrow. "When a man has a daughter with a sizable dowry, he takes no chances unless he is a fool. Do you think me a fool, Captain?"

"I thought this a friendly drink, but perhaps I was mistaken."

"Gadzooks, sir! Stand down! I came here to make amends, not to offend."

Frederick took a deep breath to steady his nerves. "Forgive me, sir." He forced a smile. "A man is only a fool if he buys me *two* drinks—that, or he is up to mischief."

Sir Percy smirked. "My wife tells me I am always up to mischief, so perhaps you are correct."

At that, Frederick inquired as to the health of Lady Blakeney and George. Assured both were well and that George would soon be on his feet, Frederick then asked the question that had been burning in his breast.

"What is being done to recover Miss Blakeney, sir?"

Sir Percy grinned foolishly. "Wheels are turning if that is what you are asking. The government gives me full assurance that they are giving this matter their upmost attention. All resources that can be brought to bear are being employed."

Frederick had nothing to lose. "Forgive me, sir, but I cannot believe you."

"Indeed?" Sir Percy remained amused.

"Yes, sir. The government is fully engaged with supporting Wellington in Belgium. There are no resources available. I fear you are on your own."

"Ah, yes. The Iron Duke playing soldier in the Low Countries. Quite an expenditure of the Crown's coin, what?"

"Necessary to stop Bonaparte." Frederick lowered his voice. "I would help you if you would let me."

"Help me? Sink me, you talk as though you were certain *I* was going to do something foolish too."

Frederick ignored him. "Sir Percy, George told me of the League. I saw the pimpernel drawing he showed to those in France whom he thought could be of help." He leaned closer. "As I told Sir Andrew, I offer the League myself in service to Miss Blakeney. If you can get word to the League—"

Sir Percy's blue eyes flashed coldly. "Captain Tilney, heed my words. There is no League. Thank you for your offer, but there is nothing you can do."

"Why will you not let me be of assistance?" Frederick asked helplessly.

Sir Percy spoke slowly and relentlessly. "I never said there was any way you can help. Sir, I believe you are a brave man and, from what I witnessed, a talented one. I appreciate your offer and acknowledge your concern for my daughter's well-being. I will tell you there are forces being assembled to resolve this matter. Like me, you must trust in that, return to your duty, and be satisfied."

"If that is what you think, why did you come here to speak to me?"

"Because I was in the wrong, and my character demands I apologize in person as a gentleman does. There is no service you can perform for my daughter, save prayer."

Frederick was desperate. "Is there nothing I can say that will sway you?"

Sir Percy only shook his head. With the last of his hopes crashing about him, Frederick rose.

"I thank you for the wine and the apology, Sir Percy. I am sorry I cannot be of service to your family. Forgive me, but I must return to Horse Guards."

"I am sorry," Sir Percy said softly.

Frederick was too bitter to offer his hand. He only gave the baronet a short bow and left the place as quickly as he could without drawing attention to himself.

As he walked back to his office, Frederick grew more despondent. He felt useless and rejected. Neither his country nor his love's family had any use for him. His future seemed to hold nothing but worthless pomp and circumstance—no creditable employment that would take advantage of his skill and training.

It seems I am doomed to play at soldier for the amusement of the lords of government until I come into my inheritance, he sourly told himself. *I am unworthy of dying for my country or my beloved. All I am good for is to march back and forth until my father passes. What a glorious future that is!*

It is a wonder I am not a drunkard.

Richmond

MARGUERITE HAD JUST SAT DOWN FOR TEA WHEN IT WAS AN-nounced that the master had returned from Town. She ordered a fresh pot and waited patiently until Sir Percy joined her in the parlor. He greeted her with affection and asked about George while the servants flitted about. Once the last maid shut the door and left the two alone, Sir Percy glanced at his wife.

"Well, it is done. I saw Captain Tilney."

"And?"

"He accepted my apology. Now will you and Ffoulkes leave off?" He sipped his tea.

"So, you have not changed your mind about accepting his assistance in that mad scheme of yours?"

"Margot, my schemes may be unorthodox, but they are certainly not mad."

"You did not answer my question."

Sir Percy sighed. "No, I have not. I have no need for him."

"Percy—"

Her husband held up his hand. "My dear, I admit I was too harsh with Tilney, and I acknowledge he is a skilled swordsman. He impressed me very much at his club." He turned back to his cup. "Although I wonder how well his skill on the mat translates to the battlefield. Fencing and fighting are not the same. Still"—he returned to Marguerite—"I do not need him or anyone else for that matter. My plans require a very small party."

"How small?"

He shrugged. "Well, I have to get across the channel and to Paris, so a few men will have to be involved—a handful, I would say."

"And at the heart of it? Who will be by your side?"

Sir Percy looked over his glasses at his wife. "I will act in this matter as I always have."

"You mean alone!"

"I collect less notice that way."

"Percy, I beg you to reconsider."

"I recall to your attention the letter from M. Lafarge. It seems I have no choice in the matter in any case." Marguerite objected again, but Sir Percy forestalled her. "My plans are not yet fixed as I have to await another communication from Paris. There is nothing more to be said now. Pray, love, can we talk of other things?"

Knowing there was no moving him, she talked of George and Miss Wentworth. After she concluded her recounting of the visit, she asked, "Do you think you should talk to Mr. Wentworth about this? I think he should know, and George must be prepared to regulate matters if the Wentworths require it."

Sir Percy rolled his eyes. "The impetuousness of youth! Odd's fish, what was George thinking?"

"I think he loves Miss Wentworth."

"That is all well and good, but there are proper ways of going about one's courting!"

"She is out and finishing her first Season, so it is not so very bad."

"But George is still at Oxford, and he will not finish this term, thanks to his injury. He has no business attaching himself to anyone, even one as suitable and delightful as Miss Wentworth. It is too soon."

"Still, we must do right by the Wentworths. I suppose the uproar will not be too awful." Marguerite could not help smiling. "Nothing like when you brought me here from Paris."

Sir Percy smiled. "True." He then frowned. "I am sorry for your first months, though."

"We promised one another we would never speak of that time again. Let us instead recall your romantic courtship and the lovely times we enjoyed after our misunderstanding was set aside." She reached out and took his hand in hers. Sir Percy responded by placing a tender kiss on her knuckles.

"I am well rebuked, m'dear. I suppose I should have that long put-off interview with me heir." He shook his head. "Ah well, Miss Wentworth will make a fine Lady Blakeney someday. I quite approve of her."

"I am glad you do. Do not be too hard on George." She paused. "Percy, George means to share *everything* with her." Her raised eyebrow left him in no doubt of her meaning.

Sir Percy sucked in his breath through his teeth. "I suppose that is for the best—but gadzooks! I hope she is as trustworthy as she is charming. It appears I have something else I must speak to George about. He has been talking—first Captain Tilney and now Miss Wentworth. I wonder who else knows our business." He rose and made for the door.

"Captain Tilney would learn of it eventually, for Violet loves and wants him. Will you not reconsider—?"

He cut her off. "Margot, I have seen my fault with Captain Tilney and have apologized to him. Until Violet is recovered, that matter is closed. Follow my wishes, I pray you."

Marguerite saw her husband had forestalled her once again. "I disagree with you. I think you need help."

"I will gather all the help I need. Trust me in this."

Pained, Marguerite turned away. "It will be as you say."

"Thank you, m'dear. I have enough on my mind—I do not need to deal with a lovesick soldier, as well. I will see you at dinner. I think I shall have several letters to write."

Chapter 26

apitaine Bourgeois entered M. Lafarge's room to see him engaged in writing a letter. "Forgive me, monsieur," he said to his chief. "I shall return when you are finished."

"No need, Bourgeois." M. Lafarge set down his pen and lightly waved the paper. "I am done. The trap is set. This is my second letter to Blakeney."

Capitaine Bourgeois walked up to the desk. "So, everything is prepared? We are ready?"

"*Oui.* I have *invited* Blakeney to attend us here on or about the tenth of June. We will have a proper welcome for him, I assure you."

"*Bon.* I will be happy to see this matter come to a conclusion."

"Will you?" M. Lafarge regarded the officer with ill-disguised mirth. "Will you be so happy to see the last of Mlle. Blakeney?"

Capitaine Bourgeois could formulate no answer that was neither false nor foolish.

M. Lafarge laughed. "Such a face! It seems the mademoiselle has made a conquest! Do not be sad, *mon ami.* You may still get your heart's desire."

"How can that be, monsieur? Once Blakeney is here, she will be released."

"Perhaps," M. Lafarge said. "It depends on our investigation. It may be discovered she was more involved in this matter than we first believed. She may be imprisoned or held under house arrest. Now, who would be willing to keep a close eye on her, hmm?"

Capitaine Bourgeois fought against his desires. "I thought this was about justice."

M. Lafarge lost all good cheer. "Oh, it is, Bourgeois, it is. Blakeney will get the justice he so richly deserves. I have sworn it and so have you. Do not forget that."

"I will not, monsieur."

"*Bon*. Now leave me to my work. There are many preparations to make."

Richmond

MARGUERITE WALKED INTO HER HUSBAND'S STUDY. "I SAW THE express rider, Percy." She motioned to the letter in her husband's hand. "Is that from Paris?"

Sir Percy looked up, a gleam in his eye that Marguerite had not seen in twenty years. *The game is afoot!* Her stomach sank.

"Yes. It is the official summons for my deposition." He grinned, rubbing his hands together. "I must be in Paris by the tenth of June. Still a few days to finish my preparations."

Marguerite cried, "Do not go alone, I pray you. Take someone with you." At his annoyed glance, she added, "It does not have to be Captain Tilney—just anyone. Take Sir Andrew."

"Ffoulkes is involved, m'love. He is providing the boat, but he cannot come. It states here"—he indicated the letter—"that I must present myself alone at a time and place that will be made known to me once I reach Paris. So, even if I wanted to bring your captain, there is nothing for it."

Marguerite's open distress brought him to his feet. "Now, none of that! Have I not gone to France time and time again and always outfoxed those demmed Frenchies? Have no fear, m'dear."

"But your rheumatism—"

"—will not affect me," he assured her. "I know I cannot handle a sword as I once could, but my plans take that into consideration. I have no need of swords." He smiled. "But, by gad, if I find myself in a pickle, I trust I can still give a good account of myself."

"I fear for you."

Sir Percy became serious. "I know. I wish I could calm your fears. I may be old, Margot, but I still have my wits, and they will see me through this as they always have. I will bring our daughter home."

He kissed her fiercely. Breaking away, he said softly, "I must to London at once to finalize everything. But I shall return ere I depart to take my leave of you, m'lady."

"I shall await you with every regard, Percy. Be safe."

Sir Percy laughed in that high boisterous way she knew so well. "And I shall, for I will return to you!" Another kiss and Marguerite found herself alone in his study.

June: London

A DEPRESSED AND FRUSTRATED FREDERICK TILNEY RELUCTANTLY walked into the already crowded ballroom in his dress blues.

Sir Percy had been firm on the subject of France. He neither needed nor desired his help in recovering Violet. Further argument was useless.

His duties at Horse Guards had grown more distasteful by the day. His company had worked diligently, becoming the best in the regiment. The reward for their dedication was to be left behind while others were dispatched across the Channel to face the menace of Bonaparte.

The fault for both these situations lay in Frederick's own hands, he knew. His irresponsibility had cost him Sir Percy's respect and trust. His taking advantage of favoritism from on high had created personal aversion from his commanding colonel, which led to his company's humiliation.

Frederick would make things right if he could. His frustration lay in the knowledge that it was impossible. That inability led to his despair.

For some foolish reason, Frederick had thought the diversion of a few hours at a dance might ease his pain, and he accepted an invitation to a ball commemorating the great naval victory known as the

Glorious First of June. Upon entering the hall, however, Frederick realized he had made yet another mistake. The room was filled with every example of womanhood to be found in London—old and young, beautiful and plain, married and single, charming and dull, coy and obnoxious, playful and reserved, virtuous and immoral. What it lacked was the only woman he desired: Violet Blakeney.

He saw Lady Victoria Uppercross in a far corner with Mrs. Johnson and an unknown gentleman. The last thing Frederick wanted was to converse with them, so he steered well away from that part of the room. He had finally accepted the example set by John Buford. Since meeting the Blakeneys and being in the company of people of high character, he lost all taste for the so-called fashionable set. Instead, he made directly for the refreshment table.

He was having a second glass of wine, wondering whether he should just leave before the music started, when he noticed Mr. and Mrs. Darcy standing nearby with a young lady. Frederick was not intimately acquainted with the Darcys, but they had been introduced at Buford's wedding. He thought he recognized the young lady with them as Miss Georgiana Darcy.

Colonel Fitzwilliam was Mr. Darcy's cousin, he remembered. Darcy might have news of him and, therefore, Buford, for he should be serving with Fitzwilliam. Frederick had not heard from his friend since the crisis began though the talk at Horse Guards was that Buford had rejoined the —nd Light Dragoons in Belgium as their commanding colonel. Throwing back the rest of his wine, Frederick walked determinedly to greet the master of Pemberley.

Mr. Darcy was reserved and cool. "Captain Tilney, you remember my wife and sister, of course," he said in that distant manner for which he was known. Like everyone in the place, they were well aware of Frederick's reputation. In addition, Mr. Darcy's protection of his sister was legendary in Town. Mrs. Darcy was slightly more engaged, if wary. Miss Darcy spoke not a word.

"I know we are but distantly acquainted," Frederick humbly observed, "and I would not intrude upon you, but I understand Colonel Fitzwilliam is your cousin. May I ask whether you have word of him?"

Mr. Darcy relaxed. "We have indeed. He is quite well. He writes from near Brussels, I believe."

"Did he happen to mention my friend, Sir John Buford?"

"Of course," said Mrs. Darcy. "Our families are related through the Bingleys, you know. Sir John is sharing quarters with our cousin and is also very well."

Frederick smiled. "I am glad to hear it."

Miss Darcy spoke up. "Do you go to the Continent, Captain?"

Frederick colored. "No, Miss Darcy. My company remains with the Household Regiment."

A small frown marred her gentle features. "Why is that?"

"Georgiana, someone must guard the Royal family," said Mrs. Darcy.

The girl blushed at her sister's gentle reprimand. "Forgive me, I meant no insult."

"I am not offended, Miss Darcy," returned Frederick. "Mrs. Darcy is correct, and our assignment is important. Still, I would prefer to be gone."

"You would prefer to fight?"

"No soldier wants to fight. But honor triumphs all."

As he said the words, Frederick realized the truth. His love was held captive in Paris, and his friends were facing Bonaparte in Belgium while he took his ease in London. His honor was diminished. *He* was diminished. It was intolerable!

Some of his thoughts must have been apparent, for Mr. Darcy said, "We all must do our duty, Captain. No one here thinks the less of you."

"Here, here," added Mrs. Darcy.

God bless you both for that! Still, where does my duty truly lie? Frederick glanced around. *Not in a ballroom, and not in London either, that is certain!* "I thank you both. It is time I took my leave. I hope you enjoy the ball."

"Do you not dance, Captain?" asked Miss Darcy.

Frederick smiled. "Not tonight. I should return to Horse Guards."

He did not miss the look shared between the elder Darcys. He could not blame them for their relief that he would not ask Miss Darcy for a set; his reputation was still in tatters.

He was about to bow when Mrs. Darcy, looking over his shoulder, mumbled, "Oh, dear."

Out of the corner of his eye, Frederick saw Lady Victoria Uppercross, now free of her companions, was making her way towards them. He could well understand Mrs. Darcy's displeasure. Victoria Uppercross was no fit acquaintance for an innocent like Miss Darcy. In the same instant, he realized he could be of service.

"Mrs. Darcy, I observe the object of your disquiet, and I quite comprehend your feelings. May I suggest a strategic withdrawal? I would be happy to act as rear guard. I have dealt with her kind before, and we must protect the ladies." He looked pointedly at Miss Darcy.

Mr. Darcy offered a sharp nod. "Quite right. Good night, Captain. We are in your debt."

Frederick bowed. "Think nothing of it. Good night." The Darcys took their leave and moved away, while Frederick turned to intercept Lady Uppercross.

Victoria Uppercross owned a certain cold beauty. She moved with a dancer's grace, her bosom straining against her low neckline. Her thin lips curled in a feral smirk, and her dark eyes were fixed upon him.

Frederick knew Victoria years ago when, for a short time, she was John Buford's paramour. When his comrade left for the Peninsular War, she did not turn to Frederick for comfort, and all contact was broken. He had no regrets; he did not desire the doxy then or now. Apparently, Lady Uppercross had changed her mind.

"Captain Tilney," Lady Uppercross purred. "You are looking very well, I see." Her desire for an assignation was obvious, and his determination to deny her wishes was resolute, no matter how prominently she displayed her excellent assets.

"Thank you, madam." Frederick, stone-faced and cold, had no intention of encouraging the woman. His refusal to return the compliment did not escape her notice. But instead of responding, she attacked the couple who had just left his side.

"I see Mr. Darcy and his little country wife have fled to the refreshment table. Is she afraid of me?"

"I cannot say."

She smirked. "What an odd creature she is. Tell me, did she amaze you with her famous wit or astonish the room with a discussion of Greek literature?"

Frederick noticed they had attracted a small audience, and it occurred to him he could use this confrontation to repair his reputation. "Mrs. Darcy was charming, as always," he said in a voice louder than necessary. "I beg you not to impugn your betters. It is most unseemly."

The reprimand, accompanied by underserved familiarity, broke through Victoria Uppercross's veneer of composure. "*What* did you say?"

"Mrs. Darcy is a true lady in *every* sense of the word," Frederick drawled. "As for you, madam, you have disgraced your title and made yourself one of the celebrated whores in London society."

Stunned by the insult, Lady Uppercross became as white as a sheet. The noise in the rest of the room seemed to fade into nothingness. Frederick's words rang out through the hall—as did the slap they earned.

"How dare you!" Lady Uppercross screamed.

Frederick only smiled. "May I assume that our acquaintance is at an end? Excellent. I am a better man for it. Farewell, Victoria."

With a nod to those assembled, Frederick strode towards the door, refusing to rub his burning cheek. Catching the attention of the astonished Darcys, he paused to bow in their direction before continuing out of the house.

Frederick knew the news of his latest fracas would be in the London papers. By noon tomorrow, all of society would know of the painful insult to his person he suffered in defense of Mrs. Darcy.

He now put all that aside. A resolution had grown in him. He had work to do before morning.

Richmond

FREDERICK HANDED HIS HORSE'S REINS TO A POST BOY AND STRODE up the steps of Blakeney Manor. Despite tossing and turning the night before, he could come up with no better strategy for dealing with Sir Percy. He would demand to see the baronet and refuse to leave until he was given employment in service to Violet. It was not a good plan, but it was all he could conceive.

Damnation, I will insist upon it—League of the Pimpernel or no!

As it was far too early in the day for visitors, he stood outside a full ten minutes after giving his name to a surprised butler. He was about to enter without leave when the door was opened. It was not the butler.

"Lady Blakeney! How do you do this morning?"

"I am well, Captain Tilney," returned the good lady, clearly puzzled by his presence. "Will you come in?"

"Thank you. Forgive me for calling so early, but it is imperative that I speak to Sir Percy."

Lady Blakeney nodded as he walked into the house, and it appeared the news seemed to please her. "Unfortunately, my husband is away on business."

Frederick cursed under his breath and wondered whether he had been too late. "My lady, I beg you, tell me how I may contact him. I wish to be of service to your family."

"I am glad to hear it. I hoped it would be so. George said you would come around."

"That is kind of him. Milady, I do not wish to be impertinent, but pray tell me how to contact Sir Percy."

She glanced at him. "Will you not talk to me?"

"I will do anything you wish, but time is of the essence, is it not?"

"The evening tide will not go out until after midnight," she said mysteriously. "We have time."

They had entered a study, and there on a divan was the recovering George Blakeney. "Frederick!" called out the young man in good cheer. "You see, Mama? I told you."

Lady Blakeney smiled and kissed her son's forehead. "So you did, but enough of self-congratulations. We have much to talk about and little time to do it."

She turned to Frederick. "I will be frank. You said you wish to be of service to my family. Exactly what do you mean by that?" She stood before him, expectant.

"Milady, I can no longer stand by whilst Miss Blakeney is in danger. Consider me your instrument. Give me a task, and if it will help your daughter, I shall see it done—no matter the cost."

"Faith, but those are pretty words, sir. And what reward do you seek?"

Frederick pulled himself to his full height. "Nothing but Miss Blakeney's safe return."

"So you may marry her?"

"No! I-I mean…" Frederick struggled. "Milady, forgive my frankness, but I love your daughter beyond such selfish reasons. If I can do anything—*anything*—to assure her safety and happiness, I will do it."

"Including giving her up?" The lady's eyes bored unmercifully into his.

This was something Frederick had not before considered. It took only a moment for the officer to know his mind. He bowed his head. "Yes. If that is the cost, yes."

He was so wretched and drained he did not know Lady Blakeney had approached until he felt her hand under his chin, lifting it up.

"I believe you," she said softly in the light French accent that over twenty years in England had not extinguished. "And, therefore, I trust you."

Trust. That magical word strengthened him.

Lady Blakeney bid him sit and took a seat next to him. "Captain Tilney, my husband sails for France tonight. He seeks to recover Violet, but I fear a trap. Sir Percy is…is not the man he was." She sadly smiled. "Age has a way of catching up with all of us—even my husband. He is as clever as ever, but as for the rest—" She shrugged.

"I understand, milady," said Frederick. "The League did some marvelous things so many years ago."

"The League? Oh, my!" She glanced at George. "He needs to know."

"I agree," answered her son.

"Know what?" demanded Frederick.

Lady Blakeney turned to him with pride. "Sir Percy Blakeney was more than a member of the League of the Scarlet Pimpernel, Captain Tilney. Much more. Sir Percy *was* the Scarlet Pimpernel!"

"Good God!"

"But even the Pimpernel needs a good, strong right arm. With George wounded and the rest of the League crippled by age, who might that be?" She looked at him in renewed expectation.

A fierce gleam grew in Frederick's eyes as he comprehended her meaning. "That would be me."

Chapter 27

Marguerite and Captain Tilney dashed to Deal after making a short detour to Horse Guards in London, the driver pushing the team as hard as possible. The Blakeney carriage was the finest available, but by the time it reached the harbor in the early hours of the morning, its passengers had suffered greatly. The pair stumbled several times as they navigated the rough cobblestones to reach the dockside.

Their objective was a two-masted sloop. It was small with a narrow beam, built for speed rather than transport. No guns marred the gleaming deck; this was a pleasure yacht. The name *Mid-night Dream* graced its stern. Its master and owner was a familiar figure.

"By Jove, Margot!" cried Sir Andrew Ffoulkes. "I have only just received your express. You have made excellent time."

"Faith, I am happy we arrived in time, though my bones feel every mile!" She embraced her friend. "Is Percy aboard?" she asked in a low voice.

Sir Andrew answered in the same manner. "No, he went ashore for a time, but he will soon return. We sail in a few hours." He turned and shook hands with Captain Tilney. "Good evening to you, Captain. You are a welcome addition to our little band. You are just the bright, strong buck we need!"

"Thank you, sir. I am honored to join you."

"Percy will not welcome the captain's participation, I fear," said Marguerite. "We must get him below."

Sir Andrew hesitated. "He does not know? He will like surprises even less, Margot."

Captain Tilney laughed. "What can he do? Throw me overboard?" He sobered at his companion's grim countenance. "You mean… he *would*?"

Instead of answering, Marguerite spoke to Sir Andrew. "Put the captain below. I will speak to Percy."

Sir Andrew nodded. "Aye. If there is a man or woman alive who can convince Percy to change his mind, it is you, lass."

"Wish me luck, Andrew," she said as she kissed his cheeks. "Godspeed, Captain Tilney, and good hunting."

She saw Captain Tilney pause as though trying to frame something witty to say before deciding a jest was inappropriate for the occasion. He simply snapped to attention and gave her hand a proper bow before following Sir Andrew onto the yacht. Marguerite pulled her cloak tightly about her, raised the hood, and waited on the quay.

It was not long before a tall, powerfully built figure emerged from an alleyway. He was about halfway to the boat before his steps faltered.

"Margot?" Sir Percy hissed.

"My love, I must speak with you ere you go."

"Why are you here?" He approached with determined strides. Once he reached her, he lowered the hood of her cape, stared at her beloved face, and said tenderly, "I took my leave of you at home, my darling."

She embraced him. "Percy, I have brought someone to help."

"Who?"

"Captain Tilney." She heard his sharp intake of breath. "He is in the cabin below decks."

"Margot, what have you done? No! No, he will not come. I will not allow it."

"You need help."

"I need nothing."

"You do, you do need help, and Captain Tilney will come with you. I insist upon it."

"I will not take him."

"Then you will take me."

Sir Percy laughed. "You are not coming!"

"You think not? You think you can stop me? By gad, but you have a failing memory! Have you forgotten that I am a member of the League?"

"The League is no more."

"Is it, Percy? Do you really think so?" She swept her arm towards the boat. "Look there—your old comrade-at-arms, Andrew Ffoulkes, willing to risk life, limb, and his wife's displeasure to help you just because you asked it of him. And the others—oh, yes, I know you have been talking with them, gathering information. Dewhurst and all the rest, willing and happy to assist you in any way! Lud, your own son and even Captain Tilney would follow your every order right into the gates of Hades." She shook her head. "You are wrong, my dear, foolish love. The League still lives, Percy Blakeney, because England still lives. Because *you* still live."

Marguerite could see battling emotions cross his face. Finally, he said, "I cannot have you come, Margot. It is too dangerous this time."

She placed her hands on his strong arms, her eyes commanding his attention. "Then take Captain Tilney." She interrupted his refusal. "Percy, you need help. The Pimpernel is nothing without the League—you know this. You have said so yourself time and time again. The League is your only chance of success, but there are so few of us left. Ffoulkes is too old. All the others are too old. George is hurt and cannot help.

"But Tilney is young and strong and determined. He loves Violet, and he would lay down his life for her. I believe in him, and I trust him. He will follow where you lead. My love, you need him…and he needs you."

Marguerite embraced her husband, her tears falling on his broad chest. "I want my daughter back but not at the cost of losing you. I must have *all* my loves with me, or I cannot go on. Take Captain

Tilney if but for my sake!"

Sir Percy closed his eyes. "Ah, Margot, how can I refuse you?" He sighed. "Very well."

Marguerite and Percy lost themselves in a passionate kiss, and when it came to an end, Marguerite, deep in her husband's embrace, looked intensely into his blue eyes.

"You know this is a trap."

"Of course, it is a trap."

"You have a plan?"

"I do." He grinned slightly. "I may have to adjust it."

A million thoughts crossed Marguerite's mind, but all she said was, "Come back to me."

"Violet will be safe in Merry Olde England before you know it."

"Of that, I have no doubt," she said for his sake. "But I want *you* back too."

"That is my intent." He kissed her again. "Margot, my darling, you must go. I have much to do if I am to be successful."

Marguerite studied his beloved face, memorizing every detail. "I love you," she whispered. She kissed him one last time and broke away, stumbling to the coach, blinded by tears.

FREDERICK JUMPED OUT OF HIS CHAIR AS THE DOOR TO THE CAP-tain's cabin opened, and he watched Sir Percy and Sir Andrew enter the room. He made no sound; instead, he steeled himself for the onslaught that was sure to come. Not for the first time, Sir Percy surprised him.

"Well, sink me! I see there is no telling what sort of riffraff will stow away, eh Ffoulkes? Good evening, Captain Tilney. To what do I owe the honor of your presence, may I ask?"

Frederick bowed to the two gentlemen. "I am here to aid you in your quest, Sir Percy."

"I see you have brought your sword—but what of your wits, sir? Will you not be missed at Horse Guards?"

Frederick stood as tall as he could. "I have resigned my commission in the Blues."

Sir Andrew was startled, and Sir Percy asked incredulously, "You resigned? In the middle of the night?"

"True, my colonel was still abed," Frederick admitted. "I informed the officer of the watch, Lieutenant Brookings, of my intention and left a letter of formal resignation for my commander in his care. In my letter, I recommended that Mr. Brookings, an outstanding officer, assume command of the company in my stead. I have left the Blues in better hands than my own."

"Odd's fish, the army may have a different opinion!" Sir Percy shook his head. "You know this could be considered desertion in time of war?"

"Yes, sir."

"And the punishment can be of the most severe kind?"

Frederick took a deep breath. "That is my understanding. Men have been hung for less."

"By gad, you are rather calm about it!"

"Lad, you should think twice about this," said Sir Andrew.

Frederick stared Sir Percy in the eye. "I am determined to do what I can to rescue Violet. I will no longer stand by while she remains in peril. I well know this is a dangerous mission, and I may not survive. However, should I prove to be successful and see Violet safely home, I intend to immediately surrender myself to the proper authorities. After that, it is in God's hands."

Hard was Sir Percy's look at this speech. "Ffoulkes, pray excuse us."

Sir Andrew hesitated. "Percy—" He stopped at Sir Percy's glare. "It is time to shove off anyway." He turned to Frederick. "I hope you know what you are about, lad. I am glad to see you in any case. I will be on deck." With that, Sir Andrew left the room, closing the door behind him.

Sir Percy's stare made Frederick uncomfortable, but he withstood it. Finally, the baronet said, "By what right do you call my daughter by her Christian name?"

"By her leave, sir. I pledge my sword arm for her defense; she already owns my heart."

Sir Percy rolled his eyes. "Phiff! Pretty words, my good captain.

Wait—I suppose you are no longer a captain. Just what the devil are you now?"

"Son of a gentleman farmer, waiting for his inheritance like so many others. In a word—useless."

Sir Percy laughed at that. "Faith! It is well to see you have not lost your sense of humor! You will need it on this trip."

Frederick brightened at that. Perhaps convincing Sir Percy would not be so difficult after all. "Is there some sort of oath I need take?"

"Eh?"

"I assume I am joining the League of the Scarlet Pimpernel."

"Why do you—?" Sir Percy paused and gasped. "Margot told you?"

"That you are the Pimpernel? Yes. I am honored to serve with you."

"God's life!" Sir Percy cried. "What demmed power do you have over the Blakeneys, Tilney? First George, then Violet, and now me own wife? What have they *not* told you?"

Frederick thought it best to remain silent while the baronet paced about the cabin, rubbing his forehead. "The oath you speak of, Mr. Tilney," he finally allowed, "is one of fealty and *secrecy*. Apparently, that is as old and rusty as the remaining members of my merry band."

"I will take it if you will allow me."

The baronet glanced at him. "No, those days are long gone. Tell me, Tilney, what is it you mean to do?"

"Whatever you wish."

"Including staying on board the *Mid-night Dream*?"

Frederick did not answer, but his sour face told the tale.

Sir Percy gestured at him. "See? How can I trust you if you will not follow orders?"

Frederick was insistent. "I will see Violet safe and will do whatever you say, but I will not be left behind."

"My plans do not include anyone but myself."

"Sir Percy, forgive me, but I have been a soldier long enough to understand two things. One, plans never survive contact with the enemy. Two, never turn down reinforcements."

"You think I need reinforcements?"

"I do not boast when I say I am proficient with the blade."

"Yes, I have seen your skill at fencing." Sir Percy looked about the cabin, leaving Frederick to wonder whether he had heard a slight emphasis on the last word. The baronet removed two staffs hanging on the wall—each a yard long—and handed one to Frederick.

"Will you humor an old man and allow me to test my talents against yours?" Sir Percy said with a smile.

Frederick hefted the length of wood, considering the baronet's odd request. "If you wish."

"Excellent. Shall we?" Sir Percy stepped about six feet away.

Frederick assumed the en guarde position, irritated by the obvious test of his abilities. Suppressing a desire to satisfy his pride and finish off this opponent as quickly as possible, he told himself to treat him carefully. It would not do to shame the man he hoped make his father-in-law.

The two men reached forward until the ends of the staffs just touched. Then, Frederick advanced in a *froissement*, trying to displace Sir Percy's staff using a strong grazing action. It was different from using a foil, Frederick immediately discovered. The balance of the wood was all wrong. Still, by paying close attention to Sir Percy's response, Frederick intended to gauge the baronet's abilities. Sir Percy successfully parried and answered with a riposte of middling quality. Frederick gave a bit of ground, setting up the second intention. The moment was there, he feinted, but Frederick's change of engagement was met with a beat. Suddenly Sir Percy pressed, and in the next instant, the two were *corps-à-corps*—body-to-body with the baronet's left thumb jammed hard against Frederick's right side.

"A hit, Captain," he whispered.

Frederick shoved the older man away. "That was illegal, sir!"

"Indeed it was—in *fencing*," Sir Percy replied. "In fighting, there are no rules. Had I a blade in my hand, you would be dead."

Frederick tossed the staff away in disgust. "You play games with me! I assure you, I know how to fight!"

"Do you? I suppose you mean your duels." Sir Percy's staff joined the other. "That you have won them all speaks of your skill, I will allow. But exactly how much danger were you in? I know no one has died as a result of your duels, thank the Lord. But do you truly know what you are about?"

"I remind you that I was trained as a soldier."

"Yes, but it is not an insult to point out that you have never seen battle."

Frederick turned white. He had hoped never to speak of this. "Your information is not correct, sir."

"Indeed? I know for a fact you have never left Britain."

"You know I was in the Twelfth. Do you recall the Luddite riots in the north about five years ago?"

"I do. You were there?"

"Yes." Frederick swallowed and turned his mind back to his nightmare. "The riots were scattered all over Nottinghamshire and Yorkshire. I was a lieutenant serving in a company charged with guarding a storehouse when, one evening, a mass of starving people approached. My captain ordered us forward to break up the mob." He turned to the stern window. "We used the flat of our swords—we only wanted them to disperse—but when one man with a sickle threatened my horse, I…I acted in the only manner that would serve. His screams were terrible. The mob broke after that." He paused. "The man was a tenant farmer, and he left a wife and three children, I understand." He looked at Sir Percy, pain and anger clear in his face. "In the same situation, I would do it again. Does that satisfy you?"

Sir Percy colored and looked at the deck. "My apologies. A bad business, that, but I would think you had no other option." He looked up and saw Frederick's face. "You disagree?"

"My commanders spoke as you do, but I had the misfortune to come across the man's funeral a few days later. I do not know what grieved the family more: that they lost their loved one or that their only means of survival had been taken away. People died of starvation that winter. I cannot help but think it was not a fair fight—a trained soldier with horse and sword against a desperate peasant. I try not to dwell on it, as you can see."

"You have not the heart of a soldier."

"Not if that means I must kill without remorse. My brother has told me I am meant to be a farmer, and I shall be one when I come into my inheritance. But until then, it is my father's wish that I follow in his footsteps."

"Until now."

"Yes. From now on, I am my own man. Take me with you, Sir Percy. I shall serve you and protect you. You shall not regret it."

"Protect me?"

"Forgive me, but Lady Blakeney has told me of your infirmity."

"She did, did she? Bah! I just bested you!"

"By trickery. Would you like to try again? I warn you that I will be ready for you." Frederick's demeanor spoke of his determination not to be fooled again.

Sir Percy flexed his hand. "You are a cocky bastard when you want to be."

"Only confident in my abilities. Look at me as your troops, my commander."

"You will do as I say? Without question?"

"I swear it. You are the Pimpernel. Where you lead, I will follow."

Sir Percy stared at Frederick for a long moment. The former captain of dragoons knew he was being judged.

A sharp movement of the boat almost caused the gentlemen to lose their footing.

"Forsooth!" said Sir Percy good-naturedly. "It seems that Ffoulkes has set sail. I suppose I am well stuck with you, Tilney, as it is too late for you to go ashore. Come—sit and have a drink. We have much to discuss."

Frederick took his seat gladly and thanked the baronet as the older man withdrew a bottle and two glasses from a cupboard. Once the drinks were poured, Sir Percy offered a toast.

"To the king—and confusion to those demmed Frenchies!"

"To your not throwing me overboard," added Frederick.

"'Tis not too late," Sir Percy murmured before he drank, almost causing Frederick's whiskey to go down the wrong way.

"So, what is the plan? What are we to do?" asked Frederick eagerly.

"The plan, Tilney, is shot to pieces, thanks to your presence." He tapped his forehead with a finger. "I am adjusting the details even now. But there are things I can tell you—things you need to know."

"Before we start, I would be honored if you would call me Frederick."

"Very well, Frederick. I will ask you a question. What is the most deadly weapon in the world?"

Many ideas came to Frederick's mind, but he just as quickly dismissed them. He knew Sir Percy was trying to tell him something important. "I cannot think of just one."

Sir Percy leaned over the table. "It is the mind—a well-trained human brain. It can overcome mountains, rivers, cannons, armies. Any plan that can be devised can be defeated. Brute force is nothing. You must always *think*, Frederick. I have been successful because I have always out-witted my enemies. It is one of the great secrets of the Pimpernel."

Frederick nodded. "And the others?"

"There is only one more secret. Always do the unexpected. That is the basis of my plan for the rescue of Violet."

"What is it you mean to do?"

Sir Percy grinned. "Surrender."

Chapter 28

The *Mid-Night Dream* sailed a whole day and night to a point off the French coast near Saint-Malo, taking great care to avoid detection by French coast watchers. There was no fear of the French fleet, for it had been suppressed and blockaded by the Royal Navy.

"George made a mistake, going so close to Calais," Sir Percy told Frederick as they watched the shore in the far distance, the afternoon sun peeking through the partly cloudy skies. "French agents are as thick as thieves there and near the Channel Islands too. Brittany is much better. The people here in Saint-Malo are an independent folk: privateers and devout Catholics with no love of Paris. They will keep our secrets as long as we bring gold."

Frederick thought about that. "Privateers *and* devout? That seems an odd mixture."

Sir Percy laughed. "They are an odd people. I quite like them."

Frederick smiled in return. During the voyage, over discussions of plans and tactics, Frederick had earned a measure of respect and even admiration from Sir Percy. To pass the time when not plotting, the two told stories about themselves. Frederick spoke of the scrapes he and John Buford had gotten into while mere lieutenants, and the baronet, along with Sir Andrew, regaled Tilney with tales of the Pimpernel.

Camaraderie had grown between the men, and Frederick felt a sense of belonging in Sir Percy's company that he had never enjoyed with General Tilney. *This* was the type of fellowship he wished to have with his own father and did not.

Violet's rescue was paramount in Frederick's mind, but there was a new sensation growing too. Frederick was determined to support and serve his leader and new friend. The idea of disappointing Sir Percy was unbearable now.

After dark, the two, accompanied by Sir Andrew, were rowed ashore in the ship's launch. A secluded cove served as their landing spot. They quickly disembarked, each carrying a pair of carpetbags.

Sir Percy shook his friend's hand. "Get word to Margot that we have landed safely, Ffoulkes. Keep to the schedule. I have no idea how long we will be."

"As soon as I touch England, an express will be sent to Richmond, never fear." Sir Andrew turned to Frederick with a stern look. "Watch out for my old friend, or you will answer to me."

"Aye, aye, Captain," Frederick said with a grin. "I will not let him out of my sight."

"Odd's fish, I do not require a nursemaid, Ffoulkes," Sir Percy grumbled.

"So you say," Sir Andrew responded. "I know better. Godspeed, gentlemen. Shove off, boys," he said to the boat crew. The two watched the small craft disappear into the murk before Sir Percy spoke again.

"*N'oubliez pas de parler français à partir de maintenant,*[7] Frederick. You need the practice."

Frederick answered in the same language. "*Et je dois aussi me souvenir que je suis votre serviteur,*[8] monsieur. Should I carry your baggage?"

"Not for the moment. Your clothing reveals your station as servant well enough."

Frederick wore a rough white shirt under the plain black coat

---

7 Remember to speak French from now on.
8 And I also remember that I am your servant.

of a servant while the baronet was dressed in his usual fashionable style. The two moved inland off the long, flat beach, climbed past the rocks, and took refuge in a patch of trees and scrub brush. They waited, seated on an overturned log.

The night stretched on, but thanks to his training, Frederick sat patiently. The army had its measure of hurry-up-and-wait, and he developed an ability to be deep in contemplation while keeping his senses alert. He reviewed the details of Sir Percy's plan, and while impressed with its audacity, he could not like it. Frederick was a man who preferred to attack things straight on. It went against the grain to have so much dependent upon the work of others. Too many things could go wrong.

He glanced at his companion, awed at his calm countenance. If Frederick had not known better, he could imagine the baronet was fishing in a stream at Richmond. The tales of the Pimpernel said he was a master of disguise. Surely, that would require great fortitude, serenity, and intelligence.

I have chosen to follow the Pimpernel. I must put my trust in his abilities. Follow the plan, Frederick, follow the plan.

About an hour after they landed, they heard a soft noise from inland. Sir Percy put a finger to his lips and then pointed at the long bundle at their feet. Frederick quietly removed his sword from the bundle as Sir Percy stood, turned around, and crept towards the sound.

Frederick rose to his feet, sheathed sword in hand, shoulders tense. Time had no meaning as he strained to hear. Then, a whistle—the tune the first six notes of "God Save the King." Frederick relaxed and followed in Sir Percy's wake.

He found the gentleman standing by a cart, a short man beside him holding the reins to the team of horses. Sir Percy waved him closer. "Frederick, this is the man who will get us to Paris. His family is known to me. His late uncle helped me many years ago."

"*Oui*," said the man. "My uncle was a victim of *la Révolution* —forced to steal to live. They branded him with the 'M' of a criminal. M. Blakeney helped my family during *la Terreur* and afterwards. My uncle used the gold from monsieur to buy a farm where my family lives today. Monsieur knew him as Rateau. I would ask you call me the same."

Sir Percy patted the man on the shoulder. "Your uncle was a good man. I am sorry he is gone." Frederick gasped as Sir Percy pulled up his sleeve to reveal an M-shaped scar. "I had to have this done the last time I was here to fool the demmed Frenchies," he said in English. "Rateau swore I was his brother after I did that. It is well for us his family does not forget."

Frederick was flabbergasted. Sir Percy—a baronet and knight, particular friend of the Regent, and one of the wealthiest men in the kingdom—had suffered to be branded like a common thief to accomplish a mission? *Would I do the same?* he asked himself. He did not know. Frederick's determination not to fail Sir Percy increased threefold.

"Messieurs," said Rateau, "we must not remain. The patrols, they are everywhere."

"Frederick," said Sir Percy, "before we retrieve our belongings, we shall change into more…rustic garb."

Rateau handed a bundle to Frederick, and he followed Sir Percy back into the woods. They found their carpetbags, but instead of picking them up, the two changed into peasant clothing.

"We cannot let the Frenchies know where we came ashore, so we shall play-act as farmers," Sir Percy said as they dressed. "Rateau will carry us up to the Calais Road where *Sir Percy and his servant* will reappear with more suitable transportation. The Frenchies will think we slipped past them at the port."

"Meanwhile, our back door out of France remains hidden," observed Frederick. "Brilliant. How long before we arrive in Paris?"

"We will travel this night and rest. On Wednesday, we will start for Paris. Rateau has arranged a carriage for us. I believe we will reach the city by Thursday evening." The baronet looked at his companion. "Sink me, you are far too clean, m'boy. While I appreciate the lack of stench, it will not do! We must be a little disgusting, what? Rub a bit of dirt on your face before you gather the bags."

He demonstrated, dirtying his hands and running them over his cheeks and forehead. "We must be as unassuming as possible."

Frederick followed suit as Sir Percy continued. "Remember, we must give no indication that we are English until Paris. Speak French from now on." He hefted his carpetbags. "Onward, mon ami!"

The two made their way back to Rateau's cart.

Paris

THE LAST NOTES OF THE SONATA SOFTLY DIED IN THE AFTERNOON air, interrupted by the sound of applause. "That was beautiful, mademoiselle!" cried *Capitaine* Bourgeois.

"Merci beaucoup, Honoré," said Violet.

"What is the name of the piece?"

"*Moonlight*, by Herr Beethoven. It is one of my favorites."

Violet was still uncomfortable calling the *capitaine* by his given name even after a month, but she made herself do it. She needed all the friends she could find in this place. Lafarge was her true enemy, and if she could earn *Capitaine* Bourgeois's empathy, she might yet devise a way to escape.

"A shame this Beethoven is not French," he said. "His music touches the soul." He rose from the sofa. "I understand he dedicated one of his symphonies to the emperor."

Violet chose not to remind him that Herr Beethoven had withdrawn the dedication for the Third Symphony before the piece had premiered because the composer was outraged over Bonaparte making himself a king.

"I enjoy listening to you," *Capitaine* Bourgeois continued. "Perhaps you might favor me with another song after dinner?"

Violet picked through her sheets of music. "After dinner? Perhaps. When do you eat?"

"I-I," Bourgeois stuttered. Violet was amazed the *capitaine* seemed downright timid. "I thought we might dine together."

The *capitaine's* words sent a bolt of fear through Violet. Her tolerance of Bourgeois's attentions had encouraged the man—something that was dangerous. It was a complication she did not need. She wanted his friendship but nothing more. What would *Capitaine* Bourgeois do when he learned his feelings were not returned? At best, her chance of escape was gone. At worst—could he act as badly as the man Bernard?

Before she could fashion an answer, there was a knock on the door. *"Vous pouvez entrer,"* *Capitaine* Bourgeois called out.

A guard came in. *"Capitaine*, M. Lafarge requests your attendance."

The officer grimaced, and Violet prayed he did not know how relieved she was at the news. "I shall be down directly." *Capitaine* Bourgeois turned to Violet. "I must go. Until later, Mlle. Violet."

She watched him go, trembling. At least he had not tried to kiss her hand! But what would happen if he returned before dinner? What could she do?

"Mademoiselle, are you well?" asked Claudette. Violet did not answer, but the maid plainly saw her mistress's distress. "He is a handsome man, *oui*, but he is not the one, *n'est pas?* Do not fear. I shall not leave you alone. I promise."

"Merci beaucoup, Claudette. I do not know what I would do without you."

The maid's lips tightened. "I do not know why you are here. There has been a great mistake, I think."

Violet gripped Claudette's hand tightly. "Could you help me? Could you get word to my cousins in Paris?"

"Non. I am followed, you see. I wish I could do something, but…" She shrugged.

"I know," Violet said sadly. "I wish you could too."

"YOU WANTED TO SEE ME, MONSIEUR?" BOURGEOIS SAID AS HE entered the third-floor room.

"Oui," said an irate M. Lafarge. "What have you heard from your people watching the ports? Anything?" Told that there had been no reports, the old man cursed. "Blakeney was supposed to be in France three days ago! Where the devil is he?"

Bourgeois pursed his lips. "Perhaps he did not come?"

"And abandon his daughter? Impossible! I know him. He must

be here. Redouble your efforts! Tell those lazy fools at the coast—"

They were interrupted by a knock on the door. "What is it?" M. Lafarge barked.

One of M. Lafarge's men came in bearing a letter. "This just came for you, monsieur."

M. Lafarge nearly tore it out of the man's hand and opened it. *"Merde!"* he breathed. He leapt to his feet and took the frightened guard by the shirt. "Who brought this? Where is he?"

"It…it was a man—short, unremarkable. He left—"

The old man's eyes were aflame. "Damnation! You incompetent imbecile! Get some men and find him!" The guard hurried out of the room as Lafarge fell back into his chair.

Bourgeois could restrain his curiosity no longer. "What has happened?"

M. Lafarge looked up at the officer. "Blakeney is in Paris." He tossed the letter to Bourgeois, who looked at it for a moment before returning it to his chief.

"It is in English. I cannot read it."

M. Lafarge grunted and translated:

My dear M. Lafarge,
  They seek him here, they seek him there,
  those Frenchies seek him everywhere.
  Is he in heaven or is he in hell?
  No—but if you call at the Hôtel __,
  I will be available after dinner.

Cordially,
SIR PERCY BLAKENEY, BART.

The old man angrily tossed the note on the desk. "You see? He mocks us."

Bourgeois frowned. "The Hôtel __? He did not go to his wife's cousin's house?"

"We have been watching the wrong place!" M. Lafarge glowered at the letter. "He thinks he is clever, but we have some surprises for him yet. He has fooled me for the final time."

"He did not send this to the ministry," Bourgeois observed. "He knew where we were. How did he find us?"

"I do not know." M. Lafarge slammed a fist on the desk. "It matters not! We have him now. After twenty years, the quest ends tonight!"

"Should I go arrest him?"

"No, not yet. Let him eat his last meal. We must prepare a fitting welcome for *Le Mouron Rouge*." M. Lafarge stroked his beard.

Excitement warred with sorrow in Bourgeois's breast. "I suppose I should let mademoiselle know to pack her things."

"She is not leaving," M. Lafarge barked.

"But monsieur! You said—"

"Silence! You will not question my orders! Mlle. Blakeney leaves when I say she does and not a moment before!"

Bourgeois was taken aback at this apparent betrayal, but his military training ran too deep for him to protest aloud.

"Go prepare the men," M. Lafarge ordered. "I have work to do."

Bourgeois hesitated a moment before slowly nodding, turning on his heel, and striding to the door. As he left, he heard M. Lafarge tell a servant he wanted a bath and a shave.

Chapter 29

"Que diable, Frederick!" cried Sir Percy as he tied his cravat in the mirror over the hotel room dressing table. "Stop that demmed pacing. You will wear out the carpet."

Frederick halted and watched with amusement as Sir Percy labored to achieve his usual sartorial splendor. He had to wonder at the man. From their long discussions aboard the *Mid-night Dream*, he knew Sir Percy assumed the guise of a foppish nincompoop during his days as the Scarlet Pimpernel to throw off the suspicions of French spies and British traitors.

That was twenty years ago. By his own admission, Sir Percy had given up adventuring and applied himself to the care and advancement of his family and estates. Yet, he still played the part. There was never a time Frederick could recall that Sir Percy was not dressed faultlessly.

The baronet was undoubtedly clever and brave. His plans balanced on the edge between genius and madness. Frederick wondered whether this was the one time the Pimpernel made a mistake. It was simply bizarre that, before Sir Percy walked straight into the clutches of his mysterious adversaries, he was perfecting the look of his cravat! Where did the fop end and the Pimpernel begin? Could it be they were eternally one and the same?

Finally satisfied with his appearance, Sir Percy turned to his companions. His eyes, behind his spectacles, were obscured by the glare from the oil lamp on the dressing table. The baronet looked rather unearthly.

"Are you troubled, Frederick?"

"*Oui*, I must admit I am. This plan is beyond perilous. For you to go in alone—"

"M. Blakeney, a coach has arrived," interjected Rateau from his post by the window. "A man with a floppy hat has descended from it and is making for the front door of the hotel."

"How would you describe the man?" asked Frederick.

Shrewd eyes met his. "I could not see his face. He wears a soldier's coat, but he is certainly not one. He is too careless in his carriage. He does not walk like you, monsieur. You—you place each step right where you intend."

"Sloppy, eh?"

"Enough of that," said Sir Percy. "Everyone to their places. He will be here in a moment."

"Sir Percy, perhaps—"

"It is far too late for changes, Frederick. Follow the plan."

THE STREET BEFORE THE HÔTEL ⸺ WAS LIT ONLY BY THE OIL LAMPS framing the entrance, but it was enough light to see two men exit the building and climb into the coach. One was a well-dressed gentleman, the other a soldier in a floppy hat. Once the coach door was shut, the driver set off down the street.

A shadowy form at the corner of the hotel building stepped back away from the street and into the darkness beyond. A moment later, he reappeared on horseback and followed the coach from some distance behind. Where it turned, he turned, the rider not losing ground or gaining.

Up and down the dark streets of Paris, this strange parade traveled until, near the ruins of *la Bastille,* the coach came to a stop before a narrow, four-story building in the middle of a block of decaying houses. The shadow on horseback did not hesitate. He rode slowly up the lane and surreptitiously watched as the gentleman and the floppy-hatted soldier went inside the tall building.

Without another glance, the horseman rode off into the gloomy Parisian night.

Capitaine Bourgeois waited anxiously in the lobby of La-farge's building. He remained neither comfortable nor content with the men his chief had assembled. True, they had acted better since the incident with Bernard. Whatever happened to *him* seemed to terrify the remaining guards. Some had been replaced, but overall, they were still slovenly and insolent. They would not even remove the hats from their heads in the presence of their betters without a direct order. Oh, if only he had a free hand with them! Two weeks and a few lashings and he would turn them all into proper soldiers.

Bourgeois did not know all the men by sight—they seemed to come and go so often. It did not bother him. They were not soldiers, therefore they were not worthy of his notice. Only lately had Bourgeois begun to wonder who the devil they really were.

One of them, a greasy specimen if ever there was one, called out. "The coach is back, *mon Capitaine*."

Finally! "Excellent. Stand back and give them room."

A minute later, the recipient of his thoughts for over a year walked into the lobby as though he owned it, the guard Bourgeois sent to fetch him close behind. The man babbled something in English.

"*Parlez français,* monsieur." Bourgeois ordered the Englishman. He turned to the guard. "Have you searched him?"

The man shook his head. Bourgeois rolled his eyes, cursed under his breath, and conducted the search himself. As he accomplished his task, he noted that the old man was taller than he had anticipated and more powerfully built than his fine clothes revealed. Indeed, based only on appearances—from his expensive coat and intricate cravat to his bored countenance—the man seemed just another useless aristocrat.

Satisfied that the man was unarmed, he asked, "You are Sir Percy Blakeney?"

The fool stifled a yawn. "I was when I left England, *old man*. I had a devil of a trip. Dreadful country!"

Bourgeois had no idea just what an *old man* was, but he trusted it was some sort of insult.

Sir Percy looked down his nose at him. "Are you to bring me to my daughter?"

"*Oui.* You will come with me."

"*Très bien.* I would prefer your company to some of these others." He looked at the assembled guards. "A fellow might get something catching from your friends," he said as he waved a handkerchief before his nose.

This creature is the feared Mouron Rouge? I cannot believe it! Swallowing his indignation, Bourgeois waved at M. Blakeney's guard, who was still wearing his confounded hat to Bourgeois's annoyance, to accompany them. Bourgeois led the way, the guard behind, and the prisoner sandwiched between.

VIOLET SAT ON THE SOFA, NERVOUSLY WATCHING M. LAFARGE at the desk. She was surprised when the man came into the room and commandeered the only table in the apartment. When he dismissed Claudette, she grew frightened. Now, observing the man's agitation, she knew something of importance was going to happen.

One thing puzzled her. Why did M. Lafarge shave off his beard? It certainly did not improve his looks; in fact, he appeared more sinister than before.

The large windows behind M. Lafarge were open, but not a breath of air relieved the stuffiness of the room. The apartment felt hot, close, and oppressive.

Just then, there was a noise at the door. M. Lafarge froze, straightened his coat, touched his cravat, and took a deep breath. "Come in," he called out.

The door swung open, and everything after that seemed to move very slowly. *Capitaine* Bourgeois came in, his eyes lingering on her form before he stepped to the side to allow entrance to another man. The air in Violet's lungs disappeared. She could not breathe. She could not speak. She could not move.

For walking into the room was a tall, broad-shouldered man

with white hair, glasses perched on his aristocratic nose. His coat and breeches were black, but his vest was a riot of color. His cravat was fastened in an elaborate knot perfectly tied at his throat. But what drew her attention were his bright blue eyes, fixed upon hers —eyes she knew as well as her own.

"Papa!" she finally gasped.

"Violet, m'love," Sir Percy said softly.

Violet finally recovered her wits. "Papa! Papa, run away! It is a trap!"

Sir Percy grinned. "I have come to bring you home, m'dear. Are you ready to go?"

"Not so fast, Sir Percy," M. Lafarge said in English.

Violet saw her father start, and he slowly turned to the man still seated behind the desk, the smile sliding from his dear countenance.

M. Lafarge smiled malevolently. "Surprised to see me?"

Sir Percy's jaw dropped, and his face turned deathly pale.

"Chauvelin!"

Chapter 30

Sir Percy's cry rang through the night air of the gloomy room. Violet was confused. Her father remained frozen still, his shocked countenance clearly visible to all. *Capitaine* Bourgeois, standing a few feet behind Sir Percy, wore a baffled expression as he gazed at their captive. As for M. Lafarge, the man only laughed!

"Excellent! You remember me!" he said in English. "I am flattered."

Sir Percy blinked. "Odd's fish, are you a ghost?"

"Perhaps I am. I have come back to haunt you for your crimes against France, Blakeney."

Violet's world spun. Raised as she was on the adventures of the Scarlet Pimpernel, she knew very well the name of *Citoyen* Chauvelin—the dangerous, clever, and ill-dressed nemesis of the Pimpernel, the fiend who had captured her mother and threatened her father time after time, and whose wickedness could only be defeated by her papa's derring-do. *Citoyen* Chauvelin was the stuff of her nightmares.

Violet found her voice. "Papa, why do you call this man Chauvelin? You told me *Citoyen* Chauvelin was dead."

Sir Percy's eyes never left his enemy. "Sink me, I thought he was. So you are Lafarge now?"

"Yes, for the last twenty years I have been Lafarge, waiting and plotting to have my revenge upon you. This is a happy day, Blakeney."

"My God," cried Violet. "I was right. You are a monster!"

Citoyen Chauvelin turned his cruel eyes on her. "If doing what

I must to protect my country and satisfy my honor makes me a monster, Miss Blakeney, then so be it." He laughed again. "You are your mother's daughter—just as amusingly emotional."

The man's nasty slur against Lady Blakeney removed all doubt in Violet's mind. Somehow, Chauvelin had survived the aftermath of the Terror and had waited patiently for twenty years for his opportunity to bedevil the Blakeney family again.

Sir Percy seemed to recover. "Well, you have what you want. Let my daughter go, and do with me as you will."

"Papa, no!"

Chauvelin smiled. "Why, Sir Percy, you have just been reunited with your daughter. You would want her to quit your company so soon? I thought better of you." His face darkened. "I assure you, other fathers given your opportunity would not be so unfeeling."

Sir Percy continued as though he were negotiating the purchase of a horse. "Come, *Citoyen*, your argument is with me, not her. Let her go."

Chauvelin waved him off. "*Citoyen*—bah! That title is as dead as the Revolution, Blakeney. And as for your daughter's fate, that is entirely in my hands." He smiled again—an evil, cruel smile. "However, I should be happy to hear you beg for her. Pray continue; it would be most diverting."

Violet grew angry. "Papa, no! Do not do as he says! I would not leave you alone with this horrible man." She turned to the man she now knew was Chauvelin. "You disgust me."

"Your opinion means nothing to me."

During all this time, a visibly confused *Capitaine* Bourgeois had been standing halfway to the door. "Monsieur," the *capitaine* finally said, "what would you have me do? Should I silence the prisoner?"

Chauvelin glared at him. "You have searched him, have you not?" he snapped in French.

"*Oui.*"

"*You* have searched him—*personally*?"

Capitaine Bourgeois was clearly offended by his superior's tone. "That was your order, and I have followed it to the letter."

"*Très bien*. This man is devious. We cannot take any chances." Chauvelin then spoke English to Sir Percy. "Sit down, Blakeney. We shall be here for some time."

Sir Percy assumed a bored countenance. "I imagine so. Lud, I was wondering when you would recall your manners." Sir Percy crossed by Violet, gave her an encouraging smile, and took a chair on the far side of the room. He crossed his legs, acting as though he had not a care in the world. "I see the years have done nothing for your sense of fashion, sir. Did a blind man tie your cravat?"

Chauvelin showed his teeth. "Mock me all you wish, Blakeney. It will do you no good. I will have the final laugh this time!"

Just then, the front door opened and one of the guards entered. He was disheveled. His uniform jacket hung loosely on his bent frame while a floppy hat hid his features.

"What are you doing in here?" *Capitaine* Bourgeois bellowed. "I told you to stay without! Why can you not follow simple orders? And why are you still wearing that damned hat?"

Before the guard said anything, Sir Percy cried in French, "Bonjour! It is my friend from the carriage!" He turned to *Capitaine* Bourgeois. "Are you in charge of this rabble, monsieur? I know you Frogs do not think much of bathing, but really! Where did you find him—in a pig sty?"

The next moment, a hat struck *Capitaine* Bourgeois in the face, and the room exploded in shouts.

"What is the meaning of this?" Chauvelin roared.

"Oh, jolly good toss," said Sir Percy.

Stunned, all eyes flew to the guard, who looked quite different now that the uniform jacket lay in a heap on the floor. He stood tall in a white shirt and black breaches, a scabbarded sword at his waist. Standing feet apart and fists by his side, he glowered, his eyes aflame, loose blond hair falling to his shoulders.

Violet could not believe her eyes. "Frederick!"

"You will release Sir Percy Blakeney and his daughter into my custody tout de suite!" Frederick Tilney ordered, one hand fingering his sword.

"Who the devil are you?" demanded Chauvelin.

Frederick raised his chin. "I am Frederick Tilney, *capitaine* of Hussars in the service of his Britannic majesty, George III. These people present are citizens of *la Grande-Bretagne*. In the name of the King, surrender them this moment or face the consequences!"

"Frederick?" snarled *Capitaine* Bourgeois. His eyes shot to Violet. She could not hide her feelings, and the Frenchman grew enraged. "You made a great mistake coming here, *salaud d'anglais!* Hello, the guard!" he bellowed at the closed door. *"J'ai besoin d'aide!"*

One side of Frederick's mouth curled up. "Are you calling for help, monsieur? I am sorry. It seems your friend outside is taking a nap in a closet at the moment. He is all tied up, you might say. Your other friends on the ground floor, I do not think they can hear you, for they are too busy drinking. Good help is hard to find, what?"

"I need no help, *salaud!*" *Capitaine* Bourgeois drew his saber.

With a single, elegant motion, Frederick's sword leapt from its scabbard and cut the air, the light from the candles and lamps glistening on the blade. "I was told you Frogs were all cowards —hiding behind old men and young ladies, after all."

"Arrghh!" screamed *Capitaine* Bourgeois, and he came on Frederick at a run, his saber high in the air. He swung with all his might at the Englishman, but the captain's sword blocked him expertly, and the battle began in earnest.

The air was filled with the grunt of exertion and the clink of metal on metal as the two captains fought in mortal combat. The Frenchman was large and broad-shouldered, and he took great swipes with his saber. Frederick Tilney's slimmer build hid wire-taut powerful muscles as he danced on the balls of his feet, expertly blocking one attack after another.

This was not a battle to Frederick's liking. The Frenchman fought with a much heavier blade than the Englishman's short sword. Frederick's elegant weapon, forged of the finest steel, was designed for thrusting with the point, while his enemy's crude saber could cut him in half with a slash. The room, filled with furniture, made a poor battlefield; there was precious little ground to relinquish while looking for chinks in the Frenchman's defenses.

The most onerous restriction was that Frederick could not kill his opponent. Sir Percy had insisted they carry out their mission without bloodshed. How Frederick was to accomplish that while this brute tried to murder him vexed Tilney no end.

Frederick did have some advantages, however. His mind was free of all emotion. He was calm and focused on the task before him. He was in his element, and he could fall back onto years of training and duels.

Meanwhile, his opponent was enraged, fighting as hard as he could. Blind anger often led to crucial mistakes. The greater weight of the heavy saber would tire his enemy quickly. Frederick's lighter short sword handled like a foil, and he could peel a grape with a foil. Victory was possible if the Englishman could survive the next few minutes.

"You have me at a disadvantage, monsieur," Frederick said after parrying a particularly aggressive attack. "You know who I am. I would hate to kill a man whose name is unknown to me."

Bourgeois, panting, gritted his teeth. "*Je suis le Capitaine* Honoré Bourgeois, English dog! The only one dying today is you!" Bourgeois moved in, but his slippery opponent avoided him yet again. "Stand still and fight, *poltron!*"

"Interesting," Frederick said with a smirk. "You call me a coward, yet you are the one who kidnaps young ladies. It is not surprising since you Frogs have a different idea about honor."

"*Salaud!*" *Capitaine* Bourgeois yelled, but his attack was foiled again. Suddenly, they were body to body, two strong men grappling with each other. Sweat flowed into Bourgeois's eyes, but Frederick was unaffected by the combat.

"If you have touched Mlle. Blakeney, you French bastard," Frederick growled at Bourgeois, "I shall kill you." As he said those words, Frederick knew it was no lie, Sir Percy's orders be damned.

"She has been safe with me," Bourgeois shot back, "and she will be well cared for after I dispose of you!"

Frederick smiled and kicked Bourgeois in the knee. The Frenchman fell back with a grunt of pain, raising his saber just in time to parry the Englishman's thrust.

"Bourgeois, enough of this foolishness!" cried Chauvelin. "Finish him!"

Capitaine Bourgeois, panting and favoring his injured leg, lowered his head, staring at his opponent. He grew calmer and waved his free hand at the Englishman. "Come again, monsieur, if you are not afraid."

Frederick assumed an exaggerated en garde position. "Will this do?" he taunted.

Bourgeois huffed and attacked. Once again, Frederick successfully blocked, but his counter-parry failed badly. Falling back, he reconsidered his foe. *Capitaine* Bourgeois was now far more deliberate, reserving his strength, showing more skill than before. That did not bode well for Frederick. He knew he had to finish this fight *now*.

"There are no rules in fighting," Sir Percy had advised him. *"Always do the unexpected."*

Frederick recalled a favorite counter-attack from his duels. Could that serve? To use it required that he bring the French *capitaine* closer—*much* closer. It would take all his skill to survive.

A few passes and Frederick slowed his attack slightly. As he expected, Bourgeois took that as a sign he was weakening. The Frenchman drew on his last reserves and pressed his attack, causing Frederick to retreat quickly.

Frederick was soon out of room. He stumbled. He was on one knee.

"Now! Now!" shouted Chauvelin.

Bourgeois, grinning in triumph, raised his blade to deliver the killing blow.

Violet screamed in terror.

At the last possible instant, Frederick flicked his short sword upward, its point sinking into the Frenchman's descending arm just above the elbow, using the same move he used over a year ago.

Capitaine Bourgeois cried out as his saber fell from his nerveless hand. The next moment, Frederick grasped his enemy by the shirt collar, holding the Frenchman up, the point of his sword against his opponent's throat.

Blazing eyes filled with death stared the Frenchman in the face. Frederick snarled in a dangerous voice, "Violet, did his man harm you?"

"No!" gasped Violet in relief. "*Non*, Frederick, *mon amour*, he did not. He protected me."

Frederick blinked and glanced at his beloved for an instant. "Did he?"

"Yes. The guards—he protected me from the guards."

A calmer Frederick returned his attention to the exhausted man before him. Even in defeat, *Capitaine* Bourgeois did not cower.

"You are fortunate, monsieur. Will you yield?"

Fear and resignation painted Bourgeois's face. "Do your worst, *Anglais*. I will not surrender to you."

Frederick saw blood running down the Frenchman's right arm. "You will bleed to death, monsieur. Will that help your misbegotten country? Do not be a fool! I come not to conquer but to retrieve what is mine. I only want to take Violet and her father far away from this place and never return. You can have France, and go to the devil, for all I care." He shook the man. "What will it be? Will you die for your pride or live for France? Decide!"

He saw Bourgeois's eyes move to Violet's face one more time. A moment and then the life went out of them. "*Je me rends, mon capitaine*," he gasped.

Frederick released his hold, and *Capitaine* Bourgeois collapsed to the floor in shame and pain. The next moment Violet was in his arms.

"Oh, Frederick, Frederick!" she declared between kisses, "I knew you would come for me!"

"Harrumph!" said Sir Percy. "Odd's fish, m'dear! And what am I?"

She turned and smiled. "Oh, Papa! I love—*LOOK OUT!*"

Everyone in the room, even the defeated *Capitaine* Bourgeois, turned toward the desk in response to Violet's scream. Chauvelin had drawn two double-barreled pistols, one in each hand, and cocked them both.

"Stand or I will shoot!" the old man shouted. Frederick tried to pull Violet away, but Chauvelin saw him. "Do not move! I am in earnest!"

Frederick grimaced, looking for a way of attacking the man without endangering Violet. His sword moved in tiny circles on its own accord.

"Come now, sir, there are two of us," said Sir Percy, placidly. "Lud, you would be lucky to hit the back wall. You certainly will miss one of us, and he will be upon you. I cannot speak for Tilney's state of mind, but I do not forgive those who shoot at me. Surrender and things will go easier for you."

Chauvelin chuckled. "Oh, I will not shoot *you*, Blakeney—at least, not yet. Surrender immediately, both of you, or I will kill Miss Blakeney!"

Chapter 31

Frederick tightened his hold on Violet and prepared to pull her away from the line of fire, but Chauvelin waved the pistols slightly.

"Do not move if you wish to live, Miss Blakeney! I may be old, but both these pistols are loaded with shot. At this distance, I cannot miss." His attention turned to Frederick. "Release the girl. This is your last warning." His long, thin fingers caressed the triggers.

Frederick hesitated, so Violet decided for both of them. Slowly, she stepped away from Frederick's embrace.

"Excellent," said Chauvelin. "Now, sir, drop your sword."

Frederick was grim as he did so, and the blade clanked loudly on the floor.

Chauvelin gestured at his comrade. "Miss Blakeney, tend to *Capitaine* Bourgeois's wound. You"—he indicated Frederick—"step over closer to Blakeney, very slowly if you please."

Frederick's countenance was severe as he joined his leader. "My apologies, Sir Percy," he mumbled.

"Tish! Think nothing of it, Frederick. You did everything you could. You fought exceedingly well." Sir Percy's eyes had never left Chauvelin. "Chauvelin, your quarrel is with me, not the young people. Let them go."

"Not this time, Blakeney," said Chauvelin menacingly.

"*Chauvelin?*" exclaimed Frederick. He turned to Sir Percy.

Sir Percy nodded. "Armand Chauvelin, the late chief agent for the Committee of Public Safety, back from the grave! You are looking very well for a dead man, what? You are wasting your time kidnapping young ladies, monsieur. You should sell your secret for resurrection. Zounds, that would set you up for life, I declare!"

Chauvelin glowered. "I am immune to your jokes, Blakeney."

Meanwhile, working to stem *Capitaine* Bourgeois's bleeding, Violet could see the man was agitated. "Rest easy, *Capitaine*, I am working as carefully as I can," she said in French.

"*Non*, mademoiselle," Bourgeois said softly, "you cause me no discomfort. I am very grateful for your help, as little as I deserve it. But, what is it they are all talking about, *s'il vous plaît*? Why do they keep saying Chauvelin? What does it mean?"

Violet stared at the *capitaine*, recalling he did not speak English. An idea came to her. She turned and said in French, "Frederick, I need your cravat to bind *Capitaine* Bourgeois's arm. Yours too, Papa. Quickly, *s'il vous plaît*."

Frederick was astonished, while Sir Percy regarded his daughter with an unreadable expression. He began to untie his cravat, stopping only to jolt Frederick out of his daze. "Come, *mon ami*," he said distinctly. "What sort of husband will you be if you cannot follow a simple order?" He unwound the neck cloth from his throat and handed it to Frederick. Frederick followed suit and extended the cloths to Violet.

"*Merci, mon chéri*," Violet said, and with the eye farthermost away from Chauvelin, winked.

Sir Percy turned back to Chauvelin, who now held one pistol on the men while keeping the other trained on Violet. "So, Chauvelin," he continued in French, "you were telling us how you came to be here when all the world thought you had passed on to whatever judgment awaits you. Did you invent the name Lafarge, or was he a real person?"

Chauvelin sneered. "I have been Lafarge these twenty years. That is all you need know."

Frederick glanced at Sir Percy. "What do you know of his fate?"

"I know that he was arrested while trying to escape Paris, and the reports all said he was guillotined the next day." Sir Percy suddenly smiled at Chauvelin. "Of course! Lafarge went in your place, did he not? However did you manage that?"

Chauvelin laughed. "When the Temple guards came in the morning, they took the man dressed in Chauvelin's clothes. I became M. Lafarge that day."

"I cannot believe that M. Lafarge went willingly."

"He was not in a state to complain," spat Chauvelin. "All night I kept him awake, learning everything about him, waiting for the changing of the prison guards. For hours, I listened to the details of his miserable existence, all the time assuring him he was to be my heir and successor as protector of Revolutionary France. Finally, the moment came. I fell upon him and beat him senseless. It only took a few moments; his days in the Temple had made him as weak as an infant. He made hardly a sound. I switched our clothing and, for good measure, broke his jaw with a chair leg. Even if he had awakened in the tumbrel, he could not protest. No doubt he looked rather like Robespierre at the end."

Sir Percy smiled softy, but his blue eyes were cold. "So they released you instead of Lafarge. My apologies, my dear Chauvelin. I had overestimated your humanity."

"Your jests are no longer amusing, Blakeney. Do you have any idea how I lived after that? I had to go into hiding for over a year using the fortune I collected during *la Révolution*, building a new life for myself. I had to buy my position in the Department of the Interior and play lackey to men who, only a few months earlier, shook in their boots at the very mention of my true name! For twenty years, I waited for the opportunity to avenge myself on you. I will receive my reward tonight!"

"You…you lied to me!"

Everyone in the room turned to the wounded *Capitaine* Bourgeois, still on the floor.

"You told me you were Lafarge—that Chauvelin entrusted you with his mission. You told me you had taken up his work. You used me!"

"Silence, you incompetent fool!" cried Chauvelin. "You cannot question me. The methods I use are justified by my sacred cause: the protection of France! What difference does the life of an insignificant clerk make against my duty! And your duty too! Did you not take an oath to safeguard France? Of course you did. You swore to follow me, to obey my every order, so keep your naïve morality to yourself."

"Chauvelin," said Sir Percy, "the young people are not a threat to France. You have me in your power, so let your vengeance fall upon me. Release my daughter and the captain."

Chauvelin's eyes were blazing. "Your daughter *is* my vengeance, Blakeney." He smiled. "You might say she is *my* way of *hitting back*."

Sir Percy blanched. "What did you say?"

"Have you not heard of an eye for an eye?"

Frederick looked at Violet in confusion, but she was as mystified as he.

Sir Percy gasped. "What? Is this about...Fleurette?" he cried in an incredulous voice.

"You stole her from me! My only love—my only daughter!"

"You asked for my help! Your enemies were trying to kill her and her lover. I took them from France to save their lives."

"Papa, what are you saying?" cried Violet. "You helped Chauvelin?"

Sir Percy spoke to the entire room. "It was 1794. I learned that a young lady named Fleurette had been arrested in Orange, and her life was in jeopardy. She was the daughter of someone high in the Revolutionary government, and that man's enemies had decided to attack him through her. How surprised I was to learn that the sweet child's father was none other than Armand Chauvelin!"

Chauvelin glowered. "*Oui*. How it tore my soul to turn to you to protect my precious Fleurette from the jackals after my hide. But I would do anything to save her, even making a bargain with my worst enemy—the man I hated with every fiber of my being. But you betrayed me!"

"How is this? I saved Fleurette and her sweetheart, Amédé Colombe, from the very clutches of the guillotine and spirited them to England. I even took them into my home for a time, and they were attended to by my own wife. I did everything I said I would."

"But they did not return! You turned them against me!"

"Return? Chauvelin, may I remind you that France tried to kill them both? As far as Fleurette knows, her beloved father—Bibi, she called you—was destroyed by *la Révolution*. Why should they come back to a place of heartbreaking memories? They have made a new life for themselves in Bath, where Amédé is a successful merchant. Their children have grown healthy and happy." Sir Percy lowered his voice. "Chauvelin, you are *un grand-père* three times."

A wild-eyed Chauvelin shouted, "English grandchildren, you mean!" He continued, as if speaking to himself. "They should have come back. We would have made a home together somewhere in the country—Fleurette, Amédé, and I." His voice rose. "Instead, you poisoned her against France, and they have raised their children as English! I still have some contacts in England. You think I do not know you helped finance Amédé's shop? That Fleurette's only son is in your Royal Navy? You have turned my child into a traitor!"

"She might have come back for you, but she thinks you dead," Sir Percy said reasonably. "Why did you not write?"

"And let the English know I was still alive? You think I do not know your government intercepts all correspondence from France? I am no fool, Blakeney!"

Listening to Chauvelin's increasingly incoherent ravings, Frederick shared a look with Violet, still kneeling at *Capitaine* Bourgeois's side. Their expressions reflected the same thought: *this man is mad.*

"So, you want my life in exchange for losing your daughter?" Sir Percy extended his arms. "Here I am. Let Violet go."

Chauvelin's laugh was chilling. "But then, you would not lose your daughter, Blakeney! No, that is not fair. If my Fleurette is forever lost to France, then your Violet will be forever lost to England!" He raised the double-barreled pistols.

Suddenly, there was a great disturbance below stairs. Violet dashed from *Capitaine* Bourgeois's side to her father's, and Frederick threw his body before both, shielding them from Chauvelin's aim. Bourgeois cried out for Chauvelin to halt, and the madman waved his weapons from left to right.

The door to the room crashed open, and the space was filled with French soldiers brandishing muskets—true soldiers from the look of their uniforms. An officer was at the head of the group, his sword in hand.

The officer of the detail cried out, "In the name of the Emperor, I order you to drop your weapons!"

"What are you doing here?" roared Chauvelin. "You dare interrupt my investigation? I am with the Department of the Interior! Be gone!"

Sir Percy laughed. "Ah, it took you long enough to get here! Well met, monsieur!"

The officer, confused, took in the scene before him. "I do not know what you mean. We were told there were spies in this place, and we were sent to arrest them."

"Excellent!" said Sir Percy. "I surrender! I am ready to leave at your convenience."

"*Non*! These prisoners are mine!" cried Chauvelin.

"Monsieur, I do not know who you are, but I insist you lower your pistols. You will have to come with us to headquarters. All of you," he said to the others, "will come now!"

"I am M. Lafarge," barked Chauvelin, "and my investigation takes precedence over yours! Leave us!"

"*NON*!" cried Bourgeois.

All eyes turned to the wounded man. He staggered to his feet, his right arm bound to his chest, a bit of blood staining his clothes. "I am *Capitaine* Bourgeois of the French army!" He pointed at Chauvelin with his good arm. "This man is not who he says. His name is Armand Chauvelin, and I denounce him as a murderer and kidnapper! He is a traitor to *l'Empire!* Arrest him!"

"Silence!" cried the officer. "Everyone is under arrest! You will all come with me." He turned to Chauvelin once more. "Drop those pistols, or I will order my men to shoot!"

"You might as well do it, Chauvelin," drawled Sir Percy as he tried to escape the protection of Violet and Frederick. "These men are here at my request. Do you recall the man Rateau? I had his nephew report that spies were in Paris. He led real French troops here so I can surrender to the proper authorities."

Chauvelin was flabbergasted. "You…you planned this?"

"Of course! Did you think I did not smell a trap? Zounds, I may be old, but I assure you my wits are not the least addled. I knew there was never a reason for the French government to arrest Violet. I had never taken up arms against their little Corsican emperor. Therefore, the people behind Violet's abduction were only pretending to be part of the government. I judged the real authorities might take a dim view of these activities, so my plan was to surrender to the government *after* I led them to whoever was holding Violet." Sir Percy smiled. "The French might dress dreadfully, but I wager they are as reasonable as the next fellow. They might put me up for a while, but at least Violet would be safe. Brilliant, if I say so myself!

"I will admit it was a surprise seeing *you* behind this. You have my congratulations, Chauvelin. However, it never affected my overall plan. In fact, with your testimony, the government might release my people and me more quickly than not. *Merci beaucoup*!

"We will all go to prison, where you can explain your plans to the judge. Who knows, he might believe you. Or perhaps you can finally fulfill your appointment with *Madame Guillotine.* I am certain they have kept her sharp for you." Sir Percy paused, and then with an air of satisfaction, concluded, "In any case, I am finally rid of you, once and for all."

A stunned and crushed Chauvelin lowered the guns, hands shaking. Everyone else in the room breathed a sigh of relief. But, as the officer stepped forward to take possession of the pistols, Chauvelin stirred and quickly raised them again.

"Stand back—I warn you!" This time Chauvelin aimed at the officer.

The officer stumbled backwards, his hands in the air. The armed detail raised their muskets to their shoulders.

"Chauvelin, do not be a fool!" called out Sir Percy. "Surrender is the only way out of here!"

Chauvelin's eyes flew to his archenemy. His eyes were filled with dejection and defeat, but also something else: an iron resolution. "The only way, Blakeney?" the madman replied in a soft voice. "I think not." He turned his attention back to the troops.

"Monsieur, you must put down your weapons!" the officer insisted. "This is your last warning."

"No one is in danger if you stay where you are," Chauvelin said in an unnaturally calm voice. "But I must tell you I shall not go to the guillotine. That is for criminals and traitors, not for patriots. All my life I have been loyal to France. There will be no traitor's death for me." He moved backwards towards the open window and smiled at Sir Percy. "You think you have won, but I refuse to give you the final victory. I am a free man! I choose when and where I go!"

Sir Percy's eyes grew cold. "Then choose, and for Heaven's sake, stop boring us to death."

Chauvelin gave Sir Percy one last look of hate and flung himself though the open window. The officer of the detail called out and rushed to the scene, his men following close behind.

"Où est-il? Where is he?" cried the officer. After a moment, one of the soldiers pointed below. The officer turned to him. "Take three men and see if he still lives. Hurry!"

Sir Percy moved to the group gathered about the window. "I beg your pardon, but might I take a look?" he said pleasantly. The officer blinked at the request, and with a perfect Gallic shrug, gave way to the baronet.

Sir Percy leaned out the window, looking to the street below, and Frederick and Violet joined him. Four stories down, directly below the window, was a crumpled dark form, barely lit by the street lamps. Four soldiers came out of the building with a lantern and inspected the wreckage. Frederick could just make out the gleam of light reflected in a growing dark pool about the body.

A soldier looked up and called out, *"Il est mort!"*

Violet gasped and fell into Frederick's open arms. Sir Percy's expression did not change, but they heard him speak softly, almost to himself.

"It is over. Finally, it is over."

Chapter 32

apitaine Bourgeois nodded at the guard in the lobby of the apartment building previously owned by Chauvelin before heading up the stairs. The place had been seized by the government in the wake of the criminal's suicide. The given justification was that the investigation found evidence among Chauvelin's papers that he had embezzled ministry funds for years. This, along with other information from his late chief's files, allowed Bourgeois to escape from the worst of the scandal. He was exonerated from any charges of malfeasance or collaboration.

Bourgeois knew he was fortunate. Mlle. Blakeney's sympathetic affidavit had proven critical, as did the gallant testimony from both Sir Percy and Captain Tilney. He was grateful and astonished, particularly with the Englishmen. These were men of high honor, it seemed—a quality that until lately Bourgeois did not think could be owned by any outside of France. Bourgeois was not a man given to reflection; therefore, the pain he experienced was intensified by self-reproach for his prejudice and folly.

I have been wrong about so many things, he had told himself. *I have been given an opportunity to start anew. It is time I put the past behind me and start living again.*

Bourgeois knocked on the door of the top-floor flat. A moment later, it was opened by Claudette, who bade him enter. He bowed to the well-dressed gentleman behind the desk.

"Bonjour, Sir Percy. I hope I find you well."

"Bonjour, *Capitaine* Bourgeois." Sir Percy was in good spirits. "To what do we humble prisoners owe your visit today?"

"I bring you news." Bourgeois looked about the room and noticed two of the inhabitants of the flat were missing. "Are Mlle. Blakeney and *Capitaine* Tilney in good health?"

"Very well, I thank you. *Capitaine* Tilney is indisposed. We have received very sad news from home. A comrade-in-arms was gravely wounded at Waterloo."

"I am grieved," Bourgeois said sincerely. "I know well the cost of battle. A close friend, I take it?"

"*Oui.* Frederick and Sir John are like brothers. He is grief-stricken. Violet attends him."

"There could be no kinder nurse. I hope my news will lift his spirits." Bourgeois was generous. It had been weeks since the confrontation in this very room, during which Bourgeois learned just how blind he had been. But the pain of knowing Mlle. Blakeney's true preference was still fresh and strong.

"As you know, my superiors have held you here until your case was decided. With the Emperor's defeat in Belgium, you can readily understand their concerns have been directed elsewhere. A few days ago, the Emperor abdicated, and yesterday he left the city. The Allies will be here within a week, and Louis's restoration to the throne cannot be far behind. Therefore, my superiors have dropped all charges and have released you from custody. You are free to go."

Sir Percy rose from his chair and crossed over to offer his hand. "This is good news and no mistake! *Merci beaucoup, Capitaine.*"

Bourgeois shook the baronet's hand. "It is the least I can do."

Just then, a door to one of the bedrooms opened and Captain Tilney appeared with Violet on his arm. The man was stiff and formal, but Bourgeois could see his eyes were red and puffy. Miss Blakeney seemed to be supporting him. Sir Percy immediately apprised them both of Bourgeois's news. Tilney's expression changed not a whit while Violet gave Bourgeois a reserved smile.

"You indeed bring welcome news, monsieur," she said. The lack of passion in her voice cut Bourgeois like a knife.

Sir Percy rubbed his hands together. "Zounds, we have packing to do! *Capitaine,* I am sure you will excuse us."

Bourgeois's jaw dropped. "Surely, you do not mean to depart immediately!"

"I most certainly do."

"But monsieur, I must ask you to reconsider! With the uncertainly of government, there is much lawlessness, both inside the city and without. The roads are not safe. Surely, you can wait until your armies arrive."

Sir Percy patted the officer on the arm. "By gad, thank you for your warning, but there is nothing for it. I can wait until Wellington comes, but I am afraid Frederick cannot. He has a pressing appointment with Horse Guards. Do you not, m'boy?"

"Indeed, I do, sir," Tilney said in a level voice. To Bourgeois's surprise, he looked not relieved but resigned.

"Steady, lad," Sir Percy said softly. "I will be by your side, never fear." He turned to Bourgeois. "His appointment is of a peculiar kind. It would be best if he presented himself to his superiors as soon as may be, without—shall we say—the *assistance* of our troops on the Continent."

This made no sense to Bourgeois, but he could see there was no talking the baronet out of his plans. The English were all mad in any case. "Very well, as you please. I am afraid we can offer no protection to your party."

"Oh, I believe we can bumble about on our own. Do not concern yourself over us."

Miss Blakeney spoke up. "And what of you, *Capitaine*? What are your plans?"

Bourgeois silently blessed the lady for remembering him. "Thanks to your testimonies, I am not in danger of being punished for M. Chauvelin's crimes. Indeed, the evidence has led to the arrest of a M. Robineaux, a criminal who has long eluded the authorities, and all of his followers. I am actually in line for a commendation."

"That is wonderful!" Violet exclaimed.

"*Merci.* Despite this, my days at the ministry are coming to a close. I am not entirely trusted, and there will be changes made with the new regime. Returning to active service does not suit me, and there are too many unhappy memories for me in France. I need a fresh start, I believe.

"Therefore, my request for passage to our colonies in the West Indies has been accepted. There is a position in the customs office in Martinique that is mine for the asking. I sail in two weeks."

Sir Percy grinned. "Ah, a warm climate in the balmy Caribbean. Just the thing—for the right man. Odd's fish, I would soon grow to loathe it, I am sure. What would I be without proper English weather—wet and cold, what? Still, I trust it will suit you. Congratulations, *Capitaine.*"

Captain Tilney simply nodded while Miss Blakeney shook his hand. "Good luck, *Capitaine.* May you find your heart's desire."

Bourgeois almost said that what he wanted could be found in England, but he did not. What good would it do? He must learn to live without the smiles of Violet Blakeney.

Instead he replied, "*Merci beaucoup*, mademoiselle. I am certain I shall. I wish you—all of you—health and happiness." He looked Tilney in the eye. Jealous as he was, Bourgeois could not pretend to like the Englishman, but he could give Miss Blakeney the parting gift of his civility. "I am afraid we shall not meet again."

Captain Tilney nodded.

Bourgeois prepared to go. "Farewell and safe journey." He paused, and even though he had not attended Mass in years—in fact, he was not even certain he still believed—he added, "Go with God, *mes amis.*"

"God bless you, Honoré," replied Miss Blakeney.

His heart in his throat, Bourgeois could say no more. With a bow, he turned and left the room, hoping no one saw the tears forming in his eyes.

Chapter 33

Off Saint-Malo, France

Thanks to the assistance of Rateau, the travelers made good time on the roads, taking a direct route to Saint-Malo. Once they arrived, Sir Percy and his party waited a full day and night in the town before a sloop was spotted in the sound. Sir Percy arranged for a fishing boat to intercept the craft, and by late afternoon, the launch from the *Mid-night Dream* was taking Frederick and the Blakeneys to the little ship.

"Zounds, Ffoulkes! Well met!" cried Sir Percy as he made his way up the accommodation ladder to grasp his old friend's hand. "You are right on time."

"You said to stay to the schedule," Ffoulkes replied. "I instructed the *Mid-Night Dream* to visit Saint-Malo every three days since you landed. I was not on board until we got your message from Paris. Margo is overjoyed and wanted to come—and George too—but Suzanne talked them into remaining at Richmond and helping her to prepare a proper welcome for you all. The Good Lord only knows what your wife and mine will arrange. A ball, most likely —ho, take a care there!"

A bo'sun's chair gingerly lifted Violet out of the launch. The two men watched anxiously until the young lady was safely on deck. Violet greeted her godfather with great affection, while Frederick scampered up the accommodation ladder.

"And here is our young hero!" cried Sir Andrew. "The Frenchies did not put any holes in you, I trust?"

"Nary a scratch, Sir Andrew." Frederick's smile disappeared. "I will be able to appear before their lordships at Whitehall hale and whole and await their pleasure to name the date of my court-martial."

Sir Andrew could see that the once-joyful Violet was close to tears. He made to speak, but the bustle of the crew as they recovered the launch was distracting.

"Here, lad—none o'that! Come below to the cabin. I have news for you."

"Good God!" cried Frederick as his eyes scanned the dispatch in his hands. "Is this really from the Duke of York?"

"What is it? What does it say?" implored Violet.

Frederick could not speak for a few moments. His gaze moved between an astonishing pronouncement, an anxious Violet, an expectant Sir Percy, and an exceedingly pleased Sir Andrew.

"This is—I cannot believe it! What have you done, Sir Andrew?"

Ffoulkes chuckled. "'Tis only what you deserve, lad. Read it aloud."

Frederick shook his head. *"For services to the crown above and beyond the call of duty, now let it be known to all men that we, HRH Frederick, Duke of York and Albany, Commander-in-Chief of the Forces*—* 'Odd's life! I've been promoted to major, and I have been reassigned to the Twelfth Dragoons Guards, as well!" He looked at Sir Andrew again. "Forgive me, sir, but is this in earnest? I am a major and back with the Twelfth?"

"Aye, lad."

Violet squealed. "Frederick, there will be no court-martial!"

Frederick was dazed. "It…it seems there will not. How did you manage it, sir?"

Sir Andrew's grin threatened to split his face. "Well, let us say that the daughter of the Regent's particular friend was in peril of her life and that the young lady was also the sister of the Regent's own godson. In addition, the self-same Regent was the patron of an irregular force dedicated to the protection of the realm, namely the League of the Scarlet Pimpernel. And the Pimpernel, being of a rather advanced age and infirmity—"

"Ffoulkes!" bellowed Sir Percy.

Sir Andrew ignored him. "—was in need of a strong, young soldier to protect and aid him in this quest, a mission of intense interest to the Crown. But the only volunteer to step forward was forced to take extraordinary and unconventional measures to make himself available to Prince and Pimpernel.

"It was not too difficult to secure the young soldier's promotion and reassignment, seeing as that gentleman accomplished his mission, recovered the young lady, and protected the hide of the Pimpernel. The Crown certainly was not going to hang such a hero, I can tell you."

Frederick sat heavily in his chair, overcome with relief. He would not have to justify his actions before a court-martial! His constant worry since Violet's deliverance had been that, just as he had finally won his heart's desire, he could lose it all to prison, transportation, or worse.

Now, like sunlight breaking through the clouds, Frederick's path became clear. He turned to Violet, to see her attention solely on him. The same thought seemed to occur to them at the same instant.

"We can marry!" they exclaimed in union.

Violet turned to her bemused father. "We can, can we not? You said we had to wait until Frederick's case was settled."

"So I did, m'dear," Sir Percy said. "By gad, Major Tilney, it seems you are to become me son-in-law. That is, unless you have come to your senses."

"Papa!"

Frederick shook off his stupor. "If being sensible means I shall not have the high honor of Miss Blakeney's hand in marriage, then let the world call me mad, for I cannot live without her."

"Ah. So the match was made in Paris?" asked Sir Andrew.

Sir Percy gestured in mock exasperation. "For Heaven's sake, Ffoulkes, it is not as if we had much choice in the matter! For several weeks, Violet was shut in a two-bedroom apartment with her father and her admirer. Even with my admittedly superb chaperonage —stop giggling, Violet—my daughter would be considered at least somewhat compromised by the all-seeing, all-knowing denizens of the *ton*. There was nothing for it! Fortunately, Captain—now *Major* Tilney realized the level of his culpability for the situation in which we found ourselves, and with very little prodding from me, took the proper steps to regulate matters to everyone's satisfaction —to a point."

Violet attempted to stem her laughter with middling success. "What Papa means, Godfather, is that Frederick finally wore him down, once I assured him Frederick had truly won my devotion. And even then, Papa said we could not make our understanding official until we knew Frederick's fate."

"Well, that was only reasonable, my dear girl. And now you come around, Ffoulkes, and completely upset the carefully managed schedule! What am I to do with you?"

"Percy, for shame!" Sir Andrew turned to the others. "I thank you for my share, Tilney, but the greatest of your thanks must go to my friend here. Everything that was done was at Percy's direction. His was the mind that solved the fine pickle we were in—namely, how to extract you from the all-but-certain consequences of your honorable but dangerous decision to resign from the Blues. We planned it when we crossed the Channel weeks ago. I was but the messenger between Percy and Prinny."

With a cry, Violet threw herself into her father's arms while Frederick seized one of Sir Percy's hands and attempted to shake it off.

"Yes, I did write a letter or two," he admitted. "I apologize for keeping you both in the dark, as it were. I had no idea whether Prinny could talk York into it, and I did not want to raise expectations."

"I owe you my life, sir."

"Lud, that sounds droll. I expect I owe you me life as well, Frederick. Let us declare it a draw and speak of more pleasant things."

"Yes, Papa!" said a radiant Violet. "You are certainly the best of men! Now, dearest father, when shall the wedding be?"

"You want to plan such an event without your mother having her share of the conversation? Forsooth, I shall not attempt it, for I know well her ladyship's wrath!"

"Papa," she said in a manner that had brought Sir Percy to his knees countless times, "may I marry soon?"

"Beware of that voice, Frederick! She will have you dancing to her tune!" In a serious tone, he said to his darling daughter, "M'love, I remember the impatience of youth, but there are other matters that must be considered. For better or worse, we are members of the First Circles, and there are expectations of those in our class. We would not want it said that Violet Blakeney had reason to marry in haste, eh? A proper public engagement of three months—three months, m'dear, and not a day shorter—and I do not see why we cannot host a wedding breakfast at Richmond in October."

At Violet's pout, he added. "Remember, you will wed before your brother. He cannot marry Miss Wentworth until he finishes at Oxford, and that will not be until the New Year at least. We cannot even announce his engagement to Miss Wentworth until your wedding breakfast, so pray remember your unfortunate brother's agony and have some mercy for your poor father's feelings."

Violet hugged him. "Very well, Papa."

As for Frederick, the fact that he and Violet might be married as soon as October was better than he had hoped. Exceedingly boisterous were his thanks.

"Enough, enough!" cried Sir Percy in good humor. "Let us have a bit of supper, and then you two can plan your wedding to your heart's desire! You do have food on this tub, do you not, Ffoulkes?"

Off the English coast

EVENING TURNED INTO NIGHT AS THE *MID-NIGHT DREAM* BEAT northwards up the English Channel. The wind out of the northwest forbade a direct course to Deal. Therefore, the helmsman set a course to take the little ship beyond Ramsgate before coming about for the run into harbor. The additional distance would add at least another half day to the voyage, but the passengers were sanguine.

Two of them, the master of the *Mid-night Dream* and his best friend, leaned against the stern railing and took in the freshening breeze as they enjoyed their pipes, the boat creaking agreeably as it gently rolled with the sea.

"So, it was Chauvelin all along," said an incredulous Sir Andrew. "All these years we thought him dead, he was alive and plotting in plain sight in Paris. By gad, it gives me the shivers! But, he is gone for good now?"

Sir Percy removed his fine Meerschaum and gazed at it. "Zounds, I am happy that demmed war with the Americans is done, and we can again get proper Virginia tobacco. Yes, Ffoulkes, the devil has finally gone to his infernal reward! I saw his carcass myself. We are free of him forever."

Sir Percy took a thoughtful puff of his pipe. "You know, it was only after seeing him there, broken on the cobblestones, that I realized I had doubts about his execution all those years ago. The relief I felt! I should be quite ashamed of myself if I did not recall all the poor souls he sent to the guillotine. Justice has finally been done and no mistake."

Sir Andrew gestured at the quarterdeck. "It seems we have company. Finished the wedding plans, have you, Violet?"

Violet, a boat-cloak pulled tightly about her, her expression serious, made her way to the stern with Frederick beside her. "Papa, Godfather, Frederick has something to say."

A determined Frederick stood before them, his feet spread wide on account of the rolling deck. "Sirs, I cannot thank you enough for what you have done for me. But this honor, this promotion... I cannot accept them. Honors should go to men like Uxbridge, Brandon, and Buford who stood before Bonaparte at Waterloo. The Duke of York called me a hero, but I am no hero. " His voice choked a little. "Heroes are those who fell in Belgium. I am not worthy to be named among them."

Sir Percy and Sir Andrew shared a look. "What will you do then, Son?" asked Sir Percy gently.

"I must accept the appointment—that I know. But I intend to

leave the army as soon as practical, properly this time, I should add. After that, my destiny is to be a gentleman farmer, but I know little of my intended profession." He grasped Violet's hand. "Between us, we will have money to live on from what my mother left me and the income from Violet's fortune. However, I cannot be idle like so many of my fellows. My character demands employment. I need to learn my duties as a landowner.

"Normally, a son learns at his father's knee. But even though I am for Northanger Abbey, my father will be unwelcoming. The general's joy at my new *connections*," he spat the word, "will be quite offset by his anger at my retiring from the king's service at a rank lower than colonel. He will not soon forgive my failure to bend to his will, so there is no place for me at Northanger.

"I thought"—he smiled at Violet—"*we* thought that perhaps we could live at Richmond for a while, and I could be trained by your steward. We would not be an imposition. I will work hard, learning my craft, and Violet can be a companion to Lady Blakeney."

Sir Percy and Sir Andrew glanced at each other again, this time with a smile. "Sink me, the boy does have a brain, Ffoulkes!"

"Indeed he does," Sir Andrew agreed. "Tilney, we fully expected that you would refuse your new assignment."

"You did?" Frederick stuttered, flabbergasted.

"Of course," Sir Percy laughed. "I told you I still have my wits about me. We both know the army is not for you, m'boy." He turned to his friend. "What say you, Ffoulkes? Do you think I can find a nice, cozy cottage at Richmond just right for a young couple making their start in the world?"

"I believe so. But what of the dowager house? It is certainly not in use."

"Even better!"

"Papa!" cried Violet as she embraced him. "Oh, Papa, thank you!"

"Oh, do not thank me overmuch, m'dear! Your mother would have me head if I sent you away. And do not think it will be easy for you, Frederick. My steward is a hard master. You will be going from sunup to sundown!"

"A life to which I am perfectly accustomed. I shall not disappoint you, sir."

"It will be agreeable to have another gentleman about the place. We must find a bit of time for sport, eh? I have yet to learn whether you are as good with a bird-gun as you are with your sword."

As Violet returned to her lover's embrace, Sir Andrew observed, "Ah, what a fine night, eh Percy? It reminds me of another one, long ago—on the *Daydream* in October of '92."

Sir Percy leaned back and smiled. "I do remember. It was before you were born, Violet. Your mother and I were sailing back from France on a night much like this one, having rescued your Uncle Armand from the clutches of that devil Chauvelin, may he rot. Ffoulkes here"—he gestured with his pipe—"was impatient to get back to England and his fair Suzanne. And your mother and I —well, it was after some unfortunate misunderstandings were set straight, and we spent most of the time forgiving each other. Dover had just come into sight. Ah, it was a time!"

"It sounds so romantic, Papa."

Sir Percy was silent on the subject, but his wistful smile spoke volumes.

"We had some adventures back then, eh?" Sir Andrew slapped his friend on the back. "Dashing off to save those poor unfortunates from right under the noses of Robespierre and his cronies. What sport!"

"Do you miss it, sir?" asked Frederick.

Sir Percy took a puff and looked out to sea. "Everything Ffoulkes said is true, Son. We were young and brave and clever. It was sport more than anything else. That is why we never accepted any recognition for what we did."

He turned to the railing. "There, out there somewhere, is France —site of some hair-raising times, I can tell you. It was a game, Frederick, a game with the highest of stakes. Life and death—not just for me or Ffoulkes and Dewhurst and the rest, but also for the intended victims of the Terror. We saved our share, but we could not save them all. That haunts me a little."

He turned back to his companions. "That sort of game, like war, is for young men. As the years go by, a man's interests change. I no longer dream of matching wits against evil. Instead, I long for the peace of Richmond with Lady Blakeney at my side and my grandchildren at my feet. I have earned that life, Frederick, and I mean to live it.

"So, do I miss it? No. The time of the Pimpernel is done. I know I have said it before, Ffoulkes, but this time I believe I can say without fear of contradiction that indeed this has been the last adventure."

The End

Suggested Readings

Austen, Jane. *Northanger Abbey.*
    —. *Pride and Prejudice.*
Caldwell, Jack. *The Three Colonels: Jane Austen's Fighting Men.*
    Naperville: Sourcebooks Landmark, 2012.
    —. *Mr. Darcy Came to Dinner – A Jane Austen Farce.*
    Venice: White Soup Press, 2013.
    —. *The Companion of His Future Life.* Venice: White
    Soup Press, 2014.
Orczy, Baroness Emma. *The Scarlet Pimpernel.* 1905.
    —. *I Will Repay.* 1906.
    —. *The Elusive Pimpernel.* 1908.
    —. *Eldorado.* 1913.
    —. *Lord Tony's Wife.* 1917.
    —. *The Triumph of the Scarlet Pimpernel.* 1922.
    —. *Sir Percy Hits Back.* 1927.

About the Author

Jack Caldwell is an author, amateur historian, professional economic developer, playwright, and like many Cajuns, a darn good cook.

Jack is the author of four Jane Austen–themed books. **Pemberley Ranch** is a retelling of *Pride & Prejudice* set in Reconstruction Texas. **Mr. Darcy Came To Dinner** and **The Companion of His Future Life** are *Pride & Prejudice*–flavored farces. **The Three Colonels**, the first of his **JANE AUSTEN'S FIGHTING MEN SERIES**, is a sequel to *Pride & Prejudice* and *Sense & Sensibility*.

In 2015, he released the first four of a series of historical novels about New Orleans, titled **THE CRESCENT CITY SERIES**. **The Plains of Chalmette** begins the series, commemorating the Bicentennial of the Battle of New Orleans. Jack marked the tenth anniversary of Hurricane Katrina with three modern novels: **Bourbon Street Nights**, **Elysian Dreams**, and **Ruin and Renewal**.

When not writing or traveling with his wife, Barbara, Jack attempts to play golf. A devout convert to Roman Catholicism, Jack is married with three grown sons. Jack's blog postings—**The Cajun Cheesehead Chronicles**—appear regularly at **Austen Variations**.

WEB SITES: **Ramblings of a Cajun in Exile**
https://cajuncheesehead.com
Austen Variations - http://austenvariations.com/
Facebook - https://www.facebook.com/pages/Jack-Caldwell-author/132047236805555
Twitter - @JCaldwell25

JANE AUSTEN'S FIGHTING MEN SERIES

THE THREE COLONELS

THE LAST ADVENTURE OF THE SCARLET PIMPERNEL

PERSUADED TO SAIL
Coming Soon!

ROSINGS PARK
Coming Soon!

THE CRESCENT CITY SERIES

THE PLAINS OF CHALMETTE:
A Story of Crescent City

BOURBON STREET NIGHTS:
Volume One of Crescent City

ELYSIAN DREAMS:
Volume Two of Crescent City

RUIN AND RENEWAL:
Volume Three of Crescent City

OTHER NOVELS BY JACK CALDWELL

PEMBERLEY RANCH

MR. DARCY CAME TO DINNER
A Jane Austen Farce

THE COMPANION OF HIS FUTURE LIFE